PHANTOM BEAST

By
LUKE PH

CH01508925

Print Book ISBN: 978-0-9562987-5-1
e-book ISBN: 978-0-9562987-6-8

For my niece and nephews Ava, Noah, and Joshua.

Acknowledgements

The book you are about to read would not have reached you without the considerable help of a great number of people. In recent years, it's become something of a trend for acknowledgements to be placed at the back of a book – because otherwise, it may serve as a distraction to eager readers who just want to get to the story. If that's you, please feel free to skip a page or so ahead. However, as an independent author, it's important to me to buck that trend. I couldn't write books without the help and support I get from others, especially friends and family.

A first round of thanks should go to my brilliant BETA readers, Lauren, Crystal, and Ian especially. Your insights and thoughts helped bring the finishing touches to the story.

In part, this book was also made possible by the successful Kickstarter campaign which helped get it off the ground and get things up and running. So, to everyone who backed the Kickstarter, a huge thank you for your faith in me and for being so patient. You'll find your name immortalized in print on the next page.

It's been a tough journey this time round, and my family have been especially supportive, as have my close friends. Without you all, I'd probably still be tinkering with it, or have given up entirely.

And finally, to you, the readers, a huge thank you for coming with me, Thomas, and Catherine on the journey so far.

Kickstarter Backers

A huge thank you for making this happen

Mhairi and Mike Harris

Connor Schwartz

Caroline Edwards

Jemmel Matheson

Gilbert Zenner

Laura Page

Andrea Reyes

Andrew Fishtal

Ben England

Tom Scott

Andrew Keech

Sheona Hartnup-Hoolachan

Arn Radtke

Gill Coventry

Liz, Stephen and Becca Ford

Kenneth Ramsey Jnr

Mike McGreggor

Seth Breedlove

Ian Pearse

Chase Kelly

Adam Starkey

Ashley McLeod

Ben Carter

Jose Maguina

Pete Harwood

Cindy Sherwood

Spencer Warhurst

George Kouchakji

Author's Note

When this book was first concepted and I thrashed out the storyline, COVID was not a word the world was yet familiar with. In my stories, I often take on real-world issues, such as how wildlife crime funds terrorism, in The Daughters of the Darkness. In Phantom Beast, a small part of the story focused on wildlife markets and their part in spreading zoonotic diseases. Since then, COVID, and the part such markets played in its spread has become well known. I only explore it lightly in the story, but the "plague" vision one of the antagonists' experiences, was never intended to be COVID, hence why I kept it so generic. Again, it has become something of a trend to jump on the COVID bandwagon, but I think it is in a little poor taste given this is a disease that has negatively impacted lives (mine included) and caused over five million deaths to date.

You'll also find a reference to cloned black-footed ferrets in the book. In the story, this is a project controlled and run by a fictional organization, but, again, there are links to reality. In December 2020, the first cloned black-footed ferret was born, from a genetic line cryopreserved in 1988. So again, the fiction has mirrored reality.

CHAPTER ONE
JOHNSON COUNTY, WYOMING

Jesse Logan woke with a start, rising onto his elbows and half rolling away the covers through muscle memory. His heart thumped noticeably in his chest – biochemistry doing its best to rouse him from sleep, fast. His eyes darted to the door and then the cracked-open windows out of instinct. He knew he still felt uncomfortable sleeping in what had been his father's room. It was worse now Nina had left – she had brought warmth and life back to the upper floor of the old ranch house. But even before then, the room had never disturbed him this much before. Then he heard it. The horses were whinnying and neighing in anger and panic. Rhythmic thumps sounded out as the stallion kicked at the enclosing walls of the wooden stable. It wanted out, and so did the mare. But it was the heifers that were making the most noise. They were on the move and calling to each other in unbridled fear.

Jesse wiped the sweat from his brow and flung back the covers, dropping his feet to the floor. He moved to the window and peered out. The unforgiving Wyoming landscape, gripped by the icy tendrils of winter, loomed back. The foothills and woodland that bordered the Caterwaul Ranch to the west, eventually gave way to the more impressive Bighorn mountains and forest. A heavy mist was descending from them now, reminding Jesse of the movie 'The Fog', or the original version at least. He'd never seen the remake. The cattle were breaking from one side of the field to the other, constantly on the move and bunched together in a tight herd. He cursed, stuffing his naked feet into his boots and throwing on a thick padded sweater from the drawer. He shuffled downstairs, leaning heavily on the open banister as he went. As he passed the gun cabinet in the hallway, he opened it and pulled out a Winchester 12-gauge shotgun, padding the sweater's pockets with shells of buckshot at the same time.

He opened the double doors of the ranch house and stepped out onto the veranda covered deck. It helped block some of the bright moonlight illuminating the yard and meadows beyond. Both the cattle and horses were quiet now, although the livestock were still on the move. He let his gaze wander from right to left before stepping off the porch and making his way across the yard.

He was halfway when the silence struck him. Jesse was overcome by a feeling he hadn't experienced for some time. Somewhere, out in the dark, he knew a big cat was watching him. Most of the county's mountain lions had learnt a long time ago to avoid the ranch. The efforts of his father and his team of hunters had meant generations of cats now avoided the area. Known as the 'hole in the wall gang', they had taken the name from the group of infamous outlaws, including Butch Cassidy and the Sundance Kid. They in turn had taken the name from the nearby gorge that served as their base of operations. Mountain lion numbers in Wyoming were dropping, to the point where even lion hunters had suggested reducing the availability of permits, after seeing less than ten percent success one season. But if a cat had decided to visit the ranch, that was equally troubling.

Jesse pressed on, now bringing down his feet heavily and making his presence known. Jesse had adopted the same strict protocols as his father and had sworn never to take a life without reason. If the lion hadn't attacked his animals, he would leave it be. But as he neared the boundary fence of the fields and meadows where the livestock were, he realised that was no longer an option.

He only kept a small herd of Simmental yellow cattle, mainly in remembrance of his father, but he could already see they were scared. The animals were bunched tightly between a stand of Canadian hemlock trees and the back of the stable, where the horses were kept. He could see the heavy breath of the cattle in the cold night air. Their searching eyes bulged in fright and eerily reflected the moonlight.

For many years, the family business had been predator control. Jesse didn't quite share his father's tenacity for it. He'd recently spoken out against both wolf and mountain lion hunting in Wyoming. His real passion was in breeding animals for quality and purpose. He had chosen the Simmental cattle for their ability to stand Wyoming winters and the rich marbling their meat offered. But he was also interested in improving the quality further and had recently introduced a new strain in the form of a black American Gelbvieh bull. It was an experiment, and he was keen to see the results. As he climbed the wooden fence, he straddled it and sat with his legs either side, hesitating. He looked towards the upper meadows where he knew the bull and the cows he had selected to breed from were. It was ominously quiet. As he sat there, he considered returning to the barn behind the house for his more recent breeding experiment.

His father's reputation meant that his services were still in demand. But the dogs Jesse's dad had employed had proven incapable of saving him. His father had been killed by a mysterious animal, in the Highlands of Scotland and thousands of miles away. Jesse had made it his mission to breed a hunting dog not just capable of tracking a big cat, but taking it on, either alone or by working in a pack. His animals were now second generation, but he wasn't ready, and neither were they. For now, it was just him.

He swung his legs over the fence and landed with a thud, breaking an ice-laced puddle as he did. He began the long, slow march towards the upper meadows. He swung the shotgun from left to right, covering his field of view as he went. Despite his experience as a hunter, he realised he had been holding his breath when he reached the next fence. He let out a stalled, ragged gasp as he listened to the elevated thump of his heartbeat. Fear was taking hold.

A few moments later, it was replaced by anger and shock. The six Simmental heifers he'd put in the top pasture were still there, but there was something very wrong. As his breath left his mouth in visible puffs of water vapour, he noticed no such exhalations came from the cows. They lay on their sides, some with their rear legs splayed and rigid. He could smell the blood in the air, and he knew they were all dead. He approached the nearest to him slowly and steadily. His eyes flitted to the treeline, now much closer and ominous.

Seeing the six animals strewn around the meadow, seemingly ripped down together, he began to think he had been mistaken about the cat. Only dogs would kill so brazenly, fuelled by frenzy and excitement. But he couldn't understand why he hadn't heard anything. A wolf pack would have been in full voice as they hunted, constantly communicating. Coyotes, coy-wolfs or a pack of feral dogs would have been even louder and haphazard in their attack. For a moment, the thought that this was some kind of retaliation for speaking out against predator hunting crossed his mind. But he soon dismissed it when he saw the savagery up close.

As he examined the carcass, any thought of it being dogs or wolves also vanished from his mind. The precision and neatness of the kill affirmed his suspicions. It was undoubtedly a cat. The heifer had been opened along its stomach. The blood loss had been so instant and dramatic it had poured onto the ground like rain. The ribs had been snipped through as if by shears, leaving a neat line of cut-through bone. Splinters and shards around the carcass indicated the ribs had also been broken open to extract the fatty marrow. The heart and liver had been removed, and presumably devoured. It was only when he got to the head that he discovered something that surprised him.

The heifer's throat had been ripped out completely. A gaping hole, marked by shredded clumps of fur and flesh at its edges, was all that remained. The cow's eyes had rolled over into the back of its skull. They were lifeless and frosted over. He couldn't tell if it was due to the temperature or the first signs of rigor mortis. He shuddered, but it wasn't the cold that made him do so. It was the enormous paw print, etched into the frozen lake of blood. It had to be at least six inches wide, and even more in length. He'd never seen anything like it.

Hell, African lions don't get that big, let alone cougars, he thought.

He examined the five remaining cows, finding the same results. Then he headed for the top pasture. He was surprised to find the bull standing there, in the middle of the field. It let out strained, icy blasts of breath from its nostrils. Jesse had named the bull Fabian, hinting at its German ancestry. He had often considered 'Ferdinand', like the cartoon character, would have been more appropriate, given the animal's placid and affectionate nature.

As Jesse appeared at the gate, Fabian began to trundle towards him. But immediately, he saw the bull was in trouble. It veered from side to side, unsteady on its feet. It let out a distraught bellow as it tripped and hit the ground. Jesse was up and over the gate and running to the bull's side before it was down.

Fabian lay where he had fallen but held his head up as Jesse came close.

"Easy big fella," Jesse exclaimed, patting the bull on his neck and shoulder.

The source of the animal's distress was obvious. A set of deep claw slashes, starting at the hock of his front left leg and ending on his rump were bleeding freely. The animal was weak and exhausted. Jesse tried to comfort the animal, eyeing the treeline again. As his gaze settled on a patch of darkness between the firs, he thought he glimpsed something. Two green spots of glowing light. As he watched, they would slowly blink in and out of visibility. Finally, they faded away into nothing. He shuddered again, realising they had been the eyes of the predator, reflecting the moonlight.

He backed his way through the pastures, never fully turning around or shifting his line of sight from the trees. The cows in the bottom field watched him all the way to the ranch house. He closed the front door behind him and locked it, noticing the shake in his hands as he did so. He went into the office and picked up the phone. He flipped through the old-fashioned rolodex on the desk and found the number for the veterinarian, a woman named Walke, who like his cows, also had German ancestry. He took out the card, looking at it and turning it over in his fingers as the line rang.

After apologizing and explaining the situation to a sleepy Anabel Walke, Jesse went to put the card back in his father's rolodex. He paused, staring at the next card in the slot behind. He picked it out and lay it on the desk. He reached for the phone again, glancing quickly at the clock. It was a little after three in the morning. He didn't know how far ahead Scotland was, but he didn't hesitate to dial the number. He hadn't spoken to Thomas Walker in five years, but something in his gut told him it was time to talk.

CHAPTER TWO

Thomas Walker eyed the cat with an unblinking stare. Its own gold-green iris met his gaze with equal confidence. The long black tufts at the end of each of its ears flicked once as it raised a paw to step forward. Thomas matched the movement, pushing his chest out as a sign of dominance. The cat was silent but dropped its chin and bobbed its head from side to side as it sized him up. He wondered if this was perhaps another reason why its smaller cousin was called the bobcat, not just because of its lack of tail. This cat, a northern lynx, was a fine specimen. Male, fully grown at nearly three years old, weighing close to 110lbs, and nearly four feet in length. Thomas had given the cat the name Loki, befitting both its temperament and its Norwegian ancestry.

As the cat pounced, so did Thomas, whisking the little four-year-old girl up into his arms, feeling the thud of her heavy outdoor clothes against his chest as he clutched her tightly. Loki rose onto his hind legs, reaching out with his front paws towards Thomas and the girl. The pads of the cat's paws met the wire-mesh fence harmlessly, which flexed a little under his weight. Thomas met the stare of the cat with a smug look of his own as he dropped the girl back to her feet.

"Cassie Walker, what have we said about going near the enclosure?" Thomas demanded, gently.

"Loki wants me to be friends with him, daddy," the girl answered adamantly.

Thomas smiled, brushing away her red curls and meeting her vivid green eyes, which burned with resolve.

"Loki wants you for lunch, munchkin," Thomas sighed.

"No claws daddy, no claws!" Cassie replied, thumping him on his calf with a scowl.

Thomas looked at the cat. He could see his daughter was right. Loki had not extended his claws. But it was no reassurance its predatory instinct hadn't kicked in.

"I was going to accuse you of having your mother's good looks and my brains, but it seems you're using your head. It's still my job to make sure it stays attached to you though, okay."

"Silly daddy," Cassie sighed.

Thomas took his daughter's hand and led her back to the house. Named Sàsadh, an old Gaelic word meaning a place of comfort, it was now homelier than ever. The grand old farmhouse had changed rather dramatically over the last few years. First had come an impressive extension, incorporating a bedroom, bathroom and playroom for Cassie on the ground floor. Then had come the further addition to the grounds, with enclosures for the lynx. Part of a reintroduction programme, the Mullardoch forest on their doorstep was one of three test sites where the cats were being released as part of a pilot scheme. Thomas's wife, Catherine, and the Highland Wildlife Research Centre, which they ran together, were overseeing the reintroduction.

He walked in with Cassie through the back, into the boot room, where both he and Cassie removed their shoes and left them by the door. He again whisked Cassie up into his arms, lifting her up from behind and making her giggle. A good-natured bark sounded from the hallway as two dogs trotted down the corridor to greet them: Meg, Thomas's three-legged chocolate merle Border collie, and Arturo, a slate-grey cane corso mastiff he and Catherine had adopted. Cassie began to squirm, signifying she wanted to get down to greet the dogs. Meg eyed Thomas sheepishly as Cassie's feet hit the floor and she rushed forward, licking and yipping at the little girl with loving affection.

"Traitor," Thomas sighed.

Meg instantly came to his side and leaned into him. He lent down and patted her side tenderly.

"Daddy, I want a doggy," Cassie declared.

"Looks like you've got two already, greedy-guts," Thomas replied.

"No," Cassie shrugged, as if tired at having to explain. "Meg your dog, Atty mummy's."

"Well, they're *our* dogs really Cassie," Thomas explained. "They're as much yours as mine and mum's."

Cassie seemed to think about it for a moment, then stomped off down the corridor.

"Mummy, want a doggy," he heard Cassie whine to Catherine, who was in the kitchen.

"That's a kind offer darling, but I've got two already," he heard his wife reply snappily.

Thomas couldn't help but smile as he saw Cassie storm out of the kitchen towards her room, scowling, and with both dogs in tow.

"Don't think she liked either of our answers," Thomas said, raising an eyebrow as he lent up against the kitchen doorframe.

"That's the price she pays for having parents with over-developed sarcasm glands," Catherine laughed.

Thomas admired his wife from the doorway. There was no doubt where Cassie got her red hair and striking turquoise eyes from. Whereas Catherine's hair was short and gave her something of an elfin look, Cassie's was longer with a curl. Catherine often remarked Thomas's black hair and pale blue eyes had been traded for his stubbornness. Her temper was all redhead though, something he could again blame Catherine for.

"By the way," Catherine remarked, closing the fridge door slowly. "With everything that's been going on at work, and with Loki's arrival, we plain forgot to do any shopping. There isn't any food in the house."

"That's alright, I'll take Cassie out for a ride, and we can go to the farm shop. I spoke to Annie during the week about keeping the cat's diets varied, and she thinks she can help out."

Annie Patterson ran a farm shop in the nearby village of Cannich. It specialised in the high-end produce of the local area and its farms. Thomas had always preferred to get his groceries there as it was, but now, Annie also served as a conduit of communication between the farmers and Thomas and Catherine. Not everyone was thrilled by the idea of having large cats reintroduced into the area. For many, it was a very sensitive subject. The potential killing of livestock by the lynx was one aspect of the residual resistance. But as Thomas well knew, the events of his past had also dramatically impacted the Highland hamlet. A big cat had been here before. Its existence was denied by the government, and it had killed over a dozen people before he had stopped its rampage. Although the lynx was considerably smaller, he empathised with the local community's hesitance in welcoming the species

"Settled then," Catherine smirked. "But hurry up, I'm hungry," she thumped him playfully on the arm.

"What is it with you two hitting me?" Thomas grumbled playfully.

Thomas walked to Cassie's room and pushed open the door. Arturo was laid out on the white rug that covered the floor, with Meg by his side. Cassie was slumped on top of the big grey dog, her arms trailing either side of his rib cage, her eyes firmly fixed on the expansive picture window opposite. Thomas went and sat on her bed, shaking his head but smiling.

"Come on kiddo, we're going into town to do some shopping. We need to feed mummy, and then we need to feed Loki. Wanna help?"

"Wanna dog," Cassie said quietly and sulkily.

"There's one underneath you, hon," Thomas pointed out helpfully.

Cassie tried to stop herself smiling but couldn't quite help the corners of her mouth turning up. With a sigh, she picked herself up and walked over to Thomas, leaning into him. He put an arm around her shoulders and scooped her up again, brushing away some of her curls. He carried her back through to the hallway, where they grabbed fresh coats and shoes. Cassie took his hand as she impatiently dragged him out through the front door.

Thomas walked across the gravel drive to the converted stables that were now a garage and workshop. He clicked the remote from inside his Barbour jacket, and the double-fronted, fire-station style doors began to open. Inside was another reminder that Sàsadh was now a family home. The Land Rovers he favoured had proven a little impractical, and Catherine had put her foot down about a replacement. Inside was what he had called a compromise. At first glance, it looked like a classic three-door Range Rover. But the matt yellow paintwork, smoked black alloy wheels, and aggressive stance hinted this was something else. The vehicle was a bespoke creation called a Chieftain Xtreme. It combined classic good looks with high-end, meticulously engineered modern running gear, including a 6.2 litre supercharged V8 good for 700bhp. He had a penchant for more unique vehicles, and this was as close to a modern car he could willingly go. He opened the door and lifted Cassie into her seat in the rear.

As they drove towards the village, Thomas pointed at birds in the sky and asked Cassie to name them. It was one of her favourite games, and she participated eagerly. As they wove through the wooded lanes that surrounded Sàsadh, she picked out the flocks of siskin and chaffinches. As they got nearer to the village and the forest gave way to arable fields, she called out the lapwings and hooded crows with pride. As they passed the sign that indicated the village boundary, she shrugged and sat back in her chair, declaring all they would see now were sparrows. Thomas smiled at both her intelligence and stubbornness.

Patterson's Farm Shop was close to the village border, making it logistically convenient for the local producers. Most of the groceries had travelled fewer food-miles than he'd covered in the drive over. He pulled into the gravel parking area to the side of the wooden barn-like building and stopped the car. Cassie was pushing against the restraints of her car seat by the time Thomas got to her. He unbuckled her and tried to control her hasty descent to the ground.

Thomas often thought the inside of the store was probably what markets used to look like. Annie was strict about only stocking seasonal produce that met her high standards for quality. Today, the steeply angled displays were filled with cauliflower, purple-sprouting broccoli, leeks, rhubarb, and cabbages. Thomas knew he would also find cockles, clams, mussels, and oysters on the fish counter, taken from the Beauly and Moray Firths, and the cold, clear waters of the Scottish east coast. But today, it was the meat counter, or even the cold store that he was interested in. Cassie dragged him impatiently towards a room to their left, which was home to popular pets like rabbits, hamsters, and guinea pigs – as well as kittens and puppies from the local area looking for homes. But he pulled her back as he caught the eye of Annie, who was watching him make his way over. She smiled when she saw him coming.

"You've got a lot of nerve showing your face around these parts," Annie joked.

A few of the customers looked around to see the object of her mirth. Some smiled as they recognised him. But one older man studied him with a cold, stern gaze.

"Hello Cassie, how are you today?" Annie asked.

Cassie swayed to and fro in silence but beamed a brilliant smile back.

"Why don't I ask my friend Alex here to take you to the pet section?" Annie asked, nodding at one of the store assistants, who was unpacking some boxes behind her. "I think the rabbits need feeding."

Cassie nodded her head enthusiastically and looked up at Thomas for permission. He laughed and let go of her hand. She immediately dashed over to the surprised Alex and took his, dragging him off in the direction of the animal room.

"Speaking of feeding, I've come to take you up on your kind offer of helping out with supplying my charges with their meals," Thomas said.

"Aye, I guessed as much," Annie smiled. "Better follow me."

Thomas followed her through to a room filled with cold cabinets and steel counter tops. She opened one of the largest fridges, a big industrial metal one.

"I'll need a hand," she indicated.

Thomas stepped over and helped her haul out a large sackcloth bag. It was long and thin, reminding him a little of a body bag. He realised that was pretty much what it was as Annie opened it. Inside, was a pristine rib cage from a red deer, and some meaty lower leg bones. It was much more than he had expected.

"Loki will love them," Thomas exclaimed.

"It makes me happy to see them not go to waste," Annie replied. "We could also look at the heads, offal, and other bits that don't get used. And of course, there's also pork, mutton, lamb, and beef carcasses to make the most of."

"That'd be great," Thomas said. "Although I'd prefer if we stuck to their more natural prey items as much as possible. I don't want him getting a taste for livestock." He appreciated the support and was determined to make it go as far as he could. "And I want to make sure we pay a more than fair market price. I want the suppliers to know my animals, and theirs, are going to contribute positively to the local economy."

"You'll need to do more than that," Annie shrugged, "but it's a start."

"How bad is it, is it even worth trying?" Thomas asked. His concern was all too evident in his voice.

"Of course it's worth trying," Annie replied. "I'd say you have as much support as you do resistance. Most people know you understand the community. To a certain extent it's not even you they don't trust."

"It's the government," Thomas added.

Annie nodded. "If the last few years has shown us anything, governments and leaders come and go at a fair rate of knots these days. This scheme could lose official support as quickly as it got it. And it has only been six years since..."

"Since a big cat killed a dozen people here," Thomas nodded, finishing her sentence.

"I don't think you've even seen the start of that part of the uproar," Annie sighed. "We're a small village Thomas, but we've got a big grudge there. And long memories."

"I know," Thomas said. "I once hunted every big cat I could. I was motivated by vengeance and hurt. I was a force of destruction." Thomas paused as he remembered his time in the Mato Grosso of Brazil, hunting jaguars and in the wake of his first wife's death. She had been killed by an unusual pride of lions, descendants of the infamous man-eaters of Tsavo. It had taken him seven years to return and settle the score, steering himself right in the process with Catherine's help. He now knew more than ever that big cats needed human protection. It was something he had learnt in Wyoming, under the mentorship of a skilled hunter and trapper named Lee Logan, who had also been one of those killed by the Cannich cat six years ago.

Annie seemed to be able to read his thoughts through his distracted look.

"People know you once lost someone too," she offered. "We know you're not an outsider on this, and that makes a big difference."

"Hopefully, so will this," Thomas nodded, pulling out his wallet.

After grabbing some venison, mushrooms, kale, and potatoes for their own dinner, he went to find Cassie. She was still with Alex. He reported that Cassie had helped him feed the fish, and the rabbits, but had become immovable from a pen that held a new batch of puppies. There were four of them, leftovers from the unplanned mating of a farm collie and terrier. The black and white, wire-haired bundles were lapping up the attention Cassie was lavishing them with. Thomas guessed they were about fourteen weeks old.

"I've already told her they're all reserved," Alex explained, reading Thomas's worried expression. "We only take the ones the owners can't find homes for, and word gets out pretty fast."

"Come on munchkin, you can help me feed Loki if you're good," Thomas suggested, hoping it would be a strong enough pull to draw her away from the overload of cuteness.

"Bye boys," Cassie chirped, getting up from the straw-covered floor of the pen.

Despite having been born in the local village of Drumnadrochit, Thomas had lost his natural accent after moving to England whilst still young. It had been the same for Catherine. So, it gave him great delight to hear Cassie's soft Highland lilt well and truly established. He lifted her up and over the wooden rail of the pen, rubbing noses with her as he drew her close to his face. She laughed as he dropped her down to the floor in a fast swing. By the time they got back to the car, Annie was waiting for them with the big sackcloth bag on a trolley.

Annie crouched down and began to frisk Cassie. "Just need to make sure you're not smuggling any puppies out," she joked, gently tickling Cassie under her arms. The little girl laughed shrilly and uncontrollably.

Thomas loaded the deer meat into the back of the car, thanking Annie for her help again. As they drove back, Cassie explained to Thomas that they hadn't been the right puppies for her anyway, but she was going to keep looking. Thomas was in no doubt she would.

When they arrived back at Sàsadh, Thomas dragged the sackcloth bag over to Loki's pen with Cassie's help. The lynx bounded over to the fence with eager interest. It didn't escape Thomas's attention that the cat rubbed the side of its head and chin against the mesh close to where Cassie stood. In fact, Loki seemed to follow Cassie rather than Thomas as they headed to the gated door of the enclosure. Thomas went in first. Loki retreated to the rear of the pen, watching intently as Thomas pulled out the rib cage from the bag. He kept an eye on Loki as he hid it in a log pile and covered it with some brush. He then closed the sackcloth bag and headed back to the gated door. He picked Cassie up and took her into the enclosure with him. From a distance, they watched Loki dig through the rocks and scrub of his pen until he found the meat.

Having seemingly not noticed them whilst he ate, Loki lifted his head as Thomas and Cassie went to leave. He made a short, foxlike yowl as they headed to the door. The cat took two swift bounds towards them, putting Thomas on alert. When it was just him in the enclosure, Thomas let Loki be quite playful, but he was wary, having Cassie with him. Loki was watching him now, still as a statue.

"Don't get any ideas," Thomas warned the cat. He moved to Cassie's right, getting between her and the lynx. He could see Loki wasn't hunting from his upright stance. But being Labrador-sized, he wasn't an insignificant animal, and was not to be underestimated. Loki bounded forward again, flanking Thomas as if trying to approach from the front. Thomas was a little amused as he watched Cassie instinctively pick up a good-sized rock.

"No need for that, look at his behaviour. What's he trying to tell us?" Thomas asked Cassie.

"He wants to play," Cassie remarked.

"Exactly. He's approaching from the front. He's had a good meal. But he's lonely."

Thomas knew it was a slight risk, but he decided to crouch down and see how Loki reacted. The lynx seemed to relax and walked casually over to him. Thomas kept Cassie to his side, still separating her from the cat. But Loki was in a good mood. He greeted Thomas as he had a few times before, butting his chest with his head and pushing it under his arms. The cat slumped down onto the ground, and Thomas carefully began to stroke the cat, bringing Cassie in closer.

"We're trying to get Loki used to us, so that when the time comes, it will be a little easier to put a radio collar on him. That way, we'll know where he is when we let him out," Thomas explained.

Cassie nodded, her eyes wide in wonder as Thomas took her hand and ran her fingers through Loki's belly fur.

"Better than a doggy, huh?" Thomas asked,

Cassie nodded slowly, then caught herself, suddenly vigorously shaking her head, thrashing her curls from side to side. Thomas laughed. Having had enough attention, Loki jumped up and retreated to a favourite rock, which he sprang to the top of to watch them leave.

Thomas went to a small shed on the other side of the enclosure and put the rest of the deer meat into a chest freezer inside. As he came back out, he heard Catherine calling him. She had a concerned expression on her face as he walked up.

"You have a phone call," she explained. "He says his name is Jesse Logan."

CHAPTER THREE

Thomas picked up the phone. His breath caught in his throat as he held it to his ear.

"Thomas?" Jesse asked, his western United States drawl cutting through the silence.

"Jesse," Thomas replied. "This is a surprise. A welcome one though."

"I've been meaning to, you know," Jesse said quietly. "Just couldn't find the words, or the time, I guess. Bit too much like my old man," he laughed. Thomas felt the tension and nervousness.

"That's no bad thing," Thomas offered. "He was old school, and one of the best."

"It's not been nothing deliberate like," Jesse continued. "I just…I guess I just thought there was nothing to talk about. Pops did what he did. Died doing it."

"I don't know what to say Jesse. I've always felt responsible…"

Jesse's short, shallow breaths were the only thing he heard on the other end of the line. There was no forgiveness there. Maybe there was none to give. Or like him, Jesse didn't know what to say.

"What can I do for you Jesse?" Thomas asked gently.

"Well, would you believe it, I've got myself something of a cat problem. But it's a strange one. I still can't believe…never seen anything like it."

"What happened?"

"I've just had to hire a box truck to come take away six of my heifers," Jesse continued. "All gutted, organs and best bits removed. My bull also has some fresh new scars to impress the ladies with."

Thomas smiled. Jesse sounded like his dad.

"I didn't get much of a look," Jesse added, "but I saw eye-shine from the treeline. It hung around to watch."

Thomas knew that mountain lions were known as ghost or phantom cats by some of the Native American tribes, partly because of their habit of following hunters. Rather than the aggressive behaviour it was often interpreted as, curiosity was something the cat of the Americas was well known for. The number of cows attacked had made Thomas first consider Jesse was describing a dog attack, but he knew Jesse was his father's son, and recognised the difference. And being watched from the trees confirmed it. Only a big cat was likely to do that. Cats weren't just predators driven by instinct. They observed their prey, learnt their routines and behaviours. And struck at the perfect moment.

"I'd say maybe a female with older cubs, but I can't see them taking down six heifers," Thomas exclaimed.

"Thanks for not insulting my intelligence," Jesse replied. "The kills are clean. Rib bones sheered in a straight line. Organs fished out from the cavity. Claw marks are almost surgical they're so neat."

"Sounds like a cat alright," Thomas sighed.

"There's something else, but I didn't feel like sharing with anyone else."

"What?" Thomas asked.

"I'm sure you remember Wyoming winters. I got a print. I'm going to send it to you. Once you seen it, call me back."

Thomas confirmed his contact details and hung up the phone. He walked through to the study and opened his laptop. He scrolled through the messages in his inbox and paused as he saw a new, unopened email appear. He clicked on it, wondering why Jesse had been so mysterious. Jesse could probably identify a mountain lion print better than he could. What he saw made him stiffen in his chair as a sudden chill built in his chest.

The image filled the screen. Jesse had put his own hand down to show its comparative size, and the tip of his boot could be seen in the bottom corner of the frame. The pug mark, frozen into the ice and stained by the pooled blood, was longer than Jesse's hand, and nearly twice as wide. He remembered the Cannich cat, and the first time he had seen its pug marks. He had compared them to his own hand then, having to spread his fingers out to do so. The prints were eerily similar in size. But the Cannich cat was dead. This was something new.

"Never seen anything like it," Jesse exclaimed when Thomas called him back.

"Unfortunately, I can't say the same," Thomas replied.

"Whatever did this, it's bigger than an Amur tiger," Jesse stated. "It's no mountain lion."

"The only thing I can think of is, you're dealing with something like what your father and I faced here in Cannich. A hybrid of some kind, like a liger."

"I'll come straight out with it," Jesse replied. "I figure you owe me. But if I'm being honest, I don't know who else to ask for help anyways. Whatever this thing is, it isn't ordinary. I figure that's your specialty these days."

Thomas paused. He was offended by Jesse's accusation of owing him. He hadn't been the one to involve Lee Logan in the hunt for the Cannich cat. He couldn't decide if Jesse was being arrogant, or if like his father would have, was shielding his pride by not directly asking for help outright. He also didn't know if that meant he knew Jesse well, or hardly at all.

"Jesse, I have a family now. We're right in the middle of a project. Dropping everything would be extremely difficult. I'm not saying no, but I'd need to look into it. If that's not good enough..."

"I'm not going anywhere," Jesse replied. Thomas could hear the nervous hope in his voice.

"Well let's hope your mysterious visitor is," Thomas replied, his own tone softening.

"It was good to talk to you Thomas. I'll hear from you then?"

"You can count on it."

The line went dead. Thomas looked up, meeting Catherine's curious gaze. The corners of her mouth were turned upward, stifling a smug smile.

"We can call in a favour from Paleo Park and have one of the keepers feed Loki. At a push, Annie might even do it. Mum would look after the dogs," Catherine suggested.

Paleo Park was a zoological attraction in the next glen. The collection was made up of native animals, as well as more exotic species that had once called Britain home, before and after the ravages of the ice age. They had worked closely with them ever since the Cannich cat had rampaged through the park, seeking sex and sustenance. The cat had killed a keeper, and several of the animals, including a full wolf pack. Thomas was again reminded of the similarities of the attacks on Jesse's cattle.

"Cath, it's not a mountain lion, I don't know what it is," Thomas replied. "I wouldn't feel comfortable taking you or

Cassie on any kind of hunt."

"As far as I'm concerned, my part isn't your decision," Catherine stated, raising an eyebrow and walking over. She twisted on to his lap and lifted his chin with her fingers. "And as for Cassie, I'm not saying take her out in the field or anything. But Wyoming isn't exactly the wilds of Africa."

"You really want to go, don't you?" Thomas asked, surprised.

"I think you *need* to go, and I'm not prepared to stay behind," she explained. "And I've never been to America. Yosemite…"

"Has more people go missing in it than any other National Park," Thomas quipped.

"Guess we should take a map, then," Catherine laughed, hugging him closer and resting her cheek on his. "Wyoming was a second home to you," she nodded towards the numerous pictures on the wall of the study.

Thomas's eyes went straight to a picture of him, Lee, and the other members of the Hole-in-the-Wall gang. They stood with their backs to a huge mountain range. He didn't want to say it out loud to Catherine, but it perhaps felt even more of a home than Sàsadh had before they'd married.

He turned and kissed his wife on the cheek.

"Then we're homeward bound," he declared, his eyes lifting to the window and the mountains beyond.

He felt a slight tightening in his stomach as he realised they would soon be replaced by ones more impressive, dangerous, and harbouring a new, mysterious predator.

CHAPTER FOUR

Elijah Garrett looked up at the swaying tops of the Ponderosa pines and Douglas firs, gauging the strength of the incoming storm. He'd seen worse, but he was beginning to question his judgement in heading out. His camp was set up in a small clearing, in a secluded woodland on land his nephew owned. The Bighorn National Forest was a few miles north, and was connected by corridors of woodland and patches of wilderness like the one he was camped in. It made for good hunting land, and he was appreciative of his nephew letting him use it. The kid was a rich suit in Denver. Elijah couldn't remember the last time his nephew had hunted with him or been up here.

He leaned over and added a fresh log to the fire. It cracked and fizzed as the cold breeze fed the flames. There was something else in the air too. Something that had both him and the dogs on edge. His two blue-tick coonhounds were brothers, and they stuck to each other like glue. But as he watched them standing by the tent, their shoulders hunched and their heads low, he realised he wouldn't have gotten a piece of sandpaper between their shivering butts. His other coonhound, a redbone, was perhaps the meanest yet best hunting dog he'd ever owned. But even he was pacing the camp, occasionally throwing a growl into the night.

Elijah put it down to the storm, but he piled another two logs onto the fire. The red and yellow licks of flame jumped high into the air, pirouetting and sparking wildly as the cold mountain breeze fueled them into frenzy. The dogs padded over to him, whining their delight at the warmth, light, and safety the flames brought. Even the redbone wagged his tail and shoved his head into Elijah's chest.

"Don't know what you boys are so happy 'bout," Elijah declared. "You're still sleeping in the truck."

By Elijah's standards, that was a kindness. The dogs were workers, born, bred, and trained tough. He knew they could see out a Wyoming storm. But their behaviour was getting to him, and he wasn't mean-spirited. Their coop in the back of the truck was as good as anywhere. They'd feel secure, but he knew they'd miss the warmth of the snow some time during the night. Their fleece blankets weren't nearly as good insulation as the flakes of white that would naturally cover them when the storm hit. He always enjoyed watching them erupt from their covering of white in the morning, playful as pups when they did so. Maybe he'd see what they wanted to do. They might settle down after a few moments by the fire.

He made his way to the cooler and opened it. He pulled out a large tin of bacon and beans, and grabbed the pan and a long, cast-iron hook to hang it from. He didn't usually cook right in camp if he could help it, but he was too tired and jittery to do anything else. Besides, the dogs were usually good enough deterrent. They were big and bold enough to see off most black bears, and grizzlies were few and far between outside of Yellowstone. In any case, most would still be curled up in their dens, sleeping out the colder months of early Spring. He still paused, and walked to the truck, which faced back down the trail leading to the clearing. He opened the driver's door and grabbed his knapsack. Inside was a flare gun, his hatchet, and his Taurus 44. Tracker revolver.

From the bed of the truck, he also took three kerosene lamps and hooked them onto trees around the camp. They formed a tight triangle of illumination around his tent and working area. He shrugged off the thought that from the dark trees beyond, his camp now looked like a shining beacon. But he walked back to the fire more confidently, nonetheless.

He soon had the can of beans and bacon on the go. He took the hatchet from the knapsack and used it to split some more logs for the fire, expertly stripping the dried wood he'd already stacked and put aside. He threw the hatchet down, the blade striking deep into the large, smooth log he was using as a bench. He slumped back down. Lost in thought, he stirred the beans occasionally. He liked to let them simmer until the sauce had reduced a bit, leaving a thick stew of mushed beans and soft meat. The sweetness of the beans and the salt of the bacon lifted from the pan in deep wafts. He set about feeding the dogs, knowing they would never leave him alone whilst he ate if he didn't. Their chow came out of cans too.

"Don't think you're getting anything better than I am," Elijah commented, taking a curious sniff at the contents. "Actually, you might be," he chuckled, emptying the rest.

He gave them generous portions and made a little fuss of each dog. The heat of the fire and the warmth of a good meal were helping to distil the uneasiness from earlier.

As Elijah finally sat back down on the log by the fire, the redbone stood up and walked several feet towards the treeline. Elijah froze, a spoon of beans halfway to his mouth as the dog let out a menacing growl. As Elijah watched the dog, he knew the difference between the dog's nervous behaviour before, and the absolute certainty it was now showing. Its ears were pricked, and its spine and tail straight. Then it pinned its ears back and started to snap its teeth in fevered barks. The two blue ticks were by its side instantly, adding their baying howls to the mix. As the dogs began to pace frantically along the perimeter of the clearing, Elijah heard the sound he'd been dreading. The sorrowful, rumbling grunts of a bear on the move.

As he listened, he heard the snap of twigs underneath its feet, and brush being moved aside by its bulk. The animal was being brazen. Perhaps it had just woken from its torpor state unexpectedly and early. Or perhaps it had sensed an intruder in its territory, equally brazen, flaunting food and bringing dogs. If recently woken from its slumber, it was hungry – perhaps not fattening up pre-winter. If it was investigating a stranger, it would be anxious. Either way, it would be bad-tempered.

Elijah stood up and joined the dogs. He edged forward, the three hounds falling silent as he did so. He walked over to the nearest kerosene lamp, lifting it high as he stared into the trees. It threw long, drawn shadows into the surrounding forest. He lifted a hand to shield his eyes and squinted into the gloom.

The face that lunged out of the darkness towards him was hideous. A twisted, crumpled nose and mahogany, bloodshot eyes that seemed to glow red as the light touched them. Curved, yellowed fangs set in pink, drawn-back gums against a black void of the throat. The bear bellowed as it came for him. In his fright, Elijah swung the only thing he had in his arms, the kerosene lamp. It smashed against the bear's jaws, the glass turning to shards and the liquid fuel bursting from the container and soaking the bear's face and muzzle. The bear reared up on its hind legs, pawing at its face and howling with rage. It seemed to stumble backwards, and Elijah realised the fuel had gotten into its eyes.

Elijah scrambled backwards as the dogs rushed forwards, surrounding the bear and baiting it with mad barks and lunges of their own. That's when Elijah's heel hit the log and he spun backwards through the fire, scattering the burning logs. The bear lifted its head and roared. It batted one of the blue ticks aside with a cuff of its paw and charged across the clearing towards Elijah, rolling its head. The hump on its back shook as it powered its heavy forelimbs. The knapsack was just in arm's reach, and Elijah fumbled for it in a maddened panic. His hand slipped through the open top. He felt relief wash over him as his fingertips found the pistol grip of the gun. He clawed at it, dragging it into his palm and out from the bag with a cry of triumph.

The bear was enormous. He'd never seen a grizzly so big. Its fur was dark, almost chocolate coloured, with red and blonde patches on its hump and forelimbs. The hair was long and spike-like. As it rolled its head and popped its jaws now mere feet from him, he aimed the gun and fired.

It was only then, dazzled as he was by the eruption from the barrel, that he realised he was holding the flare gun. The projectile slammed into the right side of the bear's face, which burst into flame and engulfed the animal's lower jaw. The fuel in its fur ignited instantly, the flare still burning and scorching deep into the flesh. The bear yowled, driving its face into the snow and screaming with pain. Elijah watched in horror as the bear reared up again onto its hind legs. It then slammed back to the ground and charged into the trees. It broke the second kerosene lantern from its mooring, as it brushed aside the sapling it was hanging on. It too shattered and ignited a new fire along the bear's back. The animal roared, attacking the tree and throwing itself onto its back in panic. It shuddered as it righted itself, turning to look at Elijah.

If he thought it had been ugly before, now it was nothing

short of hell-spawn. Raw, pink, blistered flesh had replaced the fur on the right side of its face. An opaque, misty white eye twisted madly in its socket. The remaining fur on the right side of its muzzle was singed black. The skin there had shrunk and withered, revealing the yellowed teeth. It growled. It was a sound unlike anything Elijah had heard before. Full of rage, sorrow, intent, and despair all at the same time. It huffed and then lumbered into the trees, letting out a morose whine as it went.

Elijah sat there in the silence, his hand trembling, the flare gun still pointed in the bear's direction. As the whimpering of the dogs brought him back to reality, he tried to get to his feet. He was shaking so badly it took three attempts. The blue tick the bear had struck was dead. He left it and the rest of his things where they were, hurrying the redbone and the dead dog's brother into the back of the truck. He dropped the keys twice before he got them into the ignition. Tears streamed down his cheeks in shock as he tore back down the trail, headed for town.

Above him, the first flurries of the brewing storm began to descend on the Wyoming landscape.

CHAPTER FIVE

Thomas had insisted on flying first class, which meant a trip to London beforehand. It had also been a good excuse for Catherine's brother to meet up with them. He had been only too happy to take the keys of the modified Range Rover in exchange for giving them a lift to the airport. Thomas still wasn't exactly sure when they would be returning, and he had no intention of letting it sit in an airport car park for weeks on end.

By the time they reached Denver International, Catherine was glad of Thomas's insistence in their more exclusive travel arrangements. The private escort through security had been nothing short of a godsend, especially with Thomas's extra and unusual luggage. She hadn't known that Thomas had dual citizenship in both the U.S. and U.K. until she had brought up the subject of where they were going to stay.

"I have to confess, I still own a lodge on what is now Jesse's land," Thomas admitted. "I've had it cleaned and prepped for our arrival."

"You're good at forgetting to mention things like that," Catherine scolded. "And why couldn't it be an island in the Caribbean rather than a shack in the Wyoming wilderness?"

"I didn't say it was a shack," Thomas laughed. "It's not like I've been paying rent or anything. To tell the truth, it was a little too easy to forget, along with Jesse and the rest of my memories here."

Catherine stroked his hand and lay her head on his shoulder as they waited in the first-class lounge for the concierge to return. When he did so, he was carrying Thomas's rifle case and a large envelope. He handed them both over with a smile.

"If you'll just follow me Mr. and Mrs. Walker, I'll escort you to the freight terminal, where your car is waiting for you. Your luggage has already been packed, except for this of course." The smart-suited young man handed Thomas the gun case.

"Why do we need to go to the freight terminal for our car?" Catherine asked, surprised.

Thomas smiled sheepishly.

"We're picking up another one of your toys, aren't we?" Catherine realised, unimpressed again.

"Mummy says you have more toys than me, Daddy," Cassie declared, a cheeky grin spreading across her face.

"And then some," Catherine muttered under her breath.

"I don't like normal cars," Thomas shrugged. "They're too claustrophobic and they're made out of plastic."

They got up and followed the concierge to a golf buggy. They climbed in for their brisk ride across the airport to the freight terminal. Cassie thought it was even better than the first-class seats on the airplane. They were dropped at a large, private hanger and Thomas tipped and dismissed their escort.

Sitting in the centre of the hangar was a large 4x4 truck. It had started out in life as a 1979 Chevrolet Blazer K5, but it had been seriously upgraded since. It was a dark, matt, slate-grey colour. It had a black powder-coated front grille, side steps, and a matching light rig over the cab. Oversized panels flanked the wheel arches. The only flash of colour was a turquoise coach stripe running the length of the vehicle. The back of the truck had a black, windowed cover for the rear section. Catherine could see their bags and cases of equipment had already been expertly packed into the compartment. Thomas took the keys from the envelope and blipped the remote, before opening the back window of the truck bed cover and sliding his rifle in on top of the luggage.

The truck sat high on rugged, off-road tyres and black powder-coated wheels. Even with the flash of turquoise, the truck looked mean and menacing. His eye caught the badge displaying the simple logo for a company called Tinker Industries, and he smiled. Thomas walked around the truck once, admiring the handiwork of the storage garage. He could see it had been money well spent over the last few years after all.

"So, what's this one called," Catherine asked, punching him on the arm.

"Beast," Thomas replied, grinning. "Mainly due to its supercharged, V8 diesel engine. It's one of a kind."

"So are you," Catherine chimed.

He opened the driver's door, and watched Cassie scramble up onto the grey-coloured leather bench seat. Again, the only flash of colour was the aqua-toned piping of the seats and the matching turquoise stain of the brushed aluminium dashboard. Cassie squinted at the folded down 'occasional' rear bench, a confused expression on her face. She ran a finger over the embossed dials and the leather sports steering wheel that matched the upholstery.

"Where's my seat, Daddy?"

"Well in America, in older cars at least, you get to sit up front with Mummy and me," Thomas explained.

"I like this car," Cassie declared in awe.

They headed out of Denver, following Interstate 25 towards Cheyenne and the Wyoming border. After that, Thomas headed west on the 80 towards Laramie and settled in for the drive, Cassie cuddled up close on the bench seat beside him. She soon fell asleep, despite the impressive vistas appearing and disappearing in the windscreen. After a few hours, Thomas decided to head towards Casper, taking the quieter route 30. Soon after, Thomas spotted a silver building and bright neon lights up ahead on the side of the road. The sign read 'The Flirty 30 Diner'.

"How about your first real taste of America?" Thomas suggested, pulling into the parking area.

"I could definitely use a coffee," Catherine nodded in sleepy agreement.

She gently began to wake Cassie up too, concerned she wouldn't sleep later.

They walked in, and were immediately greeted by a young blonde girl, her hair tied back in a no-nonsense ponytail.

"Howdy folks," came the Western drawl. "My name is Toni, and I'll be your waitress today, what can I do for y'all?"

Thomas laughed as he saw Cassie was mesmerised by Toni and her accent, as well as her natural all-American enthusiasm.

"These two have never been stateside before…"

"Say no more, right this way please," Toni exclaimed, escorting them to a booth with wrap-around red leather seats and a shiny, linoleum table at its centre.

Cassie was even more impressed when Toni brought over a banana milkshake, in a glass large enough for her arm to fit in. She slurped it happily whilst Thomas and Catherine supped at the boiling hot coffee Toni continually topped up for them. Catherine ordered a chicken salad with extra bacon and ranch dressing. Thomas ignored her good intentions, selecting deep-fried dill pickle chips, buttermilk fried chicken wings, and a chili cheese dog with sweet potato fries. Catherine picked at his side dishes, and he stole some of her salad, as if to balance out both their meals.

As Thomas stretched out across his side of the booth, he looked up to an old TV that was showing the news. The words 'BEAR ATTACK!' scrolled across the screen. Thomas asked Toni if she could turn the sound up, which she did. Thomas watched as Elijah Garret told his harrowing tale of being attacked at his camp and losing one of his dogs. The crew were quick to also blame the marauding animal for a spate of livestock deaths in the area.

"The bear from hell by the sounds of it," the cocky anchor quipped to his co-host.

"With the scars to prove it, Jed," the brunette wearing too much makeup replied.

"Maybe we should call him Lucifer," the anchor declared. "Either way, it looks like a local farmer has hell to pay for speaking out against Wyoming hunting laws."

"Hope he can make a decent humble pie," the brunette joked, before moving onto the next item.

Thomas was already dialling Jesse Logan.

"I don't care what they're saying, it weren't no bear that got my heifers," Jesse confirmed over the phone. From what Thomas had already seen, he was inclined to agree.

"Still, maybe don't completely dismiss it as a possibility," Thomas suggested, delicately. We'll be there in a couple of hours in any case."

"Thanks for the warning," Jesse replied. Thomas got the feeling Jesse was smiling. The mobile phone went dead. Jesse was still a man of few words, whatever his mood.

Thomas reached across the table for his phone. The number he'd dialled rang, then picked up. He was surprised, expecting to hear the international ringtone. But the line was good, and Kelly Keelson's voice came in clear and loud.

"Hello Thomas, this is unexpected," she said.

"Sorry for calling so early, but..."

"It's okay, I'm actually in the good old U.S of A, so it's pretty late in the day as it happens."

"Strange," Thomas laughed, "I was just calling to say the same thing. I didn't get a chance to give you a heads up."

"Anything I can stick my beak into?" Keelson enquired.

Thomas smiled. Keelson was a brilliant TV producer, but her journalistic roots always showed at the first sign of a storm. They'd worked together many times since they'd first met when the story of the Cannich cat had been big news and turned into Keelson's big break.

"Maybe later...how come you're in the land of the free?" Thomas asked.

"I have a potential interview with a billionaire recluse. Can't say no to that," Kelly laughed.

"Okay, well, watch your six and keep in touch...it's good to know you're around Kelly."

"Likewise," Kelly replied. The line went dead.

Thomas was lost in thought, questioning whether he believed in coincidence or not. He pushed his food around his plate for a few minutes, trying to make sense of things. He was surprised to hear the phone ring again. As he looked down, he saw the name Jericho O'Connell flash up on the screen. Jericho had been through thick and thin with Thomas, and they had hunted side by side. Five years ago, they had taken on the pride of lions that had killed his first wife. Kelly had been with them then too. Somehow, together, they had also overthrown an African weapons trafficker to boot. They'd been in regular contact since, but he was still surprised to be getting the call. He hadn't had time to let Jericho know they were going away either.

"Heard you're back in the land of the free?" came the Irish accent, clear and crisp down the line.

"It was a little sudden," Thomas explained, almost defensively. "I'm in Wyoming, helping Jesse Logan with an unusual cat problem."

"So I hear," Jericho replied.

"Really, from whom?" Thomas enquired, surprised.

"Word gets around my friend." Thomas could feel Jericho's grin even down the line.

"So, where do you find yourself these days?" Thomas asked.

"Just flew into Boston, the only real home of the Irish this side of the big blue," Jericho exclaimed.

"Well how about that," Thomas jeered in mock surprise. "In that case, why don't you make yourself useful and head my way?"

"I intend to, but need to sort a few things out before I do. Should be with you in a couple of days though."

"Okay, now I'm really confused," Thomas replied. "It sounds like you aren't here by accident. Who told you I was out here?"

"I'll try and explain when I get there," Jericho said, more serious now. "But in the meantime, watch your back."

The line went dead, Jericho having apparently hung up. Thomas stared at the phone in disbelief.

"Sounds like we'll be having company?" Catherine asked.

"Doesn't it just?" Thomas replied.

CHAPTER SIX

It was four hours later when Thomas turned into a long, straight drive, lined by prairie meadows filled with swathes of buffalo grass and blue grama. A small sign hung over the arched entranceway – Caterwaul Ranch. Below that was a smaller sign that read "Home of Tinker Industries". Piebald and chestnut American Saddlebred horses grazed lazily in bright winter sunshine that hinted at the spring to come, before the punishing cold of the night would erase it again. For Wyoming, the Caterwaul ranch was a small affair of 1,700 acres. The 'big house' as it had been called when Thomas had lived here, was about half a mile up ahead. Cassie scrambled up from her seat, clambering over Catherine's lap to look out of the window at the horses as they passed.

"Maybe Jesse will let us take some of the horses out?" Catherine suggested.

"I'm sure of it," Thomas replied, a knowing smile spreading across his lips.

Stands of bur oak, common hackberry, and paper birch lined the pastures and meadows, and Thomas could see bunches of woodland had sprung up further out in his absence. Jesse preferred natural and native trees and plants, and his livestock needs were small. Thomas was looking forward to exploring the land on horseback again and seeing what else had changed. But the thought slipped from his mind as the big house came into view. Standing in the centre of the trail, Jesse Logan watched them pull up, his hands on his hips and a quizzical smile on his face. He reminded Thomas of a young Tom Berenger and looked every bit the cowboy, from the boots to the flannel shirt. His hair was short and blondish brown, and his eyes shone a bright blue through an unblinking and piercing squint. Thomas stopped the car and cracked the door. They all climbed out and shuffled over.

"Evening folks," Jesse greeted them, studying them quietly.

"Hello Jesse, how goes?" Thomas replied.

There was a hesitation, neither man really knowing what to do. Thomas couldn't quite bring himself to offer a handshake, worried it might be refused. As if reading his thoughts, Jesse shrugged and extended his hand. Thomas gladly took it and shook vigorously.

"It *is* good to see you Jesse," Thomas offered.

"You too, it's been too long. I 'preciate you coming out."

"Couldn't stop them once I suggested it," Thomas added, nodding at Catherine and Cassie. "Catherine, Cassie, meet Jesse Logan."

Catherine came forward, dragging Cassie with the momentum, who clung to her mother's legs bashfully, but still didn't take her eyes off the cowboy in front of her.

"Cassie was admiring your horses on the drive in," Catherine explained.

"Is that so?" Jesse exclaimed, squatting down to Cassie's height. "Well, your daddy and I used to ride all over the ranch. Figure you might be up for doing the same, little lady?"

Cassie nodded her head enthusiastically.

"One thing we're still not short of here is critters," Jesse laughed. "I figure you still know where your place is. I'll let you get settled, then give you folks the nickel tour."

"Thanks Jesse – shouldn't take us too long," Thomas replied.

He picked Cassie up from behind, and swung her precariously to and fro, as Catherine opened the truck door for him to lift her inside. She giggled as he let her go and she tumbled onto the bench seat. Catherine walked around the truck and climbed in the other side. Thomas waved to Jesse as they passed, then aimed the Beast down a side-track that led away from the ranch house.

About a mile and a half further down, he turned the truck onto a deeply rutted trail. Cassie laughed as the car bucked and bounced with each jolt. Coming over the brow of a slight hill, Thomas caught the roofline of a building a little way ahead. As the truck rolled down the slope on the other side, he let it gain some speed before hitting the brakes, sending a satisfying spray of gravel into the little turning area beside the cabin.

"Welcome to our little piece of Wyoming," Thomas declared. "Lodge View."

The building looked like an old wooden barn, painted in a dark green that matched the Douglas firs standing across the trail from it. The windows and doorways were framed in a dark red glaze, and as Catherine looked, she saw that the rear reached out onto a large pond that stretched nearly eighty feet in length. At its end, she found where the house got its name. An impressive beaver dam reached across its width, and a cap of insulating snow covered the mound of sticks and dried mud that made up the lodge.

"We have some of nature's best engineers and architects as neighbours," Thomas smiled, lifting Cassie up to see.

"Otters?" Cassie asked, not understanding and looking at the lodge quizzically.

"Beavers, munchkin," Thomas explained. With any luck, you'll see them later."

The house was already unlocked, and they all walked in to explore. Thomas was glad to find the house-keeping service had kept it just as he'd left it. The ground floor wasn't much more than a boat house that opened onto the pond, with a small canoe tied up to a berth. But there was also a small bathroom, a hallway, and a stairwell that led upstairs.

As they climbed the stairs, they found themselves in the kitchen. It was separated from the living area beyond by a breakfast bar that curved around the front. The wooden floorboards creaked as the three of them shifted their weight. Thomas crossed to the other end of the room, where large double carriage doors with windows in their upper panes looked out onto the pond. He checked the bottom sections were locked before opening the top halves to let in some air.

To his left were two rooms, a bedroom and a bathroom, separated from each other and the main living area by wooden panel walls. He scooped Cassie up and walked into the bedroom.

"This is your room, Cassie, what do you think?" Thomas asked.

Cassie's eyes lingered on the large wooden bed with a patchwork quilt, the warm rugs lining the floors, and the bay window with a seat covered in oversized cushions and blankets.

"Can we live here?" Cassie asked flippantly.

"For a little while at least," Thomas laughed.

Catherine sank down on one of the big couches in the living area. It was extremely soft and comfortable, and the back and sides were lined with oak bookshelves that came up to the full height of the sofa. An old lamp with a multicoloured glass shade sat on the top of the one that encased the right side. She flicked it on.

"So…where's our room," she asked, looking around.

"Right above you," Thomas called, looking down at her from a balcony that faced the living area and kitchen.

"How did you get up there?" But he had already disappeared again.

A moment later, he skirted around a column on the far side of the room. He took her hand and led her to a ladder that led straight up into the loft where he'd been. Cassie was hot on their heels in scrambling up after them. The bedroom was similarly appointed to the other rooms, with wooden furniture that matched the floor and walls, soft textiles and rugs for a homely feel, another patchwork quilt, and a log burning stove in the corner that matched the one Catherine had seen in the kitchen. The bed faced a large, cantilever window that looked out onto the pond.

"It certainly is a room with a view," Catherine declared, squeezing Thomas's hand.

They spent the next hour unpacking the car and getting settled in.

"Let's go for a walk and take Jesse up on that tour before we turn in," Thomas suggested.

As they walked out, they heard a terrific clap and a splash. Thomas quickly pointed out over the pond, where they just caught the sight of a beaver disappearing beneath the surface. It appeared again nearly twenty feet away, its long, straight back gliding effortlessly through the water towards the dam.

"Think we gave it a fright," Thomas explained. "But hopefully they'll get used to us and be a little more sociable after a while."

Rather than walk back along the trail, Thomas cut across country, leading them through meadows lined with winterfat bushes, chokecherry saplings, skunkbush sumac, and Indian paintbrush bushes. It was too early in the year, but he knew the grasses would be dotted with pussy toe flowers, purple prairie clover, wild bergamot bee balm and numerous other wildflowers too, come the late spring. He savoured the fresh scents of the shrubs and ponderosa pines that surrounded the pond and Lodge View. As he looked back, he could see they had climbed upwards to gain the viewpoint. He led them into the trees.

Cassie crunched the hard ground with her boots, looking for snow and ice that hadn't melted during the day. There was more of it here in the woods, where the temperature stayed a little colder and sunlight didn't always get to touch the ground. Thomas caught up to her in a few strides and took her hand. She looked up at him with a scowl.

"It's not like walking through the woods at home munchkin," Thomas told her. "There are things you need to be aware of. These woods are home to everything from bobcats to maybe even the odd prairie rattlesnake. Even some of the things that don't like eating little girls, like moose and elk, can be dangerous if we come across them. Stick with me or mum, okay?"

"Okay," Cassie sighed.

They crossed the patch of woodland and came out on the other side much further down the trail, with the big house now in sight. Jesse seemed to be waiting for them, sitting on a bench on the main porch. He was smiling as they approached.

"All settled in?" Jesse asked.

Thomas nodded.

"Glad to see you still know your way around," Jesse added, stepping off the porch. "Come on in."

Jesse showed them around the big house. The furnishings seemed homelier, perhaps through being used more often, Catherine thought. The textiles all had Native American motifs and patterns, giving the interior a vibrant and colourful glow. The same simple neatness, with a place for everything and everything in its place, echoed throughout the house as it had back at Lodge View. Catherine figured Thomas and Jesse were pretty alike in that way.

"Is the young'n okay round dogs?" Jesse asked. "Mine are kind of big, but they're very friendly."

"Believe me, the bigger the better," Thomas explained. "As you know, we adopted Arturo."

The Italian mastiff had originally belonged to Ryan Jackson, another member of the original hole-in-the-wall gang. Like Jesse's father, he too had been killed by the Cannich cat. Thomas saw something ignite in Jesse's eyes then flicker away as he looked down. He went to a door at the back of the kitchen and opened it. There was a sudden cacophony of barking and the sound of paws thudding over the floor. Three big dogs swarmed into the room, and Cassie in turn swarmed towards them. Thomas cast his eye over the animals.

Two stood out over the other, literally. The massive, shaggy-haired canines were Irish wolfhounds, one a dirty white colour, the other steel grey.

"These two are Fergus and Dougal," Jesse nodded, following Thomas's gaze.

"You have an American bandogge?" Catherine asked, watching Cassie walk up to the other dog.

The creamy-grey coloured bandogge was large and muscular. It had a white chest and paws, making it strikingly handsome. Cassie stopped, still some distance away, turning to her side. The big dog padded over. Cassie let it sniff at the back of her hand, and her hair. With the gentlest of touches, she let her fingers glide slowly back and forth over the dog's shoulder blade. Thomas watched with pride as she instinctively kept her hands where the dog could easily see them and kept her face and eyes away from his. The dog responded with an enthusiastic thumping of his tail, nearly knocking Cassie over in the process. She giggled.

"Looks like your little lady knows her way around dogs," Jesse stated, seemingly impressed. "And yes, he's a bandogge. I call him Arnold, because of that big ol' chest of his. They weren't originally bred for fighting, and they have a reputation they don't deserve. All dogs are individuals, and they need to be treated as such."

"You two are going to get on fine," Thomas laughed. "Catherine has been fighting something called the dangerous dogs act back home."

"Or the draconian dogs act as we prefer to call it," Catherine added.

Jesse walked over to Cassie and knelt down beside her.

"Now, these guys are okay," Jesse explained. "But in a minute, I'm going to take y'all out to the kennels. The dogs in there are workers, and they ain't so friendly. Don't go near them without me or your folks, okay?"

Cassie nodded feverishly.

Jesse walked them over from the big house to the stables behind. They were painted a stark black, in contrast to the more colourful out-buildings that made up the ranch. Thomas had expected the same outbreak of barking and excitement from the dogs inside, but they were curiously silent.

"I've trained them to keep quiet unless on the hunt, or starting one," Jesse explained, reading Thomas's surprise. He swung the large door of the barn-like stable open, and beckoned them in.

Jesse hadn't switched the lights on, and it took a moment for Thomas's eyes to adjust. The dogs were milling around a large pen that took up the majority of the stable. Right in front of him was a shed made out of corrugated iron with a large steel door.

"I originally kept the feed stored in bags here. But they soon figured out how to get over the top of the pen to get at it. Wood didn't keep them out neither. They've tried to dig under the panels, and they've had some success bending the wall nearest the pen, but it's kept them out so far."

"Resourceful," Thomas commented, concerned and impressed at the same time.

"I needed dogs that could think for themselves," Jesse replied. "This was a small price to pay."

Thomas turned his attention back to the dogs. Six sets of copper-coloured eyes were fixed on him and the others from inside the pen. The dogs had short, wiry coats that were a dirty white colour, with flecks of grey and red marking their back, tails, and chest. Their muzzles were broad and blunt, but not too short, reminding him of a Japanese Akita. They were of an imposing size. Each would easily stand shoulder to shoulder with the gigantic Irish wolfhounds they'd seen a few moments ago. But they were more streamlined and muscular – more like wiry haired Great Danes on steroids.

"They look formidable," Catherine exclaimed. "And they show incredible discipline."

"They're problem solvers," Jesse explained. "They've learnt to figure things out without getting excited or wound up."

"I'm guessing that's down to you?" Thomas asked.

Jesse nodded.

"What are they?" Cassie asked.

"They've got a bit of everything in their makeup," Jesse replied. "They have the scenting ability of an otterhound, so water won't slow them down none. Then there's tenacity of a Kentucky treeing walker, the strength of a wolfhound, the height of a great Dane, and the brains of a Belgian shepherd."

"I can't decide if that's a recipe for disaster or if you've created the ultimate hunting dog," Thomas said.

"Maybe both," Jesse added, in what sounded like a challenge. "I call them Wyoming Waheela hounds."

"After the Canadian bear-dog monsters, from Inuit legends?" Thomas asked.

Jesse nodded, smiling.

"You plan to hunt cats with these?" Thomas realised.

Jesse nodded again, dropping the smile. "Just one cat for now, but there ain't much they can't take down as a pack. That's the idea anyways."

As they left the stables, Thomas looked back at the pen. One dog lowered its head and let out a soft growl. He didn't know if it was a threat or a warning, but it didn't sound friendly. He closed the door behind him.

"Now all that's really left is the one beast on the farm I can't control. Figure you might make yourself useful," Jesse said to Thomas, as they strolled back across the track to another set of stables, these ones painted a more pleasing red like the big house.

"Khan?" Thomas asked.

Jesse laughed. "Yep. Couldn't bring myself to get rid of him, but he won't let anyone else asides the vet get near him anyways, and even that's only when sedated. Tell the truth, I'm kind of looking forward to the twos of you getting reacquainted."

Catherine shot Thomas a quizzical glance. He dismissed it with a wave of his hand, knowing she was about to find out anyway as they walked inside. The stables had a similar layout to the one the Waheela hounds were housed in, with a utility area to the front, and two, large, sectioned-off areas to the rear. Jesse approached the stable door nearest the entrance of the building. The top part was swung wide open and was immediately filled by the head of a beautiful palomino horse. Its dark honey-coloured hide and brilliant white mane were striking to look at. The horse also had large, deep-set eyes that made it look radiant.

"This is Princess, and she's real royalty. She's an Arabian, and an absolute sweetheart. Unlike her stable mate," Jesse said.

As if to make his point, Jesse opened the top half of the stable door next to the palomino's, which had been partially closed. The creaking hinge was answered with a furious snort, and a slamming kick into the wooden wall of the stable that shook the dust from the beams. No head appeared over the top, but Thomas and Catherine could see the silhouette of a large, dark coloured horse a little way in. Its tail brushed back and forth defiantly, and its breath was expunged in deep, heavy exhales from its nostrils.

"And that, is Khan," Jesse laughed. "Admittedly, my own creation. His sire was a wild black mustang stallion, and his mother an Arab with a temperament as dark as her hide. Thomas is the only one who's ever been able to ride him, but I doubt Khan remembers that now. Should be interesting."

Thomas walked over to the open stable and looked in. He didn't venture too close, letting Khan get a good look at him without encroaching on his space. Where the boundary between them lay was something to discover another day. He turned his back, only to see Cassie march past him. He turned quickly and scooped her up, which is when he felt the blast of moist air on the back of his neck. He froze and was in no way relieved by Cassie's giggle. He turned around slowly.

Khan was at the door, his muzzle held high but not crossing the open top, as if it had met some invisible barrier. The big horse sucked a wisp of Cassie's hair into its nostrils and blasted it out again. For a moment, his tail stopped moving back and forth, and rose up, which Thomas knew was a sign of happiness or curiosity. Then, just as suddenly, Khan backed off and pawed at the ground at the back of the stable.

"Never seen him do that before, approach someone new," Jesse exclaimed.

"Maybe we should change your middle name to Doolittle," Thomas laughed, nuzzling Cassie as they walked back out into the Wyoming evening air.

There was only one more outbuilding to explore after that – a large, old, blue-painted barn with a sign emblazoned with the name "Tinker Industries". Jesse opened the tall doors to the front and escorted them in. Thomas was impressed at how industrial the interior was compared to the rustic exterior. To the front sat one of Jesse's trucks, an old favourite of his. The

1951 Ford F1 panel van was a Marmon-Herrington special, with four-wheel drive. But Jesse had carried out some conversions of his own. The patina finish on the otherwise matt-grey paintwork was as deliberate as the raised suspension and the huge, all-terrain tyres it was fitted with. Although it sat high on its matt-black wheels, it had the stance of a hot rod, like a cat ready to pounce. All of the chrome had been removed, replaced with black powder-coat too. The truck looked incredibly menacing.

"She's been overhauled since you last saw her," Jesse commented with some pride to Thomas. "It now has a 427 FE Medium Riser V8, a Roush supercharger, and more besides. Spits out about 670 horses."

"Jesse is a skilled engineer and mechanic," Thomas explained to Catherine. "We used to tease him about how he was always tinkering with things."

"Built an entire business on it," Jesse said, raising an eyebrow. "Cars and guns mainly, speaking of which."

Jesse headed over to a large set of aluminium worktops that sat against the wall. In front of them was a similarly appointed workbench, on top of which sat a large, black rifle.

"This is one of two prototypes I'm working on. Completely custom made. The barrel is match grade, vanadium alloy steel, but reinforced with carbon fibre. It takes the weight down to 19lbs. I'm playing with the barrel length, but 24 inches seems right. I like the octagonal look for this one for some reason. Muzzle is threaded, the stock is also carbon fibre, but I might play with that. It shoots accurately to 2,000 yards, firing a very heavy grained 450. Rigby."

"You're very good at what you do," Thomas commented, admiring the stripped-down weapon. "Do you have a name for it yet?". Thomas knew Jesse named all his creations – nothing so common as a model number.

"Not until she's finished," Jesse admitted. "It's a hunter's weapon, so I'll think of something heroic or legendary no doubt. I used to have a friend who was into all that kind of stuff, but she was more interested in Native American legends, being Skokomish."

"How is Nina?" Thomas asked.

"Still around. She looks after her mother up on the res," Jesse shrugged. "We keep in touch."

Thomas knew Jesse and Nina had once been more than friends and very close, hence why her touch could be seen in the house's warm furnishings and textiles. He decided not to push for further details.

They headed back across towards the big house. Thomas, Catherine and Cassie said their goodbyes to Jesse and thanked him for his hospitality. As they began to walk back up the trail, he called them back and dashed into the house. He returned after a few moments, with a large brown grocery bag stashed with snacks and treats. Thomas took them from him gratefully. Jesse tipped his hat towards Catherine and Cassie with his thumb and forefinger, winking at the little girl as their eyes met.

As Thomas turned back, something made him freeze. He saw Jesse's face twist into a frown at the same time. Both of them snapped round and looked towards the mountains in the distance. The faintest of sounds carried on a whisper of wind, but it was enough to root both men to the floor. As Thomas looked back at Jesse, he was in no doubt what he had just heard. A roar.

CHAPTER SEVEN

The Bighorn Bar & Grill was one of Saddlestring's less frequented watering holes. Set on the eastern edge of the Bighorn National Forest, in the north-western corner of Johnson County, Wyoming – the town was a busy hub for those who loved to hunt, fish, or considered themselves a committed "outdoors" type. But the Bighorn Bar & Grill didn't advertise itself as friendly to either families or outsiders. It was a place you went to drink, and it was tucked away out of sight of tourists and unwelcome visitors. It was one of the reasons Chayton Reed went there. He could smoke his strong tobacco and drink his coffee in peace. And it was a good place to pick up work.

The group of chamois-shirted men had been at the bar for some time, occasionally throwing nervous glances his way. He sat, staring at them confidently as he continued to wait, knowing they would make their way over to him eventually. As he took another sip of the coffee, one of the men – a fat white guy, with a beard and a baseball cap, began to saunter over to his booth.

"Mr. Reed," the man said, nodding a greeting.

"Beau," Chayton nodded back.

"We're looking for some sport, figure you can help?"

"Perhaps."

"With all the news and all, we were wondering if you could get us a smokey?"

Chayton sighed. The man was as ignorant as he was stupid.

"Can't get you a bear," he shrugged. "Wrong time of year, most are hibernating. I'd have to dig it out. And there'd be no fight in it – it'd be weak and scared most likely."

"Jesus, Chayton," Beau exclaimed, sitting down quickly. "Why don't you shout about it?"

"No one cares Beau, that's why I come here."

"He really wanted a bear," Beau said, his face flushing with panic.

"The quarterback?" Chayton asked.

"You really do have a big mouth, don't you Tonto?" one of the other men spat in his direction, crossing the bar quickly to join them.

Chayton stared at the man, the care-free smile dropping instantly.

"So do you Jace, and that's why my fee just doubled."

"Why you no good, thieving redskin," Jace growled, sitting down next to Beau.

"And now it's tripled. Wanna keep going?" Chayton asked, the smile returning.

"We can get a bear from someone else," Jace threatened.

"No, you can't. If I can't get you one, no-one can. Let's be clear, I don't want to work with you. I think you're scum. I think the man you work for is scum. But I'll take your money – or not. It makes no difference to me."

"One of these days, I'm gonna teach that smart mouth of yours a lesson," Jace growled.

With a deft, easy push of one foot, Chayton pushed the table a little aside.

"Talk is cheap, Jace," Chayton challenged. "And it was your smart mouth that got you into trouble, not mine."

Chayton saw the fear in Jace's eyes and knew nothing was going to happen. At six-foot five inches, and a physique toned by years of working outdoors, he could give the quarterback competition, let alone his flunkies. But he'd had enough. An idea flickered through his mind and festered there.

"I can't get you a bear, but what about a cat?" Chayton asked, changing the subject.

"I ain't sure a cat can last against the dogs too long," Beau offered. "But a big, mean tom might do the trick."

"I have a female. But she's big. Bigger than any cat I've gotten for you before."

"I don't know..." Beau replied.

"And...she's been trained," Chayton threw in. "She won't run, she'll fight. I've been saving her for something special. It'll actually be worth the triple fee."

"So, what actually is your fee, before we triple it?" Jace asked, impatient and dismissive.

"Three thousand bucks," Chayton shrugged.

"You want me to pay you nine thousand bucks just because I hurt your feelings?" Jace objected.

Chayton met his accusation with a stony gaze of impassive indifference.

"Okay, but if she doesn't last more than ten minutes, we'll want six thousand bucks back," Beau challenged.

"I'm not sure your dogs will last that long against her, but I'll try to get her to take her time," Chayton smiled. "What time do you want me there?"

"Midnight fights at midnight," Jace muttered.

Chayton nodded his understanding. Aeneas 'Midnight' Martin was an NFL quarterback for the Jackson Jaguars. He owned an extensive, out-of-the-way ranch property about fifteen miles west of Saddlestring. Not many knew of its exact location, but the rumours of what went on there were infamous. Over the years, the Midnight kennels had produced some of the country's most notorious fighting dogs. Midnight's own in-house current champion was a large, grey, male pitt-bull terrier named Atlas. Along with his two brothers, Blitz and Blaze, they sported the scars of success. Midnight only fought them occasionally now, as other outfits were afraid to put their dogs in the ring with his. Fifteen million dollars a year, plus sponsorship, bought an awful lot of training and development for his animals. But Midnight filmed his fights and broadcast them on the dark web. He could easily make over $100,000 in one night.

"I'll take the three thousand now," said Chayton, "and the remainder on delivery. And you'll get all your money back if she doesn't last at least ten minutes. I'll also give you odds of thirty to one that she takes out at least one dog."

"You don't even know who she'd be up against yet," Jace laughed.

"Don't matter," Chayton shrugged.

Jace took out a roll of notes from his pocket, and passed it quickly over the table, looking over his shoulder and back at the bar as he did so. Chayton took it without even a glance. Nobody in the bar cared, and certainly nobody was stupid enough to mess with Midnight's business.

"Gentlemen," Chayton nodded in acceptance of both the money and terms.

He watched the men go as he supped down the rest of his coffee, He paid his tab with some of the money and put the rest in his back pocket. As he walked out into the street, he saw Jace and Beau sitting up front in the GMC Yukon that rolled by. It seemed out of place with its chrome finished wheels and shiny paintwork. Chayton ignored their jeering glances as he opened up his 1989 Dodge Power Wagon with faded red paintwork and climbed into the front seat.

The drive out to Story didn't take too long. He passed through the small village, nestled in the east slope foothills of the Bighorn mountains, following the North Piney Road along the North Piney Creek. The 800-odd residents were made up of an eclectic mix of the neo-liberal, wannabe artists, entrepreneurs, and the retired. The houses looked like small, unobtrusive cabins and lodges, but they were filled with as much consumer junk as any other in the mid-west. Cadillac Escalades, Lincoln Navigators and Ford Explorers stood shining on the driveways, having never turned a tyre onto a trail in their lives. The picturesque valley had once been roamed by the Crow, Cheyenne and Shoshone, but they had all been moved to the reservation further north. He bristled with disgust at how people today thought land belonged to them. His people had a connection and a respect to the land, but they had never claimed to own it. Now, it just served as a pretty backdrop to middle-class America. He watched the village pass out of sight in the rear-view mirror.

The big, straight-six, Cummins diesel engine pulled him along the road, through groves of lodgepole pine and shrub banks of Rocky Mountain juniper. The tarmac was frost-bitten and whiplashed by the unforgiving wind, which carried sediment from the mountains and peninsula to the north. It hadn't seen repairs, or a great deal of traffic in some time. The wilderness was on the doorstep of Story, but few ventured far in. This was his domain.

Chayton pulled onto the thin, winding track that took him through close-knit trees with dense, dark branches obscuring the view of what was around the bend. He coasted to a stop as the airstream trailer, and the lean-to he'd built as an extension to it, came into sight. He stepped out of the truck and stood for a minute, feeling the moisture in the air and tasting the scent of pine. There was something else too. A musky odour that smelt a little like damp hay. He opened the door of the trailer and threw the money down on the nearest counter, without stepping inside. He grabbed a canvas bag that sat close to the open doorway and pulled it out. Slinging the bag over his shoulder with one hand, he began to walk towards what looked like a wooden gate that opened into the surrounding woodland. Only as he neared did the thinly meshed fence of the enclosure sheltered within the trees come into view.

He unlocked the rusted padlock that held the gate shut. With a kick of his boot, the mesh door swung open, its hinges protesting with a prolonged, metallic groan. He stepped through, using his heel to slam it shut again. He walked carefully, placing his feet down heavily on the hard-compacted ground that still held a good amount of snowfall. Each step rang out with an echo, like a dinner bell.

Chayton pulled the dead mountain cottontail from the bag.

"Here kitty," he whispered to the trees.

CHAPTER EIGHT

Chayton had been watching from the ridge since dusk. His sharp eyes had studied the ranch-house-turned-mansion, and the big sweeping drive that curved in from the little-used track. But his main focus had been the barn and its outbuildings – the Midnight kennels in all their dishonourable glory. He closed his eyes, remembering the scratch marks on the black-painted boards of the floor and the ramps that led to the central pit. Most dogs, no matter the breed, didn't want to fight. Chayton had watched the wolves and coyotes he'd encountered and tracked. Canines were one of the few species with highly developed body language that signalled hierarchy and dominance. They had evolved this effective form of communication to avoid the physical fights that pack life might otherwise encourage. Squabbles over everything from who should be first at the dinner table to where they wanted to sleep, had the potential to escalate into a fight that risked serious injury or death. Having the ability to communicate they were willing to give in to a dominant animal, most confrontations ended quickly and peacefully.

Chayton opened his eyes again and lifted his binoculars. It had been dark for a good few hours now, and the lights were on in the barn. Preparations were under way. Beneath the soft yellow glow of a light at the front of one of the outbuildings, a door opened, and Beau stepped out into the cold night. Chayton could see the gasping puffs of the fat man hanging in the air. In his hand, he held three short leather leads, each of which belonged to a large, powerful dog. The three pit bulls didn't pull away. They stood to attention, their cropped ears erect on top of their skulls. All of their attention was focused on the barn opposite the outbuilding. The dogs wagged their tails in anticipation. It made Chayton feel sick.

Midnight's dogs also showed pack mentality. The three brothers hunted and killed together, working as a cohesive team. To them, the other dogs were outsiders, and just as with wolves, outsiders weren't tolerated – and no submission or backing down would save them. Atlas stood in front of his two slightly smaller brothers. He was slate grey, with amber-coloured eyes. His face was covered in tiny pink blotches, which from afar looked like a natural variation in his colouring, but was in fact, old, healed scar tissue. His chest had a bib of white, making him a strikingly handsome dog. He was the alpha. His brothers, Blitz, and Blaze had been sired by the same father, Midnight's former champion, but to a different bitch. They were black and white in colour, but whereas Blitz was predominantly black, with a white left ear and feet, Blaze was white, with a black eye patch and saddle. Chayton knew that on their own, each of the dogs had pleasant-enough temperaments, and he felt sorry for them in a way. But they were pure gladiators now – trained on treadmills, baited, and given smaller animals to practice on. And together, they were unstoppable killing machines. *It ends tonight*, he thought.

He waited another five minutes before making his way back down the ridge to where he'd parked the old Dodge, a little way off the same trail that led to the ranch. In the back of the pickup was a large wooden crate, and behind the truck itself, he was towing an old horse box. He checked on both before getting behind the wheel of the truck and heading towards the Midnight ranch.

As Chayton pulled into the drive, Beau stepped out of the main barn, and quickly directed him to the back of the building. Chayton had been counting on this, and he was pleased not to have to alter his plans too much. He parked up, carefully pulling the truck round so that it faced back down the drive. He deliberately and carefully backed the horsebox up, so it's rear-opening door was close to the ramp and double doors that led directly to the pit. He stepped out and walked with Beau into the barn.

"What's in the crate?" Beau asked, correctly assuming the cat was in the horse box.

"Coyote," Chayton replied. "Warm-up act."

Beau nodded approvingly.

The barn had a stink that the other men couldn't pick up on. Their senses were dulled, even switched off to it, but he could sense it. Ghosts walked here. Dogs that had been dragged down the ramp, terrified. Their claws had gripped the concrete and boards to no avail. He had seen it many times – the dogs hunkering flat and whimpering softly as if to plead with their captors. The men used thick leather leads, or in most cases, just rope, to drag the unwilling combatants to the arena and ultimately to their demise. Chayton said a prayer for them, and the others that would die tonight. Whatever happened, they would be the last to be sacrificed here for the sportsman's entertainment.

Chayton knew he would have to be patient, and he had already resolved himself to the possibility of failure. The cat could choose not to respond to his commands when the time came or might panic when he made his move. This would be their first test working together, and quite possibly their last. Chayton studied the interior of the barn. Despite not looking like much from the outside, the building was thoroughly soundproofed, and even shielded from thermal imaging cameras. With only two entrances, it was practically a fortress. And tonight, he and the cat would bring it down.

Beau was grinning at Chayton, dumbly. The man must have weighed 300lbs. His beer-belly spilled over his jeans, which in turn were held up by dirty, tightly pulled braces. His mop of hair was now shoved under a Jackson Jaguar's cap. He epitomised everything the modern American stood for: greed, laziness, and apathy. Right there and then, Chayton wanted nothing more than to purge it from the land. But he kept his temper staid, and moved on, looking over the ground with Beau. All seemed in order for the fight, and they walked back to the truck.

As they drew close, Chayton heard the coyote in the crate snap its jaws and yikker in fear. Chayton drew closer and began to whisper to the animal through the wooden slats.

"One last trick to play my friend," Chayton said.

The coyote quieted at the sound of his voice, and then new, pleading, pup-like murmurings came from the crate instead. Chayton nodded to Beau as he climbed back into the truck to wait. There was nothing else to do now. He put the radio on and drifted off to old country and western tunes. About an hour later, he was woken by Beau knocking on the window. He looked worried. Chayton rolled down the glass.

"That's one pissed-off mountain lion," Beau exclaimed. "I ain't never heard no critter growl like that before."

"You ain't seen nothing yet," Chayton replied.

"Well, I will soon enough, it's show time," Beau said. He seemed expectant.

Chayton sighed and stepped out of the truck. He could hear them now. The barn was full of both spectators and animals. The next few moments would determine his future. He headed to the crate, speaking again to the coyote inside with soft, comforting tones. In one swift, deft move, he slid open the crate door and grabbed the animal by the ruff of the neck. Within moments, he had slipped a rope noose over its head. Obediently it stepped off the bed of the truck and followed Chayton at a casual trot a little way down the ramp.

As nervous and excited growls began to echo in the darkness, the coyote froze and cowered. As if sensing it, a symphony of barking erupted from the direction of the pit. Through his light touch on the rope, Chayton could feel the coyote trembling. He stooped gently, gathering it into his arms and walking the rest of the way.

As he entered the arena, Chayton took a moment to let his eyes adjust to the darkness. The only lights were positioned at the four corners of the pit, angled downwards at the floor. He walked down the ramp towards the drop off, still carrying the coyote. He could feel it tensing in his arms. His muscles flexed to keep it in place.

"Goodbye brother. I thank you for your honourable sacrifice," Chayton whispered.

He let his arms fall to his side and dropped the animal into the pit. It screamed in fright, encouraging a round of jeering laughs from the crowd. Chayton couldn't make out too many faces, which he knew was the idea. Anonymity was good for business. The pit was flanked on three sides by steep banks of basic wooden benches, and they were filled with Midnight's elite friends and contacts. But the man himself hadn't arrived yet. He always liked to make a big entrance, and Chayton knew the main man never arrived until the main event.

The coyote scrabbled against the wooden walls and ran its teeth against them to try and get purchase. It jumped and reared up on its hind legs, but the pit had been designed to hold much larger animals with ease. It ran back and forth in panic, then froze. A sound emanated from the back wall, where a partition was beginning to open up. A dark, square hole was left in its place, but from it came the sounds of a frantic pattering of paws and heavy, panting breaths. Two dogs erupted from the hole, one brindle-coloured, the other tan. The two pit bulls skidded to a halt when they saw the coyote and wagged their tails in anticipation. Chayton had seen the dogs before – some of Midnight's less prominent champions. But no less formidable. Expertly, they flanked the coyote, barking and snapping their teeth to drive it into the far corner of the pit.

The brindle pit bull trotted along the far wall, rubbing up against it. It wagged its tail, moving confidently but not too quickly. It was panting gently and approached the coyote directly from the front. The tan dog had skirted to the back wall and was coming up on the coyote's rear. It seemed to stop for a microsecond, then jerked forward, bouncing on its front paws and delivering a slashing bite to the coyote's rear flank. The coyote whipped its head around, snarling viciously, giving the brindle dog to the front its opening. It lunged, grabbing the coyote's jaws from the side and clamping them closed with its own. The coyote screamed high-pitched growls as it bucked and shook its head back and forth, but the pit bull would not be easily thrown. Then the tan-coloured dog rushed in for its second attack.

The first bite hadn't really done much damage. The coyote's coat was well equipped for a rough life, and the pit bull had come away with a mouth of fur. But now, it had the luxury of knowing the coyote couldn't fight back and looked for a more prominent attack. A glancing blow of its teeth to the flank again bounced the dog's head downwards, where it found the coyote's softer underbelly and genitals. It attacked mercilessly, ripping and tearing with violent shakes of its head. The brindle dog began a gruesome tug of war with its tan counterpart. It emerged from underneath the coyote, its jaws bloody. The coyote collapsed, and the tan dog adjusted its grip with a snap of its jaws, gunning for the throat. The brindle pit bull pounced too, tunnelling into the flesh just below the coyote's front left shoulder. It wouldn't be quick, but it was over. The coyote wouldn't get up again.

Over the next five minutes, Chayton felt his nerves become frayed as the dogs occasionally adjusted their grips or tore into a new part of the coyote. It made no sound now, but Chayton could see the chest still moving up and down as it gulped down its last breaths. Finally, a cheer went up from around the pit as the dogs were announced victorious. The barn went quiet again, and suddenly, Chayton knew the time had come. Fate and destiny beckoned.

As if to confirm his thoughts, a large door opened on one of the upper levels of the barn, and a huge man stepped out to look down onto the pit. It was their gracious host in the flesh. Aeneas 'Midnight' Martin was bald, black, and big even for a quarterback. At six feet and four inches tall, he weighed in at 365lbs. But although undoubtedly a heavyweight on the field, every inch of him was muscle. He was a professional and most-disciplined athlete. And this operation wouldn't be possible if he didn't have the smarts to match. As Midnight walked to the rail, he looked down towards the pit and nodded his approval to Beau and Jace, who had joined Chayton.

"Pussy time," Beau giggled.

Chayton ignored him.

"Just as you asked, the dogs will be waiting," Jace smirked.

Hearing the pit door open up again, Chayton couldn't help himself as he took a step forward and stole a quick glance. The three dogs looked up at him expectantly. Atlas, Blitz, and Blaze. The undefeated Midnight champions. Chayton walked back down the ramp towards the rear entrance, ignoring Beau and Jace's mocking leers.

As soon as he was back out in the open, Chayton made sure he was alone before he skirted around to the front. He checked the door. Locked during a fight, just as it always was. It was now or never. He headed back to the truck. Chayton began to talk gently as he moved along the side of the horse trailer, tapping the sides lightly so that the animal inside would know he was there. He unbolted the ramp at the rear and lowered it to the ground.

~

She anchored herself to the floor of the trailer, her claws extending instinctively as her haunches raised, preparing to launch her forwards and into the air instantly. As the night sky became visible again though, she relaxed, catching the earthy scent of the one that brought her food. She knew by the sweat and pheromones in the scent that this companion of sorts was male. She trusted him. She rose and padded forwards, letting out a deep purr of contentment. The strange contraption, the noise of dogs in the distance, and the scent of strangers had unsettled her. But now, she expected a meal to be provided.

Her mass made the ramp reverberate, but although she had been wary of it on entering the box, she now knew not to fear it. The man stood by the side of the contraption, and she turned around to join him. Her head came roughly to his shoulders as she came to a stop and stood by his side. She could sense from his body language that this pleased him. As he walked towards a dwelling she was unfamiliar with, she followed, only to come to a halt again. She could hear dogs inside, and the scent of others. Ones like him. Until now, he had always turned her away when they came across their scent or heard them in the distance. He took another step towards the dwelling.

~

Chayton was patient, but he couldn't risk taking too long. If somebody came out to check on him, it would be over. He couldn't let an alarm go up.

"Come Tama," he called.

Although it was meant to be a Native American name, Chayton hadn't christened the cat. It had been named by the person who had brought it into the world. The mother had been a mountain lion, the great cat of the Americas, and they had looked for an appropriate name. In numerous baby books, Tama, or Taima, was often described as a Native American girl's name that meant thunder or thunderbolt in Blackfoot or Navajo. But it didn't actually mean anything, in any native language. The closest was a historical chief of the Meskwaki. The English shortening of his name, Tewameha, was Taima, but it still didn't mean thunder. Chief Tewameha simply belonged to the thunder clan. It equally amused and annoyed Chayton that people couldn't even get that right.

Chayton stood by the door. Tama lowered her head, inquisitive, but still uncertain.

"Asá," Chayton commanded, using one of the many Crow words meaning to hunt.

~

She understood the meaning of the command, and instantly dropped to the ground. Her shoulder muscles tensed. Her ears flicked in the direction of the building. She powered forward, rippling over the ground in silence. She kept low as she worked her way to the door. She paused only momentarily as she stared into the darkness. Then she was gone. Tama was inside the barn.

~

Beau Brown looked expectantly towards the entrance ramp. There was very little light, but he had detected the movement. Something stepped forward. Something immense. The man smiled in relief. *Damn injun, he did have a bear*, he thought. He couldn't see much more than a silhouette, but the animal was huge. It certainly wasn't a mountain lion. As he strained his eyes, he was sure he could see the hump on the back. Not just any bear, a grizzly. *Worth every buck* Beau smiled. But then the bear did a strange thing. It roared. Beau jumped at the deafening sound, and his heartbeat accelerated wildly. Something didn't feel right. He felt frightened. There was a flash of reddish-brown fur, as something dropped into the pit. As it stepped into the light, Beau took a sharp intake of breath. He couldn't believe what he was seeing. It was impossible.

~

Tama tensed the muscles in her forelegs. She purred as she sensed the unease of the dogs. Their scent was flooded with pheromones that indicated fear. The nearest of the three animals was larger and seemed more dominant than the other two. Overconfidently, she turned her head in its direction. That's when, with a sudden outbreak of furious barking, the other two lunged at her, jaws agape. The mixed dark and light hues of one of the dogs made it easier to see than its counterpart. It also seemed to move quicker. She saw the attack coming, but her long whiskers flexed as they picked up the vibration. The sensed the minute changes in air flow as they moved around the alpha animal, flanking her as the other two distracted her. She reacted out of instinct.

Her left front paw, the size of a dinner plate, smashed down onto the dark-coloured dog's head almost casually. She turned her head, plucking the alpha dog from its mid-air leap and crushing its skull between her jaws. Its body went limp, hanging from her mouth in a macabre manner. She enjoyed the sensation of the thick, hot blood teasing her taste buds. As she felt a struggled movement under her left paw, black, razor-like claws extended and sliced through the dog's skull. She dropped the dog that she carried in her mouth and stepped over the body of the one under her feet. The remaining dog whimpered at her approach.

~

At first, Beau thought it must be a clever hoax. The native had somehow dressed up the beast with a hump and elongated fangs. But as the creature dispatched the dogs with vicious ease, full panic set in. This thing, whatever it was, was real. And it moved like lightning. Beau rushed forward, but it had already cleared the pit. A blur passed in front of him, racing its way upwards into the benches. He could hear the people shouting, but still couldn't comprehend what was happening. A bloody, mangled body fell to the ground ahead of him. He recognised Blaze's blood-stained fur. He stumbled backwards, making his way towards the rear door. Finding it locked didn't surprise him, but the heat he felt, and the cracking, spitting noise from the timber outside, did.

~

Chayton watched bright orange licks of flame spread across the barn. The cold mountain air fed the fire, helping it spread as a breeze whipped at the building's walls. The dry, warped wood on the outside eagerly embraced the inferno. Smoke began to billow as the black paint melted and stripped, adding to the potent scent of the fire. The outer hull of the barn began to buckle under the onslaught of the flames, the wood popping and exploding with sharp, loud cracks. Chayton readied himself, and reached into the cab for his weapon, but not before he pulled the thin, silver whistle from his pocket. He blew on it hard.

~

Tama leapt from the pit with a roar, scrabbling her way up the tightly bunched bench seats. She found soft, wriggling flesh under her feet, and she clawed and bit and bellowed as she sought a way out. The screams of her prey fuelled a frenzy of lunges and swipes, each blow bringing down a new, mangled body. She tore strips of bloody, warm meat from the bodies as she went, eating on the run.

Just like the dogs, she had sensed the fire way before the men had. The smoke within the barn was beginning to subdue them, and they tripped over each other in their panic. There was now no doubt for her that these animals were prey. They reacted like any herd, driven together by fear and her presence. She revelled in it, roaring loudly above the sound of the raging fire. Then she heard the piercing sound that penetrated the dark interior. She leapt into the air back towards the pit, clearing it and barrelling towards the dark, fiery wall ahead of her. Although this was hotter and fiercer, she had been acclimatised to it by the one who fed her. She remembered the burning tree frames he had encouraged her to pass under, with him by her side. He had made the same piercing calls then. He was letting her know that he wasn't far away and how to escape. She accelerated hard and leapt again with a roar that drowned out her fear and hesitancy. The act filled her bloodstream with adrenaline and fuelled her strength. The wood splintered at her touch, and a vacuum of cold air swept into the space behind her.

She stopped to stand by the male, whose hand patted her hard and reassuringly. She shook a few glowing embers from her fur coat and looked back at the fire. Just like the animals inside, she no longer had to fear it. He had seen to that. They watched it burn for several minutes, until the structure began to collapse in on itself.

~

Chayton was sure nobody was coming out. He walked with Tama round to the back of the trailer and allowed her to take her time to get comfortable. She lay down, seemingly unscathed by the ordeal. He would let her rest as he checked the rest of the property. He couldn't afford for there to be any stray witnesses.

As he walked back around towards the truck, he caught the movement coming from the shell of the barn and ducked back out of sight. He heard the rapport of the gun, but the shot was in no danger of hitting him. The bullet slammed into a tree about thirty feet to his left. He stepped out again, this time more confidently.

Aeneas Martin had been seriously burnt. How he was even managing to stand baffled Chayton. Raw, pink flesh hung from his scalp. Chayton could see where the skin had melted, becoming a thick, tar-like glue that had smeared itself to the quarterback's cheekbones. A hole had burnt its way through his jaw, and Chayton could see the wrinkled gum, looking like rare steak, as drool pooled over the yellowed teeth uncontrollably. Midnight stood about twenty feet from Chayton, and held a large revolver in his right hand, which shook uncontrollably.

Chayton gripped his own weapon a little tighter. It was cumbersome and heavy, but in the right hands, deadly. The buffalo jawbone war club was intricately decorated with inlaid gold thread and emblems of his own design. He had reinforced the raw bone with a natural varnish of honey, salt, and pine sap. And the large teeth set in the curved single edge had been fused into the bone by being dipped in molten steel and sharpened. The weathered leather handle allowed him to throw it with mortal accuracy or wield it up close without slipping from his hand. Until now, it had all been just practice. But now, he realised he would be required to kill, just as Tama had been.

He closed the distance between Midnight and himself with a darting, zigzagged run. The quarterback tried to follow his movements but had no hope of doing so. Chayton suspected the man would soon succumb to his wounds if he left him, but in his heart, he knew he was being tested. He had to show resolve, that he was prepared to make the sacrifices he asked of Tama. He closed in on Midnight from the left, gripping the war club with both hands as he did. He swung it sideways with incredible might, sending the athlete tumbling to the ground. Even here, the heat of the fire had melted the snow, leaving Midnight to crawl through the mud as Chayton circled him. He looked down at the charred, defeated frame of what had been a powerful man. He was both excited and shocked at how the strike from the club had lifted the flesh from the scalp, peeling it back like banana skin. Fresh blood flowed from the wound, trickling down Midnight's face.

Chayton now felt panicked and upset. He had no interest in being cruel or callous. Midnight was suffering unimaginable horrors. Chayton did not want to take pleasure, or too long, in the man's death. He spun the club in his hand and raised it above his head, bringing it back down with a decisive strike. Midnight collapsed onto the ground instantly. Life, spirit, and strength left the body all at once, as what remained slapped back into the dirt like a gut pile cut from a strung-up deer. With one hand, Chayton pulled Midnight's body to one side. He looked up and met Tama's expectant gaze.

Tama received her gift eagerly, using her teeth to drag the bloodied carcass over to her. The rough surface of her tongue removed the seared skin and scant flesh from the skull, allowing her to savour the sweet, coppery taste of the blood. By the time Chayton stood up to his full height again, she had begun to gorge herself on the chest and legs. He left her to feed, taking a final walk around the property to make sure no other fight goers, or evidence survived.

CHAPTER NINE

Thomas slowly eased from sleep to consciousness. The soft sheets and warm blankets were tucked around him, and Catherine's arm curled around his own. He was on his back, and she was on her side, facing him. She was absolutely still, in a deep sleep that had been hard earned. It was still dark outside, but Thomas had a feeling that dawn wasn't far off. He smiled, as he entertained the thought of scratching an itch he'd ignored for too long. He slipped his arm from underneath Catherine's and silently lifted his side of the covers. He crept across the floor, grabbing a pile of clothes from his only partially unpacked bags. He stepped quietly down the steeply inclined ladder. In the living area, he finished dressing, and ventured over to Cassie's bedroom. She too was sound asleep. He headed downstairs to a cupboard in the boathouse. The rickety door opened with a creak that made him wince and look upwards, listening for the sound of stirrings from above. Assured nobody was awake, he stared in at the contents.

Although nothing else had been unpacked, he'd taken care to make sure the items now in the cupboard had been. It looked as if he'd never left. His wading boots sat neatly facing him, ready and waiting for his return. Thomas's Orvis fishing rod and his custom aqua-coloured Tibor reel were both spurring him on to take a trip to the river. And on top of all of these was a small, sapphire-coloured aluminium box that Jesse had placed in the bottom of the grocery bag for him. Having waited until now, Thomas knew what he would find inside and opened it as if it were a treasure chest, which in part, it was.

Jesse's skill as a fly-tier was unsurpassed as far as Thomas was concerned. He'd never known anyone who could create anything as exquisite as Jesse. Not only did he insist that his flies were used for fishing rather than display, but he also somehow breathed life into every single one. And this box was a selection of his best. A dazzling array of colours stared back at him from the box's interior. Most were unique to Jesse. There was the orange and black striped "Jack-o'-lantern', whose bulbous thorax of twined copper wire looked just like its namesake. The "Green Hummer" was based on the iridescent wings of the magnificent hummingbird, a rare migrant in Wyoming that Jesse had once seen by chance. Others, such as the "Blue Charm" were not Jesse's design, but still bore the signature of a master fly tier. Thomas plucked the fishing vest from the hook on the back of the cupboard door, grabbed his gear, and placed the box inside one of the vest's pockets.

The air was frosty, and there was still snow higher up, but Spring was beginning to hint it was on the way. Spring was the most unpredictable season in Wyoming. From freezing blizzards to blistering sunshine, one day could be as different from the next as it was possible to be. Today, there was a suggestion of both sun and frost as he headed along a trail that skirted the beaver pond and seemed to head away from it. Thomas followed it confidently, knowing it would eventually meet up with the broad, fast-flowing river that fed the stream that in turn, emptied into the pond. The dark sky was turning pinkish orange, and he knew that he had timed his excursion perfectly. Twenty minutes later, just over a mile from Lodge View, he found himself standing on the bank of a meandering, crystal clear river of cerulean blue, just as dawn began to break. He took his time setting up the reel with a line and then feeding it into the hoops along the rod, watching the water for signs of surfacing fish as he did. Finally, he selected his fly. He settled on a "Sage Jay", one of Jesse's most subtle and beautiful designs, made with the feathers of sage grouse and Steller's jay. The cyan, charcoal, and buttercream speckled bundle caught his eye, as he hoped would be the case with the fish.

He didn't really think he would catch anything, but he knew that Jesse didn't get many visitors, and with hundreds of fishing spots across the ranch, the fish were probably less wary or 'fly-frightened' than in heavily fished rivers and streams. He made a low and wide side-cast, the movement all coming from his wrist. Muscle memory kicked in, and just as the fly kissed the water, he swept it up again and onward for another ten feet. A large, pink and silver fish broke the surface of the water, head and tailing as it slapped back down into the river. With a flick of the wrist, Thomas brought the fly down about three feet south of where he'd seen the fish. He caught the flash of its side in the clear, streaming ripples, and then felt the line go taut.

The fish fought hard but was clearly unused to being hooked. It lavishly wasted its energy, and Thomas knew he would certainly outlast the fish, at least this time round. He let it repeatedly take the line out before he drew it back in. Each time, there was less resistance. He enjoyed listening to the slowing clicks of the reel as the fish stopped fighting both the fisherman and the gentle current. He brought it close, lifting the rod high and grabbing the line. He lifted the fish, a ten-inch-long Colorado river cutthroat trout and grabbed it firmly in one hand. He dug out the hook with pliers from the vest, then smacked the fish hard, headfirst, against a nearby rock. He tied a long loop of line through the gill slits and anchored the trout in a lie of water close to where he stood on the bank. Off to such a good start, he thought he'd try his luck again.

The fish didn't stop taking his flies. In the space of half an hour, he had two more trout for the pan, and had let two undersized ones go. He picked up his catch from the stream, now all tied together on the loop of line, and slung them over his shoulder. He walked back the same way he'd come. The mixed pines were seeping their scent into the morning air, readying for winter to release its grasp. The north of the state would be covered in deep snow throughout much of both winter and spring, but further south, it was less certain. The lowland forests and waterways, such as on the ranch, often stayed green, or threw off the shackles of winter at the earliest of opportunities. But as Thomas glanced towards the sloping woodline to the north-west, he knew he wouldn't have to climb too high before he found pristine, untouched powder.

As he passed the beaver dam, he noticed the wisps of steam coming from its top. Inside, multiple tunnels would lead to densely packed bedding and feeding chambers. Dried grass and bark strips, as well as the animals themselves, would make the interior extremely snug. But even in icy water, the beaver's fine pelt and thick fat layer would protect them. It reminded him of the many hunting and hiking trips he'd been on in the surrounding country, and the times he and the others making up the Hole-in-the-Wall gang, would catch and dine on beaver. It was a very rich game meat, and the fat was unsurpassed. Many a time, beaver fat had saved a starving trapper or mountain man. He imagined he would have a hard time convincing Catherine and Cassie of its virtues though. The trout would have to do.

He skirted the house, and entered through the front door, kicking off the wading boots at the bottom of the stairs. He took off the fishing vest and hung it over the banister before climbing the wooden steps. He turned into the kitchen and put the fish down on the counter. As he plucked a sharp filleting knife from the drawer, he heard fast paced yet light footsteps scampering across the wooden floorboards towards him. He turned to see Cassie, still in her pyjamas and running towards him. He dropped the knife and scooped her up into his arms.

"Are you making breakfast?" she asked.

"Yup, had to catch it first though ma'am," Thomas replied in a mock mid-west accent.

"Fish for breakfast?" Cassie objected, screwing her face up.

"Absolutely, you just wait," Thomas said, putting her down.

He set to work on the trout, descaling, filleting and then skinning the fish. He went to the fridge and took out some of the groceries Jesse had pre-supplied them with. He picked two pans from the rack, a large, flat skillet, and a wide-bottomed saucepan. He put some water on the boil in the saucepan and laced the skillet with oil. He took a huge potato and cut it into small chunks before adding them to the pan. He let them cook for a while before adding a generous knob of butter. As it melted into a clear liquid, he placed the trout in and began to baste it. Content, he then moved to the saucepan and cracked three eggs, breaking the unprotected innards into the simmering water one by one. Cassie watched, suspiciously, but smiled when she saw him pull out three thick slices of bacon from the fridge. The bacon went into the skillet, pushing the trout fillets and potato aside. The potatoes were beginning to crisp now and soak up some of the oil and butter. Thomas remembered to baste the fish again as the bacon gave up some of its fat to the mix.

As Catherine made her way down the steep ladder from the bedroom upstairs, Thomas served up three plates of bacon, trout, fried potatoes, and poached eggs. Cassie was already climbing up one of the stools that sat the other side of the breakfast bar, and Catherine lifted her onto the cushioned seat she was trying to reach. She took a seat next to her and reached across for a plate.

"I could get used to this," she said, raising an eyebrow.

"Me too," Cassie chirped.

"First day special," Thomas warned playfully. "After this, the cooking's down to you two, especially Cassie."

The little girl fixed him with a not amused scowl that matched the one on her mother's face perfectly.

"Hope I'm not interrupting or calling too early?"

Thomas turned, finding Jesse at the top of the stairs and looking over to them.

"Not at all, come on in. Wanna grab my plate before I tuck in?" Thomas asked.

"No, I'm just fine, thank you. But could I have a word in your ear like?"

Thomas nodded.

"Ma'am, little lady," Jesse nodded, tipping his wide-brimmed hat towards them.

Catherine remembered how Jesse's father, Lee Logan, had done the same when they'd met in Scotland. It made her smile both fondly and sadly in reply.

Thomas followed Jesse back down the stairs and out of the front door.

"I've gotten the reports back from the animal doctor," Jesse explained. "I thought you might want to take a look."

"Absolutely," Thomas exclaimed.

There was a small picnic bench nestled into the bottom of an Engelmann spruce just across the trail. Jesse headed for it, with Thomas following. They sat down on either side of the bench and opposite each other. Jesse passed across an envelope. Thomas upended it, and a collection of stapled documents and some glossy, blown-up photographs fell onto the table. He ignored the reports and went straight to the images. He thumbed through them, absorbing the clean, efficient killing pattern that was the calling card of a cat. Then he stopped. The photograph he held in his hand was of a dark-coloured cow, its eyes rolled back into its head. Its throat had been torn out. Not shredded and opened up, but literally torn out. A gaping hole where enough flesh had been removed to expose the crushed vertebrae at the top of the spine. And a memory flashed in his mind.

"That one kind of gets your attention, don't it?" Jesse mused.

Thomas nodded, not taking his eyes away from the photograph. When he did look up, Jesse's gaze was fixed on him, curiosity showing on his face.

"Know any kind of cat that has a habit of ripping whole throats out, breaking the neck to be sure at the same time?"

Thomas got the impression Jesse wasn't expecting him to say no.

"Like I said, it reminds me of the hybrid animal we hunted in Cannich nearly five years ago," Thomas replied, uneasily.

Jesse nodded, as if encouraging him to go on.

"I can assure you that one's dead," Thomas said.

"This one ain't. Anymore from where your cat came from?"

"Not that I know of,"

Thomas could feel the tension between them again.

"What about your friend O'Connell. Might he know something?" Jesse asked after a while, the tension disappearing as he thought along a different line it seemed.

"I don't see why he should," Thomas frowned.

Jesse took a cellular flip phone from the back pocket of his jeans and opened it up. He accessed the messages, then tossed the phone to Thomas. He looked down at the screen. The message he was staring at came from a withheld number, but he could make out the text just fine.

Ask Walker to call O'Connell. He knows what killed your cows.

Thomas tossed the flip phone back to Jesse in the same accusing manner, taking out his own phone and stepping up from the table. He dialled Jericho O'Connell's number and impatiently listened to the line as it rang. It connected quickly, and Thomas could hear the muffled tone of road and tyre noise that indicated O'Connell was driving.

"You must be psychic, I'm practically on your doorstep," Jericho said, speaking loudly to compensate for the road noise, or perhaps the distance from the microphone in the car.

"And why would that be?" Thomas demanded. There was a short pause.

"Why Thomas, you almost don't sound pleased to hear from me," the Irish accent prodded.

"I'm the one that called you, remember. Imagine my surprise at getting an anonymous tip to do so on Jesse's phone. Word is you know what we're dealing with up here."

There was another pause.

"I can't talk on the phone, but I'll be there within an hour. We'll talk then."

The line went dead.

CHAPTER TEN

In the time it took Jericho to arrive, Thomas had changed out of his fishing gear into working boots, jeans and a thick green-check chamois shirt. The cold wasn't improving his mood. He hadn't felt it whilst he'd been walking, but his impatient pacing along the trail outside of Lodge View was too little to keep it at bay. Despite being a relatively bright day, a storm was brewing inside him. Jericho had been flippant and dismissive on the phone. And now, he found himself questioning why Jericho would even be in the United States at the same time he was. With everything that happened, it surely couldn't be a coincidence. A notorious tracker and trapper, with a flexible approach to the law, Jericho's services were in high demand from a broad range of organisations. From government departments to private collectors, Jericho O'Connell worked with anyone willing to pick up the cheque. In return, problem animals would disappear, or the rarest specimen could be found. But the secrecy was something new. Jericho usually boasted unrelentingly about his exploits.

At the sound of a large vehicle making its way up the trail, Thomas turned to look. A brand-new, jet-black SUV of enormous size was making its way towards him. Just then, Jesse emerged from the treeline on the other side of the trail. He was clearly as interested in what Jericho had to say as Thomas was. As the car got closer, Thomas could see it was a top-of-the-range GMC Yukon. He was surprised on two accounts. First, a $100,000 vehicle was an unlikely find in a rental lot. Secondly, like himself, Jericho favoured slightly more rugged trucks, at least looks wise. The tinted glass made it hard for Thomas to see inside, but he could make out the white glow of the rancher-style hat Jericho preferred. The truck pulled up on the side of the trail, a little way off. The broad driver's door opened, and out stepped the Irishman. He was wearing a leather drovers coat on top of his bright orange denim shirt and pale jeans. His sharp blue eyes shone in the shade the rim of his hat provided, and wisps of sun-bleached blonde hair poked out from under it, trailing down towards his shoulders.

"Quite the place you've got here," Jericho nodded to Jesse.

"Want to explain what you're doing in it?" Thomas accused.

"Now, let's not forget the pleasantries," Jericho replied, his eyes narrowing.

"You say you know something we don't. Figure we skip the time-wasting," Jesse remarked.

Jericho looked from one to the other and read the looks on both their faces. He quickly realised that tensions were already high.

"Okay," he sighed. "Remember your cat back in Cannich?"

Thomas nodded silently, his eyes growing wide in alarm.

"Well, he's a dad, and it's a beautiful, bouncing baby girl," Jericho chuckled.

The punch Thomas threw was so quick, Jericho never saw it coming. It connected with the right side of his chin and made him stagger a few steps to his left. For a moment, he was stunned, and he saw the anger burning in Thomas' eyes.

"How could you?" Thomas roared "you know what we went through. You know it killed people."

"Including my pa," Jesse growled, stepping forward.

"Now gents, let's be civilised about this," Jericho warned. "Besides, I can't take two of you on. Well actually, what I mean to say is, I don't want to."

Jericho shrugged off the leather coat and let it fall to the ground. He raised his arms slightly, tensing the muscles in his forearms as he did and letting his fingers curl halfway into fists.

"You're an asshole," Jesse declared, stepping back and shaking his head.

"I'm inclined to agree," Thomas spat. He walked straight up to Jericho and rammed a finger into his chest. "How could you not tell me?"

Something ignited in Jericho. Maybe it was the long drive. Maybe it was the cold weather. But he'd had enough. He shot his left palm into the centre of Thomas's chest, pushing him back and out of his face. Almost out of habit, his right fist swung in a roundhouse punch to Thomas's jaw.

"I owed you that," Jericho nodded, slightly surprised at his own reaction.

Before he could say anything else, Thomas sprang, connecting in a full charge with the Irishman's shoulder and knocking him backwards. Thomas kept the momentum going and they collapsed onto the ground. Thomas bent his arm and crossed it against Jericho's chest, who was lying on his back and trying to get up. Jericho flinched as he saw the pain and rage wash over Thomas's face. He decided to take what was coming. But he didn't have to. Thomas staggered back to his feet, distracted by the noise of another truck coming along the track. His eyes were fixed on it.

"Have you quite finished?" Catherine demanded.

Thomas helped Jericho to his feet. They both looked sheepish and avoided her steely gaze. She stood in the doorway, but her attention too was drawn to the oncoming truck.

Thomas could see it was an older truck, black in colour and relatively compact.

"Shit," sighed Jesse.

That's when Thomas recognised the car too. It was a 1991 GMC Syclone pick-up truck. In its heyday it had been capable of out accelerating a Ferrari 348. It was fairly pointless as a working vehicle though. It was too light for heavy work and too heavy for light work. All it and its supercharged V6 engine had been designed to do, was get from one set of lights to the next quicker than anything else. But Thomas already knew this one had been modified. It sat higher, on stiff, strong suspension and bulky all-terrain tyres. And he could already hear from the exhaust and the whine of the supercharger that they were not factory-issued. But he also knew all this because he knew who was behind the wheel of the truck. It belonged to Nina Lee, Jesse's former girlfriend. She pulled into the side.

Nina was Native American. Her father was Skokomish and lived in Washington state. But Nina lived with her mother, who was of the Crow nation, and Wyoming born-and-bred. Thomas knew she was a Forest Ranger and an excellent tracker. As she got out of the truck, he could see why Jesse would have taken the breakup hard. She was stunning. Dark brown hair that rolled off her shoulders, hazel-coloured eyes that shone with defiance. She was a very attractive woman.

"Looks like it's quite the party," Nina jeered. "Trouble has a habit of following you around Mr. Walker," she said with a smile.

"Joined at the hip," Thomas shrugged.

"I'm guessing we're all here and getting worked up about the same thing. Why don't we all go inside and talk about this bear and whatever else might be on a killing spree," Nina suggested.

"Finally, someone talking sense," Catherine concluded, rolling her eyes but pushing the door wide open to welcome them all in.

Thomas nodded towards the door at Jericho.

"Sorry," he said.

"Don't be," the Irishman replied. "I deserved it. I just didn't like it."

They all went inside Lodge View and headed up to the kitchen. They each took a seat around the breakfast bar. Thomas headed over to the coffee pot and began pulling mugs out of a cupboard. After filling each, he passed them over two at a time, then fetched a quart of milk from the fridge and some sugar cubes. He took a handful of spoons from a drawer and left people to adjust their drinks to their own taste.

"Okay, Jericho, time to fill us in on what we don't know, but you seem to," Thomas suggested, softly but firmly.

The Irishman sighed deeply and took a big swig of his coffee, which he'd left black but added plenty of sugar to.

"The Cannich cat," he said. "One of the highlights of its Highland fling was a visit to a wildlife park, where it killed a number of animals and a keeper. It did so to get access to a female mountain lion they had there. She had come into heat and proved too much of a temptation for the strapping lad. I'm sure you also remember the reported tragedy of how that same mountain lion then mauled the park's owner to death? Well, that part wasn't strictly true. It was her cubs."

"Her cubs?" Catherine asked. She glanced at Thomas, who had gone pale.

"Four in total," Jericho nodded. "They escaped, but two were killed pretty quickly – not my doing I might add. But as for the other two…"

"One's made it over here?" Thomas asked, barely getting the words out as his throat clammed up at the mere thought.

"The British government thought it best not to tell you. The one over here is called Tama, and she was sold to a private collector. I arranged her capture and sale a few years ago."

"So, what is Tama doing out in the wild then?" Catherine demanded.

"Beats me, obviously that was never part of the agreement," Jericho shrugged.

"Is this why Keelson hasn't been answering my calls?" Thomas asked. "Because she knows you're wrapped up in this?"

"When did you speak to Kelly?" Jericho queried, a concerned look on his face.

Kelly Keelson hadn't been contactable since they had spoken a few days ago. That was unusual. Since having started her own production company, she had worked closely with Thomas, documenting how he and Catherine had hunted down the unusual pride of lionesses that had killed his first wife. Set in the same African wilderness that had been plagued by the man-eaters of Tsavo over a century before, the programmes had been picked up worldwide. Since then, Thomas, Catherine and Kelly had become good friends. And Jericho and Kelly had become much more, at least it was rumoured.

"I haven't, and that's not like her," Thomas replied.

Jericho didn't seem relieved.

"Where's the other cub?" Jesse asked.

"That we don't know for sure, although I have a feeling she's also in the hands of a collector. Not on these shores though, that's for sure."

"So, you're on clean-up duty?" Thomas asked.

Jericho shrugged. "Kind of.".

"You didn't sell anyone a big grizzly too?" Nina accused, mockingly.

Unusually, Jericho went quiet, his eyes focusing on the mug of coffee.

"So, Tama," Thomas said, changing the subject. "How much does she resemble her old man?"

"When I last saw her, she was nearly fully grown," Jericho replied. "I've only seen your cat in the Natural History Museum in London, but I'd guess she's only a shade smaller by now. She has mountain lion colouring, sort of reddish and sandy brown. But she has the bulk, and all the equipment of dear old dad."

"A sabre-tooth?" Jesse exclaimed incredulously. "There's a god-damn sabre-tooth loose up here, that's what you're telling me?"

Jericho went quiet again. Thomas thought he could see sweat on the Irishman's brow.

"Tell me more about this buyer," Thomas demanded.

"He's not the problem, he's who I'm working for right now," Jericho replied. "If somebody is setting this cat loose here and there, it's not him."

"I'm guessing that $100,000 status symbol out there is a company car then?" Thomas added, finally making the connection that Jericho was still on the payroll.

Jericho nodded.

"So, are you here to help out, or are you going to get in the way?" Jesse growled.

"Neither," Jericho shrugged. "My first port of call is to meet the buyer in Denver. I won't know much more until then. But believe it or not, I'm feeling just as pissy about the whole thing as you are."

"I doubt that," Jesse muttered with menace. "But it clears a few things up, least ways."

"Such as?" Nina enquired, pointedly.

"It's a hybrid animal," Jesse said flippantly. "Imported illegally into the United States. I can hunt it and kill it without issue. And that's all I needed to know."

"With those *things*?" Nina accused.

"I don't remember inviting you to this party anyways," Jesse retorted back.

"I came here to warn you, not give you a reason to risk your life and let those damn things loose," Nina scolded. "We already have two potentially killer animals out there. We don't need a pack more."

"I can control them," Jesse said, dismissing her concern.

"Really?" Nina shot back, whipping up the sleeve of her arm and revealing a healed-over scar that ran along her forearm.

The room went quiet.

"I told you, I think it smelt that wolf of yours on you," Jesse said, quietly.

"But that's just it, and something you need to consider," Nina continued. "I can control a 150lb wolf better than you can those animals. He'd never bite me, or anyone. Unless I told him to, that is," she added, smiling at Thomas.

"I don't know about the killing part, but it does need hunting down Nina," Thomas added. "Guess that's what I'll be doing too."

They sat together in silence for a few moments before Nina got up. The rest of them followed suit, following her and Jericho downstairs and out the door.

"Keep in touch from now on, okay?" Thomas said to Jericho as he climbed into the GMC.

The Irishman nodded. He turned the key in the ignition and the big V8 rumbled into life. Thomas stepped back as Jericho turned the truck around. As he was passing Nina, who was making her way towards her own truck, he slowed.

"Ms. Lee," Jericho said, almost under his breath. "I don't know much about this bear, but the circles I frequent are suggesting something isn't right about it. Talk about it being dropped here by the government, that it killed people up North or something. All the normal conspiracy stuff, you know. But still, be careful."

"Not my first rodeo," Nina smirked. "But thanks for the warning."

Thomas, Catherine, and Jesse watched the two trucks as they headed back down the trail.

"Did things just get better or worse?" Jesse asked.

"Much, much worse," Thomas replied.

CHAPTER ELEVEN

Chayton could feel the change that had taken place. He and Tama had taken the next step in their relationship. The bond of trust was much stronger now, and he couldn't bring himself to lock her up again. She had returned to the enclosure, but he kept the gate open. She was free to come and go as she pleased. He trusted her to stay close without the need of restricting her movements. He had fed her during the day again. He had guessed, as with many hybrid animals, that her metabolic rate was considerably elevated. Compared to other large cats he had worked with, he knew she was much warmer to the touch. She ran "hot", as a breeder of racehorses he once knew used to say.

Chayton though, had been fasting since the day before, not having drunk or eaten anything since the meeting in the diner. The thirst and hunger were necessary for what he had planned. He walked past his trailer down a worn path that led to a small lake. On the shoreline, he had built a simple dome structure by bending saplings over and covering them with thick blankets. The makeshift lodge wasn't very high, only coming up to his chest as he stood, and it was relatively cramped inside. There was barely enough room for the two fire pits he had constructed and a place between them for him to sit. The fire pit nearest the entrance glowed red and amber, as licks of flame crept around the stones on top of the fire. A small amount of smoke had built up in his absence, but he didn't mind this.

He used a leather cloth and a wooden bucket to collect the stones from the first fire pit before depositing them in the second. Then, from a pile of smooth, roundish, flat stones he had already collected from the lake, he added a new layer of rock to the first fire pit. Satisfied, he headed back out to the lake and placed the now empty bucket on the ground. He stripped off his clothes and plunged into the water. It was bracingly cold, but it made him feel alive. He allowed himself to float downwards, about six feet into the dark green water. He closed his eyes. He could feel the icy current being fed by the melting snows higher up. He imagined the water forcing its way down mountainsides, tunnelling through rock. He saw salmon swimming against the current, leaping from the torrent and heading upstream. He hung there in the water, letting his imagination be taken by the ebb and flow of the water. It was good practice for what lay ahead.

Finally, in need of breath, he returned to the surface and lumbered out of the water. He sought out the bank of white clay he had dug out nearby and took great scoopfuls of it with his hands. He applied it all over his naked body with great care. The chalky substrate clung to his wet skin obediently. He picked up the wooden bucket from where he'd left it by the shore and filled it with lake water. He slowly made his way back to the lodge, pulling aside the blanket that covered the entrance. He knelt, pushing the bucket towards the second fire pit ahead of him. He crawled inside, folding back the blanket after him to cover the opening. The light was dying outside, and the glow from the fire pit near the door spread across the interior of the lodge. Chayton sat with his legs folded. Content his breathing and pulse were relaxed, he reached to his side for the small package of herbs he had placed there for safe keeping. Wrapped in twine, the bundle contained dried panther cap mushrooms, cannabis leaves, jimson weed, and mandrake root powder. He stared at the fire pit for a moment before casually throwing the bundle onto it. The dry stems crackled and turned black in the heat and the powders exploded as they hit the hot stones. A greenish grey mist lifted from the pit. Chayton cupped some water from the bucket and splashed it onto the still-hot rocks of the second pit. A cloud of steam burst upwards and met the green mist. He closed his eyes.

His breathing became laboured, painful as he fought the convulsions in his chest. A moment of panic gripped him as he contemplated if he had gotten the mixture or amounts wrong. But as his breathing relaxed, he settled again. He began to chant, giggling with light-headedness as he mumbled the blessings and prayers. He knew the words, but not their meaning. It was only the journey he required from the vision quest tradition. He drifted towards unconsciousness, relinquishing his hold on the present and reality.

Out of the darkness shrouding his mind stepped a crow warrior. He was a hunter, with a bare chest, a game bag made of soft leather, and a formidable looking bow. As if shrouded in fog, the warrior stepped forward, and the darkness he had come from melted away. Mountains that Chayton recognised gave way to forests he didn't. Huge prairies, where he knew ranches and even small towns now stood, extended for miles. Swathes of bison roamed them freely. He could smell their stink in the air and feel the combined thuds of their hooves in the ground beneath him. He watched the hunter. He was making his way across the meadows towards a single-story, log-walled fort on the far side. A European-looking man with a blonde beard and dressed in the wool and linen clothing of a mountain trapper from the early 1800s, walked out to greet him. The hunter took a cleaned and rolled pelt of a mountain lion from his bag and offered it to the man, who examined it, smiling. The European man beckoned the hunter towards the fort. Next in his mind's eye, Chayton saw a ledger being filled in and the hunter being handed twenty shillings for the pelt.

The scene melted away into blackness but was quickly replaced with another. The fort disappeared and so did the bison and prairie landscape. A harsher, more sparse landscape took its place. Patches of thick forest clung to steep, snow encrusted mountain sides. He noticed a strange, tawny coloured creature standing close to a group of trees. It looked like an African lion, but of enormous size. It had a scraggy looking mane, much shorter and less regal than he would have expected. It was soon joined by a smaller, darker creature which Chayton took to be a female. His mind's eye swept again across the barren landscape, where an enormous cat, that at first glance looked like Tama, was attacking what looked like a hairy elephant calf. He watched the enormous, curved teeth enter what he now recognised as a mastodon's neck, crushing the windpipe and severing the vertebrae. Then, with a considerable show of strength, the smilodon cat tore out the throat of its prey. Chayton recognised the killing method. He also recognised an ecosystem in perfect harmony without the influence of man.

Blackness again, quickly giving way to a landscape dotted with swamp and marshland, somewhere in the south Chayton guessed. The thought was confirmed as he observed a band of Santee, Cherokee, and Chicora men as they queued to get into a British colonial encampment. The tribesmen bore hides of wolves, bears, bobcats, and mountain lions. Chayton felt the tension as one hunter hesitated to hand over his pelts. When he finally produced a singular skin, Chayton watched as the hunter was stripped of his dress and whipped in punishment. A great swell of anger began to build in Chayton's heart.

The landscape melted away again. This time, Chayton found himself watching a colossal hunting party from above. For some reason, the cold climate and fall-coloured trees made him think of New England. The clothes of the hunters suggested he was still some centuries in the past. There must have been two hundred men or more, beating through the woods and ravines. Another line of gunmen awaited the prey to come to them. And it did so in droves. Chayton watched in horror as foxes, bears, bobcats, elk, deer, buffalo, otters, beavers, wolves, and mountain lions, met wave after wave of gunfire from the ridge. Hours seemed to pass. Over a thousand dead animals were tallied, stacked and burnt. The putrid stench filled Chayton's nostrils. The pelts from fifty dead mountain lions were taken by the men and worn as cloaks. In his dream state, he watched with glee as their boastfully worn trophies helped disgruntled Native American hunters easily identify them. Each of the men who wore a pelt was hunted down and dispatched by the hunters in vengeance of losing their livelihoods. He saw himself in these hunters, who acted righteously and in retaliation to the squander of the natural resources.

The scenes of slaughter drifted back into a swirling mist. Suddenly, Chayton was high, flying in the form of an enormous bronze eagle. He felt the regal bird's sadness as it gazed down at the great American continent. He saw the wild west, and towns and cities under construction springing up out of the landscape. He watched as the railroad spread west and northward, clearing forests and wildlife as it went. First, enormous herds of elk and bison were swept from the Eastern plains. As deer became scarce, predators took the blame and then the bullets of ranchers, who feared for their livestock. The disconnect from nature he was witnessing appalled him. Ranchers and politicians alike ignored the harsh landscape, the weather, disease, and all the other possible deaths that came to their cattle and flocks. Predators were blamed in all cases. Bears, wolves, and mountain lions especially, were hunted to the brink of extinction. To his horror, he watched orphaned cubs and pups wander aimlessly, starving, until they eventually committed the crimes their innocent parents had been accused of. They entered the ranches and farmsteads, taking the only meat they could find. And they paid for it dearly. The mist swirled once more, and then he could feel himself back on the ground, within the hot and humid confines of his sweat lodge.

He staggered outside, pushing aside the blankets that covered the entrance and stumbling back down the path to the lake. He struggled to breathe, and took big, rasping gasps of the clean mountain air. His foot struck a rock close to the shore, and he tripped head on, the fall broken by the icy embrace of the lake water. Time stood still. He felt instant connection with the land again. His eyes opened. The water was clear, and he saw small bubbles rise up from the lakebed to greet him. He rose up, emerging refreshed and awakened. He spent a few moments washing off the residual white clay. His clarity had returned, and he felt steady on his feet again as he exited the lake.

As he stared up the trail towards his cabin, he saw Tama standing on the brow of the hill. She was slightly crouched, staring unblinkingly at him. Her body language hinted curiosity. Chayton may have even read it as mild concern. He walked towards her, keeping his own gaze steady. He approached with his palms open, controlling his breathing and heartrate, which he knew she could sense. He whispered soft words of reassurance. When he was within fifteen feet, she rose to her full height. He paused, allowing her to come to him. Tama purred deeply. He only had to look down slightly to meet the great cat's gaze. She looked at him momentarily, then lowered her head. She sniffed at his genitals, and he fought the urge to step back, taking a quick intake of breath and stiffening slightly. As if sensing his apprehension, Tama moved past him, rubbing her fur against his ribs. He turned to watch her as she made her way down to the lake to drink. He hesitated a moment, but suddenly feeling the cold, he made his way to his cabin. As he entered, he cast a glance at the map on the wall. His eyes darted to the nearest big town, Buffalo. He smiled.

CHAPTER TWELVE

Chayton drove past the sign that announced he was entering the small town of Buffalo, Wyoming. It was as much of a postcard frontier kind-of-place as you could get. Double-fronted, flat-roofed stores lined the main street. Their dusty red brick exteriors, weathered wooden doors, and thinly glazed, painted windows wouldn't look out of place in any western. American flags hung from most, some so over-sized they created an obstacle you needed to walk around. The sidewalks were lined by battered pick-up trucks, older model SUVs and the occasional out-of-place saloon or minivan. His beaten-up Chevy was the only one moving. He rolled slowly down the road, turning off as he followed signs for the station. His eyes flicked to the rear-view mirror, and he kept a steady gaze on the silver trailer he towed behind the truck. He wound the window down, checking the side mirrors and cocking his head to see if he could hear the trailer's occupant. For now, she seemed content and unruffled by the long journey and the confinement of the trailer. He had, though, taken the precaution of sedating her.

Having called ahead, he knew where he needed to go to load cargo and turned away from the main station building. He pulled up and fished through the glove box. It had taken him several days to fill out the paperwork under a false name and address. He'd used a taxidermist right here in Buffalo, one whom he knew had gone out of business. He'd even driven past by the empty storefront on his way through. He was confident the lower paid employees of the less frequented routes of Amtrak were unlikely to check his credentials. It was a tick-box exercise for them. He just needed the right paperwork, and that, he had. In triplicate.

After a short explanation to the cargo clerk, he watched as a forklift truck swung around towards the back of the trailer. He walked around, unfastening the bolts that held the steel crate in place. He couldn't help the tension that crept over him. Tama had never experienced anything like this. As the crate rose in the air, he heard it strain under the unexpected weight. The driver of the forklift looked out, puzzled. When the box shook, and an aggressive yowl echoed from inside, the driver's look changed to one of concern.

"One pissed off prize cow," Chayton suggested. "She's used to slightly more luxurious appointments."

The driver of the forklift seemed relieved and swung the crate clear of the trailer. He drove it straight across the end of the platform and into the open side of a cargo car. Chayton looked back down the platform at the rest of the train.

"You taking a prize cow to Denver?" the cargo clerk queried?

"Cheyenne, as you'll note the paperwork says," Chayton was quick to reply. "Big rancher has a place near the national grasslands. Wants only prize animals on his prize land." Chayton rolled his eyes.

"Last chance to check on her before we get underway," the clerk indicated, accepting the story.

Chayton smiled, struggling to believe town folk could be so dumb. He stepped onto the train and walked up to the crate. The air holes were deliberately small. He hadn't wanted anybody peeking in. Chayton glanced behind to check he wasn't being watched. He fished a small wad of greaseproof paper from his coat pocket. He unwrapped it carefully and took out the piece of dried rabbit meat it contained, pushing it through the thin vent on the side of the crate. It was laced with the antidote to the mild sedative he'd given Tama. He sensed she wouldn't need much though. In a short time, she'd be very awake and very hungry. Again, he had seen to that. He had stopped feeding Tama for the last two days. He knew she had probably caught some small game on her own, just as she had on the outings he'd allowed her previously – but it still meant a considerable drop in her usual intake. He was counting on her hunger.

He stepped off the train and watched the cargo clerk close up the car. Chayton parked up the truck and trailer, then returned to the main station building. He'd already bought his ticket in advance, on the same alias. He passed through the small, one-roomed stationhouse and stood for a moment on the platform. He looked the train up and down.

At the head, was an older EMD F40PH tractor engine. It's black-painted driver cabin and silver chassis shone in the early morning sun. The rest of the train was made up of standard passenger carriages and a few cargo cars towards the back of the train. There was also a buffet car, which featured the older style, glass-panelled roof and double-decker style bar and restaurant. He headed towards it, figuring he might as well be comfortable for now. He took one last look up and down the train. The aluminium sides of the carriages, and the bright red, white and blue Amtrak colouring gleamed back at him. There was no sign of a wayward cop, on-leave military personnel, or otherwise. Just a few passengers making their way onto the train, oblivious to what else was joining them.

He stepped onto the train and made his way straight to the bar. He ordered a cup of coffee and took it to a booth to drink.

About five minutes later, the train lurched forward, with the sound of metal-on-metal groaning under the strain. Slowly, it began to build up speed as the locomotive headed south towards Casper. There was a good seventy miles in between stations. He finished his coffee and decided to do some reconnaissance on his fellow passengers. He made his way towards the front of the train, slowly but surely. He passed between compartments, stopping occasionally to pretend to take in the view out of the windows or ask for directions and time of arrival at Casper. Most ignored him. To others, he was no different to them.

Happy that there was no immediate threat to his plan, he saw no reason to stall putting it into action any longer. He began to make his way back down the carriages. He passed through the dining car, then several passenger cars. When he got to the last one, he stopped. His eyes fixed on the guard standing in the walkway that connected to the cargo compartment. Chayton suddenly realised a locked door stood between him and Tama. Chayton stole away into a seat, reaching into his coat pocket. He drew out a small, black, plastic remote. Without looking down, he pressed the single button on the casing.

Chayton couldn't hear it against the background of the moving train or through the steel door, but he knew Tama's crate had just swung open. He'd checked it many times. The mechanism worked perfectly and smoothly. He now began to watch the guard. At this point, he wasn't sure what would happen. There was a possibility he may have to intervene. He looked around the rest of the carriage at the other passengers. This last car was sparsely populated. A man in a suit, reading a newspaper; he was wiry and thin and wouldn't put up much of a fight. A middle-aged woman sat a few seats in front of him, her nose in a magazine. Towards the back of the carriage, two boys in their late teens sat together, their eyes glued to a phone screen. Their laughter echoed down the carriage. Then, a much louder sound drowned it out.

Chayton's gaze slowly moved back to the guard. He distinctly heard something thud against the locked door behind the man. Chayton willed him on. Compliantly, the guard turned and looked at the door, confused. He took a few steps towards it and drew an electronic key card. Chayton tensed, ready to spring from the chair and make his play if he needed to. The guard pressed the key card against the lock. A small green LED light flashed, and the lock clicked. The guard swung it open. A sound like thunder reverberated around the aluminium skin of the carriage. Each passenger stopped what they were doing and swung their heads around towards the now open door. There was a snarl and then a scream as the guard was engulfed by something huge.

Chayton stood, watching the scene unfold. As the two teenagers jumped from their seats, Tama sprang and knocked them to the ground. Her claws slid from their sheaths, entering the squirming flesh beneath her forepaws like flick knives. One of the boys stopped moving instantly, but the other still tried to drag himself from under the beast. Tama opened her jaws and sent her curved fangs through his shoulder, lifting him from the ground and shaking him rigorously. She dropped him again when his body drooped lifelessly.

The woman was up and running towards Chayton now. As she glanced over her shoulder at the great cat, Chayton stepped forward and sent her flying back with a straight kick to the chest. Tama didn't hesitate. Rearing up a little, she caught the woman between her forelimbs and pulled her close to her chest, as she buried her teeth into the woman's neck and shoulder. An arterial spray of blood showered the cat's muzzle and began to spill onto the floor. Chayton watched as Tama bit down again, more heavily, shattering bone and ending the life of her prey instantly.

Chayton slipped past the man in the suit, now cowering in his seat. He squeezed past Tama, who ignored him as she strolled to the aisle seat the man sat in. Chayton heard a soft whimper, and a purr, then a scream. He knew Tama was feeding this time. He made his way back to the cargo hold and slipped inside. He found Tama's empty crate and reached inside. He pulled out the buffalo jawbone axe and slipped off his coat and shirt, but not before taking a stick of black camouflage paint from a pocket. He took a moment to tie his long hair back before coating his eyes in a thick ribbon of ebony. He turned, heading back down the carriage, stepping over bodies as he went. Tama stood patiently at the door of the next carriage. He again squeezed past her and pulled it aside. He heard the rumble of her soft purr as he stood beside her.

The great cat stepped forward, as did Chayton. They stood together. Her red fur and his tan skin shone in the stream of sunlight that poured through the windows as the train continued south. Chayton studied the crowd. Every eye was on the incredible animal that stood before them. An unequivocal force of nature. A creature not seen by humankind for millennia. On a commuter train in Wyoming, next to a half-naked Native American warrior brandishing a steel-dipped, buffalo jawbone club. Chayton smiled as their perplexed expressions turned to ones of horror. They had led dull, monotonous lives without purpose. At least their deaths would not be so tedious.

It was a scream that broke the enchantment. Tama leapt forward, spurred into action by the noise and movement. Paws the size of hubcaps swiped at those trying to rush forward and escape. Her head rolled back as she roared, freezing her prey in its tracks, as a genetic memory of a thing that came for them in the night emerged from the ether of their subconscious. Nobody on the train would have known that the pitch and sonic capacity of the cat's roar had evolved to shock and stun its victims, just as it did now. But they felt it all the same. Confused and caught unawares, they panicked, tripping over themselves, or frozen in fear. Then Chayton saw it.

He'd known all along it might happen. Someone, somewhere on the train was bound to be carrying a gun. This was Wyoming after all. The man was overweight and out of shape. He had a thick head of hair and a heavy moustache. As he raised the short-barrelled revolver, his hands noticeably shook. Tama was his target. Without flinching, Chayton curled his arm and sent the jawbone club flying. The weapon carved circles in the air as it flew with force down the corridor between the two columns of seating. His aim was true, and the bladed teeth embedded themselves into the man's right shoulder, making him drop the gun and cry out in agony. Chayton dashed forward, stepping up onto the seats and jumping nimbly from row to row until he could launch himself at Tama's would-be assassin. It only took a few seconds. He delivered a straight punch as he ripped the axe from the man's flesh. He picked up the gun, then, with a kick, he opened the door to the next compartment. He realised he'd reached the dining car again.

Tama became noticeably more aggressive. She snarled menacingly as she stepped forward. She hauled herself from the ground onto the bar and paced along it, knocking cups and glasses over as she went. With an angry growl, the cat looked down and noticed the cowering waitress on the other side. Tama extended her left forelimb and effortlessly hooked the woman with her claws. The woman barely had time to scream before one of Tama's teeth cleaved through the top of her skull. Chayton was distracted as a spray of blood and brain tissue spilled over the top of the bar, as the immense pressure the cat's jaws were putting on the skull, proved too much. The woman's head folded in on itself with a series of sickening crunches. As Tama's incisors separated it from the neck, the corpse flopped back over the other side of the bar, out of sight.

Chayton was fuelled with adrenaline now. He surged ahead of Tama, swinging his axe with one hand and firing the revolver with the other. A man in a blue business suit fell to the ground, the black patch on his jacket at the base of his spine slowly spreading. Another shot ran out, and a side window instantly clouded with a red mist. The axe swung wide, catching a woman in the jaw and sending her spinning to the ground as teeth and blood spilled from her mouth. Tama indiscriminately fell upon Chayton's victims, killing some, mauling others. Some, she ignored completely, quickening her pace to make sure she stayed alongside.

At the next carriage, a group of men made the mistake of opening the door and rushing forward to investigate the commotion. Something the size of a grizzly bear engulfed them, tearing through them with savage roars. Tama's mass was enough to crush one alone. Another looked on in disbelief as four claws the size of steak knives near-severed his arm from the shoulder. The last gulped final throatfuls of air that would not save him, as a violent gurgling rasp sounded from the two open wounds Tama's fangs had left in his chest.

There was a screech of metal on metal, and Chayton nearly lost his footing, as the locomotive careened to a halt. Tama roared at the unexpected high-pitched noise and jolting of the carriages. Several of the commuters lacking Chayton's sense of balance could not stop themselves falling forward, crumpling onto the floor in terror. Chayton looked back down the train. There was a slight tremble in his arms as, for the first time, he wondered how many people had fallen at his and Tama's touch. There was another agonising metallic groan as the train came to a final stop, rolling back a little with momentum. It was as if the onboard rampage had wounded the iron horse itself, stopping it in its tracks. Whereas in the past it had brought settlers and spearheaded the purging of the land, he and Tama had struck back for the crimes committed in its wake.

Chayton only hesitated a second. It was over. He moved forward quickly to the next compartment walkway and kicked open the exit door. He jumped down to the ground, quickly glancing up and down the train as he did so. Nobody else was taking the opportunity to get off. With a severe and deafening whistle, he set out into the Wyoming landscape. He set his eyes on a ridgeline to the east that offered a copse of oak and spruce. Responding to the whistle, Tama squeezed herself through the narrow doorway and jumped down to the ground. Chayton ran, fuelled by exhilaration and elation. Tama had again performed beyond all expectations. Their bond as a team was now cemented beyond doubt. They didn't stop until they entered the shadow afforded them by the boughs of the trees. Chayton only glanced back at the train once, but, as he heard the rotors of an approaching helicopter in the distance, he turned again and headed for the wilderness where he knew he and Tama would find refuge.

CHAPTER THIRTEEN

"A God-damn sabre-toothed tiger?" the angry American voice at the other end of the phone screamed at Thomas.

"No," Thomas replied, flustered and still watching the unfolding story on the early morning news. "Well, yes, a sabre-toothed cat, there's actually no such thing as a…"

He caught Catherine's incredulous look as her face flushed red with anger.

"What I'm trying to tell you is, we know what this animal is. And it's not a bear, or a mountain lion, or a…".

Catherine watched as Thomas' face fell. The federal agent he was speaking with was clearly having a hard time believing him. Thomas gave over his contact details, including the address of the farm and Lodge View. As he hung up the phone, he couldn't hide the look of defeat he wore. His eyes moved down to his feet as he slumped back down on the sofa next to Catherine. He picked up the remote to the TV and un-muted the sound.

A train on a remote trackway was being viewed from a news helicopter, circling the engine and its cars slowly, and at a distance. Several emergency choppers were already sat on the ground, the blades of their rotors still turning as stretchers, some covered, others blood-stained and containing flailing victims, were secured and loaded onto them with tenable solemnity.

"We're still only gaining tiny fragments of insight as to what has happened here," the reporter's voice commented over the imagery. "What at first glance looks to be some kind of terrorist attack, we're now told by survivors, was actually the work of a lone assailant and some kind of animal."

Thomas stared at the screen in disbelief.

"First reports suggest a death toll of nineteen, and nearly twice as many severely wounded. The youngest victims, a pair of teenage brothers, were taking their first solo train trip to Casper to visit their father, who recently separated from their mother, based in Buffalo."

The footage cut to a door-step interview with the parents of the two teenagers at their different locations.

"This animal…what did Jericho call her? Tama? She's been trained?" Catherine asked.

"We don't know anything for sure at the moment," Thomas replied quietly. "But it certainly looks like it. Even a hybrid like we encountered back in Cannich wouldn't need to kill or feed like that. I imagine she was killing on command, or perhaps joining in the slaughter. You once pointed out to me Smilodon was possibly a pack hunter. Maybe it comes naturally to her."

Catherine half-smiled, but he could see the anguish on her face. Thomas knew that, more than most, she understood what those people on the train had faced. She had made peace with her near-death experience some years back, but he could see the story was dredging up memories that had long been buried deep. Memories of an enormous black cat, that had hunted her down and near killed her, in the mountains above their home in Scotland. He reached over and put his hand on hers, stroking her thumb with his own. She squeezed his hand.

"But, if this cat is descended from our cat, it's not a Smilodon. It's something very new, and very old." Catherine reminded him.

"A hybrid, likely exhibiting the same genetic gigantism ours did. So, we can expect a heightened metabolic rate, an insatiable appetite, and if dad was anything to go by, one of the most intelligent animals we've ever come across." Thomas agreed.

"Sounds like trouble you've courted before," came Jesse's drawn, mid-west accent from behind.

"I really need to get used to this leaving doors open thing," Catherine muttered, almost in shock, but smiling at Jesse. "I didn't hear you come in or come up the stairs."

"Plenty of practice keeping quiet," Jesse shrugged, as if a matter of fact.

Just then, Cassie ran out of her bedroom. She immediately went up to the huge bandogge that accompanied Jesse and scratched behind his ears. The dog sat down and leaned into her, clearly enjoying the sensation. Cassie giggled. Jesse watched as if in wonder.

"You bring out his soft side, lil' lady," he said, sounding surprised. He turned back towards Thomas and Catherine. "So, what's the plan?"

"I contacted the authorities, spoke to an FBI agent in Denver. I don't think he believed me," Thomas replied.

"Well, somebody did. Sheriff and a few other fellas are heading out to meet you folks. They'll be here about noon be my guess," Jesse explained.

"That's encouraging," Catherine said, looking more hopeful.

"We'll see," Thomas and Jesse said together. They caught each other's amused expression as they did.

"What they probably want to do is keep things quiet and shut up the kooks calling in with ridiculous stories," Jesse replied.

"Does anyone know anything about our mysterious lion-tamer friend?" Thomas asked, nodding at the TV.

Blurry CCTV footage from the train station in Buffalo showed a Native American man with long dark hair, talking to a clerk at the cargo entrance of the station. An artist's rendering of the same man, brandishing a large and formidable looking club, and now naked from the waist up and depicted in war paint, flashed up alongside the CCTV images.

"Nothing concrete," Jesse sighed. "Nina says she's heard talk he may be some horse whisperer type living over towards Saddlestring, but nobody knows for sure. Sheriff told me they found a truck and trailer in the parking lot of the station at Buffalo, but it's registered to some dead guy from a reservation up North."

Catherine leaned over and picked up the remote to increase the volume as another news alert flashed across the screen.

"We're now also getting reports that the premium ranch property belonging to Aeneas 'Midnight' Martin, NFL quarterback for the Jackson Jaguars, has been decimated by a fire that appears to have been started deliberately. We're going straight to the scene," the anchor explained.

The television footage flicked to another aerial shot, this time of a huge ranch. Adjoining it was a large, black-coloured barn that had collapsed in on itself. Parts of it still smoldered.

The scene cut to a female reporter on the ground, wrapped in a long raincoat that protected her from the drizzle and cold. She stood on the immaculate drive of the property. A number of emergency vehicles could be seen in the background. Their blue lights revolved slowly, and no sirens blared. There was no urgency of the medics, police, and fire personnel. There was nobody to save. The reporter began to address the camera.

"What has been discovered here, in the early hours of this morning, is a scene of absolute devastation," she explained. "But what has also been revealed, is a dark secret that 'Midnight' Martin must have harboured for a long time. What you see behind me is what remains of an elaborate building that served as a professional dog fighting stadium. Since my arrival in the early hours of the morning, nearly twenty charred corpses of large dogs have been removed. And equally as many human victims are still being examined and processed by police and medical officials." The reporter paused for effect. "But 'Midnight' Martin himself was not killed in the fire."

The TV footage flicked to an aerial photograph, with a highlighted area in some trees to the rear of the property.

"What remained of his body was found here," the reporter continued to narrate, "and although the medical examiner is yet to deliver a full report, we already know that some kind of heavy weapon was used, and there are reports of an animal attack. Then there's this."

On screen, Thomas, Catherine and Jesse saw a photograph zipped inside an evidence bag. It showed the clear imprint of a tyre track in the mud.

"Whoever murdered 'Midnight' Martin and his paying customers approximately two nights ago, they covered their tracks well, but not these ones," the reporter explained. "They are already being compared to the abandoned truck and trailer left in the Buffalo train station parking lot. We're expecting confirmation any moment that they are a perfect match."

Thomas turned the TV off as Cassie walked back into the room. The creamy grey bandogge followed behind her, loyally.

"You two hit it off?" Jesse exclaimed.

Cassie nodded enthusiastically.

"He's worried about the doggies you have in the barn," she explained, matter of fact, giving the dog a gentle pat as he came alongside. Arnold responded by leaning close to her again.

"Is that a fact?" Jesse queried, a bemused smile on his face.

"I suggest you folks head up to the Big House when you're ready," Jesse motioned, headed back towards the stairs.

Thomas nodded in acknowledgement. He walked to the window, and watched Jesse walk back up the trail until he was out of sight. He picked up his phone again and flicked to Jericho's number. He paused and put the phone away again. Jericho would call when he had something, that, at least, he could still trust him to do.

~

Jericho O'Connell's thoughts occupied him as the miles between Wyoming and Denver drifted past. He ignored the radio and kept running the scenario through his head. He knew the buyer was a very serious businessman. There was no way he would randomly have let the animal change hands. As far as the collector was concerned, there were only two hybrid sabre-tooth cats in existence, and they only knew the whereabouts of one.

Jericho pulled off the 287 and took the 36 towards Boulder. He found it slightly ironic that his secretive employer had chosen Boulder as a place to meet. The quiet, trendy, and environmentally conscious town was only thirty minutes northwest of Denver. It was a haven for those seeking a more culturally enriched, perhaps even more liberal lifestyle than other parts of the mid-west offered. But it also harboured a tragic history that revolved around big cats. In 1991, the accepting nature of the town's good-natured and well-meaning residents had allowed predators to enter their midst. In fact, when the mountain lions had first started appearing in the gardens and driveways of the town's more remote residences, they were welcomed. Even when dogs, other pets, and prize livestock started to be taken, the cats were afforded refuge and protection. But then, in broad daylight, a promising high school athlete was killed and partially eaten by a young male lion that barely weighed in at 100lbs. It marked the first healthy, young adult to be taken by a puma in over a century. Since then, there had been others. Jericho realised that America was still coming to terms with the consequences of living alongside predators such as the brown bear, wolf, and cougar. It made him think of Thomas and Catherine's lynx project, and the similar controversies it courted.

He drove the big SUV through an industrial area before pulling through a set of large, black, metal gates of what looked to be an abandoned warehouse. They had been left open; a sign he had been told to look for. As he pulled around what must have once served as a gatehouse, he found himself in a long open space between the main warehouse and storage sheds. At the end, he saw three vehicles. Two rugged-looking Jeep Wrangler trucks flanked a large, metallic maroon vehicle of impressive size. He quickly realised he was looking at a Rolls Royce Cullinan, possibly the world's most expensive off-road vehicle. As he brought his own SUV to a halt, the doors of the Jeeps opened and a set of burly, ex-military looking, professional bodyguards got out. They all faced him as he too stepped out of the car.

"Gentlemen," Jericho nodded.

The one closest to him, who sported cropped blonde hair and a pair of aviator-style sunglasses to shield his gaze from the winter sun, nodded towards an open steel door that led into the warehouse. As Jericho headed inside, he was acutely aware he was followed in by three of the goons. He decided to ignore them, his temper and patience already tested after the early morning confrontation with Thomas.

As an experienced tracker and outdoorsman, Jericho's senses told him everything he needed to know about the warehouse. It had sat empty for months. Decay and damp were setting in. He could smell the rodent urine and taste the mould in the air. The atmosphere was stale, and the building was slowly being reclaimed by nature. He could hear the soft, distant caws of crows that were exploring the holes in the roofing. He smiled to himself as he noticed the swirl of muddy scrapes along the floor. Small, elongated prints not unlike a human hand faintly showed, giving away that racoons had sought the refuge of the dilapidated building. He made his away along the corridor, watching the shadow of the man on the wall next to him, gauging how close he was getting. He ignored him for now, then turned a corner and found the entrance to the main warehouse area. He stepped inside.

Three people stood on the opposite side of the space. They were all facing him. A woman with short blonde hair, parted sharply and with a green stripe accenting her brushed-over parting curl, stepped forward. Jericho noted the charcoal-coloured suit and black T-shirt beneath. She was attractive and toned but had the definitive swagger of ex-military.

"Good morning Mr. O'Connell," she greeted him, not offering her hand.

She had fierce blue eyes that appraised him with mild interest.

Jericho stared past her to the others. Both men, one was clearly a bodyguard type, in an expensive but cheap-fitting suit and a crew cut. He seemed bored. The other man studied him with an unblinking stare, the corners of his mouth turned up in a thin, calculated smile. He was slim and relatively short, about five foot, six inches, Jericho guessed. He wore round lensed, titanium framed spectacles. Jericho sensed the man's intelligence in a single glance. He turned back to the woman.

"My name is Annika Deveraux, I am the personal assistant to your employer, Mr. Richter."

Jericho nodded. His tiredness was affecting his patience and commitment to niceties, but he didn't miss the subtle softening of her vowels that hinted at her French accent.

"Do you think Thomas Walker will be able to retrieve the animal?" Deveraux asked.

"Not much will stop him trying," Jericho shrugged.

"We need her alive Mr. O'Connell," came a dry, well-spoken voice.

The accent was American this time, highly educated and honed over decades. But again, Jericho picked up the granite-like defining of the sentences that hinted at Erasmus Richter's German parentage. But he could tell the man had been born and raised in New York. He could imagine the grand house in the Hamptons and the sprawling New England estates.

"Well, you may have to manage your expectations on that one," Jericho said with an incredulous shrug.

"No, Mr. O'Connell, you may have to manage your friend," Richter stated, stepping forward.

"That animal belongs to me. I'm suitably impressed with her and what she can do. Our noble savage has had his fun, but it's time for them both to return to the shadows. I don't want to risk further exposure, or her unnecessary death or capture. Her DNA is far too valuable."

"Surely her DNA can be secured dead or alive?" Jericho asked, confused.

"You're being paid to bring back the animal known as Tama alive," Deveraux interjected. "The next payment instalment is due to be made, I trust we don't need to re-negotiate our terms or your fee?"

"Trust me lady, nothing would make me happier," Jericho laughed. "I'm already having second thoughts about this gig. Quiet and subtle ain't quite my style, if you get my drift."

Richter smiled. He turned to the bodyguard and nodded. The man retrieved an Apple iPad in a leather case from a bag on the floor and handed it over. Richter tapped at the screen as he walked towards Jericho and Deveraux.

"On second thoughts, lets renegotiate anyway," Richter stated. "I believe you are at the beginning of a blossoming romance with a Ms. Kelly Keelson, is that correct? Don't bother answering, I already know the answer."

Richter handed over the tablet. Jericho looked down at the screen. He was watching Kelly sitting in a plush office. It looked like she was being interviewed. The black and white footage suggested a hidden camera was being used, or CCTV of some kind.

"This was taken a few days ago. Ms. Keelson believed she was being recruited for a documentary production. However, my intentions weren't quite so noble." Richter stated.

The screen changed and flicked to a different room. Jericho could tell it was inside the same complex from the décor. But this room was occupied by four men, all dressed in black tactical gear and wearing face masks. They held handguns and seemed on alert, as if they were preparing to breach a room. Jericho was in no doubt which one it would be.

"You're dangerously close to hurting my feelings there, Herr Richter," Jericho growled.

Jericho had met Kelly after she had convinced Thomas Walker to return to Kenya and face the pride of man-eating lions that had killed his wife some years previously. Jericho had worked with Thomas in Africa before and had renewed their friendship to join the hunt. Keelson on the other hand had met Thomas when she was just a reporter, investigating the rampage of an unknown predator in the Highlands of Scotland. Since then, she had set up her own production company and become friends with the Walker family, and more with Jericho.

"I am disinclined to spare your feelings any more than I am to spare Ms. Keelson an uncomfortable few hours in return for an honoured agreement," Richter scolded.

Jericho watched on the monitor as the men exploded into the room Keelson was sat in, and surrounded her instantly, their guns all trained on her with expert precision. More than anything, Jericho wanted to launch himself straight at Richter, but he knew he'd be dead before he got there. He concentrated on his breathing, keeping it steady and deep.

"It's a shame you forced my hand Mr. O'Connell," Richter said. "I can see we have your undivided attention, and that's all that was ever required. I've made my point I take it?"

"We're crystal," Jericho growled.

He was shadowed by Deveraux all the way back out to the cars. He climbed into the black SUV and tore out of the warehouse compound, putting it in his rear-view mirror quickly and without a look back.

~

The sheriff and his deputy had been accompanied by an agent from the Bureau of Land Management. Almost a stereotype of a Mid-West elected law-enforcement official, Sheriff Bowman was fair-haired with a prominent, thick, blonde moustache. Thomas guessed he was in his late-fifties, and from his generous waistline, presumed he spent more time in his office than in Wyoming's wilderness. The deputy was young, with slicked back dark hair. Thomas hadn't caught his name. Special Agent Labar of the Bureau of Land Management on the other hand, didn't seem like an office type at all. Despite being of similar age to Thomas, probably in his early forties, his skin was weathered and tan. His eyes were sharp but set in a permanent squint. He reminded Thomas of a young Clint Eastwood.

Thomas, Jesse, and Catherine had greeted them with caution, expecting suspicion, or worse, trouble and some kind of implied liability. So, it was something of a surprise when the conversation went in a different direction.

"To cut to the chase Mr. Walker, you seem uniquely qualified to help us deal with this animal," Labar confirmed. "We're willing to extend you official license to do so, as well as Mr. Logan here."

"I'd need my wife, and a tracker of the name of Jericho O'Connell added to that list too," Thomas added.

"Your wife's no problem. But let's talk about Mr. O'Connell. Your friend here," Labar said, nodding towards Jesse, "has filled us in on his involvement. But to be frank, he was already on our radar. He's like the Indiana Jones of the black-market wildlife trade – an acquirer of what can't be acquired. I can't tell you not to involve your friend, but I'd advise against it."

"We wouldn't know half as much as we do if it wasn't for Jericho coming forward," Thomas objected. "I'm not happy about it, but he's the best tracker I know. And he clearly has inside information we can use."

"Forgive my Christian principles sir," nodded Labar smiled, "but no man can serve two masters."

"And forgive my desperation," Thomas shrugged, "but I know what we're up against, and we're going to need all the help we can get."

CHAPTER FOURTEEN

Joe Garrison watched an entire afternoon of news features on the TV, and more into the early evening. With each one, and with each sip of the bourbon he kept topped up in the tumbler resting in his left hand, his anger grew. In the later broadcasts, survivors told of the attack on the train from their hospital beds. He couldn't believe what he was hearing. A Native American, and some overgrown mountain lion that had been dressed up like a god-damn sabre tooth tiger or the like, had been responsible for the attacks. He'd always hated the term Native American. They were no more native than he, as he'd often declared in drunken vents with other disgruntled ranchers of the South Stone Mountain district. After all, the tribes had come here from Siberia and Australasia thousands of years ago, at least as far as he figured. Okay, they got here first, but there was nothing native about that.

He and his kin had made the productive land of Wyoming and beyond what it was today. He and his fellow ranchers. Not these city-slicker, hobby farmers, who just wanted a few horses and cattle on their land for show when their yuppie friends came to call. No, real men, who worked the land and the animals on it. The men and women who had tamed the wilderness, beaten it back. They had rid it all threats, both foreign and domestic. He looked at the skin of the male mountain lion that was stretched out over the hearth. An idea formed in his head, and for the first time in several hours, he smiled.

He slowly got up from the armchair, nearly spilling his drink and cursing under his breath in the process. He wandered over to the corner of his lounge and stopped in front of a small and sparsely stocked bookshelf. He plucked an old, green, clothbound and moth-eaten hardback from it. Simple line etchings of a trapper overlooking a mountain range, musket in hand, adorned the front cover. Sitting underneath was the neatly printed title "The hunting of men and other varmints in Wyoming", by Gregor Wolfsbane.

Gregor Wolfsbane had been a Russian immigrant living in Wyoming in the early 1800s. He was also a famed bounty hunter. But he had also covertly worked for the government, removing "nuisance" tribes and communities. He was the epitome of a one-man army, and would today be the equivalent of a special-forces ranger. He had also seen the state's predators as a scourge to be vanquished. Joe began to flip through the pages of the book. He paused when he came to the etching he'd remembered. A Virginian trapper, wearing a mountain lion skin as a cloak, the upper jaw and face serving as a skullcap. Joe smiled again and reached for the skin mounted above the fire.

A little time, and a few phone calls later, Joe had what he needed. A deputy in the Sheriff's department had relayed their suspicions of the involvement of an animal handler, who lived near Saddlestring. Several of the ranchers had decided to gather at the town's Game and Fish offices there. The local Game Warden was one of their own and had easily been convinced to get involved.

"You all know why we're here," Joe explained, as the last of the makeshift posse joined them in a back office. "People are dying on our land, and we can't allow that," he said, with a wicked smile. "And we all lost livestock to critters this past year, ain't we?"

There was a murmuring of muttered agreement.

"Damn wolves," Chance Nelson, Joe's closest neighbour grumbled. "Weren't none here until those damned reintroductions."

"Bear too," Sysco Miller added, one of the Saddlestring ranchers. "They come in for the calves like they do the deer."

"And the lions, well, they're a menace to all. Kids ain't safe, ain't that right Warden?" Joe asked.

"I make you right," Douglas Grant, the young Game Warden replied.

He handed out signed slips of paper to each of them. The makeshift kill-orders allowed for both the bear and the mountain lion they were planning to hunt down, to be taken by any or all of the gathered men. They'd effectively been deputised. Joe knew the kid was young and stupid, and they had taken advantage of him. His daddy was higher up in Wyoming Game & Fish, and would cover his ass and theirs, Joe was sure of it. Plus, if they got the damn beast, and maybe the man too, nobody would care if their capacity was official or not. He knew everyone in the room was prepared to take the risk.

"We're gonna head out towards this critter-chief's place, see if we can find anything," Joe explained. "I'm reliably informed that the court-order for the warrant failed on a lack of evidence, but I want to go take a look-see, don't you boys?"

More nods and grumbles indicated a firm yes.

"Then let's load up and head out, but first...a little indulgence from me if you will," Joe smiled, nodding at Douglas.

The Game Warden pulled out a large box from underneath one of the office desks and placed it on top. He took out several crudely fashioned neckties. Joe had made them himself from the old mountain lion skin. Each man took one and donned it obediently.

"It's time this mountain lion met some real mountain men, don't you think?" Joe growled.

Minutes later, the posse were headed north out of Saddlestring in a convoy of beaten-up trucks. Joe led the way in his dark blue and battered 1989 Dodge Ram Heavy Duty, the Game Warden sitting beside him, and Chuck Smith, another rancher, squeezed in further along. Miller's 1994 bright red Ford F150 was behind them, and Nelson's Black 1988 Chevy C/K behind him. Each truck carried three men. Armed with both hip flasks and serious fire power to keep both the cold and the varmints away, Joe knew they had already passed the point of no return as they reached the small township of Story.

They had to stop and ask directions twice, using the Game Warden and his official uniform to knock on some doors and get a fix on where the camp they were looking for was. At the second house, the old man had fixed them with a knowing look.

"You mean Chayton Reed's place, do you?" he'd asked.

"I'd make you right," Grant replied.

"He's not so fond of visitors...or trespassers," the old man added, looking over the trucks parked up on the road.

"Just gonna ask him a few questions, unofficial like," Grant stated.

The old man had pointed them in the right direction. Joe still missed the turning onto the trail, but Miller caught it out of the corner of his eye, flashing his lights and honking his horn wildly to stop Joe speeding off down the road. When the roof of the Airstream trailer became visible further up the trail,

Joe pulled to the side and stopped the truck. The others halted behind him.

Joe pulled his rifle, a Henry Big Boy, out from the rack behind the bench seat. He could see the Game warden had his service-issue 357-magnum revolver. Chuck had an old-looking double-barrel shotgun, and 12-bore slugs stuffed into his shooting vest. A similar assortment of rifles, shotguns, and handguns were carried by each of the men as they gathered around the bonnet of Joe's truck.

"I'm looking for a show of force and your best, gentlemen," Joe explained. "We mean business, and I don't care if our company is unwanted, we're not taking no for an answer, you hear me?"

"Damn right," Miller agreed.

"Let's do this," nodded Nelson.

The posse moved off up the trail towards the trailer and the assortment of outhouses and enclosures that dotted Reed's camp. The closer they got, the louder they became, jeering at each other as they pointed at each other's neckties and admired their collective firepower. As they rounded the corner and came into the camp itself, they stopped. It was clearly deserted. Cage doors swung too and fro in the wind, open. Nothing else moved.

Joe made straight for the Airstream trailer. In his haste, he didn't notice the subtly hidden camera in the trees opposite. He wasn't surprised however to find the door to the trailer open. He moved inside, followed by the others. They half-heartedly searched it, finding nothing of real interest. Suddenly, a portable CB radio sitting on the kitchen counter, crackled into life.

"Typical encroachers," came a deep, strong voice from the speaker. "You show no respect, just as it always has been."

Joe leered as he picked up the radio. He pressed down on the transmit button on the side.

"Now, now, Tonto, don't get your wigwam in a twist, we just wanted to have a friendly little chat, that's all. Best it's with us rather than the law, wouldn't you say?" Joe replied, as the others laughed quietly in the background. "Gotta say, you kind of already look guilty, runnin' and the like."

"I'm right here," the reply came.

Joe looked around in surprise. He ducked, peering out of the windows. Unable to see anything, he grabbed the radio and pushed past the others to get back outside. The late evening light was fading, and he covered his eyes with his hand as he squinted past the trees, towards a lake, and up onto a small hill to its side. For a moment, he saw nothing. Then, at its peak, he saw the distant silhouette of a human figure rise up from a crouching position.

"You didn't come to talk," the voice came over the radio.

"No, not really, you son-bitch," Joe spat.

"Come get me, encroacher." The radio went dead.

Joe watched the figure disappear the other side of the ridge.

"Well, we've had our invitation boys," Joe gestured, slinging his rifle off of his shoulder and pointing the way with the barrel. "Let's not keep old Tonto waiting now."

They made their way through the camp together, working their way past the makeshift shelter by the lakeshore. Joe began to follow the path that edged around the lake, but Douglas stopped, drawing their attention. The game warden was studying the ground, hard. Joe and the others walked back to him. It was obvious what he was looking at. The print was still fresh, and easily the size of a man's spread-out hand. The pugmark, undoubtedly that of a cat, was larger than any in the group had ever come across.

"Geez, Joe, that's some damn mountain lion," Miller exclaimed.

"What d'ya think we were out here to hunt, cottontails?" Joe spat. His outrage seemed to silence the doubts he could see spreading across their faces.

The group followed the path again, this time a little more tightly packed than before. They were quieter too, and Joe knew they were feeling less sure of themselves. The confident arrogance of the man, as if he had been expecting them, and the size of the print, was giving them second thoughts. Joe hoped his tenacity and take-charge momentum would keep them going. He quickened his pace as they began their ascent of the hill, where they'd seen the man.

When they reached the ridgeline, Joe was disappointed to see a sharp descent, leading to a thick patch of forest, was all that met them on the other side.

"Miller, Chuck, you guys wait here to see if he doubles-back this way. The rest of us will head down into the trees, try and flush him and the critter out," Joe ordered. "My advice is don't wait around to ask questions. They're both killers."

Joe led the men down the slope. They naturally spread out as they descended, but, as they approached the trees, they saw that only one decent trail led through. Joe nodded at the two ranchers who had travelled up with Chance Nelson – Nicolas Joven, an older, wiry man with spectacles and a wispy beard and bald patch, and James Spencer, one of Chance's ranch hands – a much younger man with thick black hair and stubble to match. They knew what to do and took up position either side of the trail. Joe walked in first, followed by Nelson, the game warden, and the other two men in their party – a rancher called Ryan Blackwood and his eldest son, Karl.

About thirty feet along the trail, Joe paused. There was an opening in the trees that led off to the right, over a raised bank of foliage. Something didn't feel right. His eyes searched upwards towards the dying light of the evening sky. It was only then that he noticed that here in the trees, there was complete silence. No birdsong or woodpeckers. No nervous scurrying in the bush as they approached. Even the wind had dropped, unable to move past the densely packed pines beyond the trail. Karl Blackwood didn't seem to have noticed everybody else had stopped and pushed past. Joe raised his hand to try and stop the younger man, but as he did, Karl let out a shriek and dropped through the forest floor in front of them. Joe's hand grabbed at air as he tried to clutch the back of Karl's shirt, but it was too late. The blood-curdling, high-pitched scream made Joe freeze in his tracks. He forced himself to look down.

A pit had been dug across the entire path, and expertly covered by a thick layer of interwoven sticks and pine fronds, before a finishing layer of loose, sandy soil had added to the effect. It had blended in with the rest of the trail perfectly. It wasn't especially deep, only about four feet, but it was what was inside the pit that sickened Joe. Viciously sharpened wooden stakes were planted very compactly across the entire floor of the pit. Karl Blackwood had lost his footing as his right boot had stepped through the trap's covering, the momentum catapulting him straight down and face first. He had been harpooned through the legs, shoulder, chest, and abdomen.

Two of the spikes had pierced his right bicep and his open palm as he'd fallen. Joe was in no doubt that the boy was dead, something confirmed to him as he knelt, only to see a stream of blood pour out of Karl's open mouth.

Joe looked back, lost for words as he met the shocked gaze of Ryan Blackwood. He went to say something but couldn't find the words. The movement was so quick, Joe almost missed it. A blur passed behind the men, from left to right. Ryan suddenly cried out in pain and crumpled to the ground. As the men gathered around him, they saw something had slashed through his jeans just below his right buttock. Whatever had done it had delivered a savage cut into the three hamstring muscles. The denim was already soaking up blood at an alarming rate.

"God damn it, put some pressure on it and tie it off," Joe spat.

Joe raised the Henry rifle, peering along the sights as he scoped through the trees. He flinched as a thunderous roar rang out, loud enough to make him wince and want to cover his ears. Adrenalin surged through his arms, and he noticed the tremble along the rifle's barrel. It was only then that Joe noticed that the trail they had been following sat in a natural gulley. The banks of trees on either side of the path stood on slightly higher ground of about two feet. It occurred to Joe that the trail might have once been an old riverbed, perhaps one that originally ran to the lake. Now he looked, he could see some of the roots from the trees showing in the banks of earth either side.

"What the hell was that, Doug?" Chance asked the Game Warden.

"Sure as hell weren't no mountain lion," Ryan Blackwood spat, a look of agony on his face as Douglas Grant tried to tend to his wound. He lay on his left side, breathing heavily. "They don't roar."

The Game Warden looked up at Joe, nodding in agreement. A soft thud, and a sharp intake of breath from Ryan Blackwood made the gathered men look down. The man rolled onto his back, a muscular twitch rippling along his arms before stillness enveloped his entire body. Grant jumped to his feet, joining Joe and Nelson as they stared at the wooden arrow shaft that stuck up out of Blackwood's chest. Joe slowly turned to look back along the trail, from where he guessed the arrow had been fired from. He half expected the warrior to still be standing there, staring them down, but what he did see, he didn't quite believe.

The cat was nearly tall enough on all fours to look him in the eye. It had a powerful, muscular stance and flashing green eyes that almost glowed in the low light. The fur was a russet red colour, with a blonde chest, muzzle and ear tips. What he could see of the belly was almost white. He couldn't see any tail over the muscular hunched shoulders, which seemed to rise in a hump behind the head. But it wasn't the animal's size that had the men stunned into silence, it was the curved, gleaming fangs that protruded from the sides of its mouth.

The cat lurched towards them, breaking into a full run. Joe raised his Henry rifle and lined up on the cat's head. There was a whistling noise and then he felt a searing pain in his left shoulder and an impact that threw him off balance. The arrowhead dug in deep, rendering his arm useless and making him drop the rifle. It clattered on the hard, stony ground. He instinctively clutched at his shoulder, staggering backwards as he fought off the shock that wanted to consume him and shut his body down. He watched the game warden draw the 357 Magnum revolver from its holster, but already knew he would be too late.

Tama shifted her trajectory, as she noticed the crouching man's movement. She rose up slightly on her hindquarters, opening her mouth wide as she drove her teeth through the back of the man's neck and back. Douglas Grant didn't even have time to scream as one fang splintered his spinal cord and the other hooked through the lung on his right side. Tama's attention suddenly shifted to the man ahead of her, running back down the trail. She let the body between her jaws fall to the ground, as her instinct to chase down live and running prey kicked in. Her head only moved slightly as she caught the sweet, coppery metallic scent of blood on the man crouched to the side of the trail. Joe watched her pass as she broke into a run behind Chance Nelson.

Chance ran for his life. His heart pounded in his chest as if it were trying to burst through his ribs. He fought for air, his brain finally kicking in and telling him to scream for help. He opened his mouth wide, and a cry broke from his lips, but it was a cry of pain. It was as if four red-hot pokers had just been drawn across his back. He crumpled to the ground, but still clutched his shotgun. He felt the skin on his back stretch and split as he tried to twist around to face his attacker. He didn't quite make it, but a heavy blow from the paw of the cat spun him onto his back. He raised his head and brought the gun up, his hands shaking. The cat moved fast, despite its size. It was on top of him before he knew it. Its hot breath wet his hair, as its muzzle pressed against his forehead. He tried to angle the barrel of the gun into the cat's belly, but he lacked the strength or space to do so. He felt the cat's mouth open and a spray of spittle from its tongue wet his cheek. He was powerless as his head slipped between its jaws. There was instant pressure, something that seemed more urgent to him than the touch of its teeth on either side of his neck. Chance felt the cracking of his skull before he heard it. A feeling of calm acceptance came over him as he closed his eyes and pulled the shotgun's trigger.

~

Joe shivered as shock began to consume him in waves. He felt lightheaded and numb as he vaguely clutched at the arrow shaft sticking out of his shoulder. It had smashed its way through the lower part of his deltoid, and the agonising pain that convulsed through him with even the slightest movement told him the arrowhead had struck bone. Blood ran freely from the wound and had soaked his shirt through. He used his good arm to get back on his feet, turning slowly and ever so carefully back down the trail. As he took a step forward, he became aware of a figure slipping from the trees into the space behind him. Joe let out a breath that helped him cope with the pain as he turned back around. He shivered again at the sight that met him. He knew he was staring death in the face.

Chayton Reed wore an unbuttoned buckskin waistcoat over his torso and jeans. Vapor rose from his hot skin and muscles in the cold air. Joe noticed the very worn and heavy-duty working boots, making him even more surprised they hadn't been able to pick up the man's tracks. The Native American studied him intently, unmoving. In one hand, he gripped a half-raised and formidable looking weapon. What remained of the light glinted off the polished bone of the club, and the metal-laced teeth and blade set within the jawbone. As

Joe's eyes fell to the leather-wrapped handle, he couldn't but help notice the dyed-in blood stains that discoloured it.

"Fuck you, Tonto," Joe spat.

It was all the baiting Chayton needed. He sprang forward with the agility of a mountain goat, covering the ground with incredible and silent speed. Joe raised his one good arm to defend himself, but Chayton had anticipated that. The warrior swung the axe low and fast with an underarm thrust, catching Joe squarely in the groin. He sprang back, ready to strike again if his aim had not been true. He needn't have worried. Joe sank to his knees, howling in pain. His good hand clutched at his jeans, where a dark stain was quickly spreading. Chayton edged closer; the club now raised. Joe's eyes shone with terror masked by rage.

"You all belong in hell, all of you," Joe cried, his arms trembling as shock began to take over his body.

Chayton slipped behind the kneeling man. He brought the axe's blade up to Joe's throat.

"Keep a spot warm for me, brother," Chayton whispered as he sliced through Joe's trachea in a short, sharp, ripping motion.

Chayton pushed his knee gently into Joe's back and sent his body sprawling onto the trail. The rancher didn't move, and there was no rise and fall of breath that Chayton could see. He waited until he glimpsed the pool of blood seep from underneath Joe's corpse, then Chayton turned back towards his camp.

~

Nicolas Joven and James Spencer had retreated back up the hill towards Sysco Miller and Chuck Smith when they had heard the other men's screams. The younger men had swapped one glance between them before giving in to their fears and abandoning their posts. Nicolas Joven had made to follow but they weren't waiting for him. He decided to try and hide out down by the lake instead. He nearly made it.

A stone-strewn beach of about thirty feet led to the water, and he paced it nervously, wondering what to do. He caught his breath, taking the time to put on the worn, blue-cloth baseball cap he had in his pocket and clean his glasses. He looked to his right, into the darkness of the trees. He knew his best bet was to hide in there, rather than out in the open like he was. He took a step into the shadows.

A snap of a branch ahead of him had him peering through the densely packed trunks. Their dark mottled bark, and the falling light made it hard to see anything beyond a few feet. He lowered his head and craned his neck to try and see further as he squinted. Then he saw them. Two bright, glowing, green coals of light appeared from the space underneath a half-fallen pine leant against a more stable neighbour. It took Nicolas longer than it should have to realise they were the eyes of the cat. The roar made him shake with fear, and he dropped the ancient shotgun he had been cradling. He was frozen to the spot as the cat consumed the space between them, the thunderous blows of its paws sending shockwaves he felt in the ground beneath his boots. The second roar had the opposite effect of the first, awakening his survival instinct – but it was too late.

Tama sprang, her forelimbs outstretched for a murderous embrace. She crashed into Nicolas heavily, knocking him to the ground and smashing his head back against hard rock. He cried out in pain and whimpered as the spittle dried in his mouth. Tama growled, lowering her head to lick the blood from his forehead. Nicolas fumbled with his hand, his fingers touching a small, loose rock. He grabbed it, swinging his arm and smashing it into the side of Tama's head with as much force as he could manage. It wasn't enough. Angrily, Tama swatted Nicolas aside with a paw and unsheathed claws. His chest and side were ripped open as he tumbled over several times with the force of the blow, ending up on his back again. Tama padded over and placed a paw on his sternum. He heard the cartilage crack as she pressed down. A snort from her nostrils blew the cap from his head. His final, agonised scream was stifled, as Tama's fangs harpooned him through his stomach and lung. She tunnelled through his chest cavity, gulping down flesh quickly and ripping out his liver with a tug of her teeth. Momentarily satiated, she licked her jaws and padded out of the trees and onto the beach.

Sysco Miller, James Spencer, and Chuck Smith had traversed the slope in silence, with quick worried glances over their shoulders every few steps. Tama watched the men. The pain in her leg had returned. It had come immediately after the explosive sound had come from the stick the first man had carried. She had been frightened, and had constantly licked at the wound, but it had continued to burn her skin and flesh. Instinctively, she waded into the shallows to lie there. The cool water, and the effect of the powerful blood clogging elements within her saliva, relaxed her and helped her feel more comfortable. But her pulse still raced from the experience and the killing of the second man, and she fixated on the others now retreating over the hill. They carried similar sticks to the first man she had killed in the forest. She growled as she rose to her feet and turned around, wading deeper into the water. She set her eyes on the beach, and the small cave covered with soft hide, where the human who fed her burned the strange and strong-smelling plants. She swam, ignoring the shots of pain that rippled down her hind leg. She ignored the urge to snarl, instead slowing her momentum to match the pace of her prey.

Heading back up the slope and along the ridge took the three men much longer than it had taken to descend it. They followed the narrow trail along the other side of the ridge, the lake disappearing from view as they descended again, this time towards the far end of the Native American's camp. The trail dropped down past some bushy scrub back onto a muddy beach, where the lake water lapped in small ripples. Chuck didn't stop as he passed the homemade sweat lodge, but something made Sysco turn and look out towards the water. The lake had been flat and unmoving, and a random thought as to what was causing the ripples had popped into his head. At first, he thought it was a beaver. A large, flat object moved through the water towards him, quite quickly. He expected to hear the thwack of the tail against the water at any moment once the animal realised he was there. Their eyesight wasn't all that great, especially if you didn't move. That's when he noticed the eyes. Huge, almond-shaped, green eyes that stared him down with clear and intelligent intent. It was the face of a predator.

The impulse that sparked in Sysco's brain came fractionally too late. The giant cat erupted from the water in an explosive leap that enveloped him. The wind was knocked from his lungs as he was thrown onto his back and hit the ground. Less than a second later, the life was driven from his body as Tama sank her fangs through his neck and skull. A savage shake of her head was enough to break the vertebrae. She turned her head and growled as she noticed the two other men ahead of her.

Chuck Smith and James Spencer heard the commotion behind and froze. They turned around slowly, fear compelling them both. A shiver rippled across James' shoulders in repulsion as he saw the cat drop Sysco's head from her jaws. Broken chips of bone and brain matter spewed from the smashed in skull, which rolled to one side, unsupported as it hit the ground. It looked unnatural and grotesque, with Sysco's eyes rolled back and his jaw unhinged and broken. Chuck felt the vomit rise in his throat. The growl that came from the cat was enough to stop him throwing up. More from involuntary muscle memory and survival instinct, he realised he was halfway through slipping his shotgun from his shoulder, when the cat growled again. It sounded much more savage and filled with warning. Chuck judged the distance between him and the cat to be a matter of yards. Unlike him, it was already poised to strike, half crouched, its muscles rigid for the intended spring. But he was distracted once more, as James sunk to his knees beside him and bowed forward, the pointed tip of the arrow neatly showing through the back of his skull.

Chuck's eyes caught movement behind the cat, and he watched the man they had come here to confront, confidently walk up to the animal.

"I saw an old western once," Chayton stated calmly, his voice steady and confident. "Where a loud-mouthed cowboy won't believe a knife can be thrown faster than a gun can be drawn and shot. Do you know the one?"

Chuck nodded. A nervous tremble was evident in his hands as he did so. He still gripped the shotgun, half raised.

"Want to find out for real?" Chayton asked, seemingly genuinely.

Chuck stood frozen, not knowing what to do. If he hadn't been so shocked by the appearance of the warrior, he could have been calculating if he had time to shoot both the man and then the cat from the hip, or vice versa. Instead, his mind was still trying to process what he was seeing. The man and the cat stood side by side, and both were fixated on him. Chance knew both wanted to attack and kill him. He began to swing the barrel of the shotgun towards the warrior.

Chayton moved like lightning, whisking an antique looking revolver from underneath his buckskin waistcoat, and smashing his hand down on the back of the gun's hammer. It fired instantly. Chuck staggered backwards, tripped over his own feet, and landed on his back. His bowels and bladder emptied. The bullet had ripped through the centre of his forehead, destroying the frontal lobe of his brain. It took a few seconds for his body to shut down, the delayed reaction a result of the trauma to his synapses. With no instructions, his muscles spasmed and relaxed in a storm of movement, and his heart swelled as blood thundered through his body to no avail. A moment later, the pressure caused his heart to rupture, and he moved no more.

Chayton wasn't surprised his little distraction and deception had worked. He paused a few more seconds to make sure the man was dead, then looked at Tama. He instantly saw the blood stain on her left hind leg, and noticed she limped slightly as she fell in behind him. He knew another test of the relationship was about to present itself as he headed back to the airstream trailer, where he kept medical supplies for the animals.

CHAPTER FIFTEEN

Thomas eyed the stable door, his unease palpable to his gathered audience. Catherine sat on the top bar of a paddock fence across from the stables. Her feet were tucked underneath the lower bar, and Cassie was nestled on her lap, fidgeting against the restraining arm of her mother. Jesse stood the other side of the fence, but all eyes were fixed on Thomas as he approached the stallion's door. The idea was that Khan would run from the stable straight across into the field and paddocks. They had positioned the trucks either side of the trail to corral Khan, but the heady combination of his mustang and Arabian bloodlines made Khan anything but predictable.

"This ougtha be good," Jesse smiled, tipping his hat towards Catherine.

"He's faced worse," Catherine replied.

Cassie twisted her head around to give her mother a 'not so sure' look.

Thomas had a 45-foot looped Lariat lasso hanging from the belt of his jeans. Jesse had smirked at his over-confidence. Khan hadn't been ridden in years, and Thomas hadn't held a rope in just as long. As Thomas approached the open top of the stable door, he began to suspect that Jesse might have been right to doubt. There were no lights inside Khan's part of the barn. Only the sunlight from outside of the stable, behind Thomas, gave illumination. It was just enough to pick up the glossy shine of Khan's black coat, and two pinpricks of light that reflected like glass. The horse was watching him intently. A deep, grumble-like grunt came from the darkness, and Thomas saw Khan's expunged breath linger in the air for a moment.

Thomas reached for the bolt that secured the bottom half of the stable door. He moved slowly and deliberately, and never took his eyes off Khan. The horse in turn stood as still as a statue, returning his gaze in unblinking concentration, his head low. Thomas pulled the wooden door towards him, stepping backwards as softly as he could. The door swung out to Thomas's right, pushing him back towards the far wall of the stable building. It put him in a slightly vulnerable position, partially blocking off his escape route to the front if he needed it. Khan took a few steps forward, his ears flicking back and forth. He stepped back again, then dashed forward, stamping his front hooves down hard. He lowered his head, adjusting his stance so he again faced Thomas. There were now only a few feet between them.

Khan trotted forward. He raised his head and seemed more relaxed – curious and alert, but not nervous. As he stepped into the light, Thomas was reminded just what a special animal Khan was. He stood at just over 15 hands, which put him at five feet and two inches at the withers – the highest point of his shoulders. He was visibly taller than Thomas, and this seemed to give him confidence. Khan had the beautifully pointed head of an Arabian and his coat shone, almost taking on a purplish hue in the sunlight. His body too echoed the sleek build of a racing horse. But his rear end and his legs held the more robust, thicker and muscular look of the wild mustang. Thomas agreed this probably made Khan one of the best riding horses he could wish for. If he could get on him. As if reading his mind, Khan trotted forward, then delivered a deft and powerful kick with both his rear legs into the open stable door. Thomas was thrown back against the wall and crashed to the floor. Khan snorted, as if amused, and trotted calmly out of the stable, crossing the trail and entering the paddock without a look back.

"You haven't kept Khan locked up in that stable all this time, have you?" Catherine asked Jesse, concerned.

"No," Jesse laughed. "He normally follows Princess out into the fields just fine. Guess I could have mentioned that to our Tom there," he laughed in mock realisation.

Catherine gave Jesse a glare, but she was distracted by Thomas as he walked across the trail, following Khan. He took the lasso from his waist and began to unwind part of it.

"Is he going to try and rope him?" Catherine asked, unhooking her legs and twisting around to face the paddock, lifting her legs and Cassie at the same time.

"Not if he knows what he's doing," Jesse smiled, serious this time. "He'll use it as an extension of his arms, to try and control Khan's movement. Usually, we'd try and do it in an enclosed pen – but Tom figured Khan wouldn't take kindly to that. So, he's hoping Khan has enough interest in him to stick around close. If not, Khan has a good couple of miles of pasture to let loose in."

Thomas studied Khan. The horse's stance was relaxed yet alert. He seemed much calmer out in the open. Khan stood about forty feet away, side on to him. Thomas walked in a wide arc, slowly positioning himself so he could push Khan towards the other side of the paddock, where the same fence marked a boundary. Khan obliged, keeping the same distance between them. Thomas let out more of the rope, holding it in both hands. Then he took a step towards the horse.

Khan bolted to the right, but Thomas's hands matched the horses speed, sending a line of rope out ahead of the horse, stopping Khan in his tracks. He doubled back, heading to

Thomas's left, back along the fence. Once again, Thomas judged it right, sending the rope flying and distracting the horse.

"What's he doing?" Catherine asked.

"Wearing him down," Jesse shrugged. "Horses don't actually take to people straight off. They look at us and see a predator. We have forward facing eyes," Jesse explained, gesturing to his own with his fingers. "They don't want to communicate with us or co-operate too much. At least until we can show 'em we're worth trusting."

Catherine nodded in realisation, turning back towards Thomas. She noticed that Khan had edged slightly closer to Thomas with each turn.

"Khan's not stupid," Jesse added. "He can see Thomas isn't hurting him. But he doesn't know why he's being controlled. If he figures it out, it could go either way."

Khan's dashes back and forth were beginning to slow now. He snorted every now and then, but he wasn't stomping his hooves or holding his head too high. He seemed to be accepting Thomas's presence now. Catherine watched as Thomas edged closer, again slowly and deliberately. She caught his smile as Khan began to visibly lick and chew, as if swilling an imaginary ball of hay between his teeth. Thomas looped in the rope and began to match the horse's movements with a slow walk that mirrored Khan's pace. Now, as Thomas took a step back, Khan followed. The more space Thomas gave Khan, the more Khan seemed at ease.

"See how Khan is licking like that," Jesse pointed. "That means the adrenaline that was pumpin' through that big old body of his is dropping. You watch now, any moment, he'll drop his head."

As if on cue, Khan dropped his head. He was now walking around Thomas in a slow, tightening circle. Thomas faced the horse with his arms and hands open. Both he and Khan's body language were now much more relaxed. Catherine was then surprised to see Thomas drop to a crouch. He brought his hands in, close to his body. He dipped his head, the rim of his own hat now covering his face. Thomas then turned away from the horse completely, presenting his back to him. Jesse seemed to nod in approval and moved along the fence. A beautiful western style saddle, with heavily embroidered leather, sat on a white fleece blanket. Jesse pulled the fleece from underneath it, then turned again to watch Thomas. Both Catherine and Jesse watched as Thomas adjusted his feet to kneel on one knee. He deliberately dropped the shoulder nearest to Khan. It seemed to act as a hook to the horse, whose head followed the movement. Khan stepped in closer to Thomas, no longer side on to him. Khan made a beeline for Thomas, dropping his head with each step. Finally, with a gentle sounding snort, Khan lowered his head over Thomas' shoulder, and touched the side of his face with his mouth. Thomas raised his hand and softly rubbed the horse's jaw and throat.

"I'll be damned," Jesse laughed.

Thomas stood up slowly and walked towards them. Khan obediently followed behind. Jesse ducked through the fence of the paddock, putting a barrier between them. He tapped the top rung of the fence near Catherine to indicate her and Cassie should do the same. They obediently obliged, dropping down beside him. Thomas walked past them, keeping a healthy distance. Khan didn't seem bothered by their presence at all, acting as if Thomas had his complete attention. They watched as Thomas took the fleece blanket and walked back towards Khan. He kept his head down and allowed the horse to come in close and smell both him and it. He gently placed it on the horse's back, then rewarded the horse with a heavy pat and rub down for allowing him to do so.

Catherine, Cassie, and Jesse watched over the course of the next half hour as Thomas slowly introduced Khan to the rest of the riding gear. Thomas and Jesse lifted the saddle together from the fence – by far the biggest test for Khan. They were surprised how placid Khan was, until they noticed he had been completely distracted by Cassie. She stood the other side of the fence, looking up at the big horse in silence from a few feet away.

"Funny," Jesse remarked. "You'd think direct eye contact like that would spook him."

"Maybe he likes redheads?" Thomas smiled.

After that, the rest of the gear was easy. Thomas fixed the stirrups, the halter and the reins without Khan giving him a second glance. Now, when Thomas walked, Khan casually followed. Thomas rewarded every new acceptance with a softly spoken word of encouragement, or a hard rub between the horse's ears at the top of his muzzle. Khan would respond with rasping snorts from his nostrils. Catherine lifted Cassie to the top rung of the fence and let her watch.

"He's okay your Dad, isn't he?" she whispered into Cassie's ear, holding her close from behind.

Cassie nodded. Thomas caught their gaze and smiled as he led Khan over. He stepped up onto the fence and only hesitated for a moment before swinging his leg up and over the back of the obliging stallion, getting comfortable in the saddle. Khan instantly planted his feet and shook his head, alert and defiant. Thomas didn't touch the reins, but let Khan settle and get used to the weight on his back. As the horse lowered his head, Thomas patted his neck and leaned over. Catherine overheard him thanking the horse, and she threw him an amused smile, as he sounded incredibly genuine. She could see by his face he was, and felt a little awkward for teasing him, even if it had been just with a look. But she could see he didn't mind. He turned to look down at Cassie.

"Want to ride with your Dad back to the lodge?" Thomas asked.

Cassie nodded her head with violent exuberance.

"What about a helmet?" Catherine asked, concerned.

"Not the way it's really done out here," Thomas exclaimed.

"If she fell, she could really hurt herself," Catherine replied, looking over the giant horse.

"Guess she better not fall then," Thomas quipped, smiling. "She'll be fine. We'll go easy."

Thomas pulled Cassie up, shuffling his butt backwards and making space for her in the saddle just in front of him. She squeezed her shoulders together in delight, and beamed a huge smile at Catherine, who shook her head and rolled her eyes, but still took out her cell phone to take a picture. Thomas gently tapped his heels against Khan's sides, and the big horse moved away from the fence. Thomas gently guided Khan out of the paddock and onto the track that led past the big house and back to Lodge View.

Thomas leant forward, smoothing Khan's mane down between his ears.

"Let's show her what we can do," he whispered to the horse, leaning forward.

The horse instinctively caught the meaning from Thomas' body language, who hadn't needed to kick his heels in to goad Khan. The horse let out a triumphant whinny and reared up on his hind legs. Catherine let out a slight cry of panic, but Thomas just smiled as Khan brought his front legs down in a thunder of hooves, catapulting into an instant burst of acceleration as horse and both riders charged up the trail.

"I'm going to kill you," Catherine yelled after Thomas, but she couldn't quite hide the smile as Jesse walked back out of the barn.

"I'll walk you back," Jesse offered.

Catherine nodded.

By the time they rounded the corner and Lodge View came into sight, Thomas was adding saddlebags to Khan's back, and she could already see a bedroll and a tightly bound, thickly insulated sleeping bag tucked in behind. Cassie stood in front of Khan, who had lowered his head to let the little girl occasionally pet him. The muscular, wild-looking horse seemed fascinated with the red-headed little human, who in turn seemed to show no fear around him. Catherine could also see Thomas had added a few layers to his clothes. A waxed cotton jacket was padded out by a fleece, and his jeans had been replaced by some good-quality hiking trousers. The boots he wore looked heavy-duty, with thick soles marked by a rugged tread. She noticed that instead of wearing Lee Logan's black cattleman hat, he'd opted for a weathered-looking black baseball cap. It was clear he was planning to spend the night under the stars.

"Leaving me on my own?" Catherine challenged, good-naturedly.

"Not quite, Nina Lee has asked if you and Cassie would like to join her for dinner tonight," Thomas replied.

"Think she'd appreciate the female company," Jesse motioned with a shrug. "She lives with her mother, and that old witch would drive anybody nuts."

Catherine watched Cassie's eyes bulge at the mention of a witch. Catherine walked over and took her hand, squeezing it reassuringly. She bent down.

"Not a real witch, just a nice woman who probably doesn't let men get away with things, so they call her names," Catherine whispered. Cassie nodded, as if she understood.

"Nope, she's a self-proclaimed wise woman," Jesse smiled. "You ask her."

Jesse stood in silence, looking at Thomas's baseball cap with a smirk. "Take that damn thing off, Dad wouldn't take kindly to me letting you ride out of here with that on."

Jesse stepped into the hallway of Lodge View and found his father's hat hanging in pride of place on the first peg of a coat rack opposite the stairs. He lifted it off the peg with revered respect and took a moment in the sanctuary of the enclosed space, out of sight of the others. When he stepped back out into the open, he smiled as he handed it over to Thomas, who removed the baseball cap and fitted the cattleman hat in its place. He gave a thankful smile and tipped the rim of the hat towards Jesse in an appreciative gesture.

"Now you look like a rancher," Jesse proclaimed. "Know where you're going?"

"I'm just going to do some scouting for now. Get a lay of the land. But, if I can get over that ridge," he paused, nodding towards a distant raised treeline and a mountainous outcrop, "then I'll be close to their backyard. I have a feeling they're headed in our direction too," Thomas explained. "I might get lucky."

"When has that ever happened?" Catherine scorned. It was Thomas's turn to roll his eyes, although he did so lovingly.

"Keep an eye out for that bear too," Jesse warned.

Thomas patted his rifle and the generously stuffed pouch of ammunition on the left saddlebag, which had a sewn-in holster for two long guns. It fitted snug against Khan's haunch, and the shotgun Thomas had already packed. He checked it wouldn't rub.

"Hoping for the best, preparing for the worst," Thomas exclaimed. "And then there's always this," he added, patting his Colt Anaconda revolver in its holster.

Jesse nodded in approval.

"And this," Catherine exclaimed, adding a new-looking Garmin inReach Explorer + satellite communicator to his bag. "You have a habit of not sticking to the plan."

Thomas walked over to Catherine and held her for a moment.

"I'm okay," Catherine whispered, a little taken back.

"I know, this is for me," Thomas grinned. He kissed her firmly on the lips and lingered there for a moment. Cassie was at their feet in a moment, and he whisked her up into his arms, placing another kiss firmly on the toddler's cheek.

"You look after mum for me, okay?" he asked. "I'll be back tomorrow."

"Heard that before," Catherine said smiling. "Don't make promises you can't keep."

Thomas swung himself up onto the saddle and waved reassuringly as he walked Khan on. He then turned his gaze to

the imposing distant ridgeline and the dark grey sky beyond
it.

~

Jericho O'Connell had seen worse bars in his time, but not
many. The Bighorn Bar and Grill had either really gone all in
to make its clientele feel at home, or they'd given up on
outward appearances some time ago. Other than the saloon-
style windows at the front of the building, either side of the
door, no natural light penetrated into the long, thin room that
stretched a good-ways back. Jericho strolled to the bar, his
casual manner veiling his shrewd analysis of each and every
patron as he did so.

"Bourbon," he nodded to the young girl behind the bar.

She looked a little out of place, with short dark hair, and a
purple streak that highlighted her cow's lick fringe at the
front. She had bright blue eyes and was extremely petite.
Jericho noticed the tattooed Chinese symbols that peeked out
from beneath the sleeve of her top on her right arm.

"Anything p'ticular?" she asked, her easy, Western accent
softening his hesitance.

He looked beyond her left shoulder at the bottles on the
shelves. Most were brands he'd usually avoid, but he realised
his particular tastes were unlikely to be catered for. Then he
spotted a squarish shaped bottle, with embossed letters on the
glass.

"The Bulleit barrel strength will do," he said, a little
surprised.

"Coming right up," she replied, turning away.

Jericho used the short delay to look around the bar once
more. This time, his eye caught the inquisitive gaze of a man
sitting in a booth towards the back, staring at him. Jericho

nodded and turned back to the bar. As the young woman went to put the bottle back, Jericho placed his hand gently on hers, and took it from her.

"Run a tab to that table over there will ya, darling," he nodded, taking the bottle and his filled shot glass.

He walked over to the table and slid into the empty seat opposite the man. Jericho realised he should have really spotted him before, as it was clear that he didn't fit in. Everything about him said middle-class white guy. His brown hair was a ruffled mess – self-induced by nervously running his fingers through it, constantly. The man's dark brown eyes darted back and forth across the room, never settling on a particular corner. He wore a loose-fitting grey suit and a white shirt with no tie. He looked pasty, perhaps even scared as he studied Jericho, licking his bottom lip with anxiety. He leaned out of the booth slightly and peered back to the bar's entrance.

"You weren't followed?" the man asked.

"No idea," Jericho shrugged, too tired to even attempt lying. It had been nearly 40 hours since he'd left the ranch, Thomas and the others, and driven to Colorado and back. It was affecting his tolerance for pleasantries.

"You can't fuck around with these people, you obviously don't know what you're dealing with," the man stressed.

"I'm beginning to get an idea," Jericho menaced, remembering the look on Kelly's face when the room had been stormed by Richter's mercenaries. "Why don't you fill in the blanks for me."

The man hesitated. Jericho sighed, looked over his shoulder, then took out a stuffed brown envelope from the pocket of his drover's coat. He kept his hand on it as he slid it across the table. The man nodded, and reached for the envelope, but Jericho wasn't quite ready to relinquish his grip.

"I insist on value for money, mister...?"

"Spencer Shaw," the man replied. "I used to work for a law firm representing Richter. Needless to say, I don't work there anymore, not since I got wind of what he had his fingers into."

Jericho nodded. "Just making sure I was talking to the right person". He let go of the envelope, which Spencer pocketed inside his blazer, quickly.

"So, what has he got his fingers into?" Jericho asked, his impatience showing.

"Illegal genetic experiments for a start," Shaw replied. "He can't run them in this country safely, but he owns several Russian and Japanese laboratories – nothing direct mind you, all through front companies."

"What kind of experiments?" Jericho challenged.

"I don't know," Shaw shrugged. "But I know they must be animal based. We oversaw purchases of all kinds of animals – weird ones too, I'm not talking lab rats or monkeys here."

Jericho stared at Shaw, hoping his grimace would encourage him to get to the point.

"An Asiatic elephant – female. Amur tiger – female. Kodiak bear – female. I believe your own services were acquired for some of his more regular requests?"

Jericho nodded. "That was before I knew who I was in bed with."

"What's he got on you?" Shaw asked, seemingly genuinely.

"He's threatened to hurt someone I'm close to," Jericho replied.

"He doesn't threaten Mr. O'Connell, he makes promises. And he always keeps them."

Jericho studied Shaw for a moment, his eyes narrowing as he scanned the face for a sign of bravado or sarcasm. There was none, just a cold look of fear that sheened his brow with sweat.

"People have been known to disappear," Shaw continued. "His private security is the best, and extremely loyal. Again, I've seen the contracts. Only the best that money can buy for Erasmus Richter. All ex-military, usually special forces. I imagine they'd pretty much do anything for him, and those who don't...well, I doubt they keep him awake at night for long."

Shaw reached down to the seat beside him, and picked up a brown manila folder, secured with twine. He passed it over to Jericho. He didn't seem too troubled with keeping anything secret now, obviously relaxed after the money exchange. Jericho looked back over his shoulder again, just to reassure himself before taking the folder.

"That's everything I have on him. Holdings, suspected front companies, known assets – but there's still a lot missing. And I still don't really know what he's up to," Shaw explained.

"That's for me to work out," Jericho growled. He downed what remained of the whiskey, grabbed the folder, and walked out, passing two folded hundred-dollar bills towards to the barmaid as he left.

~

Catherine helped Cassie pack a few last things into a bag. Jesse had a couple of big projects to attend to and had suggested perhaps she could stay with Nina. Lodge View was a little isolated and he had indicated Nina could do with some female company – and reckoned Catherine probably could too.

Catherine was a skilled and light packer compared to Thomas, whom she often teased would have been better suited to times gone by, when travelling with enormous trunks and half of everything you owned, had been more acceptable. She knew this wasn't entirely accurate, as his intention to sleep rough with just a few saddlebags of supplies showed. But she still enjoyed teasing him. She rolled some fresh T-shirts and underwear together and put them in a small rucksack, along with two sweaters. For Cassie, three complete changes of clothes, a cold-weather coat and boots, and more, had been crammed into a duffle bag, before a few favourite books and toys finished off the packing.

Catherine threw their things into the back of the Chevy – or "Beast" as Thomas called it. Cassey got as much of a thrill sitting up front on the bench seat as she had the first time. She snuggled into her mother's side as they made their way up the track. Jesse stood on the porch of the big house as they passed and waved. Catherine watched in the rear-view mirror as he moved off, walking towards the barn behind the house where his Waheela hounds were kept. She didn't know why it made her feel uneasy, and she reminded herself that it was also Jesse's main workshop.

Not much later, she turned out of the entrance to the ranch and headed north on the 25. Nina lived in a small settlement called Sleepy Hollow, on the Black Peak Indian Reservation, and it had been a good excuse to watch one of her favourite classic Disney cartoons with Cassie. Worried it might scare her, but not enough to stop herself, she had been relieved when Cassie had burst into uncontrollable laughter at all the right moments. Nina was a Game Warden, and her territory covered the nearby Thunder Basin National Grasslands. The area was home to a rich tapestry of wildlife, including the endangered black-footed ferret, impressive prairie grouse with their stunning chest ruffs of white feathers, and Wyoming pronghorn. Nina had offered to take Catherine and Cassie on a guided tour the following day, and she was really looking forward to encountering wildlife she had never seen before, just as she knew Cassie was.

Nina's cottage ended up being about a mile outside of Sleepy Hollow and was secluded to say the least. Catherine pulled the truck into the drive and pushed the driver's door open with her foot. A movement out of the corner of her eye caught her unawares, and she lifted her head, freezing as her blood ran cold at what she saw. The animal was enormous. It had padded out from the far side of the house quite casually, but now its gaze was firmly fixed on her. The amber eyes of the predator surveyed her with the cool, confident, and indifferent stare that was undoubtedly reserved for any prey that was unlucky enough to walk into its path. The wolf was almost completely black, but it's chest, muzzle, brow, and tips of its ears were flecked with grey. She found it eerie that it made no sound, nor moved from where it stood, but simply lowered its head, adjusting its gaze with even more intensity. That's when Catherine realised the wolf wasn't looking directly at her, but over her right shoulder. An involuntary shiver ran down her spine as she suddenly realised Cassie was leaning in close behind her, making direct eye-contact with the wolf.

"Ar-woooo," Cassie giggled, clearly excited to see the animal.

It responded by standing up straight again. It seemed confused that the prey seemed to speak its language. Just then,

Nina walked out of the house. Catherine went to call out, but the wolf was already on her in a flash. It rose up, placing its huge paws on either side of her shoulders, burying its head beneath her chin. Catherine felt foolish, gawping with the door still half open. She remembered Nina's challenge to Jesse about being able to control a full-grown wolf and realised it must be a pet. She had heard of both wolves and wolfdogs being relatively popular pets in the states. She didn't approve and was a little surprised Nina did. She hoped it wouldn't come up in conversation, and she was still a little hesitant to get out of the car, even with the door half open and being transfixed by the scene as she was.

Nina seemed to sense Catherine's doubts.

"It's okay if you want to come and say hello," Nina indicated. "He's not tame, but he is a gentleman."

That seemed all the permission Cassie needed, who pushed past her mother's back and was about to hit the ground running when Catherine caught her. Cassie looked around, her bottom lip trembling, and her face screwed into a pensive frown. Catherine sighed, not quite ready to break her daughter's heart, and yet also not quite ready to serve her up as wolf bait.

"With me, okay?" she pressed, gently but firmly.

Cassie nodded enthusiastically, her face bursting into a huge smile again. She held Catherine's hand as they walked over. Catherine could feel the tremble of excitement in Cassie's grip. Her own fingers drew a little tighter around Cassie's as they got closer.

"Catherine, Cassie, meet Achak", Nina invited, as she knelt next to the wolf, who had returned to all fours and was casually surveying their guests.

"He's very quiet," Catherine commented, intrigued rather than wary.

"Wolves don't make noise unless they have to," Nina smiled. "He'll make all the noises you kind of expect, like barking, growling, howling, and whimpering – but not unwarranted. A bark from a dog for instance can mean anything from excitement or a greeting, to a challenge and a warning. With Achak, it has one purpose – a singular bark is a warning of something he doesn't like or understand. At the same time, when a dog growls, we know it means that is one unhappy dog. With Achak, it's the reverse – he growls when he's happy – it's a snarl that means back off. And did I hear a little howl from back there?" Nina asked.

Cassie nodded, beaming.

"Well, that's long-range communication for Achak. If you were a wolf, he'd know where you lived, how old you were, whether you were a boy or a girl, maybe even what the hunting was like where you are," Nina explained.

Cassie pulled on Catherine's hand, perhaps getting bored of the natural history lesson that seemed to be preventing her actually meeting Achak. She did as she had done with Jesse's dogs and let Achak know she was there. She avoided reaching for his head, instead, running her fingers through the coarse hair on his side. Just as Nina had indicated, a deep rumble of appreciation emitted from Achak's chest, making Cassie smile. The wolf turned, and pushed its head into Cassie's chest, which Cassie wasn't ready for, and took a stumble backwards, landing quite hard on her bottom. Catherine went to help her up, but paused when she noticed the huge canine step over Cassie in a protective stance. Even Nina seemed surprised when Cassie naturally reached up and threw an arm over Achak's neck to get herself back on her feet.

"You make friends fast, don't you Cassie," Nina laughed.

"I swear she likes animals more than people," Catherine muttered in shock.

"Good judge of character I'd say then, we're going to get on fine," Nina winked, looking down at Cassie, who beamed back at her.

"She's gifted," came a crackled voice from above them.

Catherine and Nina looked up to see an older, yet still beautiful Native American woman looking down at them. She had all of Nina's features, from the sharp nose and dark yet somehow bright eyes, to the ebony-coloured hair that shone with a touch of mahogany, although in the older woman's case, it was also streaked with natural grey and seemed incredibly long compared to Nina's short, neat crop.

"Also, meet my mother, Kayah," Nina sighed, rolling her eyes. "You're not my only house-guest, which is why we'll be spending most of your stay outdoors."

Kayah laughed, rolling her eyes in return, and disappeared back inside. Moments later, the slight, athletic looking woman was standing in the doorway, ready to greet them. She wore black jeans and a black turtle-neck sweater. Catherine thought she was stunning, although was a little surprised to see she was actually shorter and thinner than Nina was. Kayah waved sweetly to Cassie.

"Careful Cassie, she's a witch," Nina said, bending down to whisper in her ear.

Cassie's head snapped around, a very serious look on her face.

Kayah rolled her eyes again and stepped down off the porch. She held out her hand to Catherine, who went to shake it, but found her own hand being examined on both sides instead. She did the same thing with Cassie, a look of intense concentration on her face and in complete silence. Then she too bent down to whisper in Cassie's ear.

"I am a witch, but a nice one," she winked.

Cassie smiled, acceptingly.

CHAPTER SIXTEEN

Spencer Shaw walked out of the Bighorn Bar & Grill about twenty minutes after Jericho O'Connell. He stepped a little unsteadily as he crossed the parking lot to his truck, a relatively new Ford F150 that suited his country location and coloured steel grey to match his corporate career. He opened up the driver's door wide, the alcohol in his bloodstream delaying his cognitive response just enough that he didn't register the other doors opening a second afterwards. Before he knew it, three more people were in the truck with him. A large, well-built man wearing a tight suit sat beside him in the front passenger seat. Shaw didn't recognise him, but he knew the woman sitting directly behind him. Annika Deveraux, Erasmus Richter's second in command. He knew full well she was no personal assistant, although she covered the role pretty well. To her right was another well-built guy wearing an equally tight suit. Part of Richter's security force, which Shaw knew Deveraux commanded. He looked out of the window, back towards the bar. The goon next to him grunted, making Shaw turn around to look. He noticed the gun and silencer the man held at waist level, pointed at him.

"You here to give me my settlement arrears?" Shaw laughed, the strain showing as it cracked.

"We're here to settle things, if that's what you mean," Deveraux sighed. "What did you give O'Connell?"

"A shit load of bourbon, and the run-around," Shaw shrugged. "I didn't know the answers to any of the questions he asked. But if I had, I'd have given them to him."

Lying – or at least concealing the truth came naturally to Shaw. He had to present the best case possible for his clients. It was true too, that he hadn't known some of the answers to O'Connell's questions. He didn't have to though, the file he'd handed over had been comprehensive.

"Let's go for a little drive shall we, and sort this out once and for all," Deveraux suggested, fixing Shaw with an icy gaze.

~

Kelly Keelson blinked twice as she slowly came around. Having her eyes open didn't seem to help much, as the darkness was almost impenetrable. She could smell the damp earth directly beneath her, and she could feel soft, crumbly soil beneath her cheek. She realised she was lying face down, and her limbs came to life as she scrabbled to right herself. She unfolded her left arm, which she had evidently been lying on. Her wrist was sore after having been twisted back against her stomach. Whoever had dumped her here hadn't gone to the trouble to make sure she was comfortable.

Kelly was no stranger to dangerous situations. In the name of journalism and a story, she had flown into warzones, interviewed serial killers, and seen death up close and in person. Nearly five years before, she had lost a hand-picked member of her camera crew to a pride of lions she had convinced Thomas Walker to face. Watching that man die had nearly destroyed her. Had it not been for the support of Jericho O'Connell, the Irishman she had met in Kenya, she knew her life would be very different. The same could probably be said had that support not blossomed into a whirlwind romance and the consequent on-off relationship she now had with him. That said, she knew there was nobody else she'd rather see right now.

She sat up, bumping her head on a wall directly behind her as she did. The darkness still limited her vision, but she was beginning to get a sense of her surroundings. There was a thick, oozy scent in the air, and it took her a moment to place it. But, when her brain put the other smells from around her together, like hay and something akin to spoiled honey, she realised she was in a stable. As she crumbled what she had thought was dirt between her fingers, she realised it was a fine mix of sawdust and hay. Using the wall to help her, she dragged herself to her feet and paced the perimeter until she found the door. There were no bolts or fastenings on her side. She looked around, then up, and could dimly make out a partition of iron bars on the top part of each adjoining wall. Without hesitating, she took a few running steps and leapt upwards, grabbing onto the bars and lifting herself up. She peered across the opening.

There were another two stables joining the one she was locked into, and they all opened out onto a much larger open space to the front. She could see light creeping in underneath a large set of barn doors on the furthest outer wall. With a sudden creak and rattle of chains, it began to open.

~

Annika Deveraux glanced at the message on her phone again, and then at her watch. Her latest instructions now meant she was on a tight schedule, but they still had to be carried out professionally – which meant not rushing. That was how mistakes were made. And errors led to things being followed up on and eventually traced back.

Luckily, O'Connell was using a vehicle they had provided, and she could see from the tracker he wasn't too far away – ahead of them in fact by just a few miles. The rendezvous point was also just a few miles away. She decided it would be a quicker clean up if they killed two birds with one stone.

"There's a track about a mile ahead, heading east. Take it," she instructed Shaw.

Even then, Shaw nearly missed the turning. It was partially obscured by long grass and a stand of knotted pine trees, their shadow veiling the opening that led onto the track. There were no signposts or mailboxes to suggest the road led anywhere inhabited.

"Where are we going exactly?" Shaw asked.

Deveraux could tell he was sobering up now and could sense his fear and apprehension.

"There's a farmhouse up ahead," she replied. "It's a little more private for conducting business."

"So, you gonna pay up finally?" Shaw replied smugly.

"It depends on what you did in fact tell O'Connell," Deveraux replied, not looking up from her phone. "He'll be joining us too. If we verify you've been as tight-lipped as you say, there won't be any problem."

Shaw seemed convinced enough to shut up, and he remained silent until he steered the truck over a rise, and the so-called "farm" came into view. Although it clearly had been a farm once upon a time, it now looked more like an industrial logistics centre. The front of the compound was completely obscured by a high stone wall, and a set of imposing solid gates sat to the front. The style of the perimeter had originally been decorative and "residential", but it had been seriously upgraded. The wall was now as thick as any you might find at a supermax prison, and topped with ornamental-looking, but practical spiking. As Shaw pulled up to the gates, he found himself looking into a well-hidden camera built into the wall.

He had no doubt everyone in the vehicle was being looked over. The gates began to open, and another goon, armed with an AR-15, peered at them from his post just inside.

"What are you growing in there, Marines?" Shaw asked, smiling smugly. "If this is a farm, I'm the Mayor of New York."

"Drive on in, your honour," Deveraux motioned with her hand, not looking up. She pressed the dial button on her phone. She waited until it was answered.

"Mr. O'Connell. I've just sent you a map reference to a farm not far from your current location. As you've already met my other guest, a Mr. Spencer Shaw, I'd like to have a little chat with you both. This is not a request."

She put the phone down.

~

Jericho pulled the truck over. His knuckles whitened as he gripped the steering wheel. The rage that filled him threatened to consume him as his mind raced. He was cornered, and he knew it. He threw the truck into gear and turned around on the quiet highway.

~

Deveraux led Shaw and her two agents from the car towards a large barn that had been converted into stables. The white paint on the outside boards had taken a beating from the Colorado sun, rain, and sleet, depending on the season, and showed signs of its tired, neglected life. In the silence, she wondered how long it had been since it had housed horses. Probably not long, she had noticed the faint linger of animal scent earlier.

Her head tilted instinctively, as her sharp hearing picked up the sound of an engine working hard along the track that led to the farm. She turned expectantly towards the gate and nodded to the guards. A moment later, they opened, and the black SUV they'd given O'Connell grunted its way into the compound. The murderous look she was met with through the windshield amused her, but she steadied herself.

Jericho got out of the truck and began walking towards them. Deveraux held up her hand and he stopped, confused for a moment. A guard approached from the side, and shoved Jericho in the shoulder to move him around to face him, presumably to frisk him. O'Connell hooked the guard's ankle with his foot, then unbalanced him with a barge of the shoulder he was prodding, sending the smaller man to the ground. It happened so quick, even Deveraux was impressed. She smiled, noting not to underestimate the Irishman. He stood six foot five inches, she guessed, and carried 210 lbs. at least. And he clearly knew how to handle himself.

"Who's next?" Jericho growled.

"If you'll be so kind to follow us Mr. O'Connell," Deveraux nodded towards the barn.

They entered the building through a side door that opened into a small workshop, separated from the rest of the stables by wooden panels and dirty windows held in frames with peeling paint. Deveraux leaned up against a counter and faced Jericho and Shaw. Her two colleagues positioned themselves either side. It was interesting to Deveraux to observe their two charges. O'Connell stood defensively, poised to attack, standing as close to the centre of the room as possible – equal distance between him and the three he considered a threat. Having identified Deveraux as the leader, his focus was locked on her whilst still aware of everything going on in the room. Shaw on the other hand, was backed up almost against the wall, as if trying to escape, and his attention was taken by the weapons in the hands of the two agents flanking her.

Fight or flight in action, she thought, her mouth turning up at the corners in a smile.

"Well, this is your second meeting of the day, gentlemen," Deveraux quipped. "What shall we talk about?"

"Blackmail, kidnapping, extortion…do you want to narrow it down, darlin'?" Jericho sneered.

"Let's," Deveraux nodded. She brushed aside her jacket and casually removed the small pistol from its side holster. The Sig Sauer P238 was small enough not to be noticed at first glance, but punched above its weight with 380 auto rounds. Certainly, they were lethal enough at the range of a few metres. O'Connell didn't blink, but Shaw was now visibly sweating. She turned around to the counter she had leant up against and reached for a small black canvas bag. She grabbed it by its handles and threw it at Shaw's feet. Already open, some of its contents spilled out onto the ground. Shaw fell to his knees, scrabbling to get the bundles of hundred-dollar bills back inside.

"Obviously, Mr. Shaw, we need to be convinced that your settlement is still protected by non-disclosure."

"I didn't say anything," Shaw stammered, clutching the bag tightly to his chest. He looked up at O'Connell with pleading eyes.

"Why d'ya think I'm in such a good mood?" Jericho shrugged.

Deveraux thought she might actually be beginning to like O'Connell. She nodded to the mercenary nearest Shaw, who helped him back onto his feet. They headed towards the door together, Shaw still clutching the canvas bag. He gave a fevered glance and a half smile of thanks to Jericho as they passed.

"Do I get a payoff too? I'd be happily rid of this circus," Jericho growled.

"Unfortunately, no, Mr. O'Connell. We still need your services, and we still need to be convinced you're worth the trouble frankly. Follow me," Deveraux ordered.

A flare of fury swelled in Jericho, but he caught it and let it die down again before following her through to the stables. Deveraux walked over to the panelled wall at the far end of the building. She stopped by a stable door, it's top and bottom half both bolted fast from the outside. As she turned her back to snap the lock on the top half, Jericho thought about rushing her. But the armed goon behind him was keeping his distance. They weren't making mistakes, which meant he was unlikely to be able to take them both. He watched intently instead as Deveraux swung the top half of the door open.

"Who are you, and why are you keeping me here?" a voice he recognised demanded.

"Kelly?" he snapped, storming over to the opening.

Deveraux made way for him, an amused look on her face. Jericho didn't notice that she had unholstered the Sig again.

"Jericho?!" Kelly replied, stepping forward.

The light was dim, only coming from the main space behind them, but he recognised her.

"What's going on?" Kelly demanded.

"Well, you won't be surprised to learn that this is all my fault," Jericho half smiled.

"No, it's not," Kelly replied defiantly. "Whoever these people are, they're the ones responsible for what they've done."

"That's my girl," Jericho winked. "But unfortunately, they're also my employers."

"Let's keep it that way, shall we?" Deveraux smirked. "On both accounts."

The goon had reappeared, and stepped in front of Jericho, using the butt of his SP5K sub-machine gun to put some distance between him and the stable. Jericho watched, confused at first as Deveraux levelled her gun and pointed it into the stable, targeting Kelly. She lowered her aim a little and swung the gun slightly to the right. Kelly looked at Jericho with the same look of confusion. He couldn't help the slightly sick feeling he got in his stomach. Deveraux pulled the trigger. Kelly crumpled to the floor, clutching her side, just above the pelvis.

Jericho erupted into action, knocking the guard from his feet as he closed in on Deveraux. He pinned her against the wall, grabbing her by the wrist and slamming the gun-wielding hand into the wall. Deveraux smiled at him and didn't drop the gun. Her knee met his groin and her free hand spun him around, neatly connecting him to the side-cross of the other agent. Jericho hit the floor.

"No heroics Mr. O'Connell," Deveraux explained, holstering the gun. "It's a superficial wound, and it will be treated. We just might take our time – if you don't hurry yourself. Wouldn't want infection to set in. Now get up."

Jericho was already halfway to his feet. He dusted himself off and looked in at Keelson. "Are you okay?"

"Of course I'm bloody not," Kelly replied. "It doesn't feel superficial to me. It feels like something smashed in there."

"We'll check it out." Deveraux responded, with a flippant and dismissive smile. "Time to run along, Mr. O'Connell. We all have work to do."

Jericho felt the butt of the gun in his back, and he walked forward, out of the opening barn door. He gave Kelly one quick glance before ducking back out into the sunshine. He immediately noticed the canvas bag of money, dropped in the middle of the yard. Deveraux walked up to it, and took a handful of bundles from it, tossing them to Jericho.

"That'll cover your expenses," Deveraux quipped.

Jericho pocketed the money quietly in one of the pockets of his cattleman coat. He walked steadily to the truck, not taking his eyes from Deveraux. He'd seen the dark stain on the pale canvas bag and had known it was fresh blood.

CHAPTER SEVENTEEN

The ranch buildings and boundaries were a long way back now. Thomas was amidst pristine Wyoming wilderness. Khan was walking at a relaxed pace but still covering the ground quickly in the characteristic trot of an Arabian – seemingly light on his feet. Thomas got the impression the horse was enjoying the freedom too. They were following a natural track that led along a rushing, bubbling creek – probably the same one that fed the pools and streams where he'd caught the trout lower down. They were slowly gaining elevation. The sun was on his back and his lungs filled with crisp, cold air from the mountains ahead of him. On both sides of the creek, Thomas noticed healthy groves of cottonwood and aspen. He remembered how, come the fall, the canopy would be emblazoned with drifts of fiery orange and sulphur yellow respectively, thanks to their presence. Willow trees also flanked the creek's bends and curves. As he allowed Khan to pick a path, he considered the contrast to Scotland's many bare-banked mountain streams and barren mountainsides. Back home, wildflowers, songbirds, rare butterflies, and whole ecosystems were declining rapidly. He knew the reason surprisingly and for many, controversially, was the impact of deer.

This had become abundantly clear north of where he now rode, in Yellowstone. Just like in the UK, the eradication of predators had resulted in unprecedented deer numbers. They stripped the land clean, leaving very little in their wake. As the trees disappeared, so did the beaver. With the grasslands and meadows went the invertebrates, and then the songbirds. And then, when there was nothing left to eat, the deer in turn starved to death in their thousands. But the return of a very small number of wolves as part of a release programme, had a significant impact on Yellowstone. Within a decade, groves of willow and aspen once more sprang up from the riverbanks. Beaver returned, as did many other species unaccounted for across decades. Of course, as Thomas knew, it wasn't the wolves taking down huge numbers of elk. As it happened, their hunts were often unsuccessful and difficult. But their mere presence resulted in a climate of fear – especially near waterways. On the banks of a stream, or whilst crossing it, a big bulky animal like an elk would have to slow down and manoeuvre. For the comparatively dainty wolves, not so much. As a result, water courses, log jams and cutbanks became potential kill zones. And the deer avoided them. In their absence, the ecosystems thrived once more. It was exactly what they were trying to achieve with the introduction of the lynx back in Scotland.

As Thomas looked further up the mountainside, he saw a woodland of Rocky Mountain juniper, ponderosa pine, lodgepole pine, as well as bur oak and bigtooth maple, surrounded them. The bare trunks and branches of the deciduous trees creaked and moaned in the wind, whereas the sprigs and needles of the evergreens rustled and kept beat like cajon brushes on a drum. It was clear that this was a landscape that had once again, albeit cautiously and not without controversy, allowed predators back into its midst. And all the signs suggested this was a good thing.

The topsoil here was quite thin, and he was noticing more boulders and loose rock as they went. But vibrant green mosses clung to the slabs of schist and gneiss, accompanied by a myriad of mustard yellow and steel blue lichens. There was a scent of freshness and ozone in the air, more officially known as petrichor. Created by plant oils and bacteria in the soil, it was especially evident after a storm. It invigorated him and enlivening his senses. His hearing attuned to the surroundings, and he began picking out birdcalls he recognised. Somewhere in the distance, a northern flicker was drumming and yammering its high pitched, repetitive call. Pine siskins chirped and burbled as they flited through the tree branches, mocked by a cardinal that seemed to call "slow down, slow down" in its ovulating, two note song. Thomas was then alerted to a harsh shriek-like call from behind. He glanced over his shoulder. A stout, relatively large bird confidently followed in the horse's wake. Its dark head, flamboyant speckled crest, and barred, kingfisher-blue back and wings gave it a striking look, and one easy to identify. The Steller's jay hopped along behind Khan, eagerly snapping up the plethora of flies, bugs and beetles disturbed by their progress through the grassy, mulch-littered path. Thomas smiled, and reached into his saddlebag, taking out a ziplocked bag of his own brand of trail mix. It contained peanuts, M&Ms, and dried fruit chips. The jay instantly stood to attention and cocked its head. Thomas took a scoop of peanuts and crushed some banana chips in his hand, then threw them onto the trail behind him. The jay chirred in seeming appreciation and pounced on the handouts with precise pecks of its sharp, black bill. Satiated, it flew swiftly to a nearby branch and eyed Thomas with a characteristic head tilt, until he and the horse were out of sight.

Wyoming boasted one person for every 111 acres, so it was no surprise that it was something of a paradise for wildlife. Most of America's most iconic species could be found in the state's national parks and forests. Wolves, grizzlies, cougar, bison and bald eagle all called Wyoming home. However, as the news reports about the bear and Jesse's own conflicts with the farming community had shown, there were still major conservation issues impacting the wild denizens of Wyoming. Hunters still thought the approximate 550 wolves and 600 grizzlies – most of which were confined to Yellowstone National Park, took more of Wyoming's 425,000 deer than they did. As for the big cats, Wyoming had an especially bad relationship with them. In Thomas's lifetime, nearly 5,000 mountain lions had been killed in the state by sports hunters. Wyoming Game and Fish didn't publish population numbers of mountain lions, and it was widely suspected the policy was kept in place because they were so low, and making them public would lead to an immediate hunting ban. Nearly 48% of Wyoming was considered viable mountain lion habitat, so it had the potential to be a stronghold for the species, if it weren't for intolerant communities, sport hunting, and those killed on the roads. He'd read that 97% of all lion deaths recorded in Wyoming were due to human contact in one form or another.

But, he knew the further into the forest he went, the more likely he was to encounter at least one species of predator. He was happy following the river for now. First of all, carnivores needed a plentiful source of water to help digest the huge intake of protein that made up their diet. And, the moisture held in the soil surrounding the stream, as well as the numerous sandbanks made for good places to find tracks. He kept Khan's pace slow and steady as he studied the near-invisible trails that led from the forest to the water, left by animals seeking to quench their thirst. This was a fertile hunting ground for a big predator, and he hoped that since the cat had already visited the ranch, it perhaps had found new prey here in the forest, and closer to home.

The trees began to thin out a little, and rocky escarpments became more prolific across the mountainside. The river moved faster here, blasting round smooth-worn boulders that formed a maze of corridors, leading to sudden drops as the water dashed over in thundering cascades. This was ideal cat territory. Thomas looked back, realising the elevated position gave an excellent sprawling view of the forest and beyond. The beds of flat rock that made up the escarpments would hold the heat well, making perfect places to lie up, especially for an animal that spent a large proportion of its day sleeping. Thomas decided it wasn't a bad place for him to take a break either. He pulled on the reins gently and patted Khan's neck firmly, reassuring the horse he'd earnt a break too. Khan came to a halt immediately, swinging his head round and snorting approval. Thomas dismounted and pulled some of the fresher supplies he'd prepared, knowing they'd perish first – but also that the longer he left them, the more tempting they'd become for emboldened opportunists.

He took a large tin box from one of the saddlebags and went to sit down on a flat overhang. He let his legs dangle over the edge, smiling in the knowledge that Catherine would scold him if she were here. He opened up the box and took out the package on top. He unwrapped the brown wax paper to reveal sandwiches – thick cut, rare-cooked beef with generous helpings of mustard between large chunks of fresh brown bread. He tucked in greedily. He took an apple from the same tin and threw it so that it landed in front of Khan, who inhaled it, along with the mountain grass he was already chewing on.

After the sandwiches, he found something he considered a delicacy – a Baby Ruth bar. A little hard to come by in the UK, he'd already bought a significant amount of American candy on his arrival at the airport. It was then that Thomas noticed he wasn't alone. Several feet from him, close to the edge of the escarpment, a small rodent watched him intently, frozen and clinging to the rock underneath. It was a cliff chipmunk. He'd seen them before in the Grand Canyon, and knew they liked juniper woods and lived at higher elevations than their more common cousins. Thomas broke off a piece of the chocolate, complete with nuts and caramel, and went to throw it in the rodent's direction, but paused. Instead, he slowly and calmly held it out, close to the ground. The chipmunk only hesitated a second before scampering over and reaching out for the treat. Thomas let it go, watching as the tiny squirrel held it within its paws and began to eat furiously. Thomas enjoyed the company whilst he finished the sandwiches.

Refreshed, he got up and put the tin back in the saddlebags. He fished out his canteen and decided to refill it in the river. He reached it in a few strides and dunked the bottle deep into the clear, cold water. He felt content and rolled his shoulders to loosen up a little before the next leg of the ride. He was about to stand up, when he heard a two-tone, morose-sounding cry that lingered and dropped in pitch as it tailed off. It came from above, and he recognised it as a call typical of a bird of prey. His eyes instinctively searched skyward. A broad silhouette hung in the sky, just visible above the treetops. Thomas raised his hand to shield his eyes from the low winter sun, and thought he caught a flicker of brilliant white. If it was what he thought it was, the bird was a renowned opportunist, not to mention the national bird of the

United States. That hadn't stopped it almost becoming locally extinct in the late 20th century, something that would have been a little embarrassing for a country that bore it on its seal. Thomas remembered the plight of the bald eagle as one of the first conservation issues that had hit the headlines, when he was in his pre-teens during the eighties. The cross-country scramble saw the bird protected and its population recovering. Along with the historic "save the whales" campaign, the era had left its mark on Thomas and what he wanted to do with his life.

Bald eagles were very closely related to the white-tailed eagles that had recently been re-introduced to the east coast of Scotland, as well as the Hebrides before that. He'd seen white tails fly over the house and loch at Sàsadh. As he shielded his eyes, he could see they shared similar characteristics, a broad white tail and light-coloured head on a strong, muscular neck. He couldn't see them at this distance, but he knew bright yellow eyes would be fixed on the prey below. Both bald eagles and white tails were officially classed as sea eagles, so Thomas guessed there should be a large body of water somewhere not too far away. He would check on the map later. But bald eagles also wouldn't turn down a free meal – which is what he guessed the bird was circling now. He couldn't help wondering why the eagle chose to remain in the air for now. It occurred to him there was the possibility that something was still feasting below.

Thomas went back to Khan and drew the shotgun from the saddle holster. The Browning Citori 725 Feather was a lightweight model, but still packed a 12-gauge punch. The rifled barrels he had specified made it a versatile gun for whilst he was out in the wilderness. It could take standard shells for birds ranging from dove to geese, whilst when loaded with heavy duty buckshot, it could take on big game too. He also gingerly fished out the leather holster for his Colt Anaconda from the saddle bags, another weapon he had relied on heavily at close quarters before now. Armed and more confident, he found a place where he could cross the stream in the shallows, and headed into the trees, trying to keep the circling eagle in sight.

The eagle had attracted his attention because he knew it was very likely to be eyeing a kill somewhere close by on the ground. And as he moved quietly through the foliage, he soon realised he didn't need the eagle to show him where whatever it wanted to feed on might be, and why it hadn't landed yet. A chorus of strange hisses and grunts emanated through the trees. Thomas kept low and made his way forward carefully. He stopped when he spotted a small break in the trees a little way ahead of him. He saw the gathering of large birds responsible for the strange noises. Turkey vultures. As he observed them, he realised their pink, bald heads of stretched and withered skin gave them an uncanny resemblance to the turkey they took their common name from. Thomas turned his attention to their meal.

The bighorn sheep was slumped on its side, splayed across a set of uneven boulders. Thomas could see huge chunks of flesh had been taken from the animal's neck, back, and shoulders. His view beyond that was obscured by the bickering vultures, as they held out their wings and snapped at their neighbours to protect their place at the dining table. He decided he needed to break up the party. As he strode out from the trees, he pulled the shotgun up, ready to let off a shot, but the birds didn't need further encouragement. They lifted off the ground awkwardly and scattered – but didn't go far. They found perches in the surrounding woodline and watched, ready to revisit the carcass once he'd gone.

Thomas ignored them, knowing they were no threat to him. He started his examination at the head. The eyes had been plucked from their sockets, but had they been still intact, he would have expected to see them bulging – a sign of asphyxiation. However, the mouth was agape, and the tongue lolled out, another indication that the animal's throat had been crushed – a characteristic cat kill. There was no telling if that was the case, as the flesh and muscle from the lower jaw to the chest had been stripped from the ram – he could tell it was a male from the size and shape of the large, round horns. It wasn't lost on Thomas that he'd seen something kill like this before. The characteristic teeth of the sabre-toothed cats were relatively fragile. They were not used for ripping or tearing flesh, as they would have broken. Instead, they were specialist tools, used to deliver a strangling bite to the throat of the oversized prey the cats hunted, such as ancient bison, which were up to 20% larger than their modern counterparts. But the hybrid cat he had faced in Scotland had benefited from reinforced dentition thanks to its jaguar mother. As a result, it had developed a unique killing style – not only able to deliver a strangling bite, but also boasting the strength to rip out the throat with ease. The other side-effect of its hybridisation had been gigantism – something common in other crossbreeds like ligers, the offspring of a male lion and a female tiger. Tama's size meant there was very little she couldn't tackle, and whereas a bighorn sheep ram in its prime would be a significant kill for a mountain lion, for her, it would have been easy prey. He was quickly becoming convinced this was indeed her work.

The scapula, or shoulder blade of the animal, was exposed, and Thomas was surprised to see this bore several hairline fractures, as if it had suffered a significant impact. He wondered if a jackhammer sized forelimb could do that kind of damage, if harnessed to Tama's strength and size. He guessed it was possible. The rest of the carcass showed more typical damage of a big cat kill. The stomach had been split, and the ribcage exposed. The bones had been sliced through neatly as if by scissors. Cats didn't chew their food, lacking the right teeth for it. Instead, their jaws acted as cutting blades that removed chunks of flesh to be swallowed whole. And they were partial to marrow - using their carnassial teeth in the back of the jaw to break through bone to get to it. The nutrient-rich organs were priority targets and would have been consumed first. Then, the muscle-clad haunches.

Tama seemed to share another behaviour with her hybrid father – she didn't seem to attempt to store food for later. As the vultures were taking advantage of, there was still plenty of meat left on the carcass. But Tama hadn't covered the kill or made any territorial markings. She moved from kill to kill casually. Thomas couldn't be sure if this was due to her semi-domestication or, if like the cat in Scotland, she had the same raging metabolic rate that drove her to feed almost constantly.

Thomas slowly and carefully worked the kill site. A clump of red-coloured fur clung to a huckleberry bush, indicating where Tama had passed. He followed, eventually finding what he had hoped for – a track confirming the direction she had taken. It looked like it would be off trail from here on in. He knelt to examine the pugmark closer. It was undoubtedly her, the size putting it outside of any other animal, unless a freakishly large Amur tiger was loose in the Bighorn mountains. But there was something else. The track was mushy, and he could detect the distinct ammonia smell of cat urine. It was then that he noticed there was a smaller impression within Tama's track. It was hard to make out – but the well-spread, teardrop toe prints made it clear something had followed in Tama's footsteps – quite literally. Thomas smiled, recognising the traits and behaviour of a male mountain lion.

She's out of your league, believe me Thomas thought. He stood, and made his way back to Khan, ready to head into the trees.

~

The bear moved its head from side to side, its agitation growing. Saliva drooled from the corner of its misshaped mouth and raw jaws. It had followed the scent of the horse and was tired from its lumbering exploration of the trail. It could tell the horse had left, but it continued to track it to the carcass of the bighorn. There it surprised one of the turkey vultures, which it raked from the air with its claw tips. It crunched the bird to pulp, hoovering flesh from its frame and snapping wing bones as it tried to find sustenance in the small morsel. Unsatisfied, it turned its attention to what remained of the sheep. But there too, not enough remained to satiate its hunger. It growled and huffed as it nosed the air. It used its girth to part the huckleberry bushes in front of it and took up its pursuit of the horse once more.

CHAPTER EIGHTEEN

Tama pushed her nose into the wind. She purred heavily, opening her jaws wide to experience the scents more vividly. A specialist organ in the roof of her mouth, made up of a dense cluster of sensory cells, acted as a secondary station for her olfactory system. It reinforced and intensified the scents in her nasal chambers, enabling her to identify and separate them more easily. The organ was part of a cat's unique biology, and the mechanism was automatic, kicking in when she encountered something she couldn't identify. The scent was alluring and comforting. She instinctively knew it wasn't prey – but it still made her feel alert and guarded.

She moved with purpose, half crouched, passing through rocky corridors and between the trees quickly. Her sudden appearance atop an escarpment surprised a gray fox enjoying the warmth held by the stone slabs, and it shrieked in fear and cowered, unable to escape. She ignored it, padding past it with indifference. She dropped down into a small gully which had been carved out by a fast-flowing creek over millennia. She lapped at the water momentarily, but kept her gaze focused downstream. She followed it a little further, then veered into the trees, loyal to the scent.

Tama was alert to every sound and movement. She missed nothing. A tassel-eared squirrel barked at her furiously from its lofty refuge in the pine boughs. The noisy rebuttal brought her the attention of a pair of ravens, who added loud caws and cronks of alarm. The female of the pair dived at her, her menacing beak coming dangerously close to striking the back of her head. Tama turned to look at the bird and growled a single warning. The ravens left her alone as she slunk from sight.

The scent drew her further into the trees. They towered above her forming thick clusters, giving the forest an ether of eternal twilight, even during the day. Her vision suited this, naturally adapted for low light levels. In bright light, her eyesight was compromised, impacting her ability to detect motion. But here in the dark trees, and with the sun beginning to set, she was in her element. She sat crouched, her red fur blending against the bark of the fallen tree she rested against. As the light levels dropped further, movement in her peripheral vision was accented by bursts of luminescence – purple-toned ripples of glowing radiance. They only lasted a moment, but were renewed with each new movement. She watched the spotted skunk walk past her snout, within easy striking distance. Instinct alone told her that the animal's markings were a warning – but she had also encountered skunks before. She maintained her position downwind and watched it go. Then, a new wave of motion caught her attention. And this was a much larger animal, partially obscured by the trees. Her dormancy reminded her of her need to feed, and she edged forward, keen to identify the prey.

The lightest sound of an impact off to her side made her ears prick up, and she automatically shifted her gaze. She caught the scent more fully now and felt an anxious confusion of her needs. Something primal drove her towards the sound. She padded out from her hiding place, pausing only for a moment before running full pelt up the angled trunk of a fallen white ash, leaping high to intercept the carrier of the alluring smell. She landed in a crouch, her entire body on alert.

She found herself in a narrow passage between the trees and in the path of a predator.

The male mountain lion stepped out from the shadows. He dropped his head and growled. Tama was nearly twice as high as him at the shoulder, and probably had over four times his mass. But the mountain lion didn't seem intimidated. For Tama was emitting a scent of her own – one that drew the male to her in the same way she felt compelled to seek him out. Tama seemed fascinated with the male's long, sweeping tail. Her own was relatively short compared. As the male's twitched and thumped along the ground, she scampered to try and sniff it and then catch it. The male spun on his heels and cuffed her with his paw. She sat, caught unawares and baffled for a moment. But she recognised the behaviour as play, and she went to chase the male again – only to be distracted by an outraged bellow behind her. She turned, growling at the unwelcome intrusion.

The bull moose stood at the brow of an incline further along the trailway. It stood tall, its feet splayed wide, and its head elevated. Tama had not encountered an animal larger than herself before, and she growled in uncertainty. The moose answered with a guttural snort, lowering its head. Strange, savagely twisted horns, tipped red, glistened in the remnants of the sunlight. Tama could sense the strength and power of the animal, but she didn't welcome its sudden appearance. Her shoulder muscles tensed, and she dropped to the ground, unaware she automatically shifted her weight to put herself between the moose and the male.

The bull smashed its hooves into the ground, sending a trickle of small stones down the incline. Tama was not used to being challenged, and a spark of rage ignited in her. She roared, the savage sound frightening the male lion so badly that he bolted into the treeline. But the moose was old and stubborn. Confrontation and intimidation were part of his life, and something stirred in the old bull's body. Ever since a wolf had attacked and damaged his genitals, the moose had been exempt from courtship rituals and procreation. His body was now a unique mix of hormones and misfiring instincts. His once broad and sweeping antlers had dropped almost instantly, and instead, bizarre, unique horns had grown in their place. Unlike his antlers, they would never be shed – and instead of being primarily for show, they're contorted points were formidable weapons. He had killed a number of younger bulls and almost every dog, coyote, or wolf he had come across since. The moose would never know it, but his bad temper had earned him the moniker of Mr. Splitfoot with local hunters, an old nickname for the devil himself, and one which hinted at his demonic nature. He lowered his crown of daggers towards the foe before him.

Tama rippled with pent up energy, and it burst forth in a lightning-paced charge up the incline, another roar escaping her lungs as she closed in on the bull. The old moose charged, gaining rapid momentum from its mass alone. It too bellowed as the toll of its energy expenditure and the strain on its muscles showed. Tama anticipated the bull's first attack, swerving at the last moment to avoid impact. But instinct drove her to still attack, and she sank her fangs into the moose's haunch as it passed. The bull twisted its head round and harpooned Tama's own flank with his deadly points. Tama wanted to roar with the pain, but instinct willed her to complete her attack, and she bit down savagely into the moose's flesh. Her great teeth tore meat from bone, and she jumped sideways, with most of the moose's thigh in her jaws. Biology kicked in, and the moose evacuated its bowels, emptying a thick stream of shiny, slick pellets onto Tama's head.

The pungent faeces made her drop her prize, and she swiped angrily at the moose. Her claws slashed through the bull's face, opening a slit from ear to eye, obliterating the pupil and knocking the animal sideways. Dazed and now panicked, the moose tried to stumble away, dragging its hind leg and limping unsteadily down the incline. Tama moved in, enraged and confident. She could smell the change in the moose's scent, as pheromones flooded its system, driving it to run and flee. She realised with satisfaction that this animal, despite its size, was prey too. She growled with pleasure as she used her oversized shoulder muscles to unbalance the moose and tip him onto his side. Overconfident, a flailing front hoof caught her in the chest, and she yowled with the pain. She charged forward again, half pouncing onto the bull. Her dewclaws hooked into the leg and shoulder, pinning the moose down and rendering him harmless. She sank her teeth into the hump on the bull's back, tearing a basketball-sized piece of hair-covered meat from the imposing shoulder muscles. The bull slumped as tendons and ligaments were severed. An arterial spray of blood fountained from the bull as her second bite sliced through the quivering flesh and fat surrounding the spinal cord. The moose's brain fused in a second of electrical activity as pathways were suddenly cut off, forcing a systematic shutdown. Ultimately, it was unnecessary, as Tama shifted her weight and sent one fang through the moose's skull and divaricated the neck vertebrae with the other. The bull died instantly. Bleeding out might have bought it a few more seconds, but it was over.

As Tama began to feast, enjoying the taste of the blood-drenched, fatty venison and finding the slabs of meat perfectly sized for her, the male lion slunk out from the trees. She eyed him carefully, her jaws surgically removing a strip from the dead bull's chest. He moved to the other end of the moose, watching her intently. She growled a half-hearted warning out of instinct, but she tolerated the male as he began to feed on the other side of the carcass, starting with the lower half of the leg Tama had already maimed. Tama moved closer, tunnelling into the carcass and releasing the stomach. She split its contents easily, and both she and the male began to lick at the fermented plant material, even consuming some. But they quickly moved back to the meat, eating their fill before disappearing into the trees, together.

~

It was nearly dark when Thomas discovered the carcass. He dismounted Khan, who snorted and stamped at a distance whilst he examined it. He knew the horse was picking up Tama's scent. Thomas was impressed with the cat's display of power. The bull would have stood half a foot taller than him at the shoulders, and he noticed the "devil's antlers" it sported. He knew this deformity was caused by castration, and often made for a very bad-tempered animal. So much of the bull's body had been devoured, he found it hard to estimate what it would have weighed in at – but he decided somewhere in the 1,200lb region wouldn't be amiss.

As Thomas studied the blood-soaked ground, he noticed Tama's huge paw prints were not the only ones surrounding the carcass. The male cougar he had identified had joined her, and had seemingly been accepted by Tama. The tracks were fresh and mushy. He followed them a little way up the incline, noting where Tama's oversized dewclaws had dug into the ground to gain traction, something that differentiated her tracks from those of her mountain lion companion. Thomas found this interesting, given what he knew of the evolution and lineages of both cats.

In just the last few decades, it had been discovered that mountain lions were closely related to cheetahs, a species unique among the cat species, as their claws did not fully retract like those of lions or tigers. They also boasted disproportionately large dewclaws. Both physiological features had evolved to aid the cheetah in its high-speed pursuits, acting like a spiked running shoe. The dewclaws of sabretooth cats had long been thought to have developed with a dual-purpose in mind. The family were terrestrial specialists – ground predators. They were not thought to be especially good climbers, having sacrificed this as they evolved to become better hunters in open country. Like the cheetah, their preserved remains showed that their claws didn't fully retract, enabling them to maintain stability and traction at relatively moderate speeds. It was also estimated from their significant muscle mass that they could pursue with significantly more endurance than modern lions, despite not being sprinters like the cheetah. But the dewclaws in particular played a role in catching and holding down prey safely.

Thomas looked at the moose again. He noted where the neat slash marks, from the claws on what was left of the hide, were complimented by relatively large and savage tears. These undoubtedly came from the dewclaws. He could easily imagine them being used to hook and establish a hold on the prey. Then, as it was brought to the ground, they would hold the animal in position. Pinned down and motionless, sabretooths would then use their other weapon, their teeth, to deliver their surgically precise and killing bite, without risking breaking the fragile dentition. Thomas found it interesting that despite benefiting from much stronger canine teeth, Tama was still driven by this genetic instinct to kill in a certain way, whilst utilising her adaptations to feed. It occurred to him that if she were able to be captured and studied, what they could discover about sabretooth behaviour was unprecedented.

Thomas led Khan through the trees. He didn't feel comfortable setting up camp without really knowing how far ahead Tama might be. He reckoned the moose kill to be a few hours old at best. Khan in turn still showed some skittishness, which did nothing to put his mind to rest. He was about to crest a tree-lined ridge, when something told him to pause. He dropped Khan's reins, the horse stopping on cue where it stood. He removed his customised Leica Ultravid binoculars from the saddlebags. With 10x magnification and precision lenses for low light, they would give him an edge as the sun began to set. As he looked at the sky, he saw it was streaked with lavender, burnt embers of orange, velvety purples, and crimson red – night was falling fast. Thomas crept forward, dropping to his belly for the last few feet. He placed what had made him hesitate – he could smell it in the air now, as a heavy, pungent smoke drifted from the gully below. At the base of a large whitebark pine tree, he took advantage of its wide, twisted trunk and sat against it, surveying the slope that led down. It was scattered with juniper bushes and more pines, enough to give him cover, and gentle enough to descend. He traced the route he might take, a sweeping curve that led through a bank of green ash, eastern hophornbeam, and blue spruce, before dropping down into a small clearing...where he could clearly see a raging fire and the silhouette of a man sat before it.

CHAPTER NINETEEN

Chayton sat, legs crossed, the sides of his feet and thighs pressed against the ground. He rested his hands on his knees, palms facing upwards. He sat close to the fire, and the heat was fierce, forcing him to sweat. His eyes were closed, and he took in deep, long breaths, sucking up the smoke from the same mixture he'd used before. The way forward wasn't clear, and he needed guidance – to connect to the land again.

In his mind, he walked through a fog of green mist. As it began to clear, he saw he was walking through a busy and thriving market, but he didn't recognise the place or people. The men and women looked Asiatic, perhaps Mongolic, or Inuit even. He wasn't sure. The market had a stink about it, and he felt the grime and slop against his skin. He noticed that the market stalls held live, wriggling fish and crustaceans. Baby octopus writhed and curled their tentacles in futile attempts to escape their containers. He paused in horror, as he saw a stall holder leisurely hoist a small dog from a basket and dropped it into an enormous wok. He realised its ligaments had been cut to prevent it from struggling. Its cries of pain only lasted a few moments before it went into shock, as the man ladled the cooking oil over the animal, burning off the hair and melting the skin. The man showed no concern as he talked and laughed mindlessly with a fellow stallholder.

Chayton spun around, vomit rising in his throat. Everywhere he looked, more abominations greeted him. Wine made from pickled bear paws promised strength and vitality. Tiger bone powder was sold to be added to soup, for the man who really wanted to be a wildcat in bed. Bats crammed into bird cages waited their turn to be fried and skewered for the eager, hungry crowd queuing at a stall. The ground beneath his feet was soaked with blood, excrement, and more. He had heard of these markets in the news, but never knew the extent of their savagery and disregard of the natural world. His anxiety overwhelmed him as he fell to his knees, tears streaming down his cheeks. His hands began to sink into the ground, and he felt himself falling, consumed by the earth. He felt the warmth of the soaked soil encompassing him. It felt like he was in the womb, as if he were incubating. He seemed small and vulnerable. Microscopic even. He opened his eyes.

He couldn't see the soil; what surrounded him was more like a sea. He floated, as if in water, and he observed huge purple and red spheres pulse and flair around him. Sinister, tentacle-like phalanges occasionally sprouted from their surface, and tree-like appendages covered them. Little yellow spots burst across their fluid, pulsating skins like electrical storms. He realised he was looking at a virus. In a flash, he was back in the market, and he stood amongst the bustling hordes of people, all eager to get their fix or fill their bellies. But it wasn't they who he watched. At the end of the street where the market was, a beautiful Native American woman stood. She gazed at him, smiling, as she raised her upturned hand to her lips and blew. A fine purple and red mist flew from her hand. It danced in the air, moving around him. He watched as it was inhaled and ignored by those around him. He turned again to face the woman. She smiled kindly. In his heart, he recognised her as the Native deity, Pinga, a goddess of the hunt and medicine. But it wasn't the humans she was seeking to heal. It was the Earth. The virus was her creation – the natural world was fighting back against human onslaught in the only way it knew how.

The mist shrouded his view again, and as it cleared, he found himself watching an incredible blue whale rise to the surface of a vast ocean. The streamlined, cobalt-coloured body took on the hue of ice beneath the water, making it glow as its back breached, and an explosion of mist erupted from its blowhole. Suddenly, the waves began to grow pink in colour, then turned ruby red. The largest animal the world had ever known thrashed erratically as it rolled onto its side and died. Chayton watched as the whaling ship closed in on its prize. The carcass was hauled onboard by huge industrial winches and dismembered with alarming efficiency. It didn't matter that everything the whalers were doing was illegal. Whilst there was demand for the meat that paid unprecedented sums, they took the risks, and were protected by organised crime in worldwide markets. Here too though, he saw the purple mist swirl around the meat and infiltrate those working on it. Chayton watched the factory ship make port. The meat was packed and distributed in ice-filled packs and containers. As they were opened, in venues ranging from back alleys to upmarket restaurants, the virus spread.

The clouds enveloped him again, and he next found himself staring at a football stadium. He was back in familiar territory, as those around him were dressed in typical cowboy and rancher garb. But it was another market, filled with wild animals. He recognised the cougar cubs being sold at $400 each, from a dog bed on a plastic table. Wolves and wolf dogs were handed over to eager buyers. Ball pythons sat cramped in ice-cream tubs, unable to stretch out their bodies, drink, or feed. Parrots squawked in the dimly lit venue, whilst giant Madagascan cockroaches hissed as children lifted their boxes and giggled in awe. And above them all, the purple mist swirled and descended.

Chayton knew these conventions and trading fairs took place in stadiums, racecourses and other venues across the country, and in fact, across the world. He had used them himself many times to purchase animals for the fighting rings he supplied, or to train for other jobs. But only when the money was good. As this thought occurred to him, he noticed the figure of Pinga again watching him. But her expression had changed. It was one of wraith. She extended her hand, and her finger pointed at him directly. Her mouth opened in an ugly, silent scream as she began to wither, turning green, and then ash grey. Her eyes faded, dropping into the back of her skull and then disappearing altogether. The skin shrunk from her bones, and then, she was gone. She swirled as a thick cloud of lead-grey vapour, circling him, then suddenly and violently, charging at his chest. He felt her enter his body, and he began to choke. He fought to breathe, clawing at his throat, gargling as he was denied the simplest of life's free gifts – air.

As his eyes bulged, he dropped to the ground, and once more he was in front of the roaring fire. He gulped huge lungsful of air, dazed and confused by what he'd just experienced. His body was drenched in sweat, and he crawled on all fours away from the fire. As he looked towards the treeline, he watched Tama approach, and in her wake, a mountain lion followed. He had no way of telling if he was still in the grip of his abhorrent vision quest. Overwhelmed by the fear that Pinga held him to account for playing a part in the corruption of the natural world, he scrambled for the small canvas bag that lay a few feet away, pulling out an ancient looking revolver.

The 1855 Fusil Repetition was a true antique. It was all he

had ever known of his father, left to him in what had been a Civil War medicine tin. Unlike the tattered cabin he grew up in on the reservation, the gun had been immaculately kept, and he had maintained it that way throughout his life. It fired its .31 calibre bullets accurately, at about 800 feet per second. He had practiced with it regularly and had even used it to take doves and prairie grouse. Only the slightest tremble showed in his hands, as he lined it up on the mountain lion following Tama.

Tama growled, picking up on the human's fear and uncertainty. She dropped her head. She didn't fear the fire, but it caused flares in her vision, inhibiting her peripheral senses. It made her feel further on edge, and she growled steadily as she approached. She could not see what was making the human so agitated, but her body began to fuel itself for fight on instinct. Adrenaline flooded into her body, and her heart began to pump faster as it rushed blood to her muscles. She was fully braced to defend herself and the human from whatever he could sense.

Chayton felt an icy chill come over him as Tama advanced upon him, snarling angrily. The mountain lion had stopped some way behind her. He adjusted his aim and squeezed the trigger. A lick of flame erupted from the barrel of the gun. Almost instantly, the mountain lion somersaulted backwards. It landed on its feet, but its hind legs slipped, and it sat, stunned, panting. Chayton saw the red stain on its shoulder and knew that he'd hit it. His mind was still clouded by fear and chemicals, and whereas he would usually have known the revolver lacked the punch to deliver a mortal shot to the cougar, for now, it didn't occur to him. He let off another shot, this time grazing Tama's back. She froze, and twisted her gaze towards him, emitting a savage snarl as her green eyes glowed with renewed fury.

She instinctively associated the blast of noise with what stung her back. It reminded Tama of the sticks carried by the humans she'd encountered previously. They had been able to hurt her. She was conflicted as instinct fought her training and her kinship with the man. He had made the pain go away. But he was also apparently capable of inflicting it. They had hunted together, and she recognised the value in her bond with him. Like all animals that are conditioned, she was not aware of the strength and advantage she had over him. But still, something flared, and she snarled again, almost goading him in a dare to repeat his actions.

But Chayton hesitated, unsure of what to do next. Tama growled acceptingly and turned around, padding softly back to the male mountain lion. She licked at his wound. Her saliva was thick and gloopy, and her large tongue distributed it in large batches to the male's chest wound. A host of barbed spikes across her tongue helped flatten down the fur and get the saliva, containing natural antibacterial agents, into the wound. She was meticulous, and completely preoccupied, ignoring Chayton's approach from behind, the buffalo jawbone axe in his hand. She was only aware of his presence when the male cougar spat a warning and bolted back towards the trees. But by then, Chayton was already on the downswing of a blow, one intended to kill the mountain lion.

Instead, the metal-edged teeth glanced off of Tama's rear leg, the one that had been injured earlier by the moose. She roared with pain, jumping back and shaking her head in agony. She began to circle the man, her muscles flexing automatically as she prepared to fight back.

Chayton staggered backwards, his lucidity suddenly returning as the fog in his mind finally lifted. He stood up straighter and tried to control his breathing as he realised the danger he was in. He flushed with anger, struggling to believe he had been so unable to judge distance and how he was compromising the bond he'd built with Tama. He slowly lowered the club, and he looked down towards the ground. He kept Tama in his peripheral vision, but he deliberately avoided provoking her further through direct eye contact. He knew that in her current agitated state, that would be a challenge she'd be unable to ignore. He calmed himself, willing to sacrifice himself for betraying her trust. Whatever Tama decided to do now, he had brought it upon himself.

Tama growled, but Chayton thought he could detect a note of sorrow in the sound, one that pained him. She attacked with lightning speed, and the cuff of her paw sent him tumbling through the dirt. He was winded badly and came to rest on his back. A mild pain emanated from the left-hand side of his torso, and he realised Tama's claws had left an ugly set of four cuts that led from above his collar bone down to his ribs. He knew that if she had unsheathed her claws fully, his insides would be spilling out. He tried to catch his breath, wincing as he became aware of acute, painful pressure on his left ankle. He went to glance down, but suddenly, his view was engulfed by Tama's head just inches above his. Her green eyes reflected in the firelight, and he drew a sharp intake of breath in shock. There was no doubt who, in his mind, she was.

Tama growled, lowering her head further. Saliva pooled in her jaws and dripped from her exposed fangs onto Chayton's brow. He remained stock still. He spoke softly to her.

"You are Pinga, the warrior goddess of the wild and the

hunt. I am your servant. Mankind has unleashed a plague upon itself in its disregard and decimation of the natural world, but it is nothing to your power. Do what you will."

Tama huffed, then growled again. She looked towards the trees and stepped over Chayton. She turned back once and met his gaze one last time before slipping away.

~

Thomas watched the whole thing play out from his hiding place beneath the whitebark oak. He had been uncertain as to whether he should intervene or not, but when he saw Tama strike the man down, he rose to his feet and began to lead Khan carefully down the slope. He was confident the man wouldn't see him until he arrived in the clearing, the fast-approaching night further shielding his approach. As they entered a small avenue of trees, Khan snorted and started, and Thomas snapped to attention. He wondered if Tama had double backed and was waiting in the shadows, but he didn't think this was the case. Then, he noticed Khan was looking behind them, back up to the top of the slope.

~

The bear paused at the ridgeline. The horse's scent was strong here, and it could tell it had spent some time in the area. The trail was fresh, and it could follow it easily. Comparatively, its eyesight was poor, but it could still pick up the fire on the gully floor below. Hunger was replaced with a sense of pure rage, and it began a fast-paced descent of the ridge, making straight for the burning beacon. Its front limbs were longer than its hindquarters, giving it a strange rocking motion that belied the impressive turn of pace it was capable of. As it reached the flat of the gully floor, it roared as it broke into a full charge.

~

Thomas was caught off-guard by the roar that echoed several hundred feet away from him in the dark. His hand flew to the handle of the revolver in its holster, and he instinctively pushed his chest into Khan's muzzle, in an effort to keep him quiet. But the horse knew that the predator was close and had no intention of giving their position away.

The animal bellowed again, huffing and grunting as it careened through the brush. It was moving away from them, seemingly headed directly for the camp. Thomas was in awe of the speed and power it showed. The groaning, bad-tempered exhalations identified the animal as a bear beyond doubt, and then some. As Thomas listened to it collide with a tree, and the crack of splintering wood, he couldn't help thinking of a time when he had shown Catherine the wake of a large animal in Scotland, suggesting a bear could bring down trees. She had scoffed at the time. His thoughts lingered on her for a moment, and the last few years. How they had bonded facing the sabre-toothed cat in Scotland. Confronting the descendants of the world's most infamous man-eaters in Tsavo, Africa. And now, potentially one of the most powerful land predators on the planet in the wilds of Wyoming.

"Tigers, lions, and bears, oh my," Thomas whispered to the night.

He slid the shotgun from Khan's saddle holster and loaded it with slugs as he crept towards the camp, on an intercepting course with the bear.

CHAPTER TWENTY

Chayton dragged himself to his feet, haphazardly using the barrel of the revolver to push himself up from the ground and his knees. He staggered towards the fire. He caught his breath as he leaned up against the stack of firewood he had gathered, adding another log to the flames. The fire spat and crackled as it eagerly devoured the dried timber. He knew he would need to attend to his wounds. The scratches were superficial, but he could already feel the bruising and his body tightening against the sprains, pulls and knocks he had taken. But he remained by the fire, feeling some comfort from it as his mind rested and a sense of normality returned. He was exhausted and needed to regain his strength.

He felt its approach before he saw it. Impact tremors reached him as it neared, and he turned to the darkness. He felt some relief at the thought that Tama had returned so soon. But it wasn't Tama's face that loomed from the shadows. The bear was on all fours, but every inch as tall as he was at the shoulder. Its face was a distorted mess of seared flesh, shrivelled skin, and scabbed-over wounds. Wrinkled, pulled back gums exposed yellowed fangs on the left-hand side of its jaws. A milky eye seemed to stare at him, glistening as the bear raised its head, sniffing the air.

Chayton had experience with grizzlies, but this was unlike any grizzly he had ever seen. It was off-the-scale. Its broad head seemed disproportionate to its stubby muzzle, making Chayton consider it was potentially even more disfigured than he had initially thought. But its fur was wrong for a grizzly too. Its head was immense, but somehow still more streamlined than any bear he had come across. There was no ruff of coarse hair around its neck, and its pelt seemed much finer than the characteristic dense fur of brown bears. Even the colouration was wrong. The head, shoulder hump, and front legs were predominately ash black, with silvery blonde highlights on its chest and muzzle. Its sides were salt and pepper like a badger, and as it began to circle, he caught the mahogany brown merle of its rear end and hindquarters. Its movement and stance reminded him of hyenas he'd seen on TV. Its front limbs were considerably longer than its back legs, resembling paintings he'd seen in caves and Native American statues. He wondered if it was a cross between a black bear and a grizzly.

He raised the revolver high in the air and fired off two shots in quick succession. But the bear didn't flee. It roared back, drowning out the second rapport of the gun. It continued to circle until it was on the far side of the fire. Then it raised up onto its hind legs. The bear towered to over twice his height, and Chayton sucked in a breath. The bear rolled its bottom lip, something Chayton had seen grizzlies do. He knew they did this to take in a scent. He also knew that bears had one of the greatest senses of smell in the animal kingdom, having once heard an old hunter say that a grizzly had a nose eight times as good as a bloodhound. Chayton wondered what it was trying to determine as he took careful aim with the gun. He pulled the trigger, this time knowing full well he wasn't packing the stopping power he needed.

The bear was only thirty yards away, so it was a close-range shot. His aim was true, and the small calibre bullet smashed into the bear's nose at a speed of just over seven hundred feet per second. The bear roared as a spurt of blood gushed from its torn left nostril. But it didn't have the effect

Chayton wanted it to. Undeterred, the bear dropped to all fours and charged. It took less than two seconds for the bear to reach him, rearing up again as it did. Chayton suspected it would use its strange, long front limbs to swipe at him from a distance, but instead, they wrapped around him, pulling him into the bear's midriff. Then the bear dropped its head and bit down on his right shoulder.

Chayton cried out in pain as the bear effortlessly lifted him off of his feet, its jaws clamped tight across his shoulder blade and neck. The pressure was acute, seemingly pinpoint, and he gasped as he fought the wave of nausea and the light-headedness that he knew would lead to passing out. As he swung his free arm to punch and swipe at the bear, he used his teeth to bite down onto the only appendage he could see – its ear.

The bear growled through its teeth, but it was used to prey fighting back. It simply bit down harder, and dropped back down to all fours, dragging Chayton to the ground. The sickening crack he heard confirmed what the pain was already telling him. His shoulder had been broken by the bear's vice-like grip. He slumped as the bear released him, huffing and panting as it swayed too and fro, its stumpy muzzle inches from his face. Not through fighting, Chayton kicked violently at the bear's underbelly and tried to push himself away from the formidable teeth and frighteningly disfigured face above him.

Undeterred, the bear cuffed Chayton with its baseball mitt of a paw, and a new wave of agony rippled along his side. His head was spinning now, and he guessed his ribs had cracked. But the bear's blow had bulldozed him through the long grass for several feet, and he used his good arm to get on his feet. He broke into a lop-sided sprint, wheezing and gasping as he made for the fire. As he heard and felt the approach of the bear behind, he fell to his knees and plunged his hand into the flames. When he pulled it out again moments later, his fingers were wrapped around the largest burning branch he could lift. He ignored the scalded skin across his hand as he swung back around to face the bear.

It stopped in its tracks, and a low, guttural growl filled his ears. It began to sway again, chuffing and popping its jaws in warning. As Chayton swung the flaming brand, the bear shuffled backwards and again rose up onto its hind feet. Its opaque, fogged pupil rolled back into its skull, independent of its beady, black, good eye that remained fixed on Chayton. The bear seemed to instinctively turn its unblemished side away from the flaming weapon, and Chayton saw the shrivelled, raw, damaged face up close. He was certain the injuries had been inflicted by fire. He jabbed the burning branch at the bear, and considered stepping back into the fire itself, perhaps dashing through to the other side.

The bear roared, and for a second, Chayton thought it was going to retreat, as it lowered its head towards its chest. But he was wrong. There was no further warning, and the speed of the attack gave Chayton no chance of preparing for it or mustering a defence. Using the full reach of its front limbs, a smashing downward swipe slammed Chayton to ground, and the branch dropped from his hand as he once again fought unconsciousness. Blood streamed down his forehead, and it felt cold on his sweaty skin. It clouded his vison further and he struggled vainly to lift his hand to wipe it from his eyes. He realised his strength was draining quickly now, and he no longer felt in control of his body as he fell on his wounded side, screaming with agony. He almost didn't feel the momentary pressure at the base of his spine before a sound like a bursting bubble signalled the bear was on him again, and he felt a series of jerks and tugs. With one last momentous effort, Chayton tried to swivel onto his back. The pressure on his spine disappeared, then he felt a blast of warm air on the back of his head. He didn't have time to comprehend that he couldn't move his legs as the jaws clamped around his skull. He knew he had seconds to live, if that, and he stopped fighting it. But it was then that he heard a sound that he realised he'd been yearning for. A roar.

Tama stood at the edge of the clearing, on the far side of the fire. She stood frozen in a half-crouch, her green eyes blazing in the firelight. But something else burned too – an unbridled fury at the presence of this new predator in what she perceived as her territory. Then something broke her gaze. A wave of iridescence brought her attention to movement on the other side of the meadow, where an incline met the woodline again. A third predator now encroached.

~

Thomas let out a long breath he didn't realise he'd been holding, and suddenly wished he'd stayed with the horse.

CHAPTER TWENTY-ONE

Thomas was in awe of Tama, but it was the bear that he couldn't tear his gaze away from. On all fours, it was larger than the sabretooth, with considerably more bulk. Its appearance was mesmerising. The disfigured face looked almost zombified in the fierce, reddish illumination from the fire. He could certainly see why the bear had been christened Lucifer. But Thomas could also make out its merle-coloured hide, its huge head, and strange muzzle and jawline. At first, he wondered if this might be what was known as a grolar bear – a cross between a grizzly and a polar bear. They too had a strange, out-of-proportion appearance and unusual colouration, and were being documented more and more in upper parts of British Columbia. However, they'd be a bizarre find in Wyoming, and as he stared, he realised he knew what he was looking at, even though he couldn't quite believe it. The short-faced bears were a group of extinct carnivores that had disappeared from the continental United States over 11,000 years ago. But he was certain he was looking at one now. They're closest living relatives were the spectacled bears of South America, and the similarity in colouration and even the blunt muzzle they shared was evident. The size, however, was very different. A spectacled bear might weigh in at 250lbs max and come in at less than six feet in length. The bear he was looking at could be five times that mass, and it stood nearly six feet at the shoulder just on all fours.

The bear huffed, rocking back and forth on its feet. Its gaze flicked from Tama to Thomas in uncertainty. It popped its jaws again and rose up onto its hind legs. The animal was monstrous, but Thomas used its moment of hesitancy to draw closer to the Native American man on the ground. As he knelt beside him, the man let out a fevered, incomprehensible moan. Thomas could see his injuries were serious. He had brought one of the saddlebag panniers with him and fished out the first aid kit he'd packed. Thomas knew the medical help the man needed was beyond his level of expertise, but he had to try something. He bluntly plunged a morphine syrette into the man's leg and removed some tourniquets from the kit.

"This is going to be the roughest and fastest field dressing ever, but you don't exactly deserve my finest bedside manner," Thomas grumbled.

Thomas couldn't help but notice that the man didn't seem to react to any of the administrations to his legs. It was only from the waist up that flinches of pain and shock were evident. He was scared to move the man, but when he felt along the man's sides, his fingers detected the cold, damp, torn clothing that was soaking in blood. The man was bleeding out from his back. Thomas took in a deep breath and moved the man onto his side. Thomas was in no doubt that the man felt it, as he seemed to quickly pass out with the pain. As he had done with the wounds to the legs and side, Thomas hurriedly and heavy-handedly stuffed the torn flesh with haemostatic gauze, sachets of wound sealing clotting powder, and a triple-layered press known as an Israeli bandage. He secured the dressings with tape and bandage. Then he looked up.

Lucifer was still the other side of the fire and had dropped back on to all fours. Tama however, had moved much closer. Her back was to Thomas and the man, and her attention was completely on the bear. Thomas decided anywhere was better than here. If he didn't move the man, then death would come from him either in the form of blood loss, or claw and fang.

Thomas hoisted the man up from underneath his arms, and began to drag him backwards up the trail, to where he hoped Khan was still waiting. But the movement seemed to provoke the bear into action.

Lucifer's wrathful roar announced his coming charge. He swerved around the fire, headed straight for Thomas and his unconscious patient. Thomas dropped the man he was dragging with unceremonious haste, pulling the Anaconda revolver from its holster. He held the gun with both hands, cradling the handle as he lined up on the bear's massive shoulder and fired. Lucifer careened away, disappearing into the darkness. Thomas kept the gun trained on the noise of the bear's juggernaut-esque journey through the brush. His howling rage was punctuated with grunts and snorts as he circled back in an anti-clockwise loop. Just as the bear seemed to be getting farther away, it accelerated back towards the other side of the fire, heavy roars expelling from its lungs as its bowling ball sized paws smashed into the ground. But Tama was waiting for it.

All Thomas saw were two glowing coals of green light reflected by the fire, which she had retreated from. Thomas knew Tama was playing to her strengths. If records were anything to go by, he knew the bear was meant to have an unparalleled sense of smell. And, despite what many thought, their eyesight was at least equal to that of humans. Which meant, just as with humans, they had no special adaptations to help them see in the dark. But Tama did. Her eyes held nearly ten times as many light-detecting rod cells. Cats also benefited from larger corneas – and Tama's were uniquely oversized. And the glowing green orbs he could see that marked her eyes were thanks to a layer of tissue at the back of the retina that reflected and amplified light. He knew she would be tracking the bear's rampage in bursts of ultraviolet iridescence, and that she benefited from perhaps twenty percent greater peripheral vision than either he or the bear. He watched as she lay in wait, allowing her prey to come to her. Despite not wanting to be anywhere near as close as he was, Thomas couldn't help feeling a rush at the thought of the Palaeolithic showdown he was about to witness.

~

Tama lay hunkered to the ground. Her claws unsheathed and bit into the hardened topsoil for more purchase. The muscles in her neck and shoulders tightened, and she flattened herself as low as she would go. Her hindquarters bunched underneath her, centering her gravity with almost Zen-like efficiency. Like an overwound watch, her pent-up energy could only be contained for a limited few moments. But she didn't have long to wait. Lucifer was crazed after having been shot. The bear crashed its way out of the brush and came into sight again. Emboldened by rage, it didn't stop to skirt the fire, instead smashing through it with reckless speed. An explosion of burning wood and embers rained down around them as the carefully layered stack was obliterated into fiery missiles by the bear's momentum.

A relatively small splinter of a pine bough, still alight, landed on Tama's back, and she leapt forward with a scream of pain, turning back on herself to face the unseen assailant. With terrible timing, she exposed her back to the bear, which barrelled straight into her. Its bone-shattering jaws landed a glancing blow on her shoulder, but her agility saved her, as she twisted round and used her forelimbs to push herself off of the bear's flank. Now behind the bear, she sprang at its rear, sinking her claws and fangs into its hip. Lucifer roared, turning on his heels so tightly that his momentum unbalanced Tama and flung her onto her side, and before she could get to her feet, he lunged at her, pushing his muzzle towards her chest, maw open, to deliver a debilitating bite.

Tama rolled onto her back and kicked out with her hind feet, her claws raking the throat and chest of the bear as his jaws snapped shut on empty air. But as she spun back onto her feet, Lucifer used his reach to slash at her flank. Tama leapt into the air to put as much distance between her and the bear as possible, but it was in full charge and not letting up. Lucifer seemed to easily match her speed as she broke into a sprint, and she growled her displeasure at being pursued, something she had not encountered before. She changed direction, dashing to her left and turning in a tight circle. As the bear lumbered on, slowing down dramatically before he turned after her in a wider, more sweeping curve, she paused. She stood watching as she panted hard. Instinctively she broke into a trot, accelerating towards Lucifer's side.

~

Thomas continued to drag the unconscious Native American back along the trail. It was hard and slow work. As he watched Tama zone in on the bear, he couldn't help but admire her problem-solving ability. She had analysed the bear's approach and had worked out she was more agile. From what he knew of the species, the short-faced bears had the perfect anatomy for impressive locomotor efficiency. They were almost entirely carnivorous, and they used their size and strength to intimidate other predators – which would have included sabretooth cats, off of their kills. It was an extremely effective scavenger and would have been used to travelling huge distances in order to find enough food. As a result, it had evolved forward-facing feet, instead of paws turned inward like other bears. But, as Tama had found to her advantage, the bear's unique leg structure and huge bulk meant as fast as it was in a straight line, it lacked the ability to turn with any speed. In fact, he seemed to recall the leg bones were thought to be relatively thin and inflexible, meaning they risked serious injury if they were to fall or change direction quickly. It was just one of the aspects that had led scientists to conclude they were scavengers rather than hunters.

But he also knew that every test that had ever been carried out on the bear's anatomy came back with the same results. They were serious meat eaters, rather than omnivores like most other bears. Not only did they need huge amounts of flesh, but their jaw power gave them access to calorie-rich marrow contained in the carcasses of behemoth mammals like giant ground sloths, mastodons, and stag moose. The blunt muzzle concentrated the crushing power of the jaws, resulting in huge bite pressure that could split the thickest of bones. Thinking about this gave Thomas no comfort. Just because the bear might prefer the easier option of carrion, that didn't mean it couldn't hunt and kill. In fact, as he glanced at the saddlebag pannier on the ground and the shotgun he'd left next to it, he realised that this out-of-place, out-of-its-time predator, had the perfect opportunity to level up. Released into the present, nothing could stop it potentially hunting and killing smaller prey with ease – just like grizzlies did.

~

Tama accelerated, her anticipation of the impact exciting her. She slashed at the bear's flank with her claws before it could turn on her and delivered a glancing bite to its rear. By the time the bear was in a position to face her, she had retreated. Coolly and confident, she growled from her hunched position in the grass, seemingly goading the bear. Lucifer obliged, lumbering forward in a bad-tempered, but a slightly more unsure charge that lacked the pace and purpose of his previous attacks. Tama skitted sideways, but not before landing a downward swiping blow of her dagger-sharp claws to the bear's nose, which exploded in a fountain of blood.

Tama sprinted away again into the darkness, circling back quickly towards her foe. Lucifer stood up on his hind legs and roared, teetering on his back feet as he turned to face her. He was only side on when Tama leapt, her own roar drowning out his pained bellows. Her front paws spread wide, her long, curved claws reaching for the bear's shoulders like spearpoints. Her spine curled, and her hind legs bunched, ready to deliver scrabbling, eviscerating rakes to the bear's abdomen.

But the bear had claws of his own. Lucifer wasn't as agile as Tama, but his reach was longer than hers. As deftly as a heavyweight boxer blessed with lighting speed, Lucifer unleashed a debilitating jab that cut Tama's assault short. She crashed to the ground on her back, but her scrabbling hind feet left slashes on Lucifer's rear legs. He dropped to all fours and took the lower half of one of Tama's front legs into his jaws. But before he could bite down, Tama's head shot upwards, and she sank her fangs into the bear's shoulder. A roar of pain sounded out, and Lucifer lurched forwards, dragging the attached Tama with him. As his car-sized bulk trundled over Tama, she released her grip and made her escape, swiping vengefully at the bear's rear before she disappeared into the night again. Lucifer swayed back and forth on his front feet.

His breath fell in short, raspy grunts. He couldn't see the men he had tracked into the camp, but he could smell them.

~

With the fire all but destroyed, Thomas could no longer see the bear, but he could hear it. He was in no doubt that the energy it had expended, and the beating it had taken at Tama's onslaught, meant that it would be making feeding a priority. He tried to drag the unconscious Native American faster up the trail, but he knew it was only a matter of time now. The bear would be coming. He stopped, lying the man down as gently as possible on the ground. Then he took out the Colt Anaconda and unsheathed his kukri hunting knife from his belt. Despite its viciously sharp curved tip, and half-serrated edges to the top and bottom of the blade, it gave him little comfort. Somewhere in the darkness, a bear that looked like it weighed every bit of 1,500lbs was contemplating its attack. He didn't have to wait long.

The bear seemed to understand that its prey was unlikely to outrun it. Its approach seemed casual, carefully scenting the air with every few steps by lifting its nose and rolling back its bottom lip. Thomas guessed it was checking to see if Tama was still in the area. Made more confident by her seeming absence, the bear made a chuffing noise as it headed straight towards Thomas across the incline. He could feel the tiny tremors its bulk sent through the ground, announcing its presence and intent. Then, a more chaotic, thunderous ripple of seismic waves reached him, this time coming from behind. Thomas braced himself, not willing to tear his gaze from the approaching bear. In a way, he was grateful. During his time filming a series called "Hunter Hunted", he had faced many carnivores and killer animals, but he had kept bears to the minimum. Unlike big cats, they couldn't be trusted to dispatch you before they began dining. He had seen many hunters and hikers left with horrendous injuries and disfigurements from bears that were happy to eat on the run, often leaving their still live meal for dead. It wasn't the way he wanted to go out, and death by bear was a private fear of his. Tama's delivery of death would be almost instant. He closed his eyes.

But it wasn't a sabre-toothed cat that charged from behind – it was Khan. The horse snorted and whinnied, rearing up on its hind legs with flailing hooves and gnashes of his teeth – the stallion's wild mustang ancestry coming to the fore. Thomas held his breath, in awe of the horse's bravery. It was enough to make the bear pause, but not for long. It had recently faced a foe far more powerful than Khan, and it reared up onto its hindquarters again, revealing its full height. Khan was a large and powerful horse, but Lucifer towered over the animal. Khan, sensing he was outmatched, dropped down to all fours again, and snorted as he swerved around the bear. Lucifer swiped at the horse, just catching him on the saddle. The momentum was enough to topple the horse, and Khan crashed over onto his back. Thomas let out a gasp as he rolled over the pannier he'd left on the ground. But Khan was up on his feet in an instant. As if enraged at his fall, the stallion kicked out backwards with his legs, smashing his hooves into the bear's side. Then, before disappearing into the woodline, the horse kicked at what was left of the pannier, maddened, and focusing on it as if it had been what caused it to fall. The rifle was all but destroyed, its wooden stock splintered and the barrel bent. Thomas felt a pang of despair as he noticed the pristine satellite communicator was also distributed over the ground in several pieces. Catherine would have been tracking his progress with it, and he wondered if the SOS function would have kicked in and sent out a signal whilst Khan was busy obliterating it. Either way, help was not going to be immediately available. He knew there was no cell phone signal here in the mountains, and even if there had been, his phone was in the other pannier, still attached to the fast-retreating Khan. Fear washed over him again, but he readied himself as Lucifer began to traverse the incline, this time at a much faster and more determined pace.

Thomas's mind was racing. Everything about the situation was wrong. If this was a grizzly, he knew that his best option was to play dead. If it had been a black bear, if it wasn't scared off, he was better off standing and fighting. But not only was this bear neither, it had the smell and taste of the Native American's blood in its system. He'd already come to the conclusion that the bear's facial and shoulder injuries had been caused by fire, and perhaps the sight of the roaring flames had triggered an aggressive response. Thomas had long postulated that major traumas impacted animals just as much as they did humans. There was a long, tragic record of mistreated circus and zoo animals that had seemingly been triggered by memory to act aggressively, sometimes years after such events. Elephants that witnessed their mothers being killed by poachers often developed anti-social behaviours with other elephants and adopted homicidal ones towards humans. And in the 1960s, two brown bear cubs whose mother had been shot by hunters, became "park killers", as they were labelled back then.

The bear stopped when it was about fifty feet away. Thomas tensed. Lucifer, as the bear had come to be called, seemed hesitant. Thomas realised that everything the bear had attacked so far had fought back – and he wondered if it was giving Lucifer pause for thought. The bear opened its jaws wide, as if in a yawn, and took a few more steps closer. Thomas instinctively took a few more steps back. It was probably pointless at this stage, but he still wanted to show the bear he was willing to put distance between them if it was an option. Lucifer trundled forward a few more steps, woofing at him in a manner not unlike the big cane corso, Arturo, he'd left at home would. At another time, it would have amused Thomas that the dog's Italian name meant "bear". Thomas lowered his gaze, avoiding staring the animal directly in the eye, but still very aware of it in his peripheral vision. Thomas recognised that the bear was showing behaviour that signalled it was unsure and uncomfortable. He hoped that he could persuade Lucifer that a confrontation wasn't worth their while. But, as Thomas went to take another step back, the bear uttered a half growl, half guttural woof that warned him not to. Then it was coming.

The charge was lightning quick, and Thomas instantly knew that this was no bluff. Whereas many bears would mock charge to scare or warn off a potential threat, every bit of the bear's behaviour was now predatory. It had changed in a split second. Lucifer kept his head low as he moved over the ground with purpose. Even on the incline, it took the bear less than three seconds to reach him. But that was long enough for him to take off the Rancher style hat and drop it to the ground at the last moment. He'd read about distraction tactics when faced with a charging bear, and incredibly, it worked. As Thomas dashed sideways, the bear stopped as if it had hit a wall and began to investigate the hat with loud sniffs. It bought him all of two seconds.

Lucifer repositioned himself, lining up on Thomas again, and broke into a run. Thomas was amazed at its speed. There was no gentle acceleration. Like a sprinter straight out of the blocks, the charge was immediate and at full pace. But Thomas now had a plan. Just as Tama had before him, he'd noted that the bear was great in a straight line, but just like a truck, its mass gave it trouble in the corners and when changing direction. Thomas could see the woodline, and he was going to zigzag his way to it. Then, it was a case of getting up a tree. He knew that the short-faced bear skeletons discovered to date had revealed a sesamoid bone in the wrist, similar to a giant panda. This suggested that they had at least some capacity for tree climbing. But he was confident its bulk would significantly limit how far it would get – if he could find and choose the right tree. As the bear bore down on him again, Thomas leapt sideways, flinging himself as far to the right as he could.

Lucifer wailed in frustration as Thomas dashed away from him, but immediately set off on an intercept course, headed straight for him at a 45-degree angle. Luckily, the bear had no ability to be stealthy. On the move, it huffed, groaned, and smashed its bulk over the ground. Thomas suspected he would have been able to hear the bear coming from a mile away, let alone forty feet. And the odds were still against him. Whereas Usain Bolt might be able to cover, say, thirty feet per second in a sprint, Thomas couldn't. And the bear could cover fifty-eight feet per second at full pelt. It was just a matter of time if he didn't reach the trees soon.

A discharge of warm air and a grunt told Thomas that Lucifer had gotten closer than he should have let him. Thomas dove into a roll, as a watermelon-sized paw, complete with a set of carving knife-like claws, passed through the air where his midriff had been. Up on his feet again, he veered away from the maddened bear, now in a full sprint for the trees. Once more, he tried the distraction tactics, jettisoning the jacket he was wearing behind him. This time, Lucifer barely slowed, but it was enough to give Thomas the time he needed. He leapt high, throwing his arms around the thin trunk of a Rocky Mountain maple tree. He'd deliberately chosen it as something the bear would be unable to climb. He instantly clamped the sides of his feet either side of the trunk and began to rip his way up into the branches, hauling himself upwards frantically.

As Thomas turned sideways to step onto the first major limb of the tree, he felt a searing pain down the length of his right calf. He looked down, straight into the face of the bear. Its claws had all but touched him yet had slashed through his jeans and into his leg, as if his muscles were warm butter. Thomas clambered higher into the tree, finding bigger and better branches the higher he went. He didn't stop until he felt them thinning out again. It was just then that the tree shook violently, and Thomas glanced back down. The bear had placed its paws against the trunk, and its shoulder muscles worked like pump jacks as it looked up at its escaping meal, roaring its displeasure. Thomas wrapped his arms around the trunk, clinging tightly with every fibre of his being as the tree took impact after impact. Thomas looked the tree up and down to get an idea of how capable it was of taking the bear's punishment. He suddenly realised that he may have misjudged things.

Standing on its hindlegs, the bear was only five or six feet below him. Thomas had his feet bunched beneath him, resting them on the last branch but one that he would risk his weight on. If he pushed his head up, he would easily be looking at sky and past the tree's tip. The tree's spread was also relatively sparse, no more than fifteen feet he estimated. And just as he began to doubt if the tree could stand up to the beating it was getting, it was confirmed as a sound of cracking and splintering rang out. The bear backed off, tired from its exertions. Then, with one final effort and shove, the tree began to give way.

Thomas had no choice but to hang on as the tree crashed to the ground. The impact loosened him from his terror-tight grip, and he was thrown against the forest floor. Branches disintegrated around him, and a rain of wooden shards and strewn boughs blanketed him. Lucifer didn't get away unscathed either. As the trunk gave way, it splintered, and a segment exploded from its base, forming a spear-like projectile that ricocheted into the bear's face. Thomas was dazed, and he knew he was hurt, but he also could hear that the bear was retreating, its roars dissipating as it disappeared into the night. As the night grew silent again, he tried to get to his feet.

Thomas realised he was banged up pretty bad. A wave of dizziness washed over him, and he slumped back down again. The leg the bear had clawed could take very little of his weight. As well as the still bleeding slashes, his knee seemed horribly twisted out of shape and looked like a bulbous, overripe tomato. Sharp, shooting pains convulsed down his left arm, and he was familiar enough with the agony of a broken rib to know he had a few of those too. He took short, painful breaths as he steadied himself. He turned onto his belly, crying out as he scuffed his sides, and stopping again until the stab of pain went away. Using his one good arm and leg, he began to crawl clear of the fallen tree. Having already been sat in its canopy, he didn't have far to go, but the branches still clawed at him as he went. One large bough stood in his way, and he used it as leverage to reach a sitting position, perching himself on top of it as he tried to control his breathing. More than anything, he wanted to gulp down huge lungsful of fresh mountain air, but doing so was like being kicked in the chest by Khan. At least he imagined so. He wondered where the horse was, and if he would automatically head home.

As he sat, he became more lucid, and realised that the knife had thankfully stayed in its sheath, but had added its own myriad of bruises to his leg where it had been caught between his thigh, the ground, and a falling tree. The revolver was gone and searching for it would be pointless. He calmed himself and readied himself to stand. Sweat poured down his face and neck with the strain, dampening his collar. It immediately made him feel cold, and he remembered the discarded coat. He decided he would try to retrace his steps and find what he could, on his way back to the destroyed pannier that held what remained of the first aid kit. It was only then that he thought of the Native American.

He found the jacket, but not the man. Thomas was unsure if it was because he couldn't remember where he'd left him, or if the bear had claimed a meal after all. He limped slowly and stiffly back down the incline. He stumbled down onto his uninjured side when he found the pannier and began routing through it. He drank thirstily from what was left of his canteen. His hands were shaking violently, and he knew he was in danger of going into shock. He started with the elementary stuff. He slowly and deliberately added antiseptic ointment to the minor cuts and bruises. There were plenty of them, so it kept him and his mind busy. He fixed up his side with padding and tape as best he could, helping limit the movement and impact it would take. He guessed his leg needed stitches, but there was no chance of that in the dark. A large amount of his dressings and kit had already been used on the Native American. As he rummaged desperately, he found two things in the bottom of the pannier that made him smile and might make good substitutes. He took a long draw from the hip flask. It contained a straight American whiskey, made in small batches by a company called Wyoming Whiskey. The Outryder, which he favoured, was 50% alcohol, 100% proof, and would double as a frontier-style disinfectant. He gritted his teeth as he splashed it onto the deep cuts across his leg. Then, he uncapped the second item.

Thomas knew that super glue, just like champagne, had been discovered by accident. A manufacturer trying to make clear plastic gunsights created it, but found it horrendous to work with, thanks to its highly adhesive nature. One of the discoveries was that it only needed a tiny amount of moisture to become reactive and work. Something that had been taken advantage of by soldiers in Vietnam, who used it to seal their wounds and stop bleeding. Thomas planned to do the same. He cried out with pain as he squeezed the rips in his flesh together and quickly applied the glue to each. His head snapped up as his outburst was answered, distantly, by the distinct, eerie call of a mountain lion. Thomas remembered Tama's potential boyfriend and began to look around for the shotgun. He found it and decided it would make an excellent makeshift crutch as well as a weapon if he needed it. Although he was sure that under normal circumstances a mountain lion would show no interest in him, the scent of blood and signs of weakness in any animal could trigger a predatory response. He slung what was left of the pannier over his shoulder and decided that it was best to keep going downhill.

Thomas half shuffled, half limped past the clearing, continuing downhill towards the treeline on the other side. He crossed back into the forest without ceremony. He took slow, deliberate steps, checking his footing, and stopping regularly. He used these moments not just to catch his breath and bring a temporary end to the ripple of pain each movement spontaneously sparked, but to also check his surroundings. He realised it had only taken a few short moments for a place he would usually go to for refuge and solace to become a place of real danger. He smiled as he thought about numerous social media posts he'd seen about 'getting lost in nature to find yourself'. He had replied to one, saying "no, you're more likely to die". The irony wasn't lost on him. Mother Nature could be a mean bitch, but she had a sharp sense of humour too.

He had been making progress for about an hour when something about the forest changed. His senses were a little dulled, but he could still pick up on it. The woods are anything but quiet at night. Predator and prey fought their eternal battle for survival in darkness even more so than during the day. The scream of a fisher had been enough to make his blood run cold, but as he calmed himself and realised what it was, he'd been happy at having heard the secretive animal's banshee-like cry. The bickering quarrels of a band of coyotes in the distance got his attention, but actually kept him company as he walked along a game trail he'd discovered. It made for easier going. The voice of a great horned owl boomed through the trees. Several times, a cry he was more than familiar with, that of the red fox, floated out into the night. Then, all of a sudden, the coyotes fell silent, and so did everything else. He felt like ice as he remembered how an old trapper had once told him how the coyotes would go quiet when there was a bear around, and how you could train yourself to pick up on the smell of a bear. Just like the other animals around him, Thomas could sense that something else had entered the woods.

He knew Wyoming was home to both grizzly and black bear, as well as the out-of-place throwback he'd encountered back at the clearing. But again, instinct told him that it wasn't the usual residents of the state he needed to worry about. His mind suddenly flooded with every article he'd ever read about bear olfactory abilities. Most biologists agreed that bears had the finest sense of smell in the animal kingdom. He'd heard accounts of polar bears following the track of a seal for over forty miles. He'd seen videos of a Hollywood-trained grizzly bear track a small fillet of chicken three miles across a valley. He looked down at his tattered, blood-stained clothing. He thought about where he would have brushed up against bushes and trees as he walked. He felt ice cold, but he was in no doubt that Lucifer was back on his trail.

Thomas realised that if that was the case, outrunning the bear was not an option. And he had no strength or desire to consider climbing another tree. Something inside him stirred, a flicker of resistance and fire. He'd make a stand and wait for the bear to come to him. He'd use his lingering scent and the bear's sense of smell to his advantage. He tore a blooded rag of material away from his shirt. He'd lace the surrounding brush with it, then work his way to a position upwind. Sit down with his back against a sizeable tree and hope the bear would doggedly follow the trail and walk straight into the welcoming blast of the shotgun and its rifled slugs. He was out of options, out of strength, and would soon be out of time.

It was just then that Thomas noticed a light off to his left. It wasn't especially bright, but it was clear, small, and round. His heart leapt. *Thank God for hunters* Thomas thought, slightly amused at his sudden turn of luck, and the fact that wasn't how he usually regarded those who killed animals for sport. But he also knew many Wyoming hunters stocked their larders with their trophies, and right now, he was glad to see another human, especially one potentially armed. He mustered his strength to cut through the trees towards the light.

As he got within about a hundred feet, he called out. Whoever it was, he wanted them to know the thing coming through the brush at them was a person, not a game animal. He paused when no reply was made and found it odd. He called again as he continued to shuffle through the trees. Then, he stepped out onto an overgrown path that had been cut through the woodland and realised his mistake. What he had taken to be a hunter's headlamp, was in fact just a reflection of the moon...in the half-broken window of ramshackle, abandoned-looking shack.

CHAPTER TWENTY-TWO

The shack had a darkness to it. It reeked of neglect. As he approached the front door, he half expected it to turn to dust at his touch, but was surprised to find it both sturdy and intact. He reached for the handle, but the door creaked open by a crack as he did so. He pushed it open. A waft of rotten wood and mossy dampness seeped from the single room before him. An old, folding canvas bed lay in ruins to one side, consumed by rust and lichens. Opposite, a wooden desk teetered on its remaining three legs. Turkey tail fungi sprang from its joints and edges. An empty gun rack, with two rungs missing, was fixed to the far wall – hinting at the lodge's original purpose. Of all things inside the room, it was the humble, unpretentious, three-legged wooden stool that he was most pleased to see. Thomas simply stopped holding himself up, dropping onto the seat and staying there for some time as he gathered his thoughts.

He was in no doubt that the bear was tracking him. In a way, he admired its unfettered, uncompromisable purpose. It would not be stopped. Its single-mindedness was astounding. It was clearly capable of carrying a grudge. But, as he also reminded himself, he was the most likely accessible prey in the area: wounded, weak, and as he had realised, leaving a convenient, blood-smeared scent trail that led straight to him. His gaze was attracted to the object on the ceiling, that swung slowly and gently in the slight breeze. He reached up and took down the old oil lantern. Spurred into action, he emptied out the pannier onto the floor, and smiled. A small hand pouch of kerosene and a pack of waterproof matches were amongst the spoils. He tore off small strips of the canvas bed and stuffed them into the lantern's chamber. Ripping the kerosene open, he poured it over the fabric and lit it with a match.

The shack seemed to come alive, as the glow of the lantern threw light up onto the walls for the first time in however long it had been. Thomas realised, for the first time, he was not alone in the cabin. A family of dusky shrews scuttled underneath the bed. A deer mouse fled through the open door, out into the night. And a bushy-tailed woodrat scampered into the darkest corner of the room, sitting on its haunches and watching him. Thomas was surprised at its size, and guessed it was a male. Including its tail, it was nearly a foot and a half long. He started at the rodent. This was the original "packrat", and we wondered if tales about its affinity for storing shiny objects were true. Thomas fished out a coin from his pocket, a quarter, and threw it gently a few feet towards the woodrat. Obligingly, it scurried forward, and picked it up in its front paws. Then, it disappeared through a hole in the floor with its prize

Thomas wasn't accepting death just yet, but he appreciated the distraction of the woodrat that had helped calm his thoughts. He often wondered at times like these if the serendipitous nature of such moments and events were somehow orchestrated, if there perhaps really was some kind of influence being pushed by the unseen universe. Or, if, in a shack that offered good shelter to rodents and humans alike, he'd simple shared a tiny fragment of his life with an arboreal animal likely to be found in a forest in Wyoming. He guessed he would never know until it was all over, but was likely to find out soon if he didn't make preparations for Lucifer's arrival.

He decided to give the cabin a look from the outside. As he limped around its perimeter, he realised it was well situated. Its rear was set snug up against a rocky outcrop, and on both sides of the narrow trail that led to it were thick-trunked, closely knit Fremont cottonwood trees. Just as he had, the bear would have to approach the shack from the front. Thomas went back inside. He doubted the walls would withstand much of an assault from a 1,500lb bear, but he shut the door anyway, and was pleased to find it had a bolt that would hold it fast. He piled up the bed against it, then broke the remaining legs off of the desk and piled them and the flat work surface on top too. He dragged the shotgun and the stool over to the far corner opposite the door and sat down.

Thomas looked the weapon over. A simple slab of camouflage material, courtesy of Jesse, housed five shotgun shells as part of a handmade side-saddle for the gun, and was attached to its side with Velcro. Thomas realised that this was all the ammo he had, and he'd have to make it count. He took out two of the shells and examined them. Jesse's penchant for overkill was something Thomas was suddenly thankful for. The shells were 8-pellet, 000 buckshot rounds. They offered enough punch to take out a black bear at close range, let alone the small game he had intended to hunt whilst camping. But the bear he was taking on was three times the size of an average blackie. And once Lucifer arrived, he knew getting off more than two shots would be pushing it. And in the time it took to reload, the bear would be on him. Two shots at most. The first would have to work hard for its money.

Thomas took out the knife and began to perform surgery on two of the shells. He left the metal bottoms of each shell alone, and instead focused on the tight plastic tube that contained the pellets. He deftly used the blade to cut through the plastic about halfway up each shell, running the knife along the circumference. He made sure that the cut did not run the complete way around, stopping just before where he'd started cutting each side. Each shell was now a bastardised slug. Buckshot had a much-reduced spread compared to birdshot, which is why it was favoured for both larger game and home defence. It offered greater penetrating power at shorter range, as long as you had decent enough aim to make up for the narrower path the shot pellets would travel. The simple customisation he had made to the shells would make them even more devastating. Instead of bursting out of the end of the shell, the cut in the plastic wrapping would mean less explosive force outwards, concentrating the pellets into an even more compact barrage of lead – which he'd be firing directly at Lucifer's chest. In short, he'd turned the pellet of shot into a missile with the same stopping power as a big bore bullet. He hoped the obstacles he'd placed at the door would force the bear to stand up, even if just for a few moments, and give him his shot.

Thomas closed his eyes and slowed his breathing by taking deep, long draws of air and holding them in for a short period before exhaling. After a little while, the rise and fall of his chest became shallower, and his hearing tuned into the sounds of the forest surrounding him. Somewhere, out in the darkness, a pure powerhouse of bad attitude was moving in on the cabin. And Thomas was relying on the forest to let him know when it got close. He didn't have to wait long. A barred owl, off in the distance and to the northwest of the cabin, let out a panicked alarm call. He listened to the bird of prey get nearer until it flew over the cabin and beyond, shrieking its warning cry on silent wings as it went. Logic dictated the owl was flying in the opposite direction from that which danger approached.

Instinct kicked in and he tensed as every living thing within a few hundred yards of the cabin fell silent. Unlike before, the bear was quiet too. No more games. No more bravado. It was a reckoning. Thomas remained silent, his eyes still closed. He tilted his head slightly, lifting his ear towards the half-smashed window. A cold breeze rushed through it into the cabin, testing the strength of the rotted wooden frame in a full-frontal blast, before it was redirected upwards through the cracks and fissures in the remaining glass, then sucking itself into the interior through the vortex of the broken pane. The movement of the air created a reverberation that sounded like a small whine, like that he'd heard made by wolves. He had no way of knowing if his mind was playing tricks on him, giving muster to the sound as he imagined Lucifer, pained with hunger and his wounds, staring through the blackness at the cabin's front door. *It was just the wind* he reminded himself. He lent forward slightly, lifting the gun up towards the hastily prepared barricade. The three-legged stool cried a creak of strain as he did.

Something hit the front of the cabin with all the force and suddenness of a freight train. Thomas opened his eyes in a flash, and locked onto the door, which buckled on its frame and then gave in entirely. It fell lopsided against the heap of furniture on the inside, and Lucifer's disfigured muzzle pushed through the space between the door and the frame. The bear let out a disgruntled huff as it stood up on to its full height. The top of its head lifted the ceiling off of the cabin, as rotted timber and rusted ironmongery were matched against

Lucifer's sheer strength. The same paws and claws that dislodged and overturned boulders weighing hundreds of pounds, flipped the corrugated sheets and latticework of beams that made up the roof with ease. As it smashed to the ground in pieces, Lucifer placed his front paws over what remained of the front of the cabin and looked down at Thomas.

Saliva dripped from the bear's jaw in a steady stream, thick like syrup. The animal had a stink about it of rotted meat. Thomas wondered if its disfigurements meant it couldn't eat properly, allowing some of its food to lodge and decay within its twisted teeth and matted fur. Lucifer yowled as he pressed his weight against the cabin. At first, it seemed as if it could take more of a beating than Thomas had thought, but then the doorframe and some of the timber to the front splintered and broke, folding on top of the pile. Lucifer began to climb the rubble, as if it were a scree slope. The bear roared as it scrabbled, rearing up again on its hind legs to bat away the debris with its front paws. Thomas saw his opening.

In a flash, Thomas was on his feet, having reserved all his remaining strength for this moment. He pushed his back against the rear wall of the cabin and hooked his good foot around the three-legged stool. With a deft kick, he sent it flying into the bear's face, making it look up and distracting it further. Thomas fired, and knew instantly that he'd hit the bear and his plan had worked. Lucifer reared up and staggered backwards, as if in shock that something had the punch to knock the wind out of him. But the blast had done more than that. The bear slammed onto its side, and it kicked and pawed at the air as it tried to scrabble back to its feet. It righted itself, and lay on the floor, panting and whoofing in wounded disbelief. As it rose to all fours, Thomas detected a distinct wobble in its stance, and as it swung its head around to look at him, he pulled the trigger again. He hadn't had time to make the same adjustments to the second shell, but at such close range, the triple aught buckshot acted as effectively as a broadside from eight cannons. Each lead sphere was a third of an inch in diameter and exploded from the barrel of the shotgun at a speed of 1,200 feet per second. The spread of the shot was limited by the few yards it had to travel, only straying slightly from its intended target of the tender spot behind the shoulder and forelimb. The heart and lungs of the animal were planted deep inside the chest cavity, much further back than most thought, especially when the bear was on all fours. Thomas had sworn at, and encouraged the prosecution of many bow hunters, stunned by an escaping bear with a broadhead buried in nothing but muscle.

The bear roared and reared up on its hindlegs again. Thomas could see the deep red stain that seeped from its chest wound, and he noticed that Lucifer no longer stood tall and confidently. Instead, he teetered violently, his right side buckling from the combined effect of his mass and the buckshot that had peppered his hide. Thomas thought he'd at least evened the odds, what with his own mobility compromised. But he wasn't done yet. He hurled the lantern at the pile of broken furniture and parts of the structure brought down by the bear with all the force he could muster. The glass smashed, and the flame leapt at its chance to escape the confinement of its prison. The oil doused the wood, and the cool mountain breeze fed the fire, building it into a blaze in a matter of seconds.

Thomas half fell, half ran at the smashed window ahead of him. Neither it, nor the remnants of the wooden wall beneath it offered him much resistance. Thomas envisaged something a little more athletic and heroic than simply falling through the timber like a dead weight, but it got the job done. His head spun as he clawed his way back to his feet, stumbling sideways as he desperately sought out the bear. It was ahead of him, staring straight at him. As the cabin burned, Thomas was unnerved by the bear's fixed gaze, as both its good eye and its opaque, frosted-over, damaged one both seemed set on him. Small embers burned at the end of its fur, and as they extinguished, wisps of grey smoke rose from its great back.

"You sure live up to you name, Lucifer," Thomas exclaimed in awe.

The bear growled its reply. The sound seemed to amplify as it crossed the ground between them. It hung low in the air, and Thomas could feel the reverberations in his chest. It reminded him of the sonar clicks he'd experienced whilst diving with sperm whales off the coast of Dominica. The sound moved through him rather than around him. Thomas realised he had dropped the shotgun as he fell, barely holding onto it with one hand as he had been. The pannier was lost, left back in the cabin – not that it would have offered much help. He accepted his luck had run out, and slowly drew the knife from its sheath.

The roar was explosive and filled with savage intent. But it didn't come from the bear. Attacking from behind, Tama launched at Lucifer. She leapt, anchoring her hind claws into the bear's rump as her front paws spread wide across its back. Before Lucifer could throw her off, she sank her fangs deep into the bear's shoulder. Her nine-inch canines passed either side of the bear's spinal column and stayed there as the bear collapsed. She lifted her head, making ready to deliver a killing bite to the back of the neck. But Lucifer wasn't done yet. However, the fight in him had gone, and survival instinct was kicking in. He shot forward, crashing dangerously into the trees as Tama slipped from his back. She growled, as the bear skirted past, giving them a wide berth as it headed back towards the higher ground. Thomas wondered how far it would get. He could feel his own strength leaving him. He knew he shouldn't stare at Tama, but he couldn't take his gaze away. A sabre-toothed cat stood before him and was likely about to kill him.

It wouldn't be the first time Thomas had faced and fought a sabretooth, but he decided it would be the last. She bore little resemblance to the creature he'd discovered in Scotland, but he knew from Jericho had told him, it had been her father. Whereas the Highland sabre had been melanistic, bearing a black coat that all but hid the spots it had inherited from its Jaguar mother, Tama was a rust red colour. Her fur was also longer and coarser, giving way to blonde tufts at the tips of her ears and on her underbelly. Thomas guessed these characteristics came from her mountain lion mother. Thomas remembered the raw intelligence and the sentient soul he had seen in the eyes of the cat he'd killed, and how that light had been extinguished when it died. Ever since, the creature had been taxidermized and put on display in the Hintze Hall at the Natural History Museum in London. It guarded the main stairway that led to the upper galleries, dwarfed only by the skeleton of "Hope", the museum's blue whale, hanging above it. Thomas had never seen it.

Thomas dropped the knife and sank to his knees. He watched Tama as she padded up to him. There was no need for caution in her approach. She paused only when her own face was inches from his own. Her nose wrinkled slightly, but she didn't growl or move closer. Instead, she huffed and brushed past him, disinterested and seemingly unimpressed.

Thomas looked down at his torn and bloodied clothing, confused. He sniffed his shirt and pulled back as he caught the scent. He knew it was only blood and sweat, and should've had the opposite effect on Tama. It would have been the equivalent of the waft of a butter-basted steak frying in a pan. It didn't make sense.

"I wouldn't eat me either," Thomas slurred as his mind began to fog.

He collapsed onto his back and watched the star-filled sky spin as he quickly drifted into unconsciousness.

CHAPTER TWENTY-THREE

Catherine looked down at Cassie, who had a huge beam of a smile on her face. She could see that bench seats and sitting upfront with the grownups was a new favourite thing for her. Nina Lee was driving Thomas's 1979 Chevy Blazer, which he called "Beast". She was going to be their tour guide for the day, as they explored the nearby Thunder Basin National Grasslands.

"So, is it Jesse that I can blame for Thomas's love affair with modified trucks?" Catherine asked, raising an eyebrow.

"I don't really have an issue you blaming Jesse for anything," Nina laughed. "But, for that, we're all kind of guilty. You kind of have to make your own kind of entertainment out here."

"You and Jesse were…?" Catherine implied, wary of saying anything in front of Cassie.

"Yeah," Nina replied. "Things stopped making sense last year, so we, uh, you know."

Catherine nodded.

"Getting bitten by one of those things of his was just an excuse. It's not like I'm not used to dangerous animals," Nina added, nodding at the wolf lying down in the back.

"I like Chakky," Cassie chirped, still smiling.

"Me too," Nina laughed. "Although I've never heard him called Chakky before. Achak is difficult to say though, isn't it?"

Cassie nodded, a serious expression on her face.

"What do you think of my office?" Nina asked Cassie, nodding at the green expanse beyond the windshield.

Catherine allowed Cassie to stand up on the seat, freeing her from the practically redundant lap belt. Cassie placed her hands on the dashboard and looked out through the glass. Her eyes bulged as she took in the sight.

A huge swathe of green swept from the bumpy dirt track they were driving along, down to the horizon. Swirls of yellow prairie grass punctuated the thick sagebrush. In the distance, they could see pinkish orange outcrops and rock towers that stood stark against the skyline. Catherine noticed that the grassland wasn't flat though. It rolled, from hillocks carpeted in blue grama grass to escarpments blanketed in vibrant green herbaceous plants.

"It's incredible," Catherine commented. Cassie nodded.

"It's completely unique," Nina explained. "The prairie is made up of things like viper grass and pepper weed – over fifty different species in fact. And there's something special about this place, in the summer, it is a blanket of different flowers, but almost all of them are purple. Western prairie clover, cottonrose, dotted blazingstar – even the cacti have purple flowers."

"It sounds beautiful," Catherine said, awed.

"But, we don't want to look at boring old grass do we?" Nina teased Cassie. "Want to check out some prairie dogs?"

"Yes!" Cassie yelled.

"Just to be clear, they're not actual dogs munchkin," Catherine explained. "They're more like big squirrels that live in the ground."

"They're still really cool though, and very important," Nina added. "And, if we're lucky, we might get to see something much rarer on the lookout for them too."

After about twenty minutes more driving, Nina pulled over on to the crest of a small hill.

"If you guys take a look through your binoculars, over there, you'll see one of our grassland specialists," Nina pointed.

Cassie pouted, impatiently waiting for Catherine to fish out her binoculars from her daypack. She had been shown how to use the robust Nikon Prostaff 7S glasses. They were light, waterproof, and fog proof, and covered in rubber armouring in case she dropped them. One thing Catherine and Thomas agreed on, was the need for good optics when it came to watching wildlife. Catherine extracted her own Zeiss Victory model, with 10x magnification, and raised them to her eyes. Nina in turn viewed through her own battered Nikon pair, but smiled when Cassie noticed they were the same brand as hers.

"What you're hopefully looking at are pronghorn," Nina said. "They're the only surviving species of their kind, leftover from the Pleistocene. They're not actually antelopes and are more closely related to giraffes and okapi from Africa than they are deer."

They watched the pronghorn graze and pass on over a ridge before Nina indicated they could get out and walk for a little while. They didn't have far to go. There was a small ridge to their west, where a weather station and some camouflage netting had been set up. Catherine noticed Nina was carrying some foam roll mats with her. She lay them on the ground, in front of the netting. She placed a finger on her lips and showed Catherine and Cassie how to get into position by crawling forward. A wide slit was cut through the fabric, and they had an uninterrupted view of a pristine patch of grassland.

"Welcome to prairie dog town," Nina whispered.

"Why are you studying them?" Catherine asked, fascinated.

"They're a vital component of the ecosystem," Nina replied. "But, I need to prove that to the powers that be. Not only are they an important prey species for predators like ferruginous hawks and swift foxes, but their tunnels also provide homes for species like burrowing owls and mountain plovers. The Forest Service is considering scrapping the current protection scheme, and I'm trying to convince them otherwise."

Nina noticed Cassie's confused look. "Let's see if we can make this a little easier, shall we?" she smiled.

Nina walked to the back of the truck and opened up the glass panel of the trunk lid. She took out what looked like a telescope, mounted on a short tripod of just a few inches. She brought it back to the little viewing hide and placed it down between her and Cassie. Nina looked through the eyepiece and made a few adjustments. The spotting scope was a Bushnell Sentry, with 50x magnification. Like most of her equipment, she had bought it personally, and through eBay.

"Okay Cassie, we have a customer for you," Nina said.

She helped Cassie get in position over the eyepiece. Then she directed Catherine where she should look with her binoculars, before picking up her own. As she turned the focus dial a few notches, the animal they were all looking at appeared in sharp detail. Sitting upright on its haunches, a relatively small, fawn coloured rodent observed the surrounding area. It looked back and forth with sharp, twitchy head movements from right to left. Nina smiled as it dropped to all fours, and its small, curved tail shook furiously as it let out a series of short barks.

"And now you can see why they're called black-tailed prairie dogs," Nina commented.

"So cute," Cassie chuffed.

"I thought you'd like them," Nina smiled.

At the sound of the barks, other prairie dogs began to appear from their burrows. Some loped and hopped a few steps from the entrances, immediately beginning to browse and feed.

"They probably heard the truck's engine and ducked back underground," Nina explained. "And that sound they were making is why they're called prairie dogs Cassie – it sounds like a bark doesn't it?"

Cassie nodded.

"And they're clever like dogs too. They have a different sounding bark for each threat they come across. It lets the others know what to do...hello? What do we have here?"

Nina raised her binoculars again and swung them left, towards a small patch of scrubby grass that edged the prairie dog town. Catherine copied her, whilst Cassie continued to happily watch the rodents through the scope.

"Black-footed ferret," Nina mouthed silently to Catherine.

Catherine tracked the progress of something moving fast and low to the ground, as she saw tussocks of grass shake and shudder as it passed. Its direction was clear, headed straight for the prairie dog town. Suddenly, a small, intelligent-looking face bearing the mask of a bandit, poked out from the grass. The ferret had an almost pure white chin, cheeks and nose, whilst its big round eyes sat in a stripe of grey and caramel. Despite being a ruthless predator, Catherine thought it made the animal look incredibly endearing.

"America's only native species of ferret," Nina explained. "There's only 600 of them left in the wild, and all of them can be traced back to just seven individuals. But here, we have introduced a small number of cloned animals. They have three times the genetic variation of their wild counterparts, helping us stave off their extinction and increase genetic diversity. Even so, they're still the most endangered animal in the United States."

"How come?" Catherine asked. She had read about the use of genetic tools developed by a group called the Richter foundation, and how they were using them to protect and preserve endangered species. She was impressed to see them already having a positive impact.

"Habitat loss, and a plague that affected prairie dog populations on the Great Plains. We're lucky here, as our burrow hounds weren't impacted. But that little predator is one of the reasons I'm trying to get them, and this area protected. The diet of a black-footed ferret is ninety percent prairie dog."

Suddenly, a series of shrill, continuous barks rose up from the sentry they'd all first observed at one of the burrow entrances, as it too spotted the approach of the predator. The ferret reacted by bounding a few steps almost casually, no longer concerned at concealing itself. The prairie dogs scattered, disappearing into the burrows as the alarm continued to sound. All except one, which the ferret seemed to zone in on as a result. The prairie dog was quite large and was sitting next to a burrow entrance. However, rather than disappear down this particular one, it dashed forwards, towards the ferret. The lithe predator was happy to oblige in the strange game of chase it seemed to be initiating. In a few seconds, the prairie dog reached a different burrow and shot into it. The ferret didn't hesitate, following it straight in. Catherine put a protective arm around Cassie, unsure about what they might see next.

"It's okay, I don't think you'll have to worry," Nina said, amused. "This is quite a young ferret, and he hasn't quite learned the ropes yet. And I think our prairie dog has a little surprise for him."

Sure enough, the ferret reappeared almost immediately, tumbling out of a tunnel entrance and leaping high into the air in a backflip, landing on its feet and facing the burrow with teeth bared, uttering a high-pitched yikker of annoyance. Hot on its heels was not a prairie dog, as Catherine had suspected, but a small bird – an owl. At first glance she mistook it for a little owl, a species she was familiar with from the UK. However, she quickly realised it was a burrowing owl, a species Nina had made reference to earlier. Just like the little owl, the species was predominantly a milk-chocolate brown colour, with white speckles and bars across its chest, head, and back. It also had the piercing – almost glowing yellow eyes, and furrowed brow, that made them look like they were in a permanent state of furiousness. The owl certainly seemed irate enough as it opened out its wings and hopped menacingly at the ferret, which backed off again. The owl tucked its wings behind its back and strutted on its out-of-proportion long legs, jutting out its head and snapping its hooked beak. The ferret took the hint and bounded back to the scrub. Once there, it raised up on its hind legs and gave a cry of retort before hopping back down to all fours and disappearing into the long grass. Catherine watched, amazed, as the prairie dog sentry reappeared and barked the all-clear. Within half a minute, the rest of the prairie dogs had joined the sentinel and got back to their breakfasts.

They kept watching for another half hour before Nina suggested they head back to the truck and perhaps down to the river. As Nina drove, Catherine checked the GPS tracker she'd been using to keep an eye on Thomas through the app on her phone. She knew reception was patchy, so she told herself not to jump to any wild conclusions when she noticed the tracker had seemingly stopped responding. But it quickly began to eat away at her. As far as she could see, the GPS hadn't moved, nor responded in over twelve hours. Nina caught her looking up at the sky and back across to a ridgeline to the west.

"What's up?" she enquired, the concern in her voice real.

"I'm sure it's nothing," Catherine shrugged, "but roughly where would you say these co-ordinates are in relation to here?"

Nina glanced at the screen as Catherine held up her phone, then lifted her head towards the ridge.

"You were thinking right – it's the other side of the ridge from here," Nina replied. "Back over towards the house and the reservation. Probably about twelve miles in a straight line. Fair few more to get close by road."

Nina followed Catherine's gaze towards the ridgeline.

"You know, a lot of things can interfere with GPS. Sunspots, weather – maybe he dropped it in a creek, or even turned if off?" she added.

"I know, you're probably right," Catherine sighed. She could half imagine Thomas turning it off, not wanting to be tracked and enjoying the outdoors. She'd like to think he wasn't quite so irresponsible, but knew full well he certainly could be on occasion.

"We'll make a call or two and head that way if it doesn't change when we get to the river, and we're a bit more out in the open," Nina offered.

Nina parked the truck up on a long sweeping bank of grassy dunes. Beyond was a slope that ran down to a bubbling river with multiple cascades. Catherine realised they had moved much closer to the mountains and the ridgeline. On the other side of the water was a woodline that became denser as she followed it upwards. Nina walked around the truck, phone in hand, as she let Achak out by opening the tailgate. The big wolf padded casually down to the water and took a drink. Nina put the phone away and opened up Catherine's door, breaking her distracted gaze.

"So, Jesse is going to get some gear together and see if he can catch up with Thomas," Nina explained. "He's also going to speak to the sheriff and see if they can get a bird up to take a looksee. I imagine nothing will thrill Jesse more than probably having to come to Thomas's aid."

"I get that," Catherine laughed, "and thank you". She paused for a moment. "That Jesse-Thomas thing...does he blame Thomas for what happened to his father?"

"Unfairly of course, but I think so. Jesse isn't great at letting things go."

"Bodes well for you."

Both women laughed and sat down on the bank, watching Achak follow Cassie around like a puppy. Suddenly, the wolf went on alert and pointed its nose towards the far bank and the woodline. They all followed suit, and soon they could hear something large moving through the brush. Whatever it was moved quickly and was making its way directly to the river. Nina and Catherine jumped up. As Nina moved to the back of the truck, to get her standard issue Smith & Wesson Model 686 .357 magnum revolver from her pack, Catherine ran forward and grabbed Cassie. A meadowlark took to the air in alarm, as a large black shape crashed past the tree it sat in. Then, with a snort, the animal broke free of the wood and thundered down the remainder of the slope before coming to a wrenching halt at the river's edge. It stared at them across the water, great billows of air venting from its nostrils as it took a moment's pause.

"Look mummy," Cassie cooed, "Kan".

"Khan," Catherine whispered in quiet disbelief.

The stallion dropped its head to the water and drank thirstily. Catherine dropped Cassie back on her feet and took a few steps towards the horse. Khan immediately raised his head and turned to look at her.

"Okay, I'd say we definitely have a problem," said Nina. "I'd better update Jesse, then we have to figure out how we're going to get that damned horse under control and somewhere safe."

"I think he's hurt," Catherine murmured as she took another step.

Khan whinnied, and stamped his foot, sending a tower of water straight up into the air with the force. Catherine froze. But Cassie moved forward and stretched out her hand. Khan took two steps into the river, and then another. He hesitated for the briefest of moments, then forded the rest of the river. It wasn't especially deep, barely touching his belly as he made his way across. He stepped out onto the bank, his jet-black hide shining with moisture from the spray. Catherine could see his nostrils rising and falling rapidly as they still worked hard to refill the air in his lungs. He dropped his head and flicked his ears in a sign of submission. Catherine took the risk of moving along his side and towards his rump. She examined the scratches and cuts, concluding they weren't serious. Her hand moved up instinctively and she ran her fingers back along the horse's back and into his mane. To her surprise, he let her do so without protest.

"Jesse is going to head out as soon as he can," Nina reassured.

Catherine looked up at the ridgeline lost in thought.

"The quickest route would still be up and over, right?" she asked Nina.

Nina nodded.

"Would you be willing to take Cassie back to yours so your mother can watch her, then make your way to me? Hopefully we'll all meet in the same place?" Catherine asked.

Nina nodded again.

~

Lucifer could find no solace for the pain. He'd plunged into a lake, completely submerging himself, and whilst the cool water soothed him a little, it didn't end the agony. He'd bitten at the wounds and torn at his own flesh, but again, the sensation acted as a distraction yet offered no cure. He wandered without purpose, instinctively taking the paths that offered him least resistance. As he left the trees, he found a wide, clear, river of stone that was easy to walk on. He followed it south and downhill. He left bloodied tracks of his paw prints in his wake. Then, a new series of scents began to waft in his direction, beckoning him. Biology kicked in, and the surge of adrenaline acted as a natural painkiller. He felt weak, which caused hesitation. He'd never experienced panic or uncertainty before, and it felt dangerous. But hunger and rage drove him on, albeit at the limited, lumbering pace his injuries afforded him.

As he rounded a corner, he stopped. The stone river led down to a dwelling similar to the one he'd encountered the man and the cat at, both of which were responsible for his wounds. He growled and huffed. He pushed down with his paws violently, sending a trickle of loose stone down along the edge of the trail. He swung his head to and fro, popping his jaws in warning as he approached. New scents came to him now, one of which he recognised as wolf. A low, penetrating rumble of warning built in his chest. No answer or challenge came back. He left the stone river, and travelled along the side of the dwelling, lifting his head and sniffing loudly. A straight and narrow path made of dead timber surrounded the dwelling. As he tested the small incline that led to it, it creaked loudly under his weight. Something stirred inside the dwelling. A soft, gentle, inquisitive call rang out. The scent of the wolf was strong, and all around. But Lucifer was certain this was prey. Perhaps the canine had been unable to get inside the dwelling. The bear saw no such obstacle.

As he had done before, he rose up on his hind legs and pressed hard against the wooden barrier. The strain on the dwelling was evident in groans from the timber, and a subtle sound of splintering that helped Lucifer zone in on the weakest point. Without hesitating, he smashed through as the wood gave way. He lumbered through the cave-like interior, which was cluttered with strange objects. A large boulder moved easily as he brushed up against it, and he was surprised to find it soft to the touch. He could smell the downy feathers inside it, and pine oil. Just as if it were a fallen tree, he tore it apart with quick slashes of his paws. He nosed through the inside, finding a strange substance that had the texture of flesh, but no scent or taste. The feathers scattered, some sticking to his blood-clotted fur. Another sound now, this time of movement. There was an opening that led deeper in, and there, something was making its way down an incline, towards him.

Lucifer recognised the animal as similar to the humans he'd encountered before, but instinctively knew this was a female. The gentle call came again, then the animal stopped in its tracks. Predator and prey met each other's gaze in an unblinking stare. The female bolted sideways, making for the outside. Lucifer's instinct kicked in and he charged, breaking through the wall between them. She skitted backwards, into another section, and Lucifer followed. He was temporarily halted by the new aromas of food. Salts, fats and oils all lingered here. But he would not be swayed by them – his prey now seemed cornered. As the female moved again, towards something dark and metallic, he saw the spark of flame and roared. He felt the heat as she threw a piece of hide onto it and it immediately ignited. Then his world went black as she flicked it in his direction, and it covered his face.

The fire hooked into his flesh, and fear flooded his body. He rose up, panicked and roaring as he thrashed. The burning hide fell away from his face, and he could see again. The female had moved again and was now holding a long black stick. Lucifer recognised the weapon as that which had caused the pain he now suffered with endlessly. He gave no warning. He charged, knocking his prey to the ground. His jaws closed over her shoulder, and he bit down with savage force. The taste of blood flooded over his tongue, and he half gulped, half chewed. But then, he felt the heat again, and he dropped his meal, turning to find its source. There was a sound like thunder, and he was suddenly unable to hold himself up anymore. He collapsed, gnashing his jaws as he watched his prey crawl and slither backwards in its own blood. He couldn't stop her as the wall behind gave way and she put further distance between them. Blood bubbled in his nostrils as he desperately tried to power his huge limbs forward. But his strength was gone. The flames reached out for him one final time, and he felt their cruel, stabbing touch. In a last act of defiance, his heart stopped beating before they could take him.

~

Catherine hadn't been sure if Khan would let her approach. But, it seemed his exertion and the presence of Cassie seemed to coerce him towards surrendering to her will. She couldn't help but wonder if the horse had somehow sought them out, if it had been his intention to find them and maybe lead them back to Thomas. She'd heard such stories, with both dogs and horses. Either way, Khan had let her mount him, and was now headed back up into the trees. She occasionally checked the GPS position on the app, but the horse seemed to know where he was headed. Catherine decided she would trust him, and only check again if he changed direction – she was anxious enough as it was already, and she knew that could make Khan nervous.

Wearing a cream-coloured Stetson hat with an orange and brown leather trim, western jeans, and a thick, plumb-coloured plaid shirt beneath her black, fleece-lined jacket, she couldn't help the excitement she felt as she guided the horse through the incredible vista of the Wyoming landscape. Under different circumstances, this was what dreams were made of. She loved Scotland and had seen Africa. But she could now understand why Thomas was so in awe of this place, why it was special to him. It wasn't just the memories and the people. Here, the mountains and forests were etched on a landscape of unprecedented scale. Untamed wildlife, including apex predators, made up pristine ecosystems that resisted, yet were still vulnerable to, the encroachment of humans. She found it devastatingly sad to think that something hunters, fishers, and the general public in the towns behind them took for granted, was something Scotland had lost. Back home, there was no balance to the ecosystem, no natural checks and balances with the lack of keystone species and predators. It proved to her how vital the lynx reintroduction project was, and why she must succeed with it. She hoped that those in America who lived side by side with wildlife would cherish what they had before they lost it, or worse, deliberately destroyed it.

She'd packed what she could from the car and Nina's own stash into her daypack, covering everything from food and water to as much first aid as she could carry. Nina had also given her a laminated sheet that showed radio frequencies for all the local authorities in the area, from the Forest Service to Fish and Wildlife units on patrol. Despite the sense of adventure, she was on alert for the slightest anomaly. The brim of the hat shielded her from the reach of the afternoon sun and allowed her to scan the hillside up to the horizon. Nothing seemed out of place. She could see Khan was traversing a well-worn game trail, noticing the deer tracks that led back down towards the river. Judging by the size, she presumed they were mule deer. She knew that what in the US were known as elk, could be found here too. But these were very closely related to the red deer at home, whose tracks she knew well – and were not to be confused with moose, which Europeans unhelpfully knew as elk. Further up, another set of tracks that resembled the wild cats she was also familiar with, caught her attention. Too small for mountain lion or even lynx, she guessed at bobcat. But still, nothing out of the ordinary – at least for Wyoming.

Catherine skirted the ridge and passed into an area of thick forest. They had been riding for three hours and Khan's calm demeanour and gentle pace reassured her that there was no immediate threat in the area. It felt colder here though, and she zipped her coat up a little more. She patted Khan hard on his neck and thanked the horse for leading the way. As far as she could tell, they were still headed straight for Thomas. But a few minutes later, Khan veered away from the steady northeast direction he'd been travelling and began to head directly east. Now, she was uncertain. She was about to pull on the reins, when she noticed that a horse had been this way before – hoofprints along the track going back the way they had come. Given that they were undisturbed she deduced they were fresh, and as she couldn't imagine another horse out here in the last 24 hours, it could only be that Khan was retracing his steps. As she realised that Khan was in fact using the terrain to his advantage and dropping down into a wide gully, she let him be. Then, as the trees gave way to scrub, she could see that it opened out into an open clearing. At its centre, she could see the scar of a burnt-out fire. She instinctively touched Khan's flanks with her heels, and the horse broke into a sudden gallop.

Reaching the remnants of the fire, she swung down from the saddle and examined the ground. The mix of charcoal and mud made reading the ground easy, even with the mismatch of overlapping prints she could see. Bear, horse, and boot tracks crossed back and forth. As she neared where the fire had been piled up, she also found the smooth-soled prints of another person. Her eyes snapped to the woodline as she realised Thomas had discovered the Native American they'd been told about. It was a threat she hadn't considered. She walked towards the trees slowly, acutely aware that she had no weapons with her. But her gaze was brought back to the ground as she noticed the grass was smeared with an oil-like stain and pushed over. As she knelt, she realised it was blood. If the Native American was still alive, he had clearly been badly hurt. But he wasn't her priority. She worked her way back to the other side of the clearing.

Catherine reached out for Khan's reins and pulled on them to lead him on, but the horse whinnied in disagreement. She looked at him, confused, and looked around again. But everything she knew about animal behaviour was telling her that Khan was not frightened, he just didn't want to follow her. She pulled on the reins again, as if to reassure him. This time, Khan reared up on his hind legs and kicked out with his front hooves, before smashing them into the ground defiantly. As she considered how she was going to win a battle of wills with a horse that weighed every bit of a 1,000lbs and had the stubbornness of a wild mustang in its DNA, Khan turned a half circle, pulling her along with him. He took a few steps, and she went with him, examining the ground as she had before. She saw the boot tracks again and smiled. She took some comfort knowing that Thomas and the Native American had apparently headed in very different directions. The smile vanished when she noticed the splashes of blood that dotted the trail. She swung herself back up into the saddle.

"You lead, I'll follow," she said, patting the horse heavily on the neck.

Khan responded with a snort of acceptance. He trotted forward, soon reaching the treeline and stepping along a new trail. Catherine kept her eyes to the ground, following the path of matted, pressed down grass. There were no footprints here, and she had to assume it was Thomas she was following, and not some irrelevant animal. For a moment, her mind wandered, and she imagined Khan leading her completely astray, becoming lost amidst the snow-capped peaks of the Bighorn mountains. But she shook it off, having faith in both the horse and herself. She'd tracked him this far, and if the blood was anything to go by, he was unlikely to have gone far.

As an hour ticked by, doubt began to creep in again, when she noticed a diversion off of the game trail Khan was following. It led left. Although severely overgrown and at first glance, as wild as the rest of the surrounding forest – something about it made her pause. The edges to the trail were square, as if they had once been shaped that way. As she stared at it harder, she realised that unlike the natural trail she was following, this new path had to have been manmade. She steered Khan towards it, and she instantly picked up on the horse's unease. Something was putting him on edge. As they passed a sandy bank of soil, she noticed the oversized pawprint etched into it. It was clear where its maker had entered the trail between two trees, sending a cascade of loosened earth down the bank in its wake. She marvelled at its size and urged Khan on. Then, for a moment, the boughs of the trees above parted, and she saw smoke rising above the canopy. It didn't seem to be coming from far away. She spurred Khan on.

Catherine smelt the smouldering remnants of the cabin before she saw them. But, as she rounded a corner, Khan whinnied and broke into a gallop. She couldn't help the smile when she saw Thomas propped up against a pile of half burnt logs. He weakly raised a hand and tried to smile. He looked about as banged up as she had ever seen him. His hair was a mop of sweat and caked, dried blood. Soot and mud did a poor job of covering the multitude of scratches over his face. His left eye was severely bloodshot. He'd torn a sleeve off of his coat to make into a temporary sling, and as she neared, she could see the heavy staining on his trouser leg.

"The first rule of getting lost is to stay where you are," Catherine addressed him in a scold, as she swung down from the saddle.

"Watch your step, we're not alone," Thomas croaked in a half-smile, pointing at a patch of ground ahead of him.

Catherine gasped at the small, coiled form that was ominously still on the path ahead of her. The midget faded rattlesnake was creamy grey in colour and blended almost perfectly with the dull sandy soil beneath it. Living up to its name, the dorsal blotches of squared patterning that lined its back seemed diluted, adding further to its camouflage.

"He may be small, but he packs quite the punch," Thomas warned. "Most potent venom of the Pacific and western rattlers".

Catherine approached carefully, but confidently.

"And, like most snakes, not deliberately aggressive," she explained as she picked up a lengthy fallen pine branch. "It's a stalemate – its waiting to see if you move away. It doesn't know you can see it."

As Catherine got closer, the snake lifted its head and swung its body in her direction. As she had suggested, the movement seemed casual and curious. The snake pulsed its coils, moving backwards a few inches towards the brush, but didn't give its namesake warning of a distinctive rattle.

"I was an RSPCA Inspector for some time, remember," Catherine chimed. "Animals aren't difficult to figure out for me."

"Just people then?" Thomas mocked.

As Catherine took another slow step forward, the snake decided that it was time to move on, and it crossed the path, disappearing into the nooks and crannies of the rocky bank beyond the path. Khan walked up to where the serpent had disappeared and snorted his disapproval. He then trotted up to Thomas, joining Catherine at his side. She already had her daypack open. She handed a large canteen of water to him as she fished out the first aid supplies. She also handed him a bag of cheeseburger flavoured beef jerky, slapping it into his chest a little flippantly. She noticed him wince and looked him over.

"Ribs," he whispered, apologetically. "Hence the sling. Keeps the pressure off."

Catherine used scissors to cut away the material from Thomas's leg. She could see the impromptu job he'd done with the superglue and was amazed it had held so well. She cleaned meticulously, pausing when she noticed the dirt embedded in the waxy residue of the glue.

"I'm going to have to open this up again and clean it out, then I'll stitch you up," she explained.

Thomas nodded. He had seen her apply veterinary care to many animals, including their own dogs. He didn't doubt or question her.

Catherine laboured intently and in silence. Despite the odd jab of pain, the jerky and the water had done much to revive him. But he knew he'd still lost a lot of blood.

"I think your ribs are just very badly bruised," Catherine stated, not looking up. "Is it painful to breathe?"

"A little, but not as much as before," Thomas admitted.

Catherine paused as she considered what to do. "I'm going to stabilise you with dressings, then I'm going to give you a shot of co-codamol, and you can have some of this as well," she said, passing him what looked like a small, green whistle. "It's methoxyflurane."

Thomas turned the cylinder around in his hand and held it up to the light to examine it in a squint.

"You inhale it, you idiot," Catherine said, shaking her head.

She strapped up Thomas's side with padding and bandages, after cleaning the scrapes and cuts. Thomas took sharp intakes of breath and winced at every touch, but otherwise didn't complain. She examined her inventory, then gave him some co-codamol tablets, as well as a dose of high-grade ibuprofen. Along with the methoxyflurane, it soon began to have an effect, and she could feel his muscles relaxing as she worked.

"I obviously have no idea if you have internal injuries or bleeding, but it doesn't seem so," Catherine determined once she had finished. "But we need to get you out of here, and to a hospital."

"How do we do that?" Thomas asked, raising an eyebrow.

"I brought the cavalry," Catherine laughed, nodding at Khan. Then she pulled a bright yellow Motorola radio out of the daypack.

~

Nina was about halfway back to her house when the radio Catherine had given her gave a loud beep. She picked it up off of the dash.

"Beast recieiving, over," Nina stated formally.

"Ten four Beast, this is Black Lightning, over," Catherine's voice confirmed.

They had come up with the callsigns on the spot, mainly to relieve some of the tension they felt, but also to parody every man in authority with a radio they'd ever come across.

"Change of plan," Catherine explained. "I need you to head straight here…".

There was a pause, and Nina could hear the scrunch of paper. She guessed that Catherine was looking at a map. She pulled the truck over to the side of the road she was on and pulled out her own. She glanced quickly behind, and saw Cassie had fallen asleep, with Achak's head nestled into her lap and her arms and head sprawled across his back. The wolf too, seemed peacefully asleep.

"Sorry, just getting my bearings," Catherine's voice chimed again. "We're exactly 44.290781 degrees north by 107.225962 degrees west. It looks like we're about a couple of miles north of a place called Meadowlark Lake. If this map is accurate, there's a trail that leads from there most of the way in."

"I see it," Nina confirmed.

"I'm going to put Thomas on Khan somehow, and we'll work our way back down the trail towards you. Again, if the map is accurate, it looks like there is a parking area also north of the lake, which makes sense, as Thomas managed to burn down an old hunting lodge here."

"He's been busy," Nina laughed. "I'm on my way."

Nina thought she knew where Catherine was talking about, but just to be safe she punched in the coordinates into the Beast's impressive and customised GPS system. She reminded herself to suggest Jesse gave her own truck an upgrade or two. She checked the map too, just to be sure, and glanced in the back again. Her two charges were still sound asleep. She pulled back onto the road, and soon took a turning north that would lead to Meadowlark Lake.

There were a few cabins around the beautiful Meadowlark Lake, but they would be empty at this time of year. There was though, a Forest Service outpost nearby, covering the popular trails, and she guessed she might be able to pick up a horse trailer there. She couldn't imagine Catherine would want to ride Khan back to the ranch, or even just back to her place despite being much nearer. She got on the radio again, this time to let the outpost know she was coming and what she needed. Being winter still, she unsurprisingly found them not overrun and happy to oblige her. Half an hour later the trailer was attached to the truck, and she was waving to the two rangers in the rear-view mirror.

Beyond a small picnic area that looked out over the crystal-clear water of the lake, a single trail headed north, gradually pulling away from the shore and ascending in a gentle curve. The track was loose and littered with boulders and scree. She had to take her time as she guided both the truck and horsebox along it. Another twenty minutes passed before she rounded a bend and saw Catherine, stood by the side of the road, holding Khan by the reins as Thomas rested in the saddle. She could see Catherine had been generous when she had described a parking area. It was simply a slightly wider area of road. Luckily though, it was wide enough to allow her to turn the truck and horsebox, but only just. She manoeuvred carefully, the wheel on full lock. She could feel the wheels slipping as the horsebox edged over the trailside and gravity gently tugged at it, encouraging it to career back down the hillside. Nina changed up a gear and put her foot down, whipping the horsebox back onto the trail, and with the truck pointing back the way she'd come.

Catherine looked in at Cassie, now awake and beaming at her.

"Hello munchkin," Catherine smiled back.

"Allo mummy," Cassie giggled. "Did you find Daddy?"

Catherine nodded in the direction of Thomas and Khan.

"Mummy to the rescue," Catherine sighed.

"As usual," Thomas added from his mount.

Cassie shook her head and rolled her eyes. Catherine couldn't help but laugh, knowing it was something she was copying from her own behaviour. Nina joined Catherine by Thomas's side, and they both helped him down from the horse. Rather ungracefully, he lowered himself straight-backed into their collective arms. He winced slightly as his feet dropped to the ground, but he had no trouble making his way to the car from there. With fresh hay, water, and oats waiting for him, Khan too seemed to welcome being coerced into the horse box and stepped in with little protest.

"Catherine talked me out of calling in a medivac team via helicopter, but other than a quick stop at home, I think you still need a hospital by the looks of it," Nina explained, once they were underway again.

"I feel okay," Thomas replied. He then caught Nina and Catherine's collective stare and changed his mind quickly. "Yes ma'am," he nodded.

He sat behind the flip-up rear bench seat of the Chevy, his arm trailing over the back as he gently played with Cassie's hair. She giggled and knocked his fingers away in mock annoyance. He tried to keep as still as possible as they passed the lake, and he distracted himself as he took in the stunning view. The sun was just beginning to drop behind the mountains and shadows from the surrounding pines reached out across the water, darkening the surface in swirls of teal against the cold cobalt lake. His eyes lifted skywards, and he noticed the heavy clouds rolling in. He could never get over how vast the horizon was here. The valleys didn't feel enclosed like in Scotland, but stretched for miles instead. And always, no matter how steep or sheer the mountains were, the sky was bigger. Everything fit beneath it and felt small in comparison. And he loved how it could change from instant to instant. One minute deep reds and purples reflected off of the snow-capped peaks, next, the entire sky changed to slate grey and inky blue.

They spent only a few short moments on a main road before turning off again. They were headed west, and it felt as if they were doubling back on themselves. Thomas realised they were skirting the other side of the lake now and travelling down the long, rarely travelled road that led back to the north side of the reservation, where Nina's cottage was. It didn't take long to reach the outskirts. Being on the very edge of the settlements, the house was the first one that came into view and was still set some distance from the others. Nina let out a long sigh as she pulled into the drive.

Achak was on his feet in an instant. The low growl of warning made Cassie flinch, and Thomas's brow furrowed. Everyone in the truck was immediately on edge. When Achak's lips rippled and a savage snarl escaped his jaws, Nina jumped from the cab and let him out. He dashed up onto the veranda and disappeared towards the back of the house.

"Something's very wrong," Nina said to herself.

As if to confirm, a long, wailing howl came from Achak. Thomas met Catherine's eyes. The strange, sick feeling in the pit of their stomachs that they'd experienced too many times before, confirmed something terrible had happened. Thomas waited for Catherine to extract herself and let him out of the trunk. By that time, Nina was halfway across the front yard.

"Nina…," he called out. "Maybe I should check first?"

Nina paused. He could see she was shaking. He moved past her, touching her elbow as he did, and then headed for the far side of the house. As he rounded the corner, he stopped in his tracks. Kayah Lee sat with her back against a post supporting the veranda. The back porch was partially destroyed, and sprawled across the decking, his muzzle just inches from Kaya's feet, was Lucifer. But unlike Kayah, Lucifer was dead.

"Nina," Thomas yelled. "Cath, keep Cassie in the car. Call 911."

Kayah turned her head slowly towards Thomas. He could see her strength was failing fast. She reached for him, and he crouched beside her. He took her hand in his and pressed it gently.

"Your little one," Kayah murmured. "She is special, she is gifted. She is in tune with the natural world."

Thomas nodded. He didn't have the heart, nor the urge to argue with her.

"Both you and your wife have it too, but you don't use it. It's why you do the work you do."

Thomas again nodded. "I feel like I do far more harm than good," he admitted, his gaze turning downwards.

Kayah took short, sharp breaths. He could see it was a struggle for her.

"Try not to talk," he murmured.

She waved her hand dismissively.

"You're not fighting nature," Kayah whispered, shaking her head and looking around despairingly. "You're fighting humankind. Things are wrong. Very wrong. Out of balance."

Nina came bolting around the corner, Achak by her side. Thomas stood up and moved back.

"Just hold on mom, help is coming," Nina assured her, tears welling in her eyes. "Killed a bear on your own, huh?" Nina laughed, veiling the shake in her voice.

"Witch," Kayah explained with a forced smile as she closed her eyes.

"Stay with me mom," Nina yelled, grabbing her mother's shoulders hard with both hands.

Thomas made his way back to the truck, nearly collapsing on it when he reached it. Catherine was by his side in an instant.

"It doesn't look good," Thomas said, shaking his head. "It was the bear. I guess it just headed downhill, broke into the first house it came to."

Catherine held his hand. He lifted his head as he picked up the sound of sirens in the distance.

"One for her, one for you," Catherine explained. "You need a hospital."

"I shot the bear and didn't follow it," Thomas explained. "I..."

"Couldn't walk," Catherine comforted him. "I've seen that look before when I got to you. You were ready to die. This is not your fault."

"You're going to need to call Jesse and Jericho," Thomas explained. "I'm not going to even bother trying to convince you, that bear...you'll see when you see it. It's not a grizzly."

Catherine looked at him, confused. "It can't possibly be a black bear, it's far too big?"

Thomas shook his head slowly, the disbelief evident on his face.

"You can't just hand it over to Fish and Wildlife. We need to know much more about it." Thomas added.

"I'll talk to them. We'll sort something out," Catherine assured him.

As he slumped against the truck, he looked up to the darkening sky as the red and white lights of the ambulances reflected off of the glass and white painted front of the house. Night and a storm were coming.

CHAPTER TWENTY-FOUR

Jesse put down the phone. For a few moments he sat in silence, contemplating his next move. Catherine had told him that Nina's mother was likely to be dead on arrival by the time she got to the South Bighorn County Hospital. The grizzly – which apparently wasn't a grizzly at all, was dead, but the cat was still out there. Thomas was also headed to the hospital, with injuries unknown. And Jericho was still on the road, heading back from Colorado. That made Jesse the last man standing. He stood up with a grunt. In the hall, he put on his thick, fleece lined coat and turned up the collar. He then lifted two guns off of the rack and filled his pockets with ammo from the safe in his study. Both weapons were Winchesters. The shotgun was an SXP Shadow Marine Defender, a gun originally designed for coastal bear hunters. It featured a pistol grip and hard-chrome plating for standing up to the elements, as well as hitting hard with three-inch, 12-gauge rounds. The rifle was a model 1886 lever-action, in a 45-70 calibre. More than a match for a grizzly, bull elk, or even a bison, as his father had proven on many occasions. But they were just backup. The real weapons were in the barn.

He left the house and slipped through a side entrance into his main workshop. He loaded the guns into the customised 1951 Ford van and slung a small pack onto the bench seat in the front. He walked around to the back and opened the tailgate, lowering the ramp he'd made and opening the six dog cages that made up the trunk, one at a time. He took a whistle from his pocket and made his way over to the pen. Six pairs of orange-coloured eyes watched him approach. He opened the gate, but none of them moved. The training had finally paid off. They were as ready as they were ever going to be. Up until this point, he hadn't been sure and had been ready to abort his plan. But not now. They were ready to do what he'd designed them to do. He blew on the whistle.

In silent formation, the pack of Waheela hounds trotted out of the pen in single file. One by one they made their way up the ramp and found a cage. Once the three on the bottom row were filled, the other three dogs lifted themselves up into the top row. There were no barks or yikkers of excitement as he might have expected from the hounds his father had used. But these were different animals entirely. He closed up the back of the truck.

Just as he was about to open the driver's side door, he heard the faintest whimper from the second pen, now closed off from the other, after his previous breeding experiments had no longer been warranted. He swung the gate open, and it creaked ominously on its unused hinges. Something in the straw moved. Something small. He knelt down and brushed aside some of the wet bedding. Big wet eyes, the colour of a pumpkin, stared back at him. He didn't know how, but the second-generation pup had somehow survived on her own. He'd thought the mother, one of the dogs now in the truck, had killed her entire litter when they were about eight weeks old. Whether this one had the smarts to play dead or just got missed, he didn't know, but it was still alive. He guessed the pup was about 12 weeks old now and was maybe living off scavenged scraps. Or maybe his mum was feeding him through the fence – although he doubted it. He reached out, and the pup pushed its head into his hand.

"You're no Spartan little'n," Jesse cooed. "Maybe that's why momma didn't want your brothers and sisters. Too friendly like."

He pushed aside the little straw nest the pup seemed to have made for itself, unearthing the skull of a woodrat as he did.

"Okay, maybe not that friendly," Jesse exclaimed in surprise, and with a little bit of pride. "But I guess you're still not part of the pack."

Jesse thought for a moment, then went to the food store on the other side of the barn. He took out a blanket that was covering some sacks and brought it out, and filled a spare bowl with water. He placed the water down in front of the pup, then, as it lapped at the dish, he placed the blanket over its back. He made another trip to the food store and dropped a pile of dry mix next to the pup.

"If you're as smart to have made it this far, you can figure out how all that works," Jesse exclaimed, scratching the pup behind its ears. "I'll sort out something a little more permanent for you when I get back, but I gotta go to work for now, little britches."

Jesse pulled the truck out of the barn, then got out and closed the doors. The supercharged V8 engine growled as it idled. He lifted his eyes to the mountains, noticing the moon was obscured by a dark and ominous cloud bank. Its eerie glow was masked, but there was still enough light to see the heavy water vapour rolling off of the mountain tops towards the forest below. It was going to be a cold and fog-filled night. But rather than deter him, he felt encouraged. The cat would be at a disadvantage. Its excellent night vision wouldn't help it in the mist. He gripped the wheel tight as he turned out of the ranch and joined the main road.

Nina had given him the coordinates and told him about the track that led to the burnt-out cabin. She'd indicated that there was a place a few miles in where he'd be able to leave the truck and trailer. Her voice had sounded hollow, like a piece of her was missing – soulless even. He knew that there would have been a conflict within her to have told him even that much. Nina would have known that he intended to hunt down Tama and kill her, not something she'd usually condone or help facilitate. Although it had been the bear that had attacked Nina's mother, it had borne the scars of its clashes with the cat. Perhaps Tama had even been responsible for driving it down the mountain and closer to civilisation. Whatever the case, something in his gut told him it was all connected. Two giant predators, seemingly straight out of a different time and place – it couldn't be coincidence.

He passed the Forest Ranger outpost, keeping the revs low and the engine quiet as he did. He didn't blink as his gaze swept over the dark, single storey building – not much more than an office with a garage and parking lot. He observed every detail. There were no lights. Nobody was home. He didn't know why he felt such unease. Tama was a hybrid animal, and as such, had no protection. She could be hunted and killed without question. She was an out of place animal, and he saw her as a threat to the ecosystem. The bear showed that. If she could near-kill that thing, her impact on the vulnerable and small population of grizzlies outside of Yellowstone could be devastating. Same went for the local wolf packs. Jesse had no qualms about putting Tama down if it meant protecting his own, and every other animal in Wyoming alongside.

He first overshot and passed the wide part of the track Nina had described, judging that what he was looking for had to be bigger. But with no alternative availing itself, he found himself backing up and carefully manoeuvring into the space. He let the dogs out and they lined up silently beside the truck. He decided on the shotgun, leaving the rifle in the rack against the back of the cab, behind the front bench seat. He didn't know how far he'd have to go, but he knew he might have to move fast. If the dogs did their job, the shotgun was best for close quarters work. If not, the rifle would still be waiting for him here.

Tama had last been sighted at the cabin, so that was where he was headed. All the dogs needed was the slightest hint of a trail or sign to scent from, and they'd be able to track her. He had no doubt about that. He was used to the dark, and it didn't bother him much. He'd done night hunts before, although admittedly for nothing in Tama's league. Cats were generally nocturnal and more active during the hours of darkness. Most of their prey benefitted from eyesight that gave them an edge during the day. Deer for instance, like most prey animals, benefited from eyes on the side of their heads, giving them up to a 310-degree field of vision – with just a 50-degree blind spot at the back of their heads. Deer could also likely see UV light, and they experienced blue and grey colours much more intensely than humans. Not a bad thing when Jesse considered that the colouration of wolves and cougars could easily be summed up in shades of grey. But turn the lights off, and the advantage went to the apex species – the hunters.

Tonight, the hunter would become the hunted, if he got his way.

Lost in his thoughts, he practically stumbled onto the remnants of the cabin. Parts of it still smouldered and embers at the end of the timbers glowed with each breath of wind. He didn't want to use torchlight, as it would ruin his night vision. But the moon was still trying to burn through the gathering mist, and there were no trees above the path to the cabin to block out its light. Somewhere, Tama must have left a print, or some kind of trail that the dogs could track. More usual hounds might have shown some unease or sign that they could smell the cat's presence, or the bear's for that matter. But the Waheela stayed silent, sitting patiently and awaiting command.

As he studied the ground, he was able to piece together part of the events that had taken place at the cabin. The bear's tracks were brazened and easy to follow, and it was by following these that he came to find a rear pawprint of Tama's. A little way from there, at the edge of the treeline, he found her claw marks etched into the bark of a western hemlock. And she had sprayed too, marking the ground after vanquishing Lucifer.

You may have beaten that devil thought Jesse, *but hell's coming for you now*, he grinned.

Jesse gave a single, short whistle which ascended in pitch and tone gently before coming to a sharp stop. Immediately, the dogs sprang to their feet and ran to the base of the tree, still in single file. Each took their time to familiarise themselves with the scent. He took it as a good sign that each of them congregated around the same group of trees, their focus on the woods beyond. He could sense their anticipation. It equalled his own. This is what they had been trained to do. Although the pack didn't have a traditional alpha – as each dog operated independently, the dog he'd named Chief was as close to it as they got. He stood apart from the rest, his head down and shoulders tensed ready for the run. Next in line were two sisters, Electra, and the mother of the pup he'd discovered, Cruella. They were lying on the ground, saving their energy. He'd named Havoc after witnessing the dog's ability to deliver both a whirlwind attack on his prey, but also serve as an unrestrained distraction, that enabled the rest of the pack to draw in. His size and strength meant he could hold his own until they arrived. Azrael was an excellent tracker but often hung back when on the trail, only to usually deliver the death blow once the prey was down. That left Zuul, as good an attack dog as he was a hunter. Jesse had considered the breed would be good for military work based on what he'd seen of the dog's abilities.

"Go," Jesse said, in barely a whisper.

As the dogs disappeared into the trees, Jesse felt a shiver run down the length of his spine. He knew the cold air was descending on the forest now, and the trees would soon be shrouded in mist.

~

Tama rested by the fallen trunk of a Fremont cottonwood. She had found the wood-lined canyon by following a creek to a pool where it slowed and deepened. Lying in the cold, crystal clear water had soothed her wounds and the rage she had carried after her fight with the bear. Conflict waged an internal war between her biological instinct and her domestic conditioning. Although she had never established or claimed a territory of her own before, the surroundings of virgin forest, and the presence of prey and water had stirred something dormant and ancient within her. And another predator that would compete with her for resources was not to be tolerated. Her second attack on the bear had therefore been far more savage and determined. She had not needed the bear to die, just to leave, and the wounds she had inflicted had seen to that. But the thick scent of the nutrient-rich blood and its volume was enough for her to know it was unlikely to return.

The smaller, male cat had followed her into the canyon. Twice he had tried to mount her, only to be rebuffed by her. But with the arrival of darkness, she could sense the restlessness building. The male wanted to hunt, but it couldn't resist Tama's allure and proximity. She stood, stretching her front paws out in front of her and arching her back. She unsheathed her claws, scraping them along the dead bark of the cottonwood. Each left a jagged scar with a depth and length a good hunting knife would struggle to compete with. Tama opened her jaws and shook her head in a grumbling, moaning roar of awakening. The forest stood still in reply. She took a few steps into the trees. There was no breeze here, and she moved further in, cutting a slow and deliberate circular path that moved her into the wind. The canyon walls weren't especially steep, so manoeuvring was easy. The high ground beckoned. She knew the male was shadowing her but ignored him for now.

By the time she reached the ridgeline, a sheet of icy fog had rolled in from the mountains and hung thick between the trees. The moisture it added to the air blunted her sense of smell, and she opened up her jaws and wrinkled her nose – forcing air into her olfactory system and filtering the scents of the forest at a micro level. Her ears flattened, and a snarl escaped her throat through drawn back lips. A new threat had entered her recently established domain, and just as with the bear before, she couldn't tolerate their presence.

Forgetting the male, she hugged the landscape as she searched the competitors out. Cover came in the form of shadows. Towers of rock and trees as wide as she was long, appeared as giant tombstone-like pillars of deep black, set against a background of slate and ash-coloured vapour. Their edges swirled, morphing their physicality and distorting their actuality into something more ethereal and nightmarishly temporal. Her heart thundered in her chest as her eyes darted to each unfamiliar shape taking form in the darkness. Each gave way up close to something recognisable and benign. She began to anticipate the inefficacy of the phantom beasts around her and grew more confident.

Approaching a void that stood in her path against the darkness, she cocked her head, curious at its sureness of form. She paused, then took a step forward. Then another. Two rust-coloured lights flickered, then she felt the press of teeth against the joint in her forelimb. A flinch of her shoulders freed her, but then she heard the clatter of her attacker's paws as it circled her in a wide and relentless run. The loud, confident bark that rang out enabled her to identify her attacker. She'd killed their kind before, at the bequest of the man. Now, she fought for herself, without confinement. But as more singular barks sounded, Tama understood that she was being hunted, and her pursuers were verging in on her.

Havoc's mistake was moving. Lying in wait as he had been, his body had been cooled by the night air, and his scent had been hidden by his position upwind. He'd heard the snarl of the quarry and set a near perfect ambush. But now, as he ran, moving his head up and down in excitement, his body began to heat up and the breeze was forced to move around his 120lb mass. A series of minute, momentary fluctuations in the air current was all it took for Tama's whiskers to register the dog's route. As she homed in, her unique feline retinas picked up flickers of purplish iridescence that accented the rise and fall of a body in motion. Tama froze and watched, turning her head as the canine drew closer. She charged, silent and fast. Her jaws snapped shut like a sprung trap around the dog's skull, yanking it from the forest floor mid-run. The yelp was more in surprise than in fear, but Tama allowed it no further time to sound out its terror. The skull cracked between her teeth with ease and for a moment, bloodied brain matter leaked across her tongue. She shook the limp body violently, snapping bone and mashing flesh as she systematically thrashed it against the ground. As quickly as she had attacked, she discarded the dog, throwing it from her jaws back into the mist with a flippant toss of her head.

Tama crept away into the fog, her senses in overdrive. Attuned to the environment, she instinctively approached a hulking, ominous void that towered over her. As she drew nearer, the ozone scent of the moss and lichen-ravaged pillar of rock, helped her to identify this was the refuge she was seeking. For the briefest of moments, the moon burnt a hole through the fog, and Tama lifted her head towards the light, her retinas drinking their fill of it. She saw the broad, flat top of the escarpment and leapt, hunkering down as both the moon and the rock disappeared again in a swirl of shadow.

Cruella padded forward softly, then paused. Her warning growl was heard by her sister, Electra, who was flanking to the left. She too froze and pricked up her ears. The wind brought two new scents to them, both of which they all too easily recognised. The first was the unique tell-tale odour of one of their own kind. The other was blood. The pungent tangs fused in the breeze and the dogs lifted their heads to filter it. Veiled by the redolence of the more vibrant scents, the musk of their quarry was also evident. The sisters moved closer together and followed their noses.

Tama listened. Her pursuers were quiet, but not silent. The clack of their claws against the stony ground. Exhales of breath carried on the wind. The rustle of an unseen branch passed in the fog. Her keen hearing caught each sound. Her own claws were retractable, and her paw pads were cosseted by fine slippers of fur that dulled her footfalls. Which meant she was able to reposition herself in complete silence as she readied for the dogs to reach her. As they did, she ambushed them directly from above. Her leap brought her down upon Cruella, who was the furthest from her. Caught underneath Tama's chest, the dog writhed and caught hold of her ear between its teeth. Tama ignored the pain as her own fangs sliced through the dog's torso, her upper and lower canines fighting to complete their scissor-like cut. Cruella went limp between her jaws, and Tama spun on her heels with a swiping hook of her paw that slashed Electra down the side. The dog went into an immediate attack, burying its teeth into the soft flesh underneath Tama's left front leg. She instantly let the dog in her jaws drop to the ground, then jumped into the air to try and dislodge the one trying to tunnel into her soft parts. This pain was excruciating, and she yowled and snarled as she bucked and twisted. But Electra clung on, shaking her head, tearing the skin with each thrust.

A rage built within Tama that she had never experienced before. The pain made her wild, but she fought it as she tried to regain control. She raised her rear left leg and stretched it forwards as steady and carefully as a surgeon wielding a scalpel. Her claws extended, and suddenly, it was Electra's hide that was pierced and torn. The dog yelped as Tama's hooked dew claw pinned it down at the hips, whilst its bowels spilled onto the ground. Tama growled as she stepped over the dying dog, her mind set on escape. But her growl was answered by three others, one to each side and directly in front. Only as she backed up did she realise she was cornered against the pillar of rock she'd executed her ambush from. Instinctively she knew there was no time to climb it. Finally, the rage erupted from her.

~

The roar was primal, savage, and deafening. It made Jesse stop in his tracks. It was like being hit by a wall of sound. He felt dizzy and nauseated. His hearing was muted, as if he were underwater, and an intense, painful, tinnitus ring echoed in his head. He staggered forward. He heard a yelp, then the sound of something breaking through the brush ahead of him. He gripped the shotgun and swung it forward, only to let out his held breath with a sharp jolt as Zuul appeared out of the fog, his head bloodied. The dog paid him no attention as it dashed past him and back into the mist. Not once had he ever seen the dogs retreat from any of their training hunts. He shuddered.

~

As one of the dogs bolted, Tama saw her opening. She moved with fleeting silence, accelerating instantly and disappearing into the night. The other two dogs were not so easily put off, although she could feel their hesitance in the cocktail of pheromones that exuded from them. But theirs wasn't the only scent she could pick up. The male cat was close, and she began to seek him out, homing in on his must. She engulfed the ground in fearless, resolute bounds. She growled with anticipation and slowed, now feeling frustration at the dog's lacklustre pursuit. She turned her head as she ran and roared, baiting them.

She quickly managed to distance her pursuers. As a huge, towering shadow appeared out of the mist, she found herself at the foot of an imposing lodgepole pine, where the male waited for her. As her body cooled and her temper dulled, she found herself more open to his attentions. She lowered herself to the ground and squirmed against the hard dirt. The male didn't hesitate, mounting her and resting his forepaws over her back. He could not reach her neck, so he placed his jaws over her spinal column in an attempt to placate and control her. As he retreated, the barbs of his penis stabbed and scraped against her, and she spun, cuffing him with her claws half sheathed. It was enough to send him reeling back. Her ears flicked, and she turned to find the source of an advancing sound. She growled, realising the dogs had held back, but not given up entirely.

She raised her head, her eyes searching upwards. She heard the splintering of the bark, and a few shards fell against her muzzle. She huffed, and it was answered by the snarl of the male from somewhere not far above. She searched the boughs through her limited vision for a few moments more, then slipped away silently. Not far from the tree she found a rock escarpment and began to climb upwards.

~

Jesse followed the baying dogs, a smile spread across his face. He knew from their barks that they had their quarry cornered. That was all he needed. In a few moments, he'd be able to end this, maybe avenge his dad in some way. He heard the scrabble of the dogs, circling in excitement. And that's when he knew something was wrong. He couldn't believe that Tama would have been treed. He knew that it wasn't impossible for her to climb, but it just didn't seem to be in her nature to run. At every opportunity, she'd turned to face a fight rather than escape it. Jesse shouldered the shotgun as he drew closer, sweeping the barrel left to right slowly, waiting for something to launch at him out of the mist. But it never came. Instead, he found himself at the foot of a pine, the dogs all standing on their hind feet with their front paws resting on the deep, rutted bark. He followed their fixed gaze, and was met with a fear-filled, savage snarl that he instantly recognised. The dogs had cornered a mountain lion, and he cursed them under his breath. He switched on the torch attachment he'd strapped to the bottom of the barrel and lifted it towards the canopy. Bared white fangs and cool green eyes were caught in the light, and he could see the cat was ready to spring. He knew he had no choice and aimed calmly at the top of the skull. He pulled the trigger, cursing the dogs once more as the lion's body hit the ground in a lifeless heap. As the dogs moved in, eager to claim their prize, they sprang back, cowering, and heads lifted with ears pricked

The savage growl of intent that reverberated around them was impossible to place. It reflected off of unseen rockfaces, cushioned by evergreen boughs, and amplified by the breeze. The snap of a twig to his right was easy to place though, and he flinched as he brought the gun up again. He traced the imaginary steps of his foe, only to spin on his heels as stones trickled gently downhill as they dislodged behind him. The two remaining dogs hugged the ground, side by side and frozen in tension. Jesse was not surprised; it was simply survival instinct kicking in. Perhaps as three, they might have had a chance. But as a pair, Tama could dispatch them as easily as she had their pack mates. It was then that Jesse realised the arrogance of his plan and thought process. The mist hung thick, and the moisture in the air was palatable. The fog did level the playing field, but only now could he see that wasn't enough. With the odds even, Tama was still an apex predator that was more accustomed to the environment than he, or even his dogs, ever could be. He needed an advantage, but Tama would always have the natural edge.

There was an explosion of sound in the tree above them, and Jesse stumbled back in terror. The sound of wood cracking and splintering echoed like dynamite charges, as something dropped from the tree with the tenacity and sureness of a bowling ball dropped from a great height. A mass of broken branches fell to the forest floor, followed by something else that hit the ground with a wet slap. Instinctively, Jesse knew there was something finite about it. Whatever it was didn't move. He was thankful that even now the dogs didn't whimper or vocalise the same feelings of terror they collectively were experiencing. Jesse realised that they, as well as he, understood their place in the food chain in this moment. If death came for them now, they would fight it as nature intended – surrender wasn't natural after all. But ultimately, they would accept it.

Jesse crept forward. He could make out the silhouette of what had dropped from the tree but little else. As he neared, the two dogs took comfort from his closeness and jumped to their feet. They moved behind him, taking up flanking positions to his left and right as they nosed forward. The veil of the enshrouding fog lifted, and he saw Zuul's mangled corpse appear at his feet in vivid clarity. The monochrome light painted his blood black against his dirty white hide. Like slow, rolling thunder, a growl from close by built into a roar filled with warning and intent. The sound seemed to move through him. A wave of nausea swept over him, and his legs threatened to give out from underneath him. As his head spun, he kept it together enough to recognise the symptoms of infrasound. He knew tigers used the same vocal ability to stun their prey. He knew what came next. As he lifted the barrel of the gun, his hands shook, and it seemed overwhelmingly heavy in his hands. He took in a breath and held it as he felt the tremors across the earth as something heavy pounded it and drew near. His hand still trembled as he worked the pump and reloaded the gun. A bolt of lightning ripped the sky apart above their heads, and the crackle of thunder echoed off the rock faces. Hidden, but not lost within it, came a savage and distant roar.

CHAPTER TWENTY-FIVE

The second roar was more distant, and Jesse knew that it came from beyond the ridge. That was bad news and put Tama beyond his reach. It marked the boundary of the reservation, and Nina had banned the use of his dogs there. He could only imagine how Tama would react if she was cornered within the confines of civilisation. As another flash lit the sky, his sharp, short whistle recalled the dogs immediately before the commanding call could be drowned out by the thunder. The dogs fell in behind him as he returned to the trail. Jesse had left the original track some ways back and was using his best guess to get them back to it. Following the thunder came blasts of ice-cold air that swept the remnants of the fog away. It was a blessing. But he knew a hard, unforgiving rain would soon follow.

The night sky appeared above, deep indigo in colour. He saw the swirls of black reach out to extinguish it. The lightning surged, forcing pathways through its cloud prison like synapses firing in a brain. The electricity rumbled and raged, looking for an exit. Unable to find one, it tore the underbelly of the cloud apart and darted towards the peaks in pinkish, orange bursts of static. It lit the way ahead for them. As they skirted a shallow, bowl-like gully, Bullet let out a low, single growl of warning. Jesse snapped to attention immediately, raising the barrel of the shotgun. But he saw the dog's nose pointing down the slope and into the scrub. Something in his gut told him not to ignore it.

"Okay, find it," Jesse encouraged the dog.

Instantly, the two dogs ploughed downhill, the hound breeds in their makeup evident as they trailed nose-to-ground.

He followed, wondering what would get their attention after, what for them, had already been a successful hunt. Just as they had been trained to, the dogs stopped to mark something they had found. Jesse stopped in his tracks. Another streak of light illuminated the splash of blood against the rock. It looked black, like tar. He could smell it too. Not exactly fresh, but not yet gone so bad to make a normal person puke. About a day old he guessed. He couldn't help wondering if it was perhaps Thomas's. If so, his sense of direction was off, as he was convinced they were headed away from the trail and where he'd parked the truck.

Bullet led the way, and Jesse noticed they passed the burnt-out remnants of a campfire. The slick of blood-stained grass grew stronger here. The storm was still chasing them, and Jesse found it easier to follow the trail with the naked eye. About fifty feet from the campfire in the clearing, the trail clearly led into the woodline. Here, Jesse hesitated. It would be harder to see anything until he was right on top of it amongst the trees. His father had often pressed the point that it was a bad idea to walk into anywhere without knowing where the exits were. And what he was dealing with here was definitely unknown. But the two dogs and a loaded shotgun gave him confidence. He stepped into the trees. As soon as he did, he knew something was coming for him. He heard the womp-womp-womp sound of it cutting through the air towards him in heavy, but slow reverberations. He glanced aside instinctively, and the jawbone club sailed past him and embedded itself in a tree ten feet behind him. The two dogs charged forward and surrounded the Native American man sprawled on the ground before them.

Jesse relaxed as soon as he saw him. The club had not been thrown with any strength, and the man certainly had none left now. From the state of him, Jesse was shocked he wasn't dead. Only sheer will could be keeping him alive. Jesse was no soft touch by any means, and he knew the hard life of the outdoors better than most, but he doubted he'd have survived with the wounds he could see the man was inflicted with. Just a glance told him that saving the man was beyond anything he or a basic first aid kit was capable of. Thankfully, the man was unconscious – no doubt from the exertion of having flailed the club at him. Jesse could only guess how long the man had lain there in agony, anticipating someone, or something, eventually following his trail.

You're lucky it was me and that Thomas distracted that damn bear, Jesse thought as he placed his pack on the ground. He pulled out the Iridium Extreme 9575 satellite phone Jericho had given him in secret. He'd found it, along with instructions, on the porch of the ranch house, after Jericho had left for Colorado. The Irishman wasn't as cavalier as he made out. And he was counting on that now. Thomas and Catherine had enough on their hands as it was. He pressed the first speed dial setting, knowing it would go through to Jericho's burner phone. It picked up immediately.

"How you doin' Irish?" Jesse asked.

"I'd say my luck's been running a little thin of late. Is this call likely to change that?" Jesse replied.

"Depends," Jesse mused. "But guess I can join the Mounties any time now."

"Found yer man then?"

"Yup. Had the cat too, but it gave me the slip. Think it might be headed for town."

Jesse filled Jericho in on what had happened to Thomas, and Nina's mother.

"I'll come straight to you…but I have a favour to ask," Jericho agreed.

"What's that?" Jesse enquired.

"Goin' on what yee've told me, I was wondering if you'd let me borrow those dogs of yers."

"Don't see why not," Jesse answered. "I'll see you when I see you. I guess I better think about calling in a medivac for our friend here."

The line went dead.

A little while later, after he'd phoned the emergency services and given them exact co-ordinates, Jesse lifted the phone once more and dialled Catherine's number. As he looked to the mountains, he noticed dawn was beginning to crack the night sky. As it advanced, the storm changed direction and fled from its light. Jesse wasn't surprised to find Catherine not only up, but at the end of the phone too.

"Thomas seems to think being made to stay overnight at hospital expires at daybreak," Catherine explained. "He's determined to check out."

"I can't say I'm surprised. And that it would go aways to helping me out," Jesse sighed. "I think you folks should know, I've chased your cat as far as I can, but it's headed for the reservation. Nina has seen to it that I can't go on the res with my dogs. I think you're pretty much the only thing that might be able to get in Tama's way now."

"We'll definitely give it a try," Catherine assured him. "Just so you know, Nina's mother…"

"Didn't make it," Jesse guessed.

Catherine's silence was all the confirmation he needed. He

hung up.

CHAPTER TWENTY-SIX

Kelly awoke, cold and damp from her sweat-soaked clothes. The fever had hit the night before and she had passed out not long after she had felt its first effects. She felt thirsty, but the thought of food made her stomach turn. She knew that wasn't good, given the meagre rations she'd had over the past few days. Sitting up made her feel dizzy but she forced herself. Her left side felt numb, which she was thankful for, as it dulled the aching pain of the scabbed-over, bruised wound from the gunshot. She couldn't bring herself to look at it, that too making her feel sick. She dragged herself over to the wooden wall separating her from the next stable-turned-jailcell and leaned her back against it. It felt cool against her body, soothing her further.

As drowsiness tugged at her gently, tempting her back towards unconsciousness, she heard the barn door creak as it opened. The fall of footsteps followed, headed in her direction. Kelly forced her eyes open. She fumbled with her necklace quickly, then hid it back under her shirt. The lock holding the stable door shut rattled and Annika Deveraux appeared as it opened. She was carrying the metal tray she had become accustomed to. On it was a carton of milk, like they gave kids at school, a bottle of water, and what constituted as her breakfast. As a journalist, Kelly had been in enough war zones to recognise an MRE when she saw it – "meal, ready to eat". The orange glow from the small white bowl revealed a soupy mix of beans, bacon, sausages, and mushrooms. She knew it was more than edible and would give her much needed energy. But she had no intention of eating it whilst Deveraux watched. Her captor placed the tray down beside Kelly and glanced at her side. Kelly knew Jericho would have rushed Deveraux at the door or would be grabbing for her holstered pistol right now in a heroic act of attempted escape. But she didn't have the strength or inclination.

"You should let me look at that," Deveraux nodded towards Kelly's side.

Kelly hesitated, then noticed the first aid kit sitting on the tray beside her breakfast. Slowly, she nodded.

Kelly rolled onto her good side, away from Deveraux. Her captor-turned-nurse lifted the cloth of her shirt. There was a pause and Kelly turned her head slightly. Deveraux remained poker faced, but she was clearly assessing something. A few moments later, she opened the first aid kit. Kelly felt the moist touch of wipes cleaning her wound, then a sharp pain as Deveraux redressed and taped it up.

"You need to eat," Deveraux commanded, closing the first aid kit.

Kelly noticed the green, brown and red stains on the wipes she'd used. Obediently, she picked up the bowl. For a moment, she let it warm her hands and wrists. It felt good.

"What exactly is it you are trying to achieve here?" she asked Deveraux, lifting a spoonful of the breakfast slush to her mouth.

"That's not really your concern, is it?" Deveraux replied. "But you may be comforted to know that we are on the same side. We are working towards a world that works in harmony with the other species living in it. We are reversing trophic cascades and the next great extinctions."

"And that requires a private army and acts of terrorism?" Kelly objected.

"Absolutely, this is a war. And we're losing," Deveraux replied. "Drastic measures are the only option available. Putting your teabags in the compost isn't going to cut it."

Kelly sensed the defiance, almost an invitation daring her to challenge the remark. She couldn't quite muster the inclination.

"I'll have someone bring more water and some fresh blankets," Deveraux added with less glee.

Deveraux left the bowl and the plastic spork but took the tray and the first aid kit. Kelly watched her leave and lock the door again. As if in reverse, she listened as the footsteps receded and the barn door swung back and forth as Deveraux exited the building. When she was sure she was gone, Kelly took out the necklace again and examined it quickly, before putting it back beneath her clothes and against her skin.

She decided to peel back the dressing on her side and see what Deveraux had seen – and done about it. The wound looked clean enough, but she guessed that was to be expected after just being tended to. She could still smell a slight hint of something akin to sewage or rot, but she couldn't quite tell if it was from the wound or the stable floor. What she did know was, just like in the movies, the bad guys never told you their plans unless they weren't expecting you to ever be able to tell anyone else. Her mind raced and she tried to convince herself that as a journalist, they could have use for her to give them exposure and a platform. But she doubted they needed her for that. Clearly, funding wasn't an issue. She considered all the potential outcomes and concluded it was unlikely they were just going to let her go. Her mental faculties felt exhausted again, and she slumped back against the wall. As she drifted back off to sleep, she thought of her cosy apartment looking over Richmond Park and if, just maybe, help was coming.

CHAPTER TWENTY-SEVEN

As Catherine rounded the corner of the hospital corridor, she saw Thomas standing at administration, checking himself out as promised. At least he'd saved her a trip to the room, two floors above. She shook her head, but knew there was no telling him otherwise. She had to admit that fluids and meds had transformed him, and x-rays had revealed no serious internal injuries. The doctors had plied him with a literal cocktail of antibiotics to counteract the potential of infection from the unknown community of bacteria that might have lived within the bear's mouth. She could tell he was extremely stiff and sore by how he was bent over a little, and grimacing with the slightest movement. Nothing was fluid or easy for him, including signing his name. As she joined him by his side, she noticed the jagged and clumsily etched signature.

"We'll have to get Cassie to give you some handwriting lessons," she said softly.

"Thanks for not fighting me on this," he replied.

"I know better than that, and I know you don't like hospitals," Catherine smiled. "Besides, we have work to do. I spoke to Nina, and the good news is, the bear was killed within the boundaries of the reservation, so it comes under the jurisdiction of the tribal police. They're keeping other interested parties at bay for now, but expect federal interference sooner or later."

"Okay, so what's the bad news then?" Thomas asked. "Your face suggests there is some?"

Catherine nodded. "Jesse can't take his dogs onto tribal land. He was tracking Tama, and although the dogs certainly left their mark, she got away. She seems to be headed towards civilisation. We obviously don't want a repeat of what happened with the bear."

"Let's get after her then."

"You think you can drive?"

"Try and stop me!"

They made their way down to the hospital parking lot via the elevator. Catherine begrudgingly handed over the keys with a sigh. Thomas did his best to hide the limp his stiffness forced, but he knew Catherine would notice. She fixed him with an unamused and serious stare, eyebrows raised.

"If I feel any pain, or if there's anything I can't do, you'll do the shooting," he offered.

"I want to talk to you about that actually," she stated. "We're not going to kill her."

"We're not?" Thomas replied. His tone suggested no surprise, just interest.

"Well, we seem to be out of guns for now, as you decided to discard yours liberally through the woods of Wyoming," Catherine said, smugly. "And I think we need some answers. I spoke with Nina; she was able to procure a toy for me."

Catherine went to the back of the truck and opened the tailgate door. Inside the trunk sat a neat, long and narrow composite box. As she opened it up, she revealed a rifle.

"DAN-INJECT IM rifle," Catherine stated. "Maximum range of 145 yards, with easily adjusted pressure gauge and scope."

"What about the anaesthetic?" Thomas asked. "If Tama has the accelerated metabolism that hybrids with gigantism often do, she might be able to burn it off."

Catherine nodded. When they had hunted Tama's father in the Highlands, the cat had been shot with an anaesthetic by a zookeeper. Although the animal had succumbed finally, it had killed the man and attacked a family after travelling some distance before its unique biology gave in.

"I've thought of that too," Catherine explained. "The dart contains a high dose of ketamine with another sedative, Xylazine. I've had to guess at the dosage, but it would be enough to knock out a shire horse, and that's without the ketamine. But I think it'll do the trick. I've prepared two darts, so we get two shots."

Thomas nodded, impressed.

Catherine's cell phone rang, and she picked it up with fervor. Thomas could tell from her expression, whoever was at the other end of the line, it wasn't someone she'd expected to be talking to. *Who is it?* He mouthed at her.

"Thank you, Special Agent Labar, I'll hand you over to Thomas," Catherine said, passing the phone to him.

Thomas took it and held it to his ear.

'Mr. Walker, your friend Mr. Logan has just seen Chayton Reed, our suspect, air-lifted to hospital – the same one you're at now. I thought you'd want to know that he was still alive, and that you probably played a part in saving his life. I'm not sure whether to thank you for that or not."

Thomas could hear the smile behind the sarcasm.

"I'm dispatching a security detail to keep him detained. But it sounds like he's not going anywhere," Labar continued.

"When I last saw him, I got the impression he was paralysed from the waist down," Thomas agreed. "The bear smashed some of his lower vertebrae, I'm sure of that."

"Well, in any case, we'll be keeping an eye on him," Labar assured. "We've used satellite tracking to find a posse of missing men from the region. Their social media profiles all suggested they were trying to hunt our man and your cat down. We were able to triangulate some of their cell phones and found a cabin and compound that looks like base camp for this whole affair. I believe Mr. O'Connell is making his way there too and has some information for us. In the meantime, our team has found a horse trailer he thinks the cat might have been transported in."

"Can they bring it to us?" Thomas asked. "We're headed to the reservation and think we can capture the cat with minimal risk to others. At least, that's what we're going to try."

"Your intentions are all well and good Mr. Walker, but my advice would be to put her in the ground," Labar offered, but not without sympathy. "However, I said I'd give you my support and co-operation when I said you're the expert here. I'll have it brought to you. I'll be in touch."

The line went dead.

"The problem with authority types is, they're so formal," Thomas teased Catherine. "Every time somebody calls me Mr. Walker, I can't help feel I'm in trouble."

"Probably something you inherited from those posh private schools you kept getting thrown out of," she winked.

~

Tama lay in the long grass, flat against the hill and shrouded from view. Her tail twitched with pent up energy. She watched. Her instinct to return to the trees and shadows was being fought by her hunger and her curiosity. Instinct was losing. A large metal thing, similar to the one the man had used to transport her, had passed along the river of stone some time ago, but all was quiet now. Her ears stood tall, craning for the slightest indication of danger. But it was her sense of smell that was being stimulated most. A sticky, sweet scent was being brought to her on the wind, and she recognised this as fresh meat being scorched by flame. Tama had seen the man prepare prey for both her and himself in this way. Somehow, the aroma stimulated her in a way different to fresh blood, or even live prey. But, as she opened her mouth and drew back her lips to take in more of the scent, a new one came to her. There was warmth to it, like dried foliage, and she could taste the animal sweat on the wind. She rose up and padded forward, crossing the stone river quickly and silently.

On the other side of the stone river, there was a slight ascent that led to a series of wooden posts, linked by beams at their top and bottom. She followed these along, cautious about crossing between them. But the scents compelled her, and her curiosity drove her forward. She stepped through one of the frames and met a little resistance as the top beam put pressure on her back. She tensed her shoulder muscles and exerted a little weight, snapping the dead wood with ease. She broke into a light run, taking her to the top of the mounded earth that lined the stone river. The descent on the other side was much steeper, but the mound was only at one end of a grass meadow that stretched off into the distance. The wooden barrier continued along the flat, creating a permanent boundary. But Tama wasn't paying attention to it. The prey she had scented stood in the field, and the three horses raised their heads in unison as she crested the ridge.

Tama hadn't expected them to be so close, and the mound that marked the boundary of the stone river had offered her no cover. She was out in the open, and despite the wind being in her favour, they had become aware of her as soon as her silhouette broke the horizon. She opened her jaws and rolled back her lips to seek out the other scent, but she quickly ascertained that it came from beyond the field, behind the horses, and at some distance. With stealth and surprise unavailable to her, she chose brute force. She broke into a run, charging directly at the nearest animal, a chestnut and white pinto. For a second, the pinto seemed dumbstruck by her approach, but as she drew near, it let out a whinny of terror and broke into a full gallop. As it passed the other two, they joined it, and all three thundered down the field. They quickly and easily outpaced Tama, but soon came to the other end, where the continuing barrier of posts and bars kept them contained. Their hooves bit into the dirt as they spun around and charged again, this time snaking away from Tama to her left. But one, a dark, tan-coloured gelding with a black mane, bolted too late and too close. Tama sprung, powered forward with an athletic bunching of her rear legs. The gelding stood no chance against the cannonball impact of Tama's mass and crashed to the ground. Tama's open jaws met the thick throat of the horse and closed with the force of a bear trap, driving her fangs through the vertebrae at the back of the neck and creating a suffocating clamp around its oesophagus. The gelding was dead in seconds.

Confident her prey would no longer resist, Tama tore out the horse's throat with a casual turn of her head. She lapped at the blood and ripped out the tongue from the fleshy tube left by the wound. Ignoring the fur-lined haunches for now, she used the force of her snout and her scissor-cut bite to slash open the belly. She tunnelled into the carcass as the intestine and stomach flopped out through the opening, the latter splitting on impact with the ground. She ate quickly, biting muscle into chunks the size of a basketball with ease and gulping them down. Some forty feet away, the two other horses stood on alert, seemingly fascinated with the creature now devouring their companion.

~

The Black Peak Reservation was a small but progressive native community. It had established important mineral rights and other natural resources as commodities early on. Like many reservations across the country, it was made up of a patchwork of privately-owned allotments that belonged to specific families, land held in trust for collectives of individuals, and common land. At least, that's how a politically correct Wikipedia description might read. The truth was, it was a political and legal mess – just less so than some. Aiden Rhames knew that was due part to his input – law school having seen to that. He used a great deal of his spare time to fight for the rights of his neighbours and for the community. Without property rights, it was almost impossible for people to build on the land, to be bonded to an address, or pass on wealth. It also meant no or little credit, which meant no or little entrepreneurism or small businesses. Aiden had fought their corner, and for the most part, won.

One of the first things he had convinced the community to do was build a commonly owned market house. This brought much of the reservation's assets together and enabled them to sell everything from organic fruits and vegetables to unique jewellery and homewares. In the past, despite the revision for reservations under the 1934 Indian Reorganization Act to protect native cultures, it effectively cut them off from the benefits of US society. The simple tragedy of common land was that, if everyone owned it, nobody did. And in the absence of title, away with it went maintenance, credit, and will. The stereotypical look of substandard housing and the barren, rundown countenance that comes with a lack of investment, was almost accepted in reservations these days. But Aiden planned to change that, starting with Black Peak. Now he, and the others like him on the reservation, had created a reliable business climate – one that secured micro-loans for the native owned small businesses he represented. There were still those that needed convincing. Some saw capitalism as a threat to their identity and traditions – the "casino effect" he called it. For others, like tribal councils, they had been incentivised for decades to keep things as they were. With over $2.5 billion of Native American "programmes" in operation, staying with the convoluted system of land ownership was safer than improving property rights. It was no wonder his days off were more precious than gold.

"Damn it, Jasper, go see what's gotten into those horses, will'ya?", yelled Aiden to his teenage son, looking up from the barbecue he was overseeing.

In Wyoming, a little thing like it still feeling like winter didn't stop you from heading outside to cook on the grill. The Italian sausage and thick-cut steaks were browning just right, and the spatchcocked chicken was charring perfectly, glazed in his wife's yellow-pepper hot sauce. Now was not the time to walk away. And her and the kids wanted the horses in the first place. He smiled, watching Jasper roll his eyes and put down the soda he was drinking.

"Go on now, food'll be done by the time you get back, so quit moaning," he laughed.

Jasper dragged his feet a little as he headed for the high paddock, cursing the horses under his breath. First outdoor meal of spring, and he was already doing chores. What was the point of that? But he still appreciated life on the res. He knew that outsiders thought reservations were akin to shanty towns, made up of ramshackle huts and uptight natives. For many, he knew this was the reality. But actually, reservations were about community more than anything else. Which still begged the question why he was doing chores on his own – where was the communal spirit in that? He smiled at his own joke, as he walked around the rusted corpse of his grandfather's 1972 Chevrolet El Camino guarding the gate to the paddock. His father had suggested it could be fixed up if he passed his test. Jasper wasn't so sure, especially as he watched a deer mouse peering out at him anxiously from a bed of stuffed straw in the radiator – no doubt stolen from the horses. Another shrill whinny came from the paddock. He looked up. The smile vanished.

~

Thomas yanked at the steering wheel, passing a dawdling and elderly Jeep Wrangler with a screech of tyres and an angry growl of the V8. The student type behind the Jeep's wheel – perhaps heading to a nearby trail, beeped the horn with a scolding blast, but the scream of the supercharger drowned it out as Thomas stomped on the gas and the truck surged forward, ravenously consuming the ascending tarmac. From the passenger seat, Catherine detected the tension of the steel beneath her feet, as the truck fought to deliver its power to the road whilst keeping its wheels straight.

"We need to get there, but we also need to get there in one piece," she warned, her fingers digging into the leather seat, though she made sure Thomas didn't see. "It's not like the reservation is going anywhere."

"But Tama might," Thomas replied, glancing at her, and showing no signs of slowing down. "She has zero fear of humans, and she'll be over-stimulated. Or, she'll run – and we have no idea if we'll track her down again – at least not before someone tracks her down and kills her. Jesse's already tried. And as for Black Peak – it's their land, their law. Nothing to stop one of them taking a shot. We're not trying to stop a potential train wreck – we're racing a runaway locomotive, and we're trying to get to the town at the end of the line before it hits."

"Put your foot down," Catherine whispered.

~

Jasper Rhames couldn't take his eyes away from the crystal-clear green ones that stared back at him. They belonged to a cat, and they were just visible above the upturned belly of his mother's gelding. From what he could see of its outline, it looked like an African lioness on steroids. He couldn't see the whole animal, but it seemed to be hunched – squatting beside its prey as it watched. That meant it was over three feet at the shoulder when practically lying down. That ruled out a cougar, and he knew it wasn't a mountain lion anyway – he'd seen those. No, this was something else. Something capable of killing and eating a horse that was three times his size and had flaying hooves and flat heavy teeth to defend itself with.

As if sensing his thoughts, the animal rose up, revealing its full head – and size. Jasper took a step back in shock. Its blood-stained chin and unblinking gaze stirred something primal in him. He'd encountered moose, bear, and cats – and he'd been taught how to react to each of them and done so. But instinctively he knew there was no rule book for this creature. He was confused by the warmth he felt against his leg, and looked down, only to realise that his bladder was emptying. His face distorted into an ugly contortion and his eyes flooded with tears as he whimpered, registering the cat as it moved up and over the dead horse. It was coming for him.

Aiden looked up from the grill, his eyes narrowing into a sharp squint that blocked out the low sun yet missed nothing. His line of sight drew towards the brow of the rise Jasper had disappeared behind. He was on alert, drawn out of the casual trance instilled by working the barbecue. At its first blare, he had been confused by the sound, unable to place it. But, as it repeated, this time clearer and without the distraction of charring meat, he recognised it. The old horn of his father's car. *Probably the only thing on it still working,* Aiden thought. He hung his prized tongs back on the side of the grill and dusted some of the accrued grease and sweat from his hands. He was half-way up the rise, when his daughter, Raven, caught up with him. She was carrying his shotgun, cradled in both arms and huffing slightly with the weight. He took it off her and smiled as she fished shells from her jeans and passed them over.

"Mum says better safe than sorry, after what happened with that bear." Raven shrugged.

Aiden nodded. The community was going to take Kayah's death hard. He'd walked over there to take a look from afar, but the maze of service vehicles and the addition of outside agencies on top of the tribal police had reminded him there was little he could do. His job was to make sure Kayah's right to a traditional funeral was observed in the next few days. The paperwork was sat on his desk, and he'd make sure it was filed tomorrow. Kayah had been the perfect example of how their traditions could be preserved whilst blended into modern society. She had run a wellbeing practice for the community and had extended it online for others. Her voice as a woman was important in Crow society, and she had been a prominent speaker and campaigner for both change and preservation. She would be missed greatly, although he knew some of the older folk feared she would become a powerful spirit in the afterlife. That's why they deemed her funeral so important.

Aiden encouraged Raven back to the house, another example of how traditional Crow society brought unexpected benefits. The house belonged to his wife, Sue, and her family, and he had moved into it with her when they had married, rather than the other way round. For the Crow, even clan lineage was traced through the mother, rather than the father. Aiden had no complaints – the house was a well-maintained, single-storey, ranch-style bungalow, with plenty of space and a fine veranda. All of which was just disappearing from view as he headed over the rise.

Aiden automatically broke the barrels of his TriStar Trinity 12-gauge and filled both tubes with shells. he had always liked the gun, as he'd read an article about the company's owner knowing his customers were likely to only afford one gun, so it had to be reliable and hard working. That was good enough for him. Aiden snapped the barrels back into place as he rounded a squat, broad oak tree, the last barrier between him and the paddock. He stopped in his tracks. In the next moment, he had raised the gun to his shoulder and was looking down the sights as his finger teased the trigger. Only the slightest increase of pressure would fire the gun. Even Aiden was surprised by how his body had reacted to the sight before him. It had taken only microseconds for him to respond. A cold sweat brought him to his senses as it doused his forehead. His eyes opened wide, drinking in the light and automatically gauging the distance between him and the threat. His muscles went taut, readying to spring away and run. For that's what his instinct told him – run. It was an odd feeling. A few seconds ago, he had been the ruler over all he surveyed. But now, suddenly and violently, he was being reminded that he was part of the food chain, and he wasn't at its top. He was prey. And so was his son.

Jasper had seen him. He sat, cowering in the driver's seat of the car and his head ducked below the dashboard. He kept glancing in panic out of the side window back at Aiden, his head each time snapping back to the windscreen. As Aiden looked at the creature down the sights of his gun, he noticed the tremble in his hands that worked its way along the barrels. He tried to calm himself, taking a deep breath and exhaling slowly, using the time to study the animal he could barely believe was standing before him.

The cat rested its two front paws on the bonnet of the Camino, and he could see the metal had buckled into creases beneath its feet.

Like crushing a soda can, Aiden thought, shocked.

The cat's front legs looked like the arms of a bodybuilder. They were long and thick, flanking the deep chest. Aiden studied it, guessing the slabs of muscle were thick enough to act as natural Kevlar for the animal. The neck looked as round and as broad as a tree stump but was relatively short compared to the rest of the body parts. But upon it, sat the most marvellous and terrifying head. The fangs were unmistakable, hanging clear of the jaw on either side. The muzzle was flat and not too pronounced, but he could see its breadth gave the animal an impressive nose. He knew a big nose didn't necessarily mean a great sense of smell, but he got the impression that nothing about this animal was for sure. Every part of its form had function, turned up to the max. Aiden thought he could see something of a mountain lion's bone structure in the bridge of the nose and the flash of the wide green eyes. It was somehow familiar yet totally foreign. Behind the head, a hump, not unlike a grizzly's, held the necessary fat and muscle to power the impressive forelimbs he'd seen. He noticed the rest of the body seemed compact. The distance between the front and rear legs seemed less than it should be, and its belly hung low – like the big Amur tigers he'd seen at the Cheyenne Mountain Zoo. The rear legs seemed squatter than the front. They lacked the long, springy look he associated with the native mountain lions. The tail was also nothing compared to the cat of the Americas, not even half the length of the animal itself.

Aiden levelled the gun, aiming squarely at the head. This was when it finally seemed to notice him and turned to look at him. A low, guttural growl emanated from the animal. Aiden hesitated, the sudden weight of what he was potentially about to do, dawning on him. There was no question in his mind what he was looking at – a sabre-toothed tiger. Its fur matched the rust of the car it was seemingly slowly pushing into the ground. Longer tufts of blonde covered its chest, underside and the back of its legs. Its short ears flicked up and turned in his direction. The animal's focus was completely on him. He knew in his heart that there couldn't be another like it in the world. Something in his spirit was telling him it would be an act of evil to kill it. But he had to get it away from Jasper, away from his son.

"Go on, get," Aiden screamed, lowering the butt of the rifle and pointing the barrels skyward. "GET OUT OF HERE," he roared.

He took a step forward, lowering his shoulders and turning slightly to his side. He lowered his gaze, as if he were approaching a stallion. The growl became a huff, and it stepped off of the car. Aiden could still see the cat easily within his peripheral vision, but he avoided direct eye contact. He knew this had worked with his dogs and horses, but he had no idea if the cat was picking up on his cues. In sabretooth, he could be telling the cat to go fuck itself, for all he knew. As it tilted its head to one side and gazed at him, he guessed whatever he was trying to tell the cat, it wasn't quite clear.

Screw it, I'll just say it, he thought.

"We can both walk away from this, if you'll allow it," Aiden nodded.

The cat levelled its gaze and took a cautious step closer. Aiden realised that if he was standing directly in front of it, he would only have to look down slightly to meet its gaze. He squeezed the trigger. It reacted to the gunshot by pinning itself to the ground, but he saw in that moment that it understood he hadn't fired at it. The next move would decide what happened next. He pressed the trigger again. The cat took off, sprinting to the side and covering the ground in impressive bounds.

~

A little over an hour later, Thomas pulled onto a service road with a parking area, where he could see a group of men in FBI jackets standing around a collection of black-coloured SUVs, and the trailer Special Agent Labar from the Bureau of Land

Management had promised him. Sitting still in the cab of the truck had only made him stiffer, and his face wizened as he climbed out and a wave of pain rippled across his back and side. One of the FBI agents noticed and quickly sprung over to meet him.

"Mr. Walker?" the agent enquired, in a tone that perfectly blended suspicion and concern.

Thomas nodded. If he hadn't been so uncomfortable, he would have smiled at how cliched the situation seemed. The agent wore the seemingly ubiquitous blue jacket with yellow FBI lettering on its back, and mirrored aviator-style sunglasses. He couldn't help but wonder how they did any kind of covert work; even without the advertising, they stuck out like flies on a wedding cake next to normal people. The slicked back hair – brown in this case, and sensible shoes in the mountains, topped with a build that only the assault courses at Langley could mass-produce, was all the advertising they needed.

"Agent Martinez, FBI. Special Agent Labar said to extend you every courtesy," the agent explained. "We don't have authority to operate on tribal land, but we can help you hook up the trailer here and we'll be available to back you up and escort you home once the job's done."

"I appreciate the help, in both respects," Thomas replied.

It didn't take long to hook up the trailer to the truck, and Thomas was impatient and uncomfortable with the eyes of the agents on him. He waved awkwardly as they pulled back onto the service road. It wasn't long until he began to recognise some of the outlying buildings of the Black Peak reservation from when he'd visited Nina's mother's house. The community was a nice one, and he could tell how close-knit they were. They had worked hard together to build up what they had. Now he was here, he realised he didn't know what the next part of the plan was. He looked to Catherine, who seemed to read his mind.

"We don't need to scare anybody, let's just see if we can find any sign of her first," she suggested.

Thomas nodded. He turned the steering wheel as he came up to a T-junction, trying to head in a direction that he thought might put them on an intercept course with Tama, based on what they knew. He knew the winding road would lead them uphill, back towards Kayah Lee's now empty house. It made him question the prospect of taking Tama alive. The cat had come out on top when matched against the bear. He couldn't have her adding to its kill tally. The road began to climb in a long, moderate curve. To the left, ponderosa and white bark pines climbed the hillside up to the ridgeline, separated from the road by a drainage ditch. On the right, they passed small homesteads and cabins. Thomas was giving them a passing glance of admiration, when he noticed movement in his peripheral vision as they rounded the curve, and he slammed on the brakes. Walking along the road in front of them was a smartly dressed Native American man. He wore a thick, tan-coloured coat and a black rancher's hat. In his hands he carried a fearsome looking over and under shotgun. The man met his gaze, and Thomas detected the man was out of sorts behind his stoic demeanour.

"Stay in the car," Thomas said to Catherine.

"Nope," Catherine replied, "you might need help getting back in, Grandpa," she teased.

They swung the doors of the truck open on each side and stepped down onto the blacktop.

"Help you folks?" the man demanded. The statement lacked friendliness.

"Guessing by what you're holding in your hand, you might be able to," Thomas challenged.

"I doubt it," the man scoffed, "unless you're looking for Arnold Schwarzekitty."

Thomas guessed that was meant to be funny, but there was a wildness to the man's eyes that Thomas suspected meant he'd seen something he couldn't quantify.

"Is everything alright...she didn't...?" Thomas asked, calmly and quietly.

"That thing's a she?" The man queried, shocked.

"My name is Thomas Walker, and I'm trying to pin her down and capture her before she does any damage. This is my wife, Catherine. We're zoologists..."

"I know who you are, you were up at Kayah's place when the bear attacked," the man acknowledged. "My name's Aiden Rhames. My smallholding is back there, and I kind of look after the community here."

"Hence the gun," Thomas said kindly. "If you don't mind me saying so, I've come across something like this before, and at the very least you're going to need backup."

"You'll get no argument from me," Aiden shrugged. "She...she didn't do any harm. But she could, I have no doubt. I'm guessing she's the same animal that's been on the news, with this vigilante?"

Thomas nodded. "I have no qualms with you taking her down if it comes to it – but we'd like to try and capture her first, if it's at all possible."

"She seemed to be headed towards Kayah's place when she left my property," Aiden indicated. "It's not much farther up."

"Jump in with us," Thomas gestured.

Catherine gave him an amused look. "And just how much jumping do you think you'll be doing?" she whispered, laughing at him.

As if to prove her right, Thomas hauled himself back into the driver's seat with an effort that caused him to break into a sweat. His two passengers waited patiently, his wife's mouth turned up at the corners, as she resisted laughing in both sympathy and at the absurdity of the situation. The flash of her green eyes helped lighten his mood though, and he was glad to have the backup of a real gun if they needed it. He put the truck into gear and moved off, headed uphill.

As they rounded the next bend, Thomas could see Kayah Lee's now empty house tucked into the hillside at the brow of the rise. Thick trees now lined each side of the road, and he took his foot off the gas, letting the truck coast gently to a stop. His gaze lingered on the darkness beneath the boughs and branches, looking for any sign of movement, or the flash of iridescent green from the cat's eye shine. He switched off the engine and turned to his puzzled passengers.

"Let's walk in from here," Thomas suggested.

Thomas eased himself down from the driver's seat, swinging the door open wide as his boots touched the ground. It was mushy, caught between the warmth of a spring day and the frost of the winter night before. The muck sucked at the tread of his shoes. Thomas felt a little sense of hope and relief flutter in his gut. Tama's mass was considerably more than his, so, if she was up here, tracking her might not be as difficult as he'd thought it would be. He walked around the truck and opened the tailgate. He methodically and carefully assembled the DAN-INJECT IM rifle. Catherine joined him, and passed him a small tin case, containing the two darts she had prepared, filled with the unique cocktail they hoped would bring Tama down quickly, and without incident.

"Mr. Rhames, if you and Catherine go the long way around, and head up the drive to the front of the house, you might flush her towards me if she's still in the area," Thomas indicated. "I'll go up the hillside here and try to cut her off if she does."

"If she's still here," Catherine shrugged, unconvinced.

"And if she ain't hungry," Aiden added, seemingly nonplussed by the idea.

He nodded solemnly and turned his back to head up the drive, closely followed by Catherine.

Thomas shouldered the rifle and set his sights on the tree-lined lip of the hill above him.

~

Tama's shoulder muscles pounded like pumpjacks as she effortlessly scaled a hillside. Instinct drove her into the shadow afforded to her by the pines, and she paused, refilling her lungs with the fuel of clean mountain air. From every direction, new sounds and scents enticed her and put her on edge simultaneously. In the distance, further back down the valley, dogs barked, no doubt reacting to her passage through their territory. They knew she was there, but not where. Her hunger pulled at her, tempting her to head back downhill towards the easy meals that voiced their exact location so freely. But another scent lingered. The bear that she had faced and defeated in the forest – laced with the coppery scent of human blood, and a myriad of harsher, chemical taints. She couldn't override the instinct to investigate.

She ascended the steep slope with silent speed, pausing at the top where the trees still afforded her cover. She lifted her head and opened her mouth to take in the scents more fully into her olfactory system. Her predatory instincts broke down each one, separating them by familiarity, distance, and age. The bear had been here but wasn't anymore. The blood too was old. The smell of humans, like the one she had kinship with, lingered stronger. She recognised the mechanical, tar-laced stink of the machines the humans used, her nose wrinkling in impulsive disgust. The other chemical odours had the same unnatural tang to them, and she dismissed them as therefore also being of human origin. Confident there was no danger here, she stepped from the trees into the sunlight that floodlit the stone river leading to the dwelling. It felt warm underneath her feet, a welcome change to the frostbitten sediment that seemed ever present just a few inches below the earthy ground of the forest. Her head whipped around as she caught the movement against the thick trunk of a limber pine. The eastern fox squirrel froze, its black beady eyes fixed on her bluish-green appraising ones. The squirrel's mouth opened as it went to deliver its warning cry, but it stayed silent. Survival instinct kicked in, as, deep within the subconscious of its rodent brain, something told it the thing before it was out of place, and dangerous. Tama dismissed the animal and wandered up to the dwelling.

She found where the bear had forced its way in, and she followed its trail. It was dark inside the dwelling, like a cave. She brushed against objects, but they moved with ease in her wake. A strange, rock-like thing sat overturned in the centre of the space. It had weight to it but was soft to the touch. Something about it attracted her to it, and she rubbed her head against it, finding the sensation pleasurable. She raked her claws against the object, only to be startled when it split like the belly of a deer, spilling an unfamiliar yellow slab out into the open. Again, she felt pleasure, and she played kitten-like with this new material, shredding it into chunks and breaking it apart with ease. It had no taste and little smell, but the texture awakened her hunger. She bit and tore off pieces, only to choke and spit them out each time. She yowled with frustration, then followed her nose. A corridor led upwards, with thin strips of dead wood beneath her feet and brushing her side. The upright branches on one side, forming some kind of barrier, buckled and splintered as she forced her girth up and through.

She found herself in a maze of much smaller caves. In one, she smelt the presence of water, and she accelerated into the space. Unlike the other spaces, the ground here was cold and stone-like, just as in the forest. She could even smell pine, but it didn't seem quite right somehow. She dismissed it, allowing her nose to lead her to a small, raised platform where she could tell water collected. But there was none there now. Her tongue flicked over the metallic objects behind it, and a few droplets teased her as they wettened its surface. Motivated and aggravated at the same time, she took the metal in her teeth and bit and wrenched. There was a sound like thunder, then an explosion. A fountain of water hosed onto the cave's ceiling, then gushed over the entire cold, stone-lined space, soaking her and everything else. She didn't care, and lapped joyfully, drinking her fill. She spent a few moments playfully splashing and stomping her paw pads through the water, enjoying the sensation. She then turned tail, leaving the newly created lake and waterfall behind.

She crossed the wooden path, ignoring the way she'd climbed up as she skirted a corner into another part of the dwelling. More dead wood, this time covered in soft skins of some kind, lay in front of her. The fur on her belly, and the long guard hairs on the lower parts of her legs, not to mention the insulating tufts between her toes, were all doused and damp. She climbed onto the flat-lain skins, purring deeply at the comfort and warmth they offered. She could scent the human much more strongly here. This space held life and offered safety. She lay, and began to groom herself with soft, long, deliberate strokes of her tongue. She used the glands on the side of her head and beneath her chin to spread her own musk, marking her territory naturally. The landscape she had traversed had been imprinted on her, and she would remember it. Comfortable, and drying, she closed her eyes. A deep, long, drawn-out exhale burbled from her nostrils as she passed into a fitful doze.

She didn't know how much time had passed when she leapt to her feet, her senses on override. Something was wrong. With a snarl, she charged out and down. Instinct drove her left, away from where she had entered the dwelling. She rippled past a large wooden mound in the centre of the space, stopping as she surveyed the gaping hole that led back to the outside. She dropped her nose to the ground. The two dark stains and drag marks looked dark blue to her, but she could still detect them and recognised them for what they were. Here was the death she had sensed earlier. She lingered in the place she sensed the human had fallen. She growled as her gaze fell upon the spot where the two bloodstains met. What had happened was as clear to her as if she'd been there herself. A protective instinct kicked in, as she associated the missing human with the sense of security the dwelling gave her, not unlike where she had lived with the man. She stepped through the gap back into the outside world. Her ears flicked and her head turned as she heard the two humans approach along the stone river. The muscles in her neck and shoulders became taut as she lowered herself towards the ground. Her claws extended and her haunches buckled as she contemplated her next move. Her thirst was satiated, but not her hunger, and it called to her now.

~

Aiden froze, then threw his arm up, palm facing behind him, to caution Catherine to do the same. His mind raced, questioning if he had indeed caught movement in his peripheral vision. He didn't hunt much, but he trusted his instincts as a rancher. They weren't alone. He moved the shotgun into a position of readiness, not completely raised, but held close to him, as if he was carrying an infant. Quietly and subtly, he pumped the gun in a slow, deliberate, single movement to minimise noise. Even so, he was keenly aware that it was the loudest sound in their vicinity. Everything else was silent. Usually, when a predator was around, like the packs of coyotes that would occasionally come snooping for an easy meal of duck or chicken, he could rely on the horses and goats putting up a stink of noise, and certainly the dogs. And as he listened, he realised the dogs farther down the valley were all baying at the top of their voices. But here, in nature, the rule of survival was to be quiet and still. That's how you stayed alive. It was a different world. He took another step forward, the crunch of gravel beneath his feet impossible to stifle. He moved his head slowly from side to side, waiting for something to be out of place.

"It's a damn shame about what happened to Kayah," he said quietly, his gaze not wavering from straight ahead.

"It's horrible," Catherine nodded.

She knew he was talking to calm his nerves and remain steady. She'd done the same many times and seen the same behaviour in Thomas. To be in the presence of a predator, an animal that saw humans as much as prey as any other animal, was not usual. Even in America, where the power of a rifle or shotgun usually bestowed the confidence of being at the top of the food chain, nature never turned down an opportunity to suggest otherwise. People just weren't used to being on the menu after dedicating centuries to eradicating anything that posed even the slightest threat. She did not feel comforted by the fact that she had grown used to the danger, that it had become natural to her.

Aiden began to edge to the side of the house, where the kitchen entrance and damaged wall were. He turned the corner, raising the shotgun into a full shooting position as he did. Nothing but the dried, red-brown stain on the veranda greeted him. He stared at it for a moment, then swung his shotgun into the interior of the house. He could hear running water. He sensed Catherine close behind him and nodded his head, indicating his intention to enter. She nodded in turn with agreement.

They made their way through the kitchen, flanking the island unit in its centre on either side. From the other side of the room, they had a clear view into the hallway, where water was pooling as it cascaded down the stairs. The living room beyond looked as if it had been ransacked. The sofa was overturned, and its cushioned covers were split. Pieces of safety foam littered the floor, sponging up the water in some places.

"Your cat?" Aiden queried.

"I guess so," Catherine exclaimed with some frustration. "I'm not sure I like how she keeps being referred to as ours though."

"Hold on for a moment," Aiden said, resting the shotgun up against the wall.

He returned to the kitchen, and Catherine heard a cabinet door open. There was a hissing sound, and she heard the unmistakable banging of pipes in the walls as Aiden turned off the water. There was a spluttering noise from upstairs, and then, slowly but surely, the stream of water slowed and then stopped. Aiden reappeared in the doorway and picked up the gun again.

"Stay here, I'll just check upstairs, but I get the feeling it's long gone," he said.

Catherine watched as he lumbered upwards, his coat brushing the wall. She noticed how the banister rails had buckled and busted where something much larger had taken the same path beforehand. She heard Aiden grumbling to himself as he checked each of the rooms upstairs. She felt uneasy being in this place now. It had only been a few days since she'd sat on the couch drinking tea with Kayah. How the sleek, attractive woman had called out to them from the bedroom window upstairs. Cassie had been totally taken with her. She wondered if Nina would stay here now. Make it her own. It was such a lovely house. It deserved to be cherished and made good. But, maybe, that would fall to a new family and owner. Catherine thought about her father and how the money he'd left in his will had enabled her to buy the building that became the wildlife research centre in Cannich. But neither her nor her mother could stay in the house they'd lived in. She knew that Nina was unlikely to stay. A lake of sorrow seemed to collect in her gut, and she turned to the kitchen, freezing when she was about three quarters of the way.

She could see the immense shape in the doorway out of the corner of her eye. She pressed her teeth into her tongue to stop the gasp of air escaping from her lips. As her mind raced towards panic and losing control, she reminded herself that although everyone knew about flight or fight, they always forgot the third natural instinct fuelled by the same hormones – to freeze. As that very urge gripped her, she fought it off, and began to slowly turn back to the open door behind her. But she could only fight it so much as she came face to face with Tama. The cat stood outside on the veranda, looking in at her with a fixed, unblinking stare. Catherine wished that the flash she saw in Tama's eyes was curiosity, but she knew it could just as likely be the indifference a tiger showed a deer just before it leapt. But, still, Catherine forced herself to look at the cat and gauge its behaviour. Tama stood tall and straight, her ears were upright and facing forwards. Their sandy coloured tips hinted at Tama's mountain lion heritage. Catherine reminded herself that Tama too was trying to gauge the threat here and wasn't exhibiting hunting behaviour. At least not typical hunting behaviour.

Tama bobbed her head slightly, still assessing Catherine. Catherine felt like she was being scanned by an airport security machine looking for hidden dangers. Then, the one thing she had hoped wouldn't happen, did. The thud of Aiden's boots against the floorboards upstairs changed the atmosphere in a heartbeat. Tama growled and crouched, a wave of movement rippling along her spine to the flick of her tail as she readied. Aiden must have heard it, as in a moment, he was on the stairs. Catherine saw the barrel of the shotgun appear as he thrust it through the first gap in the banisters he came to.

"Don't," Catherine cautioned.

She could see the barrel of the shotgun shaking as Aiden tried to control the tremble in his hands. Tama looked in the direction of the stairs, growled a second time, then bolted. One moment she was there, the next, Catherine was watching her tail disappear into the brush. Catherine ran to the door.

"She's coming," she screamed at the top of her voice.

CHAPTER TWENTY-EIGHT

Thomas was barely halfway up the slope when he heard what sounded like a bulldozer tearing down the hill at him. It was as if the giant stone from the Raiders movie had been launched from the top of the rise, and it was headed straight for him. Then he heard Catherine's warning. He tried to catch his breath as he shouldered the rifle, but he knew he wasn't ready. The roar was so loud that it rooted him to the ground, just as it was designed to do. He knew that hidden in Tama's roar was a low frequency vibration wave called infrasound, which she used to disorientate and confuse her prey. Elephants were able to use it to communicate over considerable distances, but in the case of the few big cats that counted it as part of their arsenal, it was pure weaponry. And right now, it was doing exactly what it was designed to do, slowing him down and keeping him pinned.

His hands trembled as he tried to check the dart in the rifle's chamber. Then, as his eyes skipped up to the brush ahead of him, the foliage quaked and then burst, as Tama thundered towards him. She roared again as she leapt, and Thomas stumbled backwards as he lost his footing. Gravity did the rest as he slid on his back, and as he looked up, Tama passed over him without a glance down. She wasn't on the attack; he had just been in her way. By the time he was getting back up, Catherine was on her way down to him.

"Car. Now," Thomas gasped.

Catherine nodded, slinging her arm around his side and helping him down the rest of the slope. By the time they got to the truck, Aiden was already there waiting for him.

"Do you know where she's going?" Catherine asked.

Thomas raised his head, listening. A cacophony of barking dogs sounded from the valley below. He nodded, solemnly.

"An old widow, Dyan Moon, has a pasture below here. She keeps goats," Aiden informed them. "There's a track to the south that takes us right along it."

Thomas heaved himself into the driving seat and started the engine. He stuck the truck in reverse and tore at the steering wheel, whipping it round in a J-turn. He floored the gas and the tyres bit into the dirt, sending a spray of gravel as a shake of power rippled through the truck's cabin.

~

The two Pyrenean mountain dogs slowly stood to attention, lumbering out of their kennels with intrepidness rather than slowness. Their moves were deliberate and calculated. As large dogs, energy was a premium, and they preserved it with stoic dedication. Most of their days were spent lazing in the sun, their mere presence enough to keep predators away. But something was disturbing the mixed herd of Saanen and Nigerian dwarf goats. They flocked from one side of the pasture to the other, instinctively moving away from the woodline beyond the fence. The dogs trotted over to the fence to investigate. The goats funnelled between them and moved to the very rear of their paddock. Instinctively, the dogs faced the woodline and began to bark and bay.

Tama crept to the very edge of the trees, her belly flat against the ground and her hind legs tucked up beneath her. Her claws extended in readiness as she observed the two dogs. She could tell by the way they constantly repositioned themselves that they had not detected her. As the wind changed, she rose up onto her feet and padded away softly, looping back into the trees and around to the other side of the paddock's border. The furious bout of barking that followed, informed her that they had caught her scent, but for now, she remained hidden from their sight. Although the dogs had been what had drawn her down the hillside, and had been her intended quarry, she was now fascinated by the strange herd of animals before her. She watched with great anticipation and building excitement. They had a stink that called to her like nothing she had encountered before. In their fur she could pick up the smell of their own urine, and mixed with their naturally already powerful aroma, it pulled her in. She growled softly as she glanced back to the dogs, who were now behind her and off to her side. Then she charged.

She cleared the paddock fence in a single leap and hit the ground running. The goats scattered in sheer panic as she careened into them like a wrecking ball. She ignored the larger, pure white animals, and sought out the two nearest smaller ones, with their blotched orange and white colourings. One, she reached with her claws, sending it tumbling through the long grass with its side split open. The other, she engulfed in her jaws, clamping them shut. The goat screamed in agony as its spine was crushed, then it fell silent and limp. Tama dropped it to the ground, and tore into its belly, savouring the taste of the blood. It invigorated her and she feasted, sucking the goat's heart and lungs into her mouth and severing them into swallowable chunks. She ate greedily, her hunger driving her. The goats seemed the perfect size for her to easily dismember. She stripped the flesh from the haunches with easy tugs of her jaws, splitting the hide and casting it aside as she surgically separated muscle from sinew and ligament.

In her glee, she had forgotten about the dogs, and one now neared, growling, and shaking its white, mane-like ruff as it approached. Tama gave a warning growl that stopped it in its tracks. She was confused by the dogs' behaviour. They seemed to show no interest in the animals, yet protected them as if they were a food source. Territory was something she knew by instinct, but this was something else. Regardless, the dogs were not going to be allowed to threaten her meal. She stepped forward until she stood over the other goat, its blood staining the grass where it lay dying. Tama raised her head and growled savagely and angrily, shaking her head with guttural intent. The dogs cowered, then whimpered. Tails between their legs, they parted the herd of goats as they ran back to the safety afforded by their dog houses, barrelling inside as soon as they reached them.

Tama lowered her head and began to feed. Unfettered by the guardian dogs, Tama turned her attention to the remaining goats. As if sensing her preference, the pure white Saanens deserted their Nigerian dwarf sisters and put as much distance between them as they could, heading once more for the other side of the paddock. Before Tama felt even remotely full, the blood of another five of the goats was seeping into the soil.

Dyan Moon heard the goats panicking, but didn't act immediately, as she heard the dogs barking. Any coyote or bobcat would be seen off in short order, and she had continued with preparing some goats cheese recipe notes, and even a goat milk soap 'how to' for the community newsletter. But when the dogs went silent and the goats' screams seemed to escalate to a new level of hysterics, she left her desk and headed calmly to the porch door. As a matter of precaution, she reached up and lifted the Beretta Parallelo shotgun from its rack above the frame. Her late husband had always preferred an old-fashioned side-by-side model, and this, as well as the house and enough money to buy her first goats, was all that he had left her. The cacophony and racket the goats were making made her shake her head. The number of times she had wandered down to the pasture, just to find the goats screaming for the sake of it – either out of boredom or because they knew she would come down to check on them, was beyond belief. How such little goats could make such big noises always made her chuckle. But still, something seemed more urgent and real this time. She lifted the seat of the telephone bench by the door and stuffed her cardigan pockets with ammo before strolling outside. She smiled, knowing she would look quite the picture as she did so – the barrels of the shotgun broken and resting over one arm, a floral skirt, a chunky knit cardigan too big for her, and fleece-lined moon boots. She knew they weren't quite appropriate footwear, but the path to the paddock was flat and gravelly, and unlikely to give her a hard time.

She walked, muttering under her breath and looking down as she picked out her path with unusual care. She was about halfway to the paddock when something in her gut urged her to look up.

"What the Hell...?" she stammered, not believing what she was seeing.

Her hands shook as she fumbled for the cartridges in her pocket. She cursed as she dropped one, but instinct told her to leave it where it lay and fish out a new one. She loaded and cocked the gun, then rushed to the paddock fence. She took a sharp intake of breath as she aimed at the creature that stood feasting on her livestock some sixty yards away, then pulled the trigger.

Tama heard the gunshot and saw the explosion of earth several yards away from her. She spun around and sensed the female human that stood at the far end of the pasture, leaning over the fence. Tama growled and began to charge towards the new enemy. Her system was flushed with testosterone, adrenaline and cortisol after attacking and killing her prey, and encountering the humans and dogs beforehand. Enraged and engorged, she was not prepared to give up this killing ground so easily.

Dyan cursed herself aloud again as a fountain of earth exploded some way from the cat. Then, an uncontrollable tremble ran along her arms and hands. There had been no warning. It was just coming. Straight for her. Her brain and instinct did all the hard work for her. She didn't have time to aim and pull the trigger again. She didn't have time to run back to the safety of the house. But her car was just a few yards behind her on the drive, and the keys were in her pocket. Instinct and muscle worked faster than thought as she sprinted towards the car. The 1978 AMC Pacer DL station wagon was the only vehicle she had ever owned, but it was big enough to take an ailing goat to the vets or get her into town if need be. Get up and go was not an attribute it was bestowed with, but right now, she didn't care. She threw open the driver's door and fell into the seat, thankful for never keeping the car locked. She discarded the shotgun over the backseat as she fumbled with the key, and let out the breath she hadn't realised she'd been holding, as it slid into the cylinder and connected. It was only then that she looked up and out of the side window.

The cat's face filled it. Dyan screamed, which seemed to startle the cat, as it reeled back with a snarl. She only stared for a second, but it was long enough for the image to be etched onto her memory like an instant snapshot. Up close, there was no mistaking what the animal was. To Dyan, it seemed to have the body of a bear and the head of a mountain lion, save for its formidable teeth. Now, both her brain and her instinct told her to run. Dyan turned the key in the ignition, the shake in her hands hampering her efforts. As the engine spluttered into life, the cat responded with a low, penetrating growl that sounded like distant thunder. Spurred into action, Dyan jammed the car into gear and stamped on the gas pedal.

Tama lunged out of instinct, the strike of her head against the rear side window being enough to smash it. But her prey was now moving away and picking up pace. She fell in behind, matching its speed with ease and shaking her head, clearing the effect of the impact. Suddenly, the metal thing sunk its round feet into the loose gravel of the track, just as it hit a bend. Tama had not been prepared to come to a halt and collided with her intended prey in an ungainly slam of her head. She lashed out angrily, her claws leaving ribbons of exposed steel in their wake. Then, just as she was about to send her teeth through the nearest surface, the rear bumper – the car moved off again. Tama's snarl was savage in frustration, and she lurched after it again. It moved faster this time and was slowly beginning to reel away from her. Tama charged, the roar she dispelled clearing her lungs and pushing her diaphragm flat, allowing for maximum space so they could be filled with new fuel. Her shoulders strained as her body moved from side to side with the momentum, naturally balancing her through the curves and changes in direction. Her tail did this too, although it lacked the length and tensile quality of her mountain lion mother's. But her head stayed perfectly still, her gaze locked on target. As they thundered out onto a wider trail, she didn't notice the other vehicle, as it emerged from the stone river further up the hillside and began to gain on her. She would not allow distractions now. This was the kill zone.

~

"Holy shit," Aiden exclaimed, as they watched Tama and the car she was chasing appear from the farm track.

"Yep, that about covers it," Thomas nodded.

He certainly felt inclined to agree. Tama was in full charge, her muscles rippling under her hide like a fast-flowing stream. As he watched, he marvelled at how her mixed heritage had somehow given her the best of both worlds. Her fluid pace and agility came from her mountain lion mother, whereas her size and strength she had inherited from her father. He watched in disbelief as she began to gain on the AMC Pacer ahead of her, as it careened wildly down the track.

"Where does she get the stamina from?" Catherine exclaimed.

"I was just thinking the same thing," Thomas replied, jerking the steering wheel as they bolted over the patch where the two tracks met. "You couldn't make her better suited for what she does. All the advantages of a sabretooth with none of the drawbacks."

"You're thinking it's not just a freak accident?" Catherine asked.

"It's been on my mind for a while," Thomas nodded. "There's a lot that doesn't make sense about what we discovered in Scotland."

"Like how a fossil cat only known from two specimens found in Florida could have a relative stalking the Highlands?"

Thomas nodded again.

"And how sabretooths aren't really that closely related to modern cats, so cross breeding is unlikely to be an accident?"

Thomas shot Catherine a glance, and she realised that was exactly what had been on his mind, perhaps for years.

"I mean, let's not underestimate or overstate things," Thomas replied. "I'm not suggesting a big conspiracy theory or anything. Sabretooth cats, like Xenosmilus – which we know our cat is related to, are still true cats, and belong to the Machairodontinae family. And just because we haven't found fossils, doesn't mean they weren't more widely distributed. Everyone used to say hybrids like ligers weren't sexually viable – but many are. Nature doesn't like being told no. It risks all to survive. And it doesn't care much what notions we hold about what's possible or not."

"But still?"

"But still, the odds are astronomical. I just think we're missing a piece of the puzzle still, and always have done."

Catherine nodded and turned her gaze back to the track, and the strange apex predator they were pursuing once more. Thomas changed down a gear and planted his foot on the accelerator. The transfer of torque into the driveshaft sent a shudder along the chassis, as all four wheels dug into the loose dirt and gravel to re-find their purchase. Natural kinetics took over and the truck rocketed forward with a roar from the engine. Moments later, Thomas stomped on the brakes as a vicious bend loomed ahead of them. The AMC Pacer barely whipped round it, hardly slowing. Tama bolted sideways, traversing a small slope to cut the corner and leaving the track entirely. Thomas couldn't afford the same luxury of either option, the truck having too high a centre of gravity to take the corner at full speed. And he had already left it too late to follow Tama.

As they rounded the bend, the occupants of the truck watched in wonder as Tama appeared back on the track alongside the AMC Pacer. She used her momentum to shoulder barge the vehicle, which was enough to dislodge the car's wheels from the track momentarily. Thomas was impressed the driver manged to regain control of the car, and actually brought the vehicle back towards Tama, returning the graze in kind. The roofline of the car brushed against the fur on her hump of muscle behind the neck, and was enough to throw her off balance. She skidded off the track again, where the angle of the slope made her lose her footing entirely, and she tumbled sideways, rolling over onto her back as her legs flailed helplessly.

Thomas braked hard, bringing the truck to a jittering halt.

"Gun," he yelled, his hand shooting out towards Catherine.

Catherine looked down and saw the dart rifle had been slung along the footwell. She grabbed at it and pulled it up, shoving it into Thomas' outstretched hand. Thomas lowered the window and brought the gun up, resting the forestock on the sill. He took a deep breath as he watched Tama roll back over and jump back onto her feet. That's when her gaze met his. Until now, she had seemingly ignored their pursuit of her. But they had managed to regain her undivided attention. There was perhaps fifty feet between them, but the low growl of warning rolled out towards them loud and clear. It seemed to penetrate the skin, reverberating into their insides.

"Something about her that makes my legs want to give out from under me," Aiden exclaimed, looking from the far side of the bench seat in the truck's cab.

"It's not by chance," Catherine explained, not taking her eyes away from Thomas or the big cat. "You're feeling the effects of something called infrasound, just as Thomas did back there a while. Some say it can do serious harm if focused on internal organs, making it of interest to military types and the like."

"I can believe that" Aiden confirmed.

Catherine smiled. "Luckily, the animal kingdom is a little ahead of human weapon developers. We don't really know which animals use infrasound or why for sure, but either way, they definitely seem to have it in their arsenal, without it making our heads explode."

Thomas kept both eyes open. Tama was standing head on to him, narrowing his field of shot. A thousand things raced through his mind, but in particular, he was speculating how Tama might react once he pulled the trigger. The effect of the drugs wouldn't be instantaneous. It would take some time for her to weaken and eventually succumb. In the immediate moment after being hit by the dart, she would react how any animal would when threatened or attacked. With unmitigated violence. Then there was the shot placement. Head on, he would have to go for a shoulder. The chest was too close to the heart and might result in complications. Ideal placement was on the hindquarters, which were squared away out of his line of sight, behind her taut shoulders and the hump of muscle that rippled with pent up energy. She was readying to spring and studied him with unblinking focus. It was almost as if she was daring him to pull the trigger.

"Go on, move to the side," Thomas whispered under her breath.

Suddenly, the noise of metal scraping on something sounded out from along the track. From where they were positioned, Thomas could follow the road along the curve. His eyes soon came to rest on the little AMC Pacer. It had hit a rut at speed and become stuck. It sat lopsided, its wheels on one side spinning in fresh mud that thawing snow had made into a perfect wallow. As the engine revved hard under strain from its still panicking driver, the sound wasn't unlike an animal in distress. It was enough to get Tama's attention and break her thousand-yard stare with Thomas. She took a step backwards, angling her body in the direction of the unusual sound. As she took another step, Thomas saw his opening, and pulled the trigger.

The dart flew straight and true. It stuck fast in her right hind flank. Tama reacted as if she had been stung by a wasp. Like many animals when darted, they didn't associate the dart with events that had preceded being shot. The people and the vehicle close by were forgotten as Thomas watched Tama wheel around, growling and swatting at the dart. As she arched her spine, the empty cartridge dropped harmlessly away onto the ground. A hubcap-sized paw smashed down on top of it, crumpling it into the dirt and brush. But, as Thomas had seen with other animals he had darted, he watched as Tama was distracted by the sound of the AMC Pacer finally finding traction and moving off again. Whereas she didn't associate either of the cars with the pinprick she had felt before, the chain reaction of events now seared the connection into Tama's memory. She lurched forward, picking up her pursuit again with no sign of stopping. Thomas gunned the engine once more and took off after her, watching her out of the window as she barrelled over the open ground of the scrub bordering the road. Going point to point, she would close the distance easily. He checked the rear-view mirror and watched the trailer dangerously fishtailing behind them.

"This track leads straight into town," Aiden explained. "Once we're over this ridge, it's all downhill straight into the market square."

"Great, just what we need," Thomas sighed. "I don't think she's going to go down before we reach civilisation."

The little car ahead of them was gaining speed again, and turned the corner as it reached the brow of the ridge, then disappeared. Thomas glanced to his left, watching Tama continue on her course to intercept. She stayed low, not attempting to traverse the slope back up to the track. Thomas guessed she could see where the road met the scrub further down, and was happy to let the natural lay of the land bring her prey to her, as long as she stayed on course. Thomas put his foot down, determined not to let her get that far.

As they reached the rut that had snared the little AMC Pacer, the truck and the trailer behind bounced dangerously high momentarily but ploughed on through. Thomas came off the gas for a second, then planted his foot again, eager to catch up with the Pacer. They crested the ridge a few moments later, gaining a much better view down the other side of the trail once they did. Tama was still on an intercept course, but now Thomas could tell something was off. Maybe the drugs were kicking in.

~

Tama padded beside a small creek that carved out the bottom of the canyon floor. She felt a slight urge to stop and drink, surprised by a sudden thirst. She ignored it, but it slowed her pace momentarily. Her gaze didn't drop from the metal object she pursued. As her body veered around rocks and rose and fell in line with the landscape, her head and line of sight remained in a fixed position and homed in on her prey. She accelerated, but found the effort took more of a toll than she expected. She growled, a wave of momentary weariness making her feel even more uncertain. Understanding that her strength was finite, she lowered her head and scrabbled over a rocky outcrop as she quickened her pace again.

~

"Incredible," Thomas stated, watching Tama. "Look how she moves. She just traversed that slope and outcrop like it wasn't there."

"It doesn't look natural, her head not moving like that," Aiden stated.

"It's an evolutionary adaptation a lot of big cats have," Catherine explained, perking up suddenly. "Fluid imbalance in their inner ears influences their eye muscles and stabilises their vision whilst moving. Cheetahs are most famous for it, as their ability to do it at speed is a bit of a showstopper."

"And cheetahs and mountain lions are more closely related than you might think," Thomas added. "Tama's mother was a cougar," he added, as if trying to explain his thought trajectory.

Aiden simply nodded and continued to watch the surreal events from the car window, as a sabretooth cat chased down an AMC Pacer along a track in western Wyoming. At the same time, Thomas saw his opportunity, now headed downhill and aided by gravity. He accelerated again, willing the truck forward and for the trailer to stay attached, as he pushed them harder, and they took the punishment of a belting from loose gravel, ruts, and fissures with no warning. The timing was perfect. Just as Tama joined the track again, Thomas planted his foot on the gas and brought the truck within a hair's breadth. He only grazed her with the slightest of touches, but it was enough to throw her off balance, and she slipped sideways back into the scrub. Like a missile changing trajectory, Tama realigned herself with the AMC Pacer ahead and started out across the scrub again on a direct course. Thomas was relieved she hadn't decided to vent her frustration in their direction.

"She seems unstoppable," Catherine declared.

"Those drugs can kick in any time they like," Thomas added, watching Tama pound across the patch of land between them.

As they rounded the next corner, Thomas took a short intake of breath and felt his shoulders tense as he jolted back in his seat. They had run out of time and road. As they tore down the track, he could already see that it ended in a neat little crossroads that marked the edge of town. He could see the red light of the stop sign blinking in the distance. He changed up the gears and put his foot down again, but he knew they weren't going to make it this time.

The occupants of the truck watched in horror as Tama leapt and scrabbled across the slope of the mountainside. They were close now and could see she was truly committed, her muscles rippling with power as she bounded from ledges, careened down gravel slopes and crashed violently through the low branches of the gambel oaks that lined the scrub. This was it. Thomas pushed on, skidding precariously on the dirt track as a ripple of power worked its way down to the wheels.

~

With a final leap, Tama landed on asphalt and roared with defiance. She ignored the distractions of the buildings that loomed from either side. She was aware of the small number of humans that froze in the wake of her prey, but ignored them too. On reaching the stone river, the metal contraption seemed to move with more purpose and began to accelerate again. Tama could feel she did not have the strength to mount another pursuit if it escaped again. The effort she willed from her tired muscles was the last of her reserves, but it delivered what she needed.

~

Dyan Moon screamed for help through the window of the little AMC Pacer. Those she passed looked on, wearing expressions mixed with horror and wonder. She began to panic as the enormous beast bounded closer with every passing second. In a sudden burst of survival instinct, Dyan pushed down again with all her might on the gas pedal, but panicked and stalled the car squarely in the centre of the crossroads she had been turning through. The cat was the size of a grizzly and in full charge and had no way of anticipating the sudden halt of the car in mid-flight. In fact, as Dyan watched, the animal practically did a double take as it realised the car was no longer moving. It didn't see the little green car with the orange wooden panelling until it was almost on top of it. *Could a cat smile*, Dyan found herself wondering, as she watched it turn slightly in her direction and lower its head a little. With a defiant roar the sabretooth – as that was what it was, barged into the side of the Pacer with its shoulder with all the force and impact of a heat seeking missile. The little car lurched sideways then lifted off the ground as its wheel caught the curb. It landed heavily with a sound like crumpling tin and slid a little way before coming to a stop, where it rocked back and forth as it balanced uneasily on its driver's door handle.

Dyan had fallen from her seat into the crumpled recess of the roofline. She could feel her head was bleeding and she knew she would be badly bruised, but otherwise she seemed to be okay, other than a little dazed. The windshield had cracked, and the contents of the car were strewn randomly around her. Her eyes slowly came to rest on the shotgun next to her. It somehow restored a moment of calm in her. She offered up a little prayer there and then to her husband, thankful that he had provided for her after he'd passed and even now, still protected her. Clarity returned to her now. She had only fired one charge at the cat. Her arm trembled and she let out a cry of pain as she reached for the gun. Moving made her realise just how awkwardly she must have landed, twisting her leg beneath her butt somehow. But that didn't matter now. Her outstretched fingers caressed the wooden stock and she inched it closer so she could get a grip around it.

That's when a shadow fell across her from behind. She felt a snort of breath cool the sweat on the back of her neck. And Dyan was in no doubt what it was. She knew it was too much to expect it to be a helpful passer-by, ready to lift her from the wreckage. Dyan felt no pain as she was suddenly dragged backwards, as the cat tried to remove her from the car side on. Her strength could not rival that of her attacker, but she was able to put up enough resistance to reposition herself enough to stop her spine being snapped against the doorframe as she was extracted. And her fingertips found the gun and wrapped around it.

As Dyan found herself free of the car, she realised the cat's head was so large it had only been able to snag the fabric of her cardigan with its claws as it had dragged her out. But now, as the cat's dew claw dug into her side and rolled her over, she screamed with agony. It felt as she imagined a knife would, red hot and searchingly penetrative. She knew blades did more damage than bullets for the most part. It seemed to steel her resolve, and as she rolled, she dragged the gun with her. For a moment she came face to face with the creature. Time seemed to stop. The flashing green-blue eyes were filled with intelligence and purpose. It towered over her, its legs straight. It almost seemed curious, rather than about to devour her. Then Dyan thought of how she'd seen cats play with mice as a child. *I'm no mouse*, she thought as she winced with the pain and narrowed her stare with determination. The barrels of the gun rested across her stomach and aligned roughly where the cat's belly button would be if it had one. Dyan pulled the trigger and closed her eyes. The blast of the shotgun deafened and disorientated her again, but the attack she was expecting never came.

~

Tama was knocked sideways by the explosion that erupted from the end of the metal tube. Although she had recognised the weapon, there had been something about her prey's behaviour that had stopped her from acknowledging the threat. The female had seemed calm, accepting. She had not been aware that her instincts were slowly dulling. But now, Tama growled, sensing her lucidity slipping away. Her hind legs gave way from underneath her and she scuttled backwards. The pain punched the breath from her lungs in a vacuum. Tama snarled. Her prey was still lying on the ground, and she could smell the blood as it mixed with the human's sweat. But the copper-like metallic taste had lost some of its allure. Survival instinct was kicking in. The sounds of the other nearby humans, the contraptions they travelled in, and other, less familiar noises brought back her acuity. This was not a victory, or a meal she was going to enjoy. She turned and began to lope towards the end of the street and the far side of town, where she could feel the cool mountain breeze and the scent of water calling her.

She couldn't help but be distracted by the strange lights and sounds surrounding her. Despite the urge to run, hide, and lick her wounds that she felt, there was also a draw to the buzz of the streetlights overhead and the panicked faces that watched her from beyond thin sheets of glass. It was only then, as she slowed a little, she became aware again of her pursuer. An open doorway momentarily seemed to invite her inside to safety. A waft of sweet scents poured from the dark room beyond. But as she veered towards it, the opening disappeared, and a barrier of dead wood slammed in her face. She had no doubt that she could break through, but the urgency to escape again tugged at her and directed her back towards the stone river.

~

Thomas reached the crossway with his foot still holding down the accelerator like a lead weight. His eyes fixed on Tama, he didn't realise they'd reached the end of the track, and he threw the truck into a crazy, sideways drift that threatened to upturn them alongside the bruised and battered AMC Pacer. He felt relieved to see some of the town's residents had already rushed from the small, western-style parade of shops and houses to the aid of the woman, who was sitting upright against the car, clutching her side. But the vicious turn was too much for the trailer to take, and with a loud screech of metal grinding against metal, the hitch rose up from the ball hook that held it and then dove downwards towards the asphalt. Sparks flew as it ground against the tarmac and it continued its trajectory of straight ahead with the doomed determination of a crashing airliner, ignoring the truck's change of route along the main street.

Thomas' gaze snapped to the rear-view mirror as he watched the trailer slide to a halt, the undoubtedly damaged frame of the hitch ramming into the curb and stopping with a jolt. He swept the thoughts of panic from his mind and returned his focus to Tama. The cat was limping in half bounds, lifting her damaged hind leg off of the ground. He knew that soon it would become too heavy, and she would have to drag it. Tama seemed distracted by the unfamiliar surroundings of the town, if that's what you would call it.

"This is our community centre," Aiden explained, as if reading Thomas' thoughts. "A few essential stores, some social housing, a doctor's office – she's from around here and officially serves the reservation, and a few folks beyond. Your cat seems quite taken with it, least ways," he added, nodding out beyond the windshield.

Thomas ignored the reference to Tama being his cat and watched. Aiden seemed right, Tama did not seem to be in a hurry to escape. Her head swung from side to side, seemingly mesmerised by the burning streetlights. He wondered if the buzz from the simple, low-tech cables connecting them were what enchanted her. The stimulus of such new sights and sounds must be overwhelming and tempting. He watched as Tama seemed to pause outside what looked like a store. It had broad wide windows, and although he couldn't make it out from the distance, he could see faded gilt letters etched into the glass.

"That's the pharmacy, right next door to the doctor's office," Aiden explained. They sell candies and things for the kids, and a blend of natural herbal remedies – as well as your everyday meds," he seemed quick to add. "Bet that's like a veritable gingerbread cottage for our friend."

"Oh, well at least it's our cat now," Thomas smiled.

Aiden showed no sense of humour as he shot a glance at Thomas, and then down at his gun. "They do say curiosity killed the cat," Aiden sighed. "At the very least, it's giving me time for my shot. Can't see you coaxing kitty into the trailer we left back there somehow."

"Don't, not yet," Thomas asked. "Give me – give her a chance."

Aiden hesitated, then nodded solemnly. "But" he said, "she makes a move, I can't allow anyone else to get hurt."

"Agreed," Catherine declared, throwing a warning, definitive glance at Thomas, who simply nodded.

~

Tama sensed the urgency. Whatever bounty lay beyond the wooden barrier, she no longer had the luxury of time to reach it. With an angry swipe of her paw, she sent a blue-coloured metallic box through the transparent sheet between her and the scents within. She snarled menacingly, as she took a step towards the petrified woman, who now stood looking through the smashed glass, screaming uncontrollably at the monster before her. But the sound of the thing approaching along the stone river stirred her into action once more. She set off at a run down the main street of the town, now having to drag her hind leg behind her as her strength once more began to ebb.

Tama roared with displeasure having still not lost her pursuer. She increased her pace, and those who had somehow not been alerted to her presence now fled in panic before her. A man darted into a side alley between the pioneer houses. Others stood rooted to the sidewalk. She passed and ignored them, bellowing into the evening air with disgruntled rage. As she came to another cross section, her incredible sabres gleamed in the red and amber glow of the traffic light that swayed in the wind above her. The scent of water came to her again and led her away from the stone river and back onto the mountainside.

~

"You two get out and see if anyone needs help," Thomas suggested quietly. "I'll see how far I can follow her".

Catherine hesitated and for a moment, Thomas saw a glimmer of resistance in her eyes. But then she simply nodded. Aiden was already out of the truck and walking back towards the wake of fear and destruction Tama had left behind them.

"See if the trailer can be salvaged at all," Thomas added.

"Thomas, whatever you need to do...".

Thomas answered with a half-smile, meant to reassure her. But they both knew it lacked conviction. Catherine climbed down onto the asphalt, and he turned the wheel in the direction of the scrub that Tama had headed for. As long as it didn't get too bumpy, he knew the truck could take it. A few yards from the road, a steep incline led down to the river. He traced its path back towards a small arched bridge where it passed under a road that led out of town. A dark recess of shadows met his gaze. He couldn't see Tama, something that half-surprised him given her size. But then again, he'd learnt enough from tracking big cats, and especially mountain lions, to know that they weren't called ghost or phantom cats without reason. Instinct told him that the shadows under the bridge was where Tama was waiting for him. He shook his head at the fatalistic nonsense that had just passed through his head. She wasn't waiting for him; she was holding up to see if she was still being followed and to get the lay of the land whilst concealed. She was a predator, simply following her instincts. He stopped the truck.

Taking up the dart rifle, he climbed out. He had no intention of staying quiet or concealing his approach. He wanted Tama to know he was coming. He hoped she would therefore not perceive him as a threat. He began to hum to himself out loud, just as he would if he was out for a hike in bear country. But despite his apparent casual demeanour, every muscle in his body tensed, waiting for the explosion of pissed off cat he expected to come from underneath the bridge at any second. He deliberately swung the rifle over his shoulder. He didn't want to shoot her again – knowing it was likely to kill her. The drugs in her system were hopefully already taking effect. An overdose would send her into a coma at the very least. How quickly it would do so, and whether he would have time to flee, was down to guesswork. Officially, the overdose should send her system over the edge and pretty much cause an instant reaction. But then again, Tama was no normal cat.

Thomas paused at the bottom of the incline and looked up at the bridge above him. He slowly scanned the rocky slope that led upwards and away from him. A small amount of scree gathered at the bottom, which was to be expected given the alluvial nature of the terrain. A patchwork of honeyberry and buckthorn bushes peppered the dry sandy soil further up where the sun could still reach them over the course of its daily pass. The rock formations were made up of schist and gneiss, a common bedrock for Wyoming. His A-level in geology occasionally came back to haunt him, and he knew from his past time here, that Wyoming boasted some of the oldest Archean rocks in North America. This didn't pass him by as he looked up towards a large limestone boulder, which would have to be significantly younger as a result. A flash of green caught his eye, and for a moment he got excited for the wrong reason, thinking he'd found a nugget of Wyoming jade, a gemstone the state was famed for. Then he watched a second flash of green come into view and rise from the ground silently.

"Hello Tama, old girl," Thomas said as he expelled the air from his chest, trying to control the shock.

She was close. Too close. But she wasn't in mid-air, halfway to knocking him down and ripping his throat out. That seemed like a bonus. He slowly moved his hand to the tip of the dart rifle's shoulder rest, ready to slip it from his shoulder and into his hands. He couldn't be sure if Tama's placidity was from the drugs already coursing through her system, or just simple curiosity.

At the sound of his voice, Tama tilted her head slightly in appraisal.

"Believe it or not, there's a way out of this where I don't try to kill you, and you don't eat me," Thomas said, quietly and calmly. He felt relieved that Catherine wasn't there to witness him in direct conversation with the cat. "How do you feel about following me out of here?"

Tama took a step forward. It was slow, but confident. Again, he saw no sign of aggression or hunting behaviour. He backed off a few steps and beckoned her softly. This seemed to spur Tama into action. She scurried from her hiding place out into full view. She halted again, once she had recovered the distance that had been between them before. Thomas' mind was a blur as a surging storm of thoughts rushed into his head as if they had gushed from a failing dam. Out of the eddies and whirlpools of thought that threatened to suck away any linear process of assessment, one image came to the surface and stayed there. Tama had been trained. She was used to vehicles. This wasn't impossible. He didn't have to get her to the road, he just had to get her to the truck.

He glanced behind. It wasn't that far. He just had to convince Tama that he was friend, rather than foe or a convenient snack that had walked right up to her.

"Come on Tama," Thomas urged, tapping his thigh as if he were calling Meg or one of the other dogs to him.

He took a few more steps back, slightly altering course to reach the truck as planned. Tama again closed the distance. Like other animals he had observed, they seemed to have an invisible force field around them that set how close another living thing could get to them. Usually, this would change gradually as an animal became used to your presence. A garden robin might sit on the spade handle the first time it notices you tending the flowerbeds. It will learn to pick up the bounty you leave as you toil the earth, getting closer as it does so. Eventually, with a little patience, that robin will eat from your hand. In Tama's case, Thomas hoped that she wouldn't bite his off as a matter of course. Tama adjusted to his presence and manner quickly. Now, each time he took a step backwards, she drew a little closer than before. Her intelligence and predatory nature meant she adapted much quicker. Thomas turned to his side, just as he had when working with Khan. He didn't turn his back on Tama, but his body language showed he trusted her. Again, this seemed to placate her. She took a single, gentle bound and drew alongside. For several moments, it seemed to Thomas that both of them were trying to sum the other up.

"It's not far now, and I'd say the back of the truck is a little comfier than a rock," Thomas shrugged. "I suggest we get there before you really feel the need to take a cat nap."

They walked together up the incline, several yards apart but at the same pace. Tama had the same look and grace as a lioness on the move, padding confidently along the trail just like the big cats in Africa did, weaving between tourist vehicles as they went. Her limp was barely noticeable. This wasn't alien to her. She'd done this before. Thomas' own confidence grew. They reached the truck, and Tama stopped. She let out a low grunt. It reminded Thomas of the noise a jaguar made when surprised – or angry. He slowly manoeuvred to the back of the truck, still cautious to keep some distance between him and Tama. He half-smiled, knowing the distance gave a false sense of security. The likelihood was that if Tama was within thirty yards of him, she was close enough to kill him. Several feet didn't make a lot of difference. With that in mind, he made his actions slow and deliberate so she could see what he was doing, and he kept his voice low. He reached for the tailgate and swung it down. With a single deft motion, he folded the rear bench seats to make more room.

"What do you say Tama?" Thomas asked, patting the floor of the truck as if to encourage her.

Tama stood up to her full height and extended her head to look inside the truck. She strained her neck upwards and licked her nose and opened her mouth. Although the look was quite fearsome, Thomas knew she was scenting the truck to the fullest of her abilities – opening up her entire olfactory system. She seemed to wrinkle her nose and shook her head as if to dislodge what she found there. Clearly, it was not to her liking.

"I don't know what else to offer you," Thomas shrugged. "The alternative is you pass out on the rocks, and we have to winch you out – which I can't see helping your headache when you come round."

Tama padded away from the tailgate and headed around to the front of the truck. With an effortless lifting of her tail and rear end, she jumped onto the bonnet of the truck. Thomas winced as he thought of her claws on the paintwork, but he was willing to make the sacrifice right now. But Tama didn't stop there. The bonnet was only large enough to support her in a sitting position, and she didn't seem willing to accept that. She stepped up and forward again. Thomas noticed that it seemed to take more effort as she hauled herself onto the roof, dragging her hind leg now. Once there, she sprawled across it, her limbs flopping down either side of the truck. Thomas walked around to the rear again. Tama's chin rested on the lip of the tailgate. The drugs were kicking in fast now. He didn't quite know what made him do it, but he slowly and cautiously lifted his hand. His fingers touched her coarse outer fur and delved deeper to find the soft hair underneath. She responded to his touch with a deep grumble that was half growl, half purr. He caressed her gently with his thumb, wondering if she could even feel such a soft touch under the influence of the meds. He stayed there with her until the lights behind the eyes seemingly switched off and her eyelids fell like heavy theatre curtains.

Thomas let out a long and exalted breath he didn't realise he'd been holding. At the best of times, he tried not to anthropomorphise animals. The logical, lizard side of his brain told him that Tama would have been just as likely to take his arm off as let him touch her. Just because he'd gotten away with it, it didn't mean there was any connection or trust between them. But, at the same time, he couldn't help but feel there was. He clambered back into the driving seat. He winced again as he noticed the thick crack in the glass of the windshield where Tama's mass had proven too much for it. He hoped that same mass would hold her in place as he made his way back up to the road. He went slowly and surely. As he pulled onto the road, he felt his hands tremble as they gripped the wheel. The adrenalin he'd let build up, as well as the pain from his wounds and scrapes were now coming back to haunt him. He almost envied Tama's deep unconsciousness. He knew it wouldn't be long before his own exhaustion caught up with him.

He kept his progress down the road at a slow crawl, the engine just ticking over as the truck rolled along with gentle tugs of torque from the throttle. The people that had fled from Tama's path now stepped out onto the sidewalk and even the road to look at her as he passed. Thomas gave them an unsure nod and raised his hand in an embarrassed half salute of acknowledgement. He just hoped the trailer could still be used to transport Tama from here. Far from here, he decided as he drove. It had crossed his mind that the community here would not be pleased to see Tama still alive.

Thomas passed the AMC Pacer, still on its side. A Fremont County Emergency Medical Services truck sat close to the sidewalk, its red and white flashing lights revolving slowly and soundlessly. They threw strange, elongated, pink reflections onto the sandstone dust of the road. The back of the truck was open, and he could see the woman huddled inside being attended to the paramedics. Her head snapped up and she watched Thomas pass with unblinking eyes. He wasn't sure if it was terror or rage that he saw behind them, but he looked away and continued on. It was only a little beyond that he saw Catherine and Aiden standing beside the trailer. It looked shipshape, and a lot more upright than before. He hoped that was the case as he stopped the truck and stepped out.

"How in the world...?" Catherine stammered, unable to take her eyes from the giant sleeping cat sprawled across the roof of the truck.

"I just asked nicely," Thomas shrugged.

Aiden's gaze snapped to Thomas. The look in his eyes was more questioning than accusing. It made Thomas feel a little sheepish, and he rubbed the back of his neck in a nervous, knee-jerk response. He stepped closer to Aiden.

"I kind of mean it," Thomas said, quietly. "I approached her out in the open and talked to her. I figured she was used to it. It seemed to work. I thought she might get in the back of the truck, but she thought otherwise."

"Probably woulda been a little cramped," Aiden replied, his western draw bold and broad. His delivery was matter of fact, and without judgement. "I've heard elders speak of how we used to speak with our animal brothers and sisters. We understood them, and they us. But we have offended them with how we treat the environment, so they no longer speak to us. But they still understand us," Aiden stated. "I think it's a Ho-Chunk belief," he added, as if to distance himself from the idea.

"Works for me," Thomas admitted, slumping against the side of the trailer.

"So, what's the plan? I presume you're not thinking of taking her to the nearest airstrip like that?" Catherine asked, walking up to them both.

"She won't thank me for it, but I saw we winch her down back the way she came, over the bonnet and into the trailer. We'll make her as comfortable as possible. Tend to those wounds whilst we can. She'll take a bounce or too, but I think it's the best we can do. It's not like we have a lot of time."

"Agreed," Aiden nodded. "Well, we best get started, the gang's all here".

Thomas' brow creased as he suddenly thought of Jesse and what he'd said about Jericho.

"No, we're not," he said.

CHAPTER TWENTY-NINE

Jericho wasn't one for pleasantries at the best of times. And this was far from the best of times. He met the FBI agents at the deserted camp and handed over the manilla file he'd stashed in one of the expensive GMC's many storage compartments. He told them what he knew. As the less-experienced agents catalogued their findings with all the pizazz and attentiveness of a scourge of zombies, Jericho's quick hands and the deep pockets of his cattleman's coat found things he either liked or thought he might need. They certainly weren't going to get the tender loving care they deserved with the bureau. His thoughts turned to Erasmus Richter and his army of goons. He knew they were tracking him, so they would know where he'd been, perhaps even hazard a guess as to who he'd met. But he also knew that their plans, whatever they were, had begun to unravel. Things were not working out as expected, and he was going to make the most of that. He checked he was okay to leave and was then back in the car. Jesse had agreed to meet him, and knowing that had probably been a significant strain on his generosity, he wasn't planning to be late.

Just over an hour later, Jericho pulled into a deserted service area south of Saddlestring and just off route 25. He was headed back towards Colorado and the ranch. But he had no intention of going alone. Or in a vehicle that would let them know he was coming. Jesse was already there waiting for him, leaning against the old Ford van. He greeted him with a tip of his hat but little else. Jericho pulled up and got out.

"I appreciate this Jesse," Jericho said genuinely.

"I understand you're up against it," Jesse exclaimed. "You sure this is how you want to go about things?"

"I don't take kindly to being threatened," Jericho said sourly. "People I care about being punished for something that's my fault, I can't live with that. But neither will they."

"Sounds like a one-way trip," Jesse warned.

"To Hell," Jericho laughed, a little wildly.

Jesse sighed, looking Jericho over with tired eyes that filled with pity.

"Well, in that case, you're taking the right dogs," he sighed. "That cat left me with two – both male. Cerberus and Bullet. Cerberus is your lead dog. I can't guarantee they'll follow any commands, but they'll stir things up for you, I'm sure."

"That's all I need, well, that and a car that can't be traced," Jericho grinned. "Happy to exchange keys?"

Jesse nodded. It was something Jericho had already asked on the call.

"Watch your back, and try not to do anything stupid," he warned Jericho. "I know Thomas and I were angry, but you don't owe us nothing. What's happened isn't your fault any more than it's his."

Jericho smiled, warmed by the sentiment. He felt the knot in his stomach he hadn't realised was there untighten a little.

"Don't be too tough on the man, what happened to your pa wasn't Thomas' fault either," Jericho answered.

"I know, just never had anyone else to blame," Jesse shrugged.

"Well now, why don't I go see about finding you an alternative," Jericho laughed. It had meant to be amusing, but it sounded hollow. "I have a feeling this is all connected somehow."

"Something bigger than us folks is at play, that much seems sure," Jesse nodded. "Still though, watch your six. I ain't coming to your rescue."

"Couldn't live it down if you did," Jericho laughed, more wholesomely this time.

They exchanged keys, both walking away from each other without another word. Jericho clambered into the old F1 panel van, and watched the big GMC move off in the opposite direction in the rear-view mirror. Behind the bench seat in the front of the truck, dark stained slabs of varnished oak, laid horizontally across the width of the cabin, cut him off from the cargo area. The wood went as high as his shoulders and was then replaced by a panel of mesh. It enabled him to see out the back of the truck, just, but also to view his travelling companions. Two pairs of amber, wolf-like eyes looked back at him from their respective cages in the rear.

"Okay boys, I'm guessing you want a bit of payback after the whooping you took," Jericho said, softly. He wanted them to get to know his voice and gain some trust before he opened the back doors a few hours from now. "Get comfy, and hopefully we all come out of this feeling better about ourselves."

He turned the engine over and pulled out of the service area. He was caught off guard by the truck's power at first. The supercharger kicked in almost immediately, and he grinned as the van took off like a rocket along the tarmac. He came off the gas and corrected the oversteer he was fighting as the truck came back under his control. He only knew Jesse's work from what Thomas had told him, but he could see he hadn't exaggerated. Despite being built nearly seventy years ago, the old Ford handled like a modern race car. He couldn't quite bring himself to turn on the retro-looking, yet high-end digital radio integrated into the dashboard, instead letting his thoughts provide the background noise as he found his way to interstate 25 and headed south.

Jericho was no stranger to a fight. And he knew the element of surprise was a big win. But he still knew that the odds were against him. Galway might not seem like a tough place to grow up to the tourists who flocked there in their thousands, but crime was high out of season. To make it worse, in the 80s and 90s, if you weren't willing to supplement your income by a little smuggling and local support of the IRA, like Jericho's father refused to, you made it extra hard on yourself. You also missed out on the protection it provided. As a result, Jericho had grown up a fighter. Whether defending himself from gangs that saw him as an outsider they couldn't trust, or standing up to those who questioned his father – he never walked away from a fight back then. He had learned to do that later, after expanding the family business.

Jericho remembered his father's strange taxidermy shop, situated on a back street in the main town. He had to walk up hill along a cobbled street lined with gayly coloured houses on his way home from school, but when he looked back from the top, he could still see and smell the Atlantic Ocean. The same port that made Galway both an attractive tourist town and a smuggler's delight, also made it a convenient place for American hunters to have their trophies from Europe and beyond stuffed and mounted before heading home. His father was happy to oblige them, and made beautiful exhibits and mini dioramas to showcase both the hunters' bounty and his artwork. Jericho had been barely a teenager when the business began to fail. Although not much of a reader, he'd found some books by Gerald Durrell that had belonged to his mother. It was then that he saw the potential of the burgeoning environmental movement and the demand for live capture and zoo animals.

As Jericho found a place in the middle lane of the interstate, he thought about the last time he had spoken to or seen his parents. He'd been nineteen, and they did not see his vision in the same light he did. They dismissed it, and he them. Twenty-four hours later, he had stowed onboard a merchant vessel headed for Angola. Despite being discovered, he worked his passage as a crewman and found his way to Africa, and into a civil war that had been raging for nearly twenty years. Cursed with both initiative and intelligence, as he himself put it, he found demand for many things from both sides of the fight. He would never have joined the military back home, but in the midst of a bloody and dirty war, he realised very quickly that it would be to his advantage if he learned to look after himself.

It wasn't just two guerrilla movements in a power struggle in Angola. The Soviet Union, Cuba, South Africa and the United States, all got involved too, using it as a surrogate for the cold war and providing support for their allies in the region. Jericho had gotten friendly with a CIA operative who made good use of his smuggling contacts. Just hanging around with the spec-ops types who frequented the bars on their way through, enabled him to pick up a thing or two. But it was actually a Soviet KGB agent that had shown him how to fight. He was picked up off the street and beaten savagely by her crew in an attempt to extract information. When that didn't work, she had slept with him instead. Jericho grinned as he remembered.

She had also trained him, concerned that the Americans would respond in kind, once they learnt he had probably talked. Agent Galina Malkova tutored him in hand-to-hand combat, but also where to draw the line in what information he gave and to who. She taught him how to be valuable to both sides, without making himself vulnerable. One of the men who had administered the beating, Dimitri Alexeyev, had been the one to teach him how to shoot. In a strange twist of fate, the man now headed up his operations in Tanzania, Zambia, and Mozambique. As he thought of the fight to come, Jericho sat up a little straighter in the truck. He might not be military, but he'd seen conflict. And he knew how to fight a better trained, better-equipped enemy. His eyes flicked to the dogs in the back of the truck.

"And I have two fur-coated razor blades to back me up, don't I lads," he smiled.

One of the dogs, the largest of the two, raised its head and barked confidently. Jericho took it as a good sign. He realised he had been thinking like a man headed into a fight he knew he couldn't win.

"Any man who thinks he is going to die tomorrow, will usually find a way of making it so, ain't that right boyos?" he chimed to the dogs again.

They both looked up at him, curious. It wasn't as if they were wagging their tails, thumping them with enthusiasm against the wooden bed of the truck, but he got the impression they had at least accepted him. It was less likely they would tear him to pieces when he opened the back doors of the van in any case. With that small obstacle put out of his mind and to rest, he began to consider his options. He thought he could probably park the van a little way off from the drive that led to the ranch without being spotted. He'd gotten a rough idea of the layout from his visit. Security at the gate was high, but not so much elsewhere. He thought he should be able to reach the rear of the barn without being seen. Jesse had suggested the dogs would have no problem scaling the fence, but he had bolt cutters in his bag, slung along the bench seat from him. The only other thing he had in there were a pair of binoculars. He'd spent some of Richter's money on a snazzy Zeiss set. It had somehow made him feel a little better.

His old smuggling contacts had been useful in procuring what he carried under the drover's coat too. He didn't exactly have the time for the paperwork for a high-powered rifle, so he'd had to work with what he could get hold of handgun wise. He'd done pretty well given the short notice he'd given his contacts, procuring two weapons in total. One was a real prize. The Brugger & Thomet MP9 submachine gun had been kitted out with a full law enforcement spec. An infrared scope sat on top of its picatinny-type rail, along with a laser pointer and a torch. Its barrel was obscured by a cylindrical, screw-on silencer that covered the entire mounting. Completely illegal, but that didn't concern him too much. It wasn't exactly his first rodeo in that regard. He had three 30-round magazines attached to his belt, as well as the clip already in it. Also illegal, he noted.

He'd also been able to procure a decent pistol. The Sig Sauer P320 XFIVE Legion was a 9mm, but it carried enough punch to be effective. Especially with the 147 grain hollow points he'd loaded both it and the two spare clips with. He had tucked it into his belt, a little nonchalantly, but he figured if he hadn't managed to kill or maim himself with all the gunplay, he'd enjoyed in his life to date, it was unlikely to happen now. He'd have ideally liked his own Rhino revolver by his side, but he would have had trouble getting that into the country at short notice. He was as well-equipped as he could be given the circumstances.

Given his cargo, Jericho made sure he didn't stray too far from the speed limit and kept his eyes open for sheriff and highway patrol vehicles. He didn't need to be stopped and potentially discovered carrying illegal firearms. That would complicate matters no end. He knew the van was distinct enough to perhaps get some attention anyway, so he drove "casual" – not sticking to the speed limit religiously, but not letting the 670 horses under the bonnet off the reins by any means either. It seemed to work, as just over three hours later, he was guiding the van off the interstate and onto the straight, flat, deserted roads that would bypass the city of Boulder and end at his destination. A further half an hour later he rolled the van off the road entirely, and along a remote dirt track that he didn't know or care where went. But he did know that when he drew the truck to a halt, he was less than a mile due northeast of the ranch. From here on in, the rocky, uneven terrain meant he'd have to cover the rest on foot. But luckily, it also meant that the farm's defences were built facing the approach road to the front. They didn't expect visitors at the back door.

Jericho didn't rush as he prepared for his walk cross country to the old farm. His heavy drover's coat was an old hangover from his safari days with Thomas, boasting the protection of Kevlar that had been sewn into the lining – just like a leather jacket Thomas had. This was to help in the event of a leopard attack, but the heavy weave acted as decent body armour too. Anything above an average pistol and he still probably wasn't getting up again, but it covered most of his vitals, and it was better than nothing. Beneath the coat, the submachine gun was slung via a shoulder strap against his side. He slipped the extra clip for the pistol into the pocket of his coat. He couldn't help the grin as he thought about a certain line from the film Crocodile Dundee, as he secured the oversized sawback bowie knife, safe in its sheath for now, to his belt. He fixed his hat and let out a sigh. He couldn't tell if he felt like a ronin, ready to die with honour – or Charlie Sheen in Hot Shots Part Deux. He had a suspicion it was the latter. But, as if to balance that out, he reminded himself of the nickname he'd earned during his time back in Africa – the Irish bum who was good with a gun. Not being military didn't matter – he was a crack shot among the best – and he'd probably fired more times in anger than most soldiers or mercs. The outcome wasn't fixed.

As he opened the back doors of the old Ford, the dogs stood up, alert but silent. He took a step to the side and opened the doors of the cages and lowering the ramp, letting them see it was safe to get out. As he did, he glanced at the horizon. He had about an hour of daylight left, almost all of which would be gone by the time he reached the ranch – as he had planned. The dogs stepped forward and dropped to the ground. He admired their off-white, wiry colouring, mottled with subtle shades of tan and grey. Wolf-like.

One was noticeably larger, and Jericho presumed that this was Cerberus. Bullet, as his name suggested, was leaner and faster. They both allowed him to remove their collars and he petted their heads roughly, which they again seemed to allow rather than enjoy. He threw the collars back in the truck.

"Won't be needing those huh boys, don't need anyone knowing who we are."

Jericho took his own advice and removed his wallet and ID, leaving it in the glovebox of the truck. Last but not least, he took out his cell. He sent Jesse a single ping via the map app, followed with a message that if he hadn't heard from him in two hours, it would be in his best interest to come and get the van. He then smiled, adding the dogs were fine and seemed to be along for the ride if nothing else. Then he threw the cell phone underneath the passenger seat.

Jericho set out for the ranch, the binoculars now removed from the bag and slung around his neck. The bolt cutters had found their way to a pocket in his coat. He walked straight towards the ranch for about fifteen minutes, until the border fence came into view. He stooped a little lower and slowed his pace. The dogs seemed to pick up on his cues, and also slunk into a stalking gait. Jericho dropped to one knee and raised the expensive field glasses to his eyes. Everything seemed quiet. Thin sheeting had been added to the chicken wire fence that lined the back perimeter of the ranch. It prevented anyone seeing in, but shadows of those passing by were still thrown up against it, and it certainly wouldn't keep anyone out if they were committed to getting in.

Another fifteen minutes went by as Jericho studied the routine of the guards walking the perimeter. The dogs bedded down beside him, their own gaze following his. They seemed to understand that he was hunting, and they were beginning to get an idea of where their prey may lie. Approaching as he was from the southeast, his shadow would never fall across the sheeting even when he was right up close to it. Based on what he'd seen of the patrols, he estimated he had an eight-minute window to get to the fence line. He set off across the patchy scrubland of the Colorado high plain, the dogs either side of him. They moved swiftly and silently as one, closing the gap in just a few minutes.

Cerberus made to leap and scale the fence. Jericho's heart raced. Jesse had warned him the dogs had a mind of their own and were unlikely to follow his direct commands. He didn't know what else to do other than raise his hand and say a silent prayer in his head. Whichever of the two worked, he was thankful for it, as Cerberus seemed to heed Jericho's warning and settled down again. The place he'd chosen as his point of incursion was in shadow, suggesting crates or equipment were close the other side. Jericho quickly went to work with the bolt cutters, creating a vertical slit through the fence up to about five feet. He peeled it back like wallpaper and scuttled inside, holding the fence apart so the dogs could follow. Again, they followed his cue and fell in behind him. Sure enough, as he'd seen and anticipated, a stack of crates and containers hid his approach.

Jericho had made some assumptions based on what he had seen from his previous visit and what he knew of the operation. First off, he'd presumed the ranch was used as a forwarding and response post. It wasn't a significant operations centre – just somewhere where required personnel, equipment, and things that might need to stay out of the public eye, could be kept. The second assumption he'd made was that they did not intend to let Kelly live, and maybe not even him once he'd served his purpose. They'd seen too many faces, and he had seen first-hand how they tied up loose ends. But that had been one of the few mistakes they'd made by playing their hand so directly. There was now nothing to lose in the all-out assault he was making. And if it was likely that he and Kelly were going to end up dead anyway, it might as well be on his terms. But for now, he very much wanted to live. At least long enough to cause some serious damage to Annika Deveraux, that was for sure. The third and final assumption he'd made was that the mercenaries – as he was pretty sure that's what they were, would be bored by routine and inaction, making it easier for him to take them by surprise. He surveyed the yard beyond the crates hiding him and the dogs.

Thirty yards across from him, at a roughly 45-degree angle, was the old stable building where he'd last seen Kelly. He had no reason to suspect she'd been moved. Her welfare didn't seem to have been high on the priority list of her captors. If anything, she was an additional inconvenience on top of whatever else they were doing here. Directly opposite his hiding spot, some 75 yards away, was the main gate he'd arrived at a few days earlier. A single guard walked back and forth along it, zombie-like. It reminded Jericho of carnivores like polar bears that he'd seen in zoos. The animals became so bored, they would have to stimulate themselves with repetitive behaviour. But it was also a neurosis response – similar to an unhappy person rocking back and forth. Jericho remembered the delay there had been in the opening of the gate. It didn't take much for him to imagine a sleepy guard being brought back to Earth with a thud, by a buzz on the other side of the gate.

To his left sat what remained of the ranch house. This was where the main modifications to the property had clearly taken place. The bungalow had gained an additional floor, external staircases, and reinforced entry points to the front and sides. He caught a glimpse of a merc wearing sunglasses peering out from the top of the second storey flat roof. A few moments later, the guard disappeared, walking back along his own perimeter. Jericho counted, watching the drudging cycle repeat itself several times before he was sure of the timing. He glanced at his watch. Right on time, the single guard walking the entire perimeter fence appeared from behind the main building. He was headed his way. Jericho guessed the system had been worked out so that no single section of the property was left without "eyes-on" boots on the ground at any one time – but it made them vulnerable. Perhaps they weren't expecting an attack from inside the walls, but it also meant that nobody was watching the watchers. Each was a lone wolf, a single component in the overall machine.

Jericho slowly and quietly unsheathed the knife. The guards were wearing lightweight body armour vests, but that didn't extend to any protective headgear. Jericho made a fist around the wide handle of the knife. It was a full tang blade, and he intended to make full use of it – or at least it's weight. The guard passed the crates a few seconds later. Jericho used his size and reach to yank the mercenary from his feet, bringing the flat bottom of the knife handle down onto the back of the man's head. The soldier-for-hire never knew what hit him and was out for the count before he crumpled into the ground. For a moment, Jericho had been worried the dogs would react, but they merely watched with mild curiosity. That was good, he decided. And he was certainly thankful for their lack of barking. Jesse clearly knew what he was doing.

He knew he didn't have time to think or dawdle. He left the guard where he lay, out of sight behind the crates. He sprinted across the open ground towards the stables. The dogs were behind him now, picking up on that cue by instinct. He was at the large side door in an instant. It was guarded by an ordinary-enough looking padlock. The bolt cutters were out from his pocket, and he swore at himself for not bringing a pair with longer handles. But his panic wrenched unknown strength from him, and he snipped through the shackle with only a small amount of resistance from the mild steel. He dropped the padlock and slid back the bolt, ushering the dogs inside. As he closed the door behind them, he caught the top of the roof guard's head come back into view. Jericho froze as he felt the guard's eyes on him, even though the dark, dust-veiled glass shielded him from view. The guard seemed to linger longer than he had before. Jericho could feel his heart pounding in his chest. Sweat laced his forehead, not from exertion – but from the biological impact of his flight or fight hormones kicking in. As he heard a door handle turn behind him, he realised which option he'd be taking.

Bullet, the smaller but faster dog reacted before Jericho had time to fully turn around. As the guard he had never known was there walked through the door, Bullet was in the air. A short yell erupted from the man before the dog collided with him. Jericho guessed Bullet was in the region of 90 lbs. Less hefty than Cerberus for sure, but not a small dog. And more than enough to take the guard off his feet. Jericho felt a small twinge of guilt mixed with sadness as he realised the dog's jaws were clamped around the man's throat. Bullet stood over the man, his body showing all the signs of being relaxed, as his vice-like jaws prevented his prey from uttering any sounds, other than the gargled struggle of a man drowning in his own blood. Jericho registered the shock and fear in the man's bulging eyes as they frantically darted across the ceiling, perhaps searching for the help of a god that Jericho knew would never come.

Movement behind the man caught the attention of both Cerberus and Jericho. Two more guards, following the same route as the one in front, who was now being mauled to death by Bullet. Jericho and Cerberus acted as one, both lurching forward on instinct. Bullet held his ground and his grip on the dying man's throat, but this did nothing to stop Cerberus. The huge dog used his smaller comrade as a springboard, jumping onto his back and launching himself at the nearest guard, who was to Jericho's left. Jericho remained in a crouch but had already brought up the Brugger & Thomet MP9. There was certainly no joy in the prospect he faced in the few microseconds he had before he pulled the trigger. There was nothing trivial in taking a life, and he did not do so willingly. But he felt he had no choice. The man was so distracted by Cerberus, he was turning towards his partner and the dog instead, raising his own formidable looking assault rifle as he did so. Jericho saw his opening.

"Shoot my dog, and I shoot you," Jericho stated.

The guard looked around, shocked. For what seemed like an eternity, the man just stared, and Jericho thought he wasn't going to have to do it. But, almost as if in slow motion, he watched the man's face crumple with comprehension, and the swing of his arm as he brought the rifle round to bear on him. Jericho had the drop on him and was already looking down the barrel and silencer of the MP9. He pulled the trigger, sending a spray of bullets into the guard's chest. He saw a puff of blood, as one of the projectiles caught above the protective vest the guard was wearing, tearing into the soft tissue between his collar bone and below his Adam's apple. Jericho expected the man to stagger backwards, but he didn't. He collapsed where he stood, dropping to the floor as if all of his muscles and tendons had suddenly just been removed from his body.

Jericho moved forwards, cautiously. Both Bullet and Cerberus had finished their assaults, their bloodied muzzles showing the tenacity they'd shown. Jericho felt a cold shiver run down his spine as he saw the missing flesh from the guard Cerberus had taken down. He wondered if both the dogs had looked at humans and just worked out the easiest way to take one down – ripping out the throat being their preferred option it seemed. There had been no attempt to go for the arm, perhaps like a trained military or police dog. With these dogs, there seemed to be something of a call of the wild about them. Kill or be killed was a natural instinct to them. No matter how good Jesse was, that wasn't something you could breed into a dog. These animals were intelligent, independent, and dangerous. But for now, they were on his side, and they were working as a team.

No need to fuck that up now, Jericho thought.

Jericho crept through the interim room that seemed to separate the outer storage area where he'd entered, and the main stables. From what he could see, it was used for more stockpiling. Smoked glass filled the panelled wall that separated him from the barn-like space on the other side where he knew Kelly was being held. A central door was all that stood between them now. He had no real idea how he was going to get her out of there. That's where he was expecting the real firefight to come. He paused, straining his ears and willing them to pick up the slightest sound of the guards he imagined on the other side of the door. He closed his eyes as if to boost his hearing. When he opened them again, the two dogs were sitting, watching him.

"Guess there's only one way to really find out, huh lads," Jericho shrugged.

Very quietly and slowly, he turned the spherical doorknob and cracked the door open a fraction. All seemed quiet and very dark inside the stable building. Nothing moved, and the only light he could really see was the stream of faded sunlight that poured in from atop the main barn door at the other end. It created a steeply angled ray of light that he knew was pooling in the stable where he'd last seen Kelly. Slowly, he let his eyes wander back and forth across the room, and then along its full length and back again before he pulled the door open fully.

He stepped out into the stables and stood for a moment, still not quite trusting his senses that were telling him he was alone. After one final sweep of the room, he hurried straight across to the stables.

"Kelly," he half shouted, half whispered.

There was no reply. A sense of urgency overtook him, and he raced across to the stable door. There was another simple padlock securing the bolt, which he dispatched with his cutters, just as he had done before. He threw back the door and stared in. Having heard no reply, his gut had told him that Kelly was no longer there. But she was. She lay on her side, facing away from him. Her knees were bent slightly, and he could see her arms were crossed against her chest. She had been cold and was sleeping. He rushed to her side, dropping to his knees. The rays of light coming in from above the door offered some warmth, and he could see why she had chosen to curl up here. He reached out for her arm. As his fingers touched, he froze. Her skin was cold. And there was no give to it. He rolled her over onto her back. Her body gave no resistance. As her head rolled to one side, her jaw fell open. Her eyes were open, but her pupils were dilated and rolling back into her head. She looked so pale. His fingers trembled as they pressed into her neck seeking a pulse. They didn't find it. When he saw the wet patch covering her crotch, he cried out, startling the dogs enough for them to back away several feet. He pulled her limp body up to his chest and ran his fingers through her hair. He wept, cradling her, and letting the heavy sobs send trembles through every limb of his body.

Unsupported by Jericho's grasp and bound by gravity, Kelly's left arm fell back toward the ground. As her hand hit the straw and sawdust covered floor, her hand opened, and a small object fell out of it. It was enough to bring Jericho back to reality, and his crying stopped with one, ugly, gurgled suck of breath. He looked at what Kelly had been grasping. It was a small, black pendant, and Jericho almost dismissed it at first – but his instinct told him to take a better look. He knew the last thing Kelly would care about was jewellery. He reached out for the pendant. It was a simple, flattened polygon design that seemed to be made of an opaque, dark coloured crystal – perhaps tourmaline he thought. But when he touched it, he was pretty sure it was just plastic. He turned it over in his fingers, finding a small, concealed headphone USB port on its flip side. At the same time, one of the sides of the dodecagon shape gave slightly at his touch. He suddenly realised what it was and pressed the panel a second time. Kelly had been wearing a voice recorder the whole time, disguised as the necklace. He went to put it in the pocket of his drover's coat, then had another idea. The chain of the pendant was easily big enough. He reached over to Bullet and tied the pendant around his neck. The dog let him, and it seemed as safe a place as he could think of for now.

As Jericho laid Kelly's body back down, he noticed that the padded gilet vest she was wearing was discoloured where the bullet from Annika Deveraux's bullet had grazed her. He heard a horrid, strained tearing sound as he lifted it – the sound of dried blood lifting away from the matted skin and the wound beneath. Everything became clear. The bullet had done far more damage than Annika had intended, and there had been a lot of bleeding, at least at first. Perhaps Kelly had ignored it. He undid the vest and found the dressed wound had been further padded with straw on the side where the bullet had clipped her. Either Kelly had not complained, or it had fallen on deaf ears. She had tried to do what she could with what she had, and she didn't have a lot. It didn't look like she had bled out, but he had no way of knowing what internal damage there might have been, or what kind of infection she might have picked up from the neglected environment of the stable-turned-dungeon. People talked of rages burning, but, as he vowed to kill both Annika Deveraux and Erasmus Richter, he only felt cold, numb, and surprisingly calm.

Jericho stood up and walked out of the stable without a look back. He retraced his steps, only stopping to add one of the guard's rifles to his arsenal. It was a Tavor X95 bullpup model – Israeli designed, American built, and high end. It's compact 16.5" barrel still gave it plenty of reach up to 400 yards, and the addition of the UTG scope sitting on top would help that. He fished through the belt clips of the dead man, no longer feeling any sense of guilt or conflict. Each one of these men had walked past Kelly, and either assumed she was asleep, or had ignored any pleas she made for help. He knew from how he'd found her that she couldn't have been dead more than two hours at most. Likely a lot less than that. About an hour he figured. He'd punish himself about that later, but right now, somebody else was going to pay.

He paused by the door he had entered through. Whereas he'd infiltrated the ranch through stealth, any intent of passing by quietly and unnoticed was now forgotten. He checked the Tavor – it had a full magazine and no expended rounds. It had just been another quiet, routine patrol for the guard until an unhinged dog had ripped his throat out. Jericho pressed against the door to loosen it from the frame, then readied the rifle's stock against his shoulder. He slowed his breathing down and calmed himself by closing his eyes. He counted backwards...5...4...3...2...and kicked open the door.

Before the door was fully open, Jericho had passed through the frame and the rifle was up, his eye to the scope, as he searched out the guard patrolling the roof of the old ranch building. He found him and fired. A spray of bullets met their target, leaving a puff of red vapour where the goon's head had been. Jericho brought the rifle down to his own line of sight and swept across the courtyard. He was headed straight for the building, where he hoped he would find Annika Deveraux. The other guards were inconsequential now. If they got in his way, so be it.

The sound of automatic gunfire kickstarted a chain reaction of disorder. Within a few seconds, the sound of an alarm was ringing out, and outer doors on both sides of the building opened. An armed guard appeared in each, but Jericho was ready for them. He dropped them both before they had even gotten their guns up. And now the dogs were with him too.

They raced ahead, covering the distance in no time. All they had needed from him was to identify the enemy, and they had taken the lead from there. Jericho marvelled at Bullet, whose Belgian shepherd ancestry made itself known as he scaled the outer wall and onto the second storey terrace with ease. Moments later, his teeth were ripping into the throat of a guard stepping through the outer door.

Cerberus played to his own strengths, using his size to take down a guard on the ground floor. As the dogs worked, Jericho ran, spraying bullets over their backs into the unsettled and now panicking mercenaries on both levels. He discarded the rifle and switched to the Brugger & Thomet submachine gun and the Sig Sauer pistol. He entered the side door on the ground level with a gun in each hand. It was one big room that served as a kitchen and mess. Three large dining tables separated him from two goons facing him, their heavy rifles still halfway to their shoulders. In his peripheral vision, he caught the sight of another merc descending an internal staircase along the back wall. He squeezed the trigger of the submachine gun in his right hand, the rapid fire punching the chests of the two men full of shrapnel. His left hand held the big Sig combat pistol, and he fired three times, hitting the remaining guard in the shoulder, neck, and eventually head. Cerberus was already clambering over the man's corpse when Jericho reached the bottom of the stairs and looked up. The barrel of another Tavor rifle met his gaze. If Cerberus registered the threat of the gun, he didn't show it – in fact, if anything, his charge gained momentum. Just as the mercenary went to pull the trigger, he was hit from behind by Bullet, who knocked him forward. The rifle went flying, and Jericho stepped back as it clattered down the stairs. He turned to find

Bullet burying his snout under the body armour vest the guard wore. The man went down with both dogs tearing into him.

Jericho doubled back, heading outside to climb the external staircase. He ran up the steps, the pistol held out in-front of him. He jerked backwards as a spray of bullets ricocheted off the metal rail and steps a few inches from where his head had been moments before, just above where the top of the staircase joined the terrace. Somebody was up there. He didn't have time, and blind-fired the submachine gun through the gap in the rails on the top of the terrace roof. He heard a yell and went with his gut that he'd hit his mark, instead of it being a ruse of some kind. A guard was crawling towards him, his knees and lower legs smashed by the whipcrack of bullets. Jericho ascended the last few stairs confidently, then froze. Exiting onto the terrace and heading for the external staircase on the other side was Annika Deveraux. She seemed to be in no hurry. In fact, she seemed to be smiling. He felt a presence behind him, and suddenly realised why.

He didn't hesitate, throwing all of his substantial strength and frame backwards, into the thug behind him. They tumbled heavily down the metal steps, crashing awkwardly to the ground at the bottom with a sudden stop. Jericho maintained his momentum, forcing the man down with his back to the merc's chest. He sent his left elbow up into the thug's jaw, taking some pleasure in the squelching explosion that told him he'd missed and hit his nose instead. Jericho rolled and sprang to his feet with a cat-like and predatory instinct. The man had only made it to his knees and Jericho was halfway through a reaching, roundhouse punch when he felt the cold press of metal against the back of his skull.

"I think that's enough excitement for one day, Mr. O'Connell," Deveraux said quietly and assuredly.

For a moment, Jericho considered if he could pull off a pivot kick and take her off her feet, but she had made her point and was already stepping back out of harm's way. He turned to face her. The two dogs descended the stairs behind her and paused. She turned side on, giving them a quick glance.

"If you value them, call them off," she said quietly.

"Not rightly sure I know how to," Jericho shrugged. "GET," he boomed a second later. The dogs did not hesitate and bolted for the fence. Bullet flew over it with ease, whilst Cerberus barrelled through the slit Jericho had made when they entered.

"Now, Mr. O'Connell," Deveraux smiled, "what to do with you?".

CHAPTER THIRTY

Jesse watched the seconds tick down on his watch. Jericho's three hours were up. Jesse had driven down interstate 80 as far as Walcott, then taken the state route 130 towards Saratoga. The road was known as the Snowy Range Scenic Byway, and it allowed him to kill some time taking in the stunning beauty of the Snowy mountains, some of the best the state had to offer by his account. The deep, glacial lakes glistened in the evening light. Some were still iced over, whilst the mountain pastures bordering them, showed more of the cold weather's retreat – only little salt and pepper sprinklings of snow remained. Jesse had holed up in a diner and was finishing the special – an Oaxacan BBQ chicken sandwich. He'd skipped the fries and gone for the vinegary coleslaw side instead. He wiped up what was left of that with the homemade jalapeno and cheddar roll the sandwich had been served in. He left a sizeable tip and the rest of the check.

He walked outside and took a moment to admire the pristine, snow-dusted peaks behind him, then climbed into the GMC. He fired up the engine and pulled back onto the road. At this time of the evening, it was quiet and practically abandoned. Nobody took the scenic route when they couldn't see the scenery he guessed – but they were wrong. The moonlight was weak, but it was still enough to bathe the twisted hooks of granite in silvery beams. Up there, the snow was still firmly in place and reflected a soft glow of bluish light onto the valleys below. He followed route 130 to Laramie, then took the 287 towards Fort Collins. Just 42 miles lay between him and where Jericho had pinged him with a location for the truck. Just short of an hour later, the headlights of the GMC lit up the tailgate of the old Ford. Bullet and Cerberus lay side by side next to it. They raised their heads as he pulled up but didn't get to their feet. Jesse got out and took a long sweeping look around before approaching the dogs. There was no sign of Jericho, and he had no intention of lingering. He spent a few moments looking over the Ford, finding the keys and the things Jericho had abandoned inside the cabin. He went back to the GMC, checked he had room to pass, and turned off the headlights, throwing the keys to the expensive truck on the driver's seat.

As he loaded the dogs into the old Ford, he noticed Bullet's new neckpiece immediately. Although he had no idea what it was, he recognised the USB port on its bottom lip. He removed it from the dog's neck and placed it in his pocket. He took one more lingering look around, then climbed into the driver's seat. He didn't look back or stop until he was back across the Wyoming state line, and even then, it was only for fuel. When he was about an hour from the ranch, he decided to give Thomas a call.

"I'll be back at the ranch by the time you get back," Thomas said, after Jesse explained the situation. "But I have a feeling I know what it is you've got. At least, I hope it is what I think it is. It might shed some light on things."

Jesse grunted and put the phone down. 45 minutes later, he pulled through the ranch gate. Thomas was waiting for him outside the house.

"Where's your cat?" Jesse asked.

"I won't argue with you this time, I guess it is my cat now," Thomas shrugged. "Jericho sent me a data file with a list of his contacts. She's currently sedated, in a titanium enforced crate built to Jericho's specifications. We're negotiating with the FBI about whether or not we can get a permit to take her out of the country. They'd rather she was destroyed."

"I know the feeling," Jesse smiled, but not unkindly. He fished the pendant out of his pocket. "You think you know what this is?"

"Yep," Thomas nodded. "I'm pretty sure it's a voice recorder. We'll be able to confirm that as soon as we plug it into a computer."

"Let me sort the dogs out," Jesse nodded, "I don't know when they last ate or drank something. Won't take a minute."

Thomas nodded, then looked back up the trackway. He recognised the headlights of his own truck – Catherine returning with Cassie, who had been holed up with Nina in a motel. Jesse paused and waited for them to pull up and join them.

"What's the meeting about?" Catherine asked, a tired smile on her face.

"Just following up on the breadcrumbs Jericho has left us," Thomas replied, the same tired smile on his face.

Jesse could tell they were glad to see each other. Then he remembered something.

"Say, your little'n with you?" he asked Catherine.

She nodded.

"She awake?"

Catherine again nodded.

"She might enjoy a little surprise I found in the barn," Jesse hinted.

Catherine helped Cassie down from the cab, and she happily scampered across to take Jesse's hand. He first made sure Bullet and Cerberus were fed and watered, whilst Cassie watched. The dogs seemed as glad to be home as he was. They ate and drank their fill, then collapsed into the hay of the pen. Jesse smirked as he thought he might be getting soft as he fetched some wool blankets from the store locker and placed them over the backs of each dog. They didn't seem to complain. Then he turned his attention to the pen next door.

It took a little hunting through the straw to find the pup, but he found her soon enough. She licked his hand and yikkered as he lifted her up. Her little tail wagged feverishly as he brought her out to show Cassie. He noticed Thomas and Catherine were stood in the door, watching.

"This little pup seems a little different from these boys," Jesse explained. "She's a little small, but that seemed to do her some favours. I was thinking as you're kind of small, maybe you could take care of her whilst you're here."

Cassie looked at the pup wide-eyed and reached out for it. Jessie helped her hold it. Cassie's eyes immediately flicked to Thomas and Catherine, who nodded their approval.

"Just to help Jesse out whilst we're here though, you understand?" Catherine cautioned.

Cassie nodded, although Thomas suspected that just as he did, she knew the pup was coming home with them, one way or another. He groaned at the thought of getting the paperwork for another animal exported to the UK.

"Let's take a look at this necklace," Thomas suggested.

The little pendant voice recorder contained nearly 30 hours of recordings. At first, Thomas was surprised to hear Kelly's voice. They listened through her initial kidnap and then numerous conversations with guards and someone who identified herself as an employee of Erasmus Richter, Annika Deveraux. Richter was implicated many times over in crime after crime. They skipped to the end, where they found a heart-breaking message for Jericho, and another for Thomas. It was clear that the messages were meant as goodbyes. They were the last two recordings made. Thomas and the others were left to assume the worst.

"I think we need to give Special Agent Labar a call," Thomas declared, clearing his throat.

~

The FBI acted quickly. Within the hour, they were at the ranch. Armed with both the recordings and the evidence Jericho had already passed over, a task force was set up. The recordings were analysed in their entirety by a specialist team of agents, and what they found was enough to secure warrants for Richter's arrest, as well as an immediate freeze on his state-side assets and finances. There was also an unexpected upside to their co-operation – the FBI worked with the state police and customs officials to grant Tama her export permit, under the strict agreement that she would be housed securely within an enclosure for the rest of her natural life.

It soon became clear that Richter had fled and was a step ahead of them. His accessible assets and holdings had been drained, and his facilities and properties were abandoned, with only a few bemused and uninformed staff left to take the fall for him. One of the first properties to be searched, just several hours after the warrants were signed, was the ranch in Colorado, where Kelly's body was recovered. Murder charges for both Spencer Shaw and Kelly Keelson were added to Richter's warrants, and those of his known associates, including Annika Deveraux.

Twenty-four hours later, Chayton Reed, under guard from his hospital bed, identified Annika Deveraux as the person from whom he'd procured Tama. Special Agent Labar made it clear to both Thomas and Jesse that Reed's permanent placement at the United States Penitentiary Administrative Maximum Facility – known informally as Alcatraz of the Rockies, or the Supermax, had been reserved. After another day of giving statements, procuring permits, and preparing for Tama's arrival in Scotland, there was little else for Thomas to do in Wyoming but say farewell.

~

Thomas looked out from the main bedroom of Lodge View across the water. The sky was the same cool blue as a song thrush egg, the crispness of Wyoming winter even adding a hint of spearmint where the troposphere gave way to the stratosphere some eight miles above him. To the north, the Bighorn mountains rose proudly to add drama to the view through snow-capped peaks and ice-clad slabs of granite. He revelled in the peace and beauty of the scene before his eyes dropped back down towards the water. Sure enough, moving left to right, was one of the more permanent residents of Lodge View, heading home in the early morning light after a busy night of foraging. The beaver had grown used to Thomas joining it in the first light of each morning, and no longer dived under water with a signature tail slap at his appearance. Another little piece of his past seemed put right and restored, and somehow the beaver signified that to him. Nature, and his own thoughts and feelings, were back in balance. The work was done and home beckoned.

A few hours later, Thomas shut the tailgate of the Beast and let out an audible sigh. One of the benefits of taking Tama to Scotland with them was the use of the Embraer C-390 Millennium transport aircraft the FBI had acquired from one of Richter's hangars. It had been acquisitioned with record breaking speed and was believed to be the only one of its kind in the United States. Not only could the cargo hold take Tama and his truck with ease, but it also boasted a forward passenger cabin fit for a billionaire. They were going to travel home in style.

They drove the short way down the track to the big house, where Jesse was outside waiting for them. Thomas pulled the truck over and they all got out, except Cassie, who was cradling the pup in her lap. They had become inseparable over the last day or so. Cassie had also argued, quite cleverly Thomas thought, that if mummy and daddy were allowed to have a new cat, she should be allowed to have a new doggy.

"Thought of a name yet?" Jesse asked, leaning in through the window.

Cassie nodded. "Kayah".

Jesse nodded his approval, a kind smile spreading across his face and his eyes widening a little in respect and surprise.

"I've drawn up the paperwork for the horses," Jesse explained, turning to Thomas, "I'll get them both over to you within the month. You know I'm going to have to sedate Khan, don't you?"

"For his protection?" Thomas grinned.

"Nope, everybody else's," Jesse laughed.

"Thanks for everything Jesse, I mean that" Thomas said, extending his hand. "And... I'm sorry if I didn't handle things with your Dad well. I would never want to disrespect him, or you."

Jesse nodded thoughtfully, then extended his hand. The grip was strong and warm. Thomas could feel the rough skin press into his firmly and linger.

"I'm the one who didn't handle things well. No harm done."

Thomas placed his other hand on top of Jesse's and shook it for a moment before giving in to his compulsion and warmly embracing the man. Jesse laughed and slapped him hard on the back.

"Got something for you," Jesse grinned. "Follow me."

Thomas followed Jesse over to the barn and the workshop that Tinker Enterprises called home. As they entered, he noticed two gun cases on the workbench. The first was for the rifle, which he'd seen before.

"Heard you lost those expensive, fancy guns of yours," Jesse explained.

Thomas looked from Jesse to the gun cases and back again. "You can't possibly..."

"They're yours," Jesse nodded. "Made a few modifications to the rifle. I was aiming for the love child of a military sniper model with a hunting rifle that packs real punch. I've made it less military issue and given you a stock made of black limba wood. It adds a little weight, but I've compensated for that by shortening the barrel again and the stock. Effective range is down to a mere 1,500 yards as a result, but guess you'll cope with that."

Thomas laughed. "Okay, I'll try. What have you named it?".

"The Black Morrigan," Jesse replied. "After an Irish goddess of battle. She encourages brave deeds and strikes fear into enemies. She's a guardian...a protector. And associated with banshees, which is apt given how loud the damn thing is."

"I'm honoured," Thomas nodded.

"Heard you lost your beloved Anaconda too," Jesse quipped.

Thomas nodded. "Does it make sense that hurts more than the rifle that cost fifty times as much?"

"Nope," Jesse grinned. "Try not to lose this one though, it's one of a kind," he said as he opened the smaller case.

Inside was an impressive looking revolver. It was finished in powder coated black steel and sported a five-and-a-half-inch barrel with a vented rib running along it. The handle gave it the look of something from an old western, which Thomas liked. The grips were finished in a dark, deeply veined wood that complemented the colour of the metal.

"I call it the Jade Jaeger," Jesse said softly, picking the revolver out of the case and handing it to Thomas. "It's based on a Magnum Research BFR, chambered and configured for a 500 JRH calibre. You can load it down if you need to, but I've done what I can to limit recoil. You shouldn't have any problems with it."

Thomas noticed the tinge of dark green iridescence when he caught the barrel in the light.

"I can see how it got its name," Thomas smiled. "Jesse, this is too much, I know what you sell this stuff for."

"They're yours. They won't fit or suit anyone else now," Jesse nodded.

"Thank you," Thomas replied.

They put the guns back in their cases and walked out to the truck. Catherine rolled her eyes when she saw them, but smiled. Thomas opened up the back and loaded them on top of the luggage and gifts they had acquired during their stay.

"Say goodbye to Nina for us," Catherine asked, hugging Jesse.

"I will," he replied solemnly. "I think she's planning to head up to Washington state and join her Dad. It's where she's from. Heading back home as such."

"Us too," Thomas replied. "Wish her well from us."

~

They took off from an air force base – Buckley Field in Colorado, and landed in one – RAF Lossiemouth. After a seven-hour flight, it was a drive of an hour and a half and 63 miles before they turned into the lane that led to Sàsadh, the old deer farm they called home. Tama had been sedated again on landing, and as far as they could tell, was sleeping soundly in the trailer. Jericho had provided all the details they needed to contact his crew and company, but any attempt to contact him directly had been unsuccessful. They had all the equipment they could want, including the custom-made crate and trailer Tama was being transported in. Jericho's contacts also just happened to have all the materials that would have been needed to build Tama a one-of-a-kind enclosure, which they had constructed in just a few days at Sàsadh, right next to the new lynx cage. Thomas had marvelled at their efficiency, as well as the co-operation of the British and US governments. Erasmus Richter had a lot of secrets, and a lot of money – and it seemed those in power were willing to do almost anything to get their hands on either.

Thomas was tired – almost to the point of exhaustion, but his priority was getting Tama settled. He drove the Beast through the front gate and followed the makeshift trail that had been cut by the lifters and dozers that had been there a few days before them. The enclosure was vast. Thick, cross-linked panels of oxidised titanium mesh towered twenty-five feet into the air. They bent over at the top, back into the enclosure, and boughs of leafy scots pine had been interwoven into the mesh to soften the aesthetic. Six-inch thick, powder-coated pillars of titanium-steel alloy held each panel resolutely in place. The perimeter of the two-and-a-half-acre enclosure had one entry point, with a double gate safety system. Thomas used the area the construction machines had also used to turn, pivoting the trailer expertly as he yanked the gearshift down into reverse. The trailer and the enclosure gate lined up perfectly – as if they had been made for each other. Thomas knew then that they had been – although clearly, the enclosure was intended for somebody and somewhere else. They could worry about that later.

Thomas got out of the truck and peered inside the enclosure. Jericho's crew had worked with what they had. Huge slabs of natural Scottish granite had been removed from their shallow graves and cemented in place to create a cave house for Tama. It had a concrete floor that hid underfloor heating, powered by buried cables that ran back to the small control room and viewing platform on the east side of the enclosure. A thick layer of straw also covered the floor, fresh and welcoming for the new resident. Thomas laughed at the oversized cat "tree" that must have been custom made well in advance. Triple decks married by reinforced steps and polished logs.

Where the granite had been removed, a new, deep, clear pool covered the traces of the machines. The area near the house had been a good location – it was why he had built the lynx enclosure there too. In its former life, before he had owned it, Sàsadh had been a deer farm – and the east pastures had been cleared long before his arrival. A few lofty Scots pine remained and were now also part of the enclosure. Fresh, lawn-worthy grass had been put down in a few spots to hide the disruption caused by the machines – but otherwise, natural scrub of hawthorn, fern and heather remained, for the best part, intact. They could certainly make improvements, but it was by far and away a vast improvement on what Tama had been used to at Chayton Reed's camp.

Catherine directed Thomas to back the truck up a little further, until the maglocks of the first gate clunked into place, securing the crate and trailer before it could be opened. Two green buttons glowed to the gate's side, and Catherine pressed them both. The door of the crate was levered upwards as the external and internal security doors of the cage lumbered open. Catherine went back to the truck and took out a small red case from the trunk. The antidote to the sedative had been calibrated with Tama's mass in mind, how much of the sedative it had taken to subdue her, and how long it had taken to do it. She used a blowpipe applicator to deliver the dart and its restorative loadout through the slats of the crate.

"Why don't you and Cassie go up to the viewing platform and watch her from there," Thomas suggested, joining her.

"See you up there," Catherine smiled, then paused. "Given that folks weren't exactly in love with the idea of the lynx, how do you think they'll react to her?"

"In a word – badly," Thomas replied. But, for now, it's a closely guarded secret. And unlike Loki, Tama will never set foot outside this enclosure."

Catherine nodded as she unbundled Cassie from the car and headed around the perimeter towards the external metal staircase on the adjoining stretch of fence line. It led up past the control room and supply shed that serviced the enclosure. Again, Thomas had been quite impressed with the ingenuity shown by Jericho's crew – they had simply modified a prefab garden building to suit their needs. Thomas watched Catherine hold Cassie's hand as they climbed the stairs, waving at them as they reached the top. Catherine peeked out over the top rail of the viewing platform and pointed down at him for Cassie to see, who she held in her arms.

A sound, somewhere between a huff and a purr alerted Thomas to Tama's awakening. Thomas peered through the slats and his gaze was met by a pair of bright, unblinking, emerald eyes.

"You woke up quickly," Thomas said gently.

He wasn't surprised. He remembered how once, working with vets to roundup and sedate wild Exmoor ponies, how they had commented the tough little horses needed roughly twice the amount of sedative and only half the antidote that thoroughbred stallions did. There was a lot to be said for wild spirit.

"Welcome home," Thomas said. "Why not go take a look around."

Tama huffed – a sound similar to what he'd heard tigers do when happy. She walked into the enclosure, shaking her head and at first seeming a little unsteady on her feet. As soon as she noticed it, she headed for the pool. She plunged in without hesitating, surfacing after a few moments and lapping greedily at the water. Thomas disengaged the crate and trailer, then closed the doors behind her. He jumped in the truck and pulled it over to one side, disengaging the trailer. There was still a lot of work and unpacking to do.

"Thomas," Catherine cried out, as he stepped back out of the cab.

He heard the anxiety and stress in her voice and looked up. She wasn't looking at Tama though, she was looking out past him, back towards the gate and the open pasture to the front of the property. He spun around, hearing it now. The helicopter had been practically silent, and it looked extremely modern. It's matt black finish, devoid of any numbering or designation gave it a distinctly military look. It had not one, but two pairs of rotors on top, and its tail prop faced directly backwards – like a submarine propeller. The tail too looked strange, angled down below the rear fins instead of being set vertically. Something about how quiet it had approached over the treetops and was now hovering alarmed Thomas, although he could see no obvious weapon systems. Then, the noise the helicopter was generating dramatically increased, as it dropped down towards the ground. Awkward looking wheels dropped down from the sides of the aircraft and fixed in place at a 90-degree angle to the fuselage. The cockpit looked sharp-nosed and futuristic. It touched down, blocking the drive.

Thomas took up a position to the side of the truck. The weapons were buried to the side. He wouldn't be able to get to the rifle and assemble it, but maybe the revolver if he was fast. He watched as the rear cabin door of the helicopter opened and he saw two familiar figures emerge and step out onto the ground. Erasmus Richter and Jericho O'Connell. Thomas could see immediately that Jericho was in a bad way. He was handcuffed, and on stepping out, was immediately thrown to the ground by a female with military swagger, who stood behind him. She seemed to be enjoying herself. Richter on the other hand wasn't, and was looking directly at him. Richter beckoned at him. The woman behind Jericho unholstered a pistol and held it to his friend's head. Thomas sighed and stepped out from the truck. He left the back open, hoping Catherine would take the hint.

He made his way slowly up the fifty feet of track, not taking his eyes from Richter or Jericho. The helicopter was winding down but did not fully shut down. Its twin sets of rotors continued to spin, almost noiselessly now, sending waves of disturbance out from it. Two more soldier-types stepped out from the helicopter and flanked Erasmus, the woman, and Jericho. Jericho's face was heavily bruised. He had a black eye, and ugly, purple and blue welts on his cheekbones and forehead. Richter's gaze couldn't but help veer to his left to take in the enclosure.

"I see with Mr O'Connell's help, you've put my money to good use," Richter said, raising his voice so Thomas heard him clearly.

"To be fair, I didn't know you had dibs," Thomas shrugged. "You've been a little hard to get hold of."

Richter smiled. "I see you and Mr O'Connell share the same warped sense of humour," he said. "He seemed to lose his during our little trip."

"I'm laughing on the inside," Jericho interjected, flippantly. He sent a wink and a smile towards Thomas, revealing a split lip and a missing tooth to the front.

Thomas could easily imagine the butt of an assault rifle doing the damage, probably after a similar quip.

"Your best play is to leave Jericho here and escape whilst you still can," Thomas commanded, taking a step towards Jericho. "Police and army are on their way."

As if to prove it, Catherine held up her cell phone for them to see. She had slipped down from the viewing platform and was now walking back along the track towards them. She stayed to one side, approaching the truck with caution. Thomas glanced back at her, trying to gauge where Cassie was. He caught a glimpse of her curly red hair peeking from behind the far corner perimeter post of the enclosure behind them.

"I'm here to leave Mr O'Connell with you as it is," Richter explained dryly. "But to also give you fair warning. I have my sights firmly fixed on you now. Both of you."

Thomas nodded. "I appreciate the warning, but I'm not entirely sure what we did to get your attention in the first place. If you wanted Tama, there were options that didn't include killing people."

"What I wanted Mr. Walker, was to see what would happen. To see if one of my creations could be trained."

"Your creations?"

"You don't realise it Mr. Walker, but we've crossed paths before. Your first encounter with a sabre-toothed cat..."

"That was you?"

"Not deliberately," Richter sighed. That cat and its mother were let loose by a former employee, who stumbled upon the experiment. I had a facility high in the Highlands, not far from here...not that that matters now. They forced my hand to accelerate my plans."

"And what is the plan exactly?" Thomas asked.

"A simple one. To stop the trophic cascades caused by missing megafauna. To bring back the apex predators that can stabilise and reform our ecosystems. The ones we hunted to extinction and have never seen the like of again. The ones our world needs, if it and even we are to survive. We are no longer afraid of the wild or the wild things within it. We have stripped the most powerful predators of their menace, and the land we live on of its challenges. The human race can afford to be an obese couch potato because we no longer need to run and hide from what waits in the dark. As a species, we have become emotionally muted and aesthetically disconnected from the natural world. We have become the loneliest type of predator, one indifferent to the very creatures that made us who we are. We've lost our respect for predatorial heritage. And in my experience, it's hard for people to respect something they're not afraid of. I will make the afraid once more."

"Sounds almost noble," Thomas shrugged. "Except for the killing and beating of my friends."

"Ms. Keelson's death was accidental and never intended," Richter explained.

The woman holding Jericho at gunpoint glanced at her watch and nodded towards Richter.

"You've cost me a great deal of money in the last few days Mr. Walker," Richter sighed. "That short-nosed bear was the first we'd been able to bring to maturity. Millions of dollars in development."

"What about Tama?" Thomas asked.

"Mrs. Walker," the woman called out, "I think that's far enough."

Thomas looked round and saw Catherine was approaching the rear of the truck. She froze in her tracks. Thomas picked up on the woman's accent – guessing her to be French. He could half imagine Jericho hitting on her, whilst she had been actually hitting him. Then it occurred to him that if she was Richter's bodyguard, she could have been the one to pull the trigger on Kelly.

Richter smiled. "As I'm sure you now know, the cubs were never planned for. They're an interesting and pleasant surprise, but I have no need for another...for now."

"Another?" Thomas asked, his brow furrowing with confusion.

"Tama has a sister," Richter smiled cruelly. "And she also had a brother that took after their father in a strong way. Did you know that I have spent years funding next-generation research into cloning? The Japanese are so far ahead of us, and not slowed down by cumbersome animal right treaties and conventions."

"So, the Cannich cat was no random hybrid, showing up out of nowhere?" Thomas asked.

"Anything but," Richter laughed. "Xenosmilus hodsonae was not a native to European shores, as I'm sure you're aware," he explained. "But it is an extremely robust example of the sabre-tooth family – as large and as strong as smilodon, but with heavier-set bones and stronger teeth. Not to mention, the precious few examples of its preserved remains are mainly in private hands. Although not closely related, there is a correlation to the jaguar family – and as true cats, we simply had to persuade the DNA to splice."

Thomas nodded, the pieces of the puzzle slowly falling into place.

"As it happens, close lineages don't splice as well as more distant ones. You may recall, when the Asiatic lion population fell below 200, they introduced African lion genes into the population. Genetically, there was very little difference – but the resulting offspring suffered from brittle bones and any number of health complaints. More importantly, the pure-bred animals knew they were different and ripped them to pieces.

But cross a lion with a tiger, or a puma with a leopard and you get something unique – something strong – something better," Richter added.

"A zoological superweapon," said Thomas.

Richter nodded.

"There's no need for this to get ugly," Thomas explained calmy. "I'm not interested in you, and as far as I see it, all we've ever done is clear up your mess," he nodded towards Jericho.

"In Mr. O'Connell's case, he was getting paid for it," Richter replied. "My associate here doesn't like loose ends. She'd like this to end a different way. But you'll live to fight another day, you both will. And as I say Mr. Walker, you may have no interest in me – but I have some interest in you. The inconvenience and cost alone are enough to get my attention."

"I have friends in low places too," Thomas growled. "And they're on their way, as I mentioned."

"Maybe I should just wrap things up here after all," Richter sighed.

In response, the French woman and the other guards all raised their rifles, training them on Thomas and Catherine. Then, suddenly, they all swung the barrels of the guns left in a synchronous sweep towards the enclosure. The gate was emitting an alarm, and Thomas turned. To his horror, he saw Cassie's little hand reaching back down after pressing the control buttons. Tama was at the gate in a second and stepped through. She seemed to observe the little girl, who stood to one side and looked towards them all.

Thomas tried to control his breathing. The cat wasn't showing any kind of hunting behaviour. In fact, other than a cursory glance towards Cassie, Tama stood side on to the little girl beside her, whom she dwarfed comparatively. Tama took a step forward, and Thomas took a step towards her. He thought he saw a glimmer of recognition in her glinting green eyes, but she turned her gaze away again towards Richter – who was already backing up with the woman and his men towards the helicopter. Thomas saw him mouth the words "don't shoot her" to his men. Jericho didn't seem to want to be in the middle of them, and stumbled to his feet, veering violently sideways before his legs gave way from under him and he crashed to the floor.

"Curiosity won't kill this cat Mr. Walker, but it might kill you," Richter yelled as the helicopter powered up. "Until we meet again."

Richter and his mercenaries disappeared back into the rear compartment of the helicopter. As it lifted off the ground, it made a noise like straining metal. Startled, Tama doubled back on herself and slipped back into the cage. Catherine dashed across the track and pounded the controls with the palm of her hand. The gates locked shut, and the lights on the panel went green again. In a moment, Thomas was beside her.

"She'll never set foot outside the enclosure, huh?" Catherine smirked.

"Remind me to set codes for those," he said, sweat pouring from his forehead.

Thomas looked back up at the helicopter. It held its position in the sky in a nose-high hover. As it tilted back, it regained its hushed, stealthy composure and slipped sideways towards the tree-lined ridge in the distance. As it passed overhead, Thomas met Richter's unflinching gaze in their direction. He ruffled Cassie's hair, who smiled all the while she was being scolded by Catherine. Thomas couldn't help but smile too. He made his way up the trail to Jericho, who lay where he had fallen.

"You have the worst taste in friends," Thomas laughed, offering his hand to help the Irishman up.

Jericho nodded as Thomas hauled him up, then he slapped Thomas on the back.

"Ain't that the truth," he replied with a wink.

"Police and an ambulance are on their way," Catherine said, joining them. "Jericho...I'm so sorry about Kelly."

Jericho nodded.

Thomas supported Jericho as they walked back down the trail towards the rear entrance of the house. As they passed the lynx enclosure, Loki, the male lynx they were hoping to release as part of a rewilding trial, popped his head out of his shelter and walked over to the fence line. He studied the group of people with casual interest. Then his head spun towards his new neighbour. Tama stood with her nose pressed to the mesh, taking big sniffs in – her eyes fixed on the little cat. Loki snarled and bolted back inside with a series of fluid bounds.

Jericho looked back at Tama.

"Why do you think she didn't attack any of us," he pondered out loud.

Thomas stopped and looked at Tama's immense musculature and frame. She huffed a few times as Cassie stepped forward and giggled. Tama's breath was strong enough to ruffle the little girl's curls.

"In short, I think it's because she likes us," Thomas shrugged.

"Terrible judge of character," Jericho laughed.

"Maybe it's more than that though," Thomas sighed. "Catherine told me that Tama seemed drawn to the place where Kayah, Nina's mother died. You...we've all lost Kelly. It used to be believed that cats were conduits, that they escorted souls to the other realm. Maybe there's something in that. Maybe she sympathises."

Jericho nodded, a quizzical smile spreading across his face.

They all turned as the ambulance pulled through the gate, with two police BMW SUVs behind it. As they drew up, Thomas could see an old friend was sitting in the back of the first BMW. Chief Inspector Roberts had been a part of the investigation into the Cannich cat, and had supported Thomas when he had been made a scapegoat for the bungled efforts of the government response. The man exited the car and nodded at them.

"Army is on its way, but deploying from Inverness," the Chief said.

"Don't bother with us, they need to be tracking a helicopter – it left just a few minutes ago," Thomas interjected.

"Good luck with that," Jericho said, shaking his head. "That was a Sikorsky S-97 Raider, with stealth modifications. He couldn't stop telling me about it. Pretty much the perfect getaway vehicle."

"Even so, we'll alert the air force and our counterparts in Norway, Denmark, the Netherlands and Germany. This Richter is a wanted man."

The Chief Inspector called his men over. Thomas helped Jericho over to the ambulance.

"This isn't over, is it?" Jericho asked Thomas as the paramedics began to tend to his wounds and tried to get him to lie down on the stretcher.

"Back in Wyoming, Nina showed me a population of cloned black-footed ferrets," Catherine explained, joining them again. "It didn't dawn on me until now, but they were created by the Richter foundation. I can't help but wonder what else he's been up to."

Thomas shrugged and raised his hand in a solemn farewell, as the rear doors of the ambulance closed, and it trundled back down the trail. He looked out towards the mountain range to the north, known locally as the walls of Mullardoch. They were somehow a little less dramatic than the ridge-backed bighorn and Rocky Mountain foothills of Wyoming, but no less beautiful. The furthest peak was an isolated, triangular buff called Càrn Eige. It had been where the Cannich cat had lived, retreating there after each rampage. He couldn't help wondering what Erasmus Richter, cornered and on the run after his own rampage, might unleash on the world next.

THE END

Thomas Walker will return in
Predatory Nature

Nina Lee will return in
Rogue...

...keep reading for the preview chapter!

ROGUE
CHAPTER ONE

John Henderson glanced in the rear-view mirror. His teenage daughter Maggie was staring out of the window with the same look of frustrated boredom she had worn since they'd left the house nearly nine hours ago. The expensive headphones covering her ears prevented intrusion from the deep and otherwise penetrating snores coming from her younger brother, Josh, on the seat next to her. John let out a sigh as he looked across to his wife Melinda. She was fixing him with a stare that warned her own tolerance of the journey was dangerously close to collapsing.

"Maybe we're a little too early in the season," he offered, apologetically.

"You think?" Melinda replied, a little short but as good naturedly as she could manage.

"If the next one is shut too, we'll just stop at a motel in the next town. We don't have to camp."

"And you'll cover the extra $60 a day we'll have to budget for?" she scolded.

He half-smiled at her, thinking it would be a small price to pay compared to the nagging and told-you-so attitude he'd have to put up with otherwise. And the thought of a warm, comfortable double bed certainly had more allure than the camping cots stowed away in the trunk. So far, they'd been to four camping grounds, only to find thick chains across the entrances of each.

He fixed his eyes on the road, guiding the 1967 Ford Ltd County Squire station wagon through the sweeping curves that led through the scenic forested setting of north

Washington. Towering pines, sequoia, and oak, rose in steep banks on either side, the road climbing the mountain in natural undulations and tight corners. The car leaned and wallowed in these, telling its age with tremors along the chassis and groans from the suspension.

"Even the car's had enough," Melinda said, rolling her eyes.

As they rounded the next bend, John spotted the damaged sign out of the corner of his eye. He couldn't make out the first part, but the word "campsite" was still readable. He had to stamp on the brakes to avoid shooting past, but he wasn't too worried, having not seen a car in the rear-view mirror for miles. Melinda and Maggie glared at him but weren't ready to escalate into all-out argument yet. He stared out of the window at the track that led into the darkness beneath the trees. It was heavily overgrown, but something in the pit of his stomach was telling him it was worth exploring. He turned the wheel and pushed the car over the grass verge. The suspension bucked and protested along the deeply rutted trail, but after a slight rise it was all downhill, and he coasted the car down to the campground.

The first spring flowers had already begun to push themselves through the knotted mass of overgrown grass. Red columbine, bearberry, and great camas dotted the meadow. Surrounding it were clumps of fireweed, and beyond them were the trees. By the close clumping of the trunks, John guessed it had all once been Forest Service land. He turned off the engine and looked back at Melinda, who didn't seem quite so enamoured with the place.

"You're not serious, are you?" she exclaimed.

"What's wrong. It look's great," he replied, offended.

"It looks deserted," she snapped back. "What about toilets?"

"We've got tissue and wipes. Back to nature baby," he replied, smiling smugly.

"I thought only bears shit in the woods," she said shrewdly.

John checked his phone. It had one bar of signal, and he tapped on the GPS app he'd installed. It took a while to load, but eventually the screen became populated with green and white squares, and a yellow roadway that led to the north. The area known as Paradise, on the southern slopes of Mount Rainier, was a little over three miles away.

"How about a compromise," he suggested.

"I'm listening," Melinda shrugged.

"We camp here, but we head to Paradise for dinner, at the inn. Means we don't have to do anything but set up the tents. And if it's not working out, we move on tomorrow. But for now, we get out of the car, get the tents up before dark, and don't have to cook."

"Sold," Maggie interjected from behind.

Melinda rolled her eyes but couldn't quite hide her smile.

John woke up Josh, who was slightly more taken with the campsite they apparently had to themselves. John watched as his twelve-year-old son busied himself with getting the tents from the trunk and started putting them up. There were two modern dome tents for his parents and his sister, and his own backpacking bivouac and cover, which offered slightly more basic shelter. As soon as he'd finished one of the dome tents, he offered it to his sister, who hadn't budged from her seat in the car. She grabbed her bag and flung it into the empty space beyond the door flap. Josh grinned as he bolted back to the car for one of the camp beds. He passed it to Maggie as he sped past, ready to get going on his parents' tent.

John stopped him, placing his hand on his son's shoulder.

"You set yourself up, me and mom will do ours."

"Mine won't take a minute though," Josh offered.

"Gives you more time to explore," John offered.

"It certainly looks and smells like uncharted territory," Maggie called from inside her tent.

Josh had his tent set up within a few minutes, with just a roll mat and his sleeping bag pushed inside. A clear strip of plastic that would be by his head when inside, would give him a brilliant view of the stars and any wildlife that wandered into the camp. He'd seen deer, turkey, and even a black bear once. There was just enough space in the entrance for his backpack to sit upright. He left it there and returned to the car one last time to grab his hiking boots.

He headed straight for the far tree line. It was cool and dark between the trees, and he knew he wouldn't have to go too much higher before he would find snow clinging to the frozen ground. He did his coat up and stood for a moment. He noticed a Lewis's woodpecker, flicking its tail and watching him from a branch high above. In the close grouping of the trees, it and everything else was in silhouette, but its size gave it away.

There was no real path to guide him, so Josh decided to make his own. He intended to circle the campsite in a wide arc, not straying too far, but getting a good idea of the surroundings at least. Straight through the maze of trunks, about a hundred feet ahead of him, he could see a large, wide stump. Beyond that, the trees seemed to close in, and he couldn't see further. He decided to head towards it and use the stump as a marker to turn south and back towards the far border of the camp.

He picked his way through the towering trunks, occasionally having to pull branches out of his way, or duck to avoid thicker protruding limbs. He had gone about thirty feet when something made him stop. The dripping melt water, the call of crows, even the sound of his boots digging into the dirt and slime had filled his ears until that moment, but it had all been replaced with unnerving silence. He'd been keeping his gaze trained on the ground as he picked his path, but he now looked up sharply on alert. Nothing. He squinted in the low light at the stump. For a second there, he thought he'd seen something, a glint of reflected light. It was only now how big he realised it was. At least six feet high, and nearly four feet across. It piqued his interest, making him wonder what species of tree it could be.

He looked down as he lifted his foot over a low, torn branch that lay across the ground. Immediately, there was a sharp, savage sounding grunt from up ahead. Josh froze again, this time in fear. His eyes slowly rose, once more seeking out the stump. Nothing had changed, but the remnants of an icy breath of water vapour clung to the air in front of it. Josh shuddered as he realised his own laboured breathing was creating similar clouds of mist to hang in the air in front of him.

He heard his mom calling from behind in the distance. He turned instinctively to look. The movement he caught in the corner of his eye stopped him, and his head snapped back to the stump one more time. This time something was different. It wasn't there anymore. That was as much as he could take, and he broke into a run, crashing back through the trees in a straight line towards the safety of the camp. As he burst back out into the sunlight, a rock the size of a softball flew past his head and smacked into the side of his tent. He came to a stop, and stood trembling for a moment, unsure if he should turn around. When he did, the ominous feeling he'd felt among the trees had vanished. Bird song had returned, and the sounds of his family laughing and going about camp business filled his ears. He went to join them.

~

Despite being quiet, and back from his exploration of the forest a little earlier than expected, John put Josh's edginess down to being tired from the journey. He checked on him with an occasional glance in the rear-view mirror as they headed to dinner at the Paradise Inn. The boy stared out of the window, his brow wrinkled, and his eyes darting to the trees with a nervous energy and intensity that seemed unusual. John decided to try and talk to him when they were back, after a good meal. After all, the quickest route to the heart was through the stomach.

By the time they had piled into the Paradise Inn's dining room, good spirits overtook them all and Josh's disposition became solely focused on the long, generously plated buffet table. John and Melinda also ordered some extra entrees from the menu, as a reward for the long journey and the possible cold night ahead. But John felt much more reassured that things were going well, and they would soon be settled at the campsite, despite its relatively rustic amenities. He knew they'd all cope, even Maggie, and would soon get into the spirit of things, especially if they had the place to themselves. By the time dessert came around, he had completely forgotten about trying to talk to Josh. He tipped the waiter extra for an unopened bottle of red wine to be subtly delivered to the table, which he slipped into his jacket for later. Melinda would appreciate seeing in the start of the holiday with style, and with the kids in their own tents for the first time, who knew what else she might be in the mood for. It had been a while. *No reason, other than busy, tired lives* he thought. But that's what vacations were for.

They were still laughing and rough housing as they made their way back to the car. The night had crept up on them, and John checked his watch. It was a little after nine. They'd been out longer than he thought, but that was okay. He was extremely glad they'd set the tents up and had nothing left to do but climb into their cots when they got back. He'd start a fire though, just to be sure and safe. The Washington woods at night harboured more than just trees after all. And he liked the firelight too. The warmth, the glow. It felt good to sit around a fire and put the world to rights.

John took it easy on the roads back, wary of deer that might dash across as he passed. He always wondered why they did that, wait to the last moment. Not move back, or wait, or even cross beforehand. They always waited until you were right on top of them, testing your reflexes and heart condition at the same time.

In the dark it was even more difficult to spot the entrance to the campsite, and again, he had to stamp on the brakes to avoid shooting past. He pulled the car around and onto the track. He was more confident this time, and the car bucked and strained even more than it had done before. The kids laughed it off as Melinda rolled her eyes, though smiling contentedly. As John applied the brakes sharply a second time, bringing them to an abrupt halt, the smiles and laughter vanished.

"What the hell...?" John stammered, peering over the steering wheel and out through the windshield.

Melinda followed his gaze. She felt the piercing looks of the children behind her as they did the same. It was as if a tornado had been through the meadow. Maggie's tent, to the far right, had been torn in half, revealing a mash of poles and mangled nylon. The contents of her bag were strewn around the meadow. It was the same for the others too. One of the camping cots, impossible to tell who's, had been bent and crumpled into a ball, like papier-mâché, then deposited into the boughs of an oak some twenty feet up. Josh's tent had been reduced to shreds. The split and ruined frame poked out of the ground where the rest of it had been hammered into the earth. But it was John and Melinda's tent that drew their attention. Four long slashes had been clawed along the side that faced them. They sat in silence for what seemed minutes, then John opened the door and stepped out of the car.

It hadn't rained, but a dank smell hit his nostrils. A putrid mix of must and urine. The headlights were the only source of light and offered two thin corridors of illumination that stretched out from the car to the trees at the back of the meadow. John took a few steps forward, each one revealing more of their possessions, ransacked, destroyed and distributed across the open ground. A cooler hung from a tree. Beer cans that had been ripped apart littered the floor below. A trail of Cheetos led into the grass and abruptly stopped. Blue polystyrene trays were all that remained of their meat stash. Hamburgers, steaks, sausage, and bacon had all been stripped from their packages, presumably devoured. John guessed a bear had found the campsite and taken advantage of their absence. He was surprised it had managed to get the coolers and storage containers open, which were meant to be tamper-proof.

As he took another step forward, onto the torn remains of a sleeping bag, he flinched at the sound of a heavy impact somewhere in front of him. Whatever had made the noise was beyond the reach of the headlights, but he still peered into the gloom. For a brief moment, he thought he saw a dark shape take form. It was like a void in the shadows, blacker than the night surrounding it. Then it was gone. He turned as he heard Melinda approaching from behind.

"What do you think happened?" she asked.

"It…it must have been a bear," John replied, turning back to the scene of destruction.

"I want to get out of here," Maggie whined, leaning over the open car door, gripping it by the frame with an intensity that belied her fear.

Melinda's frightened and alert eyes told John she felt the same way.

"Why don't you guys get back in the car, and I'll see if there's anything worth salvaging?" he suggested.

"Something just doesn't feel right," Melinda said, her eyes darting left and right as she began to back up.

John looked back towards the car, intending to call Josh over to help him. But the boy was still as a statute, sat in the car with his seat belt fastened. He had twisted his head around to look through the window towards the nearest grouping of trees. Something there held his attention. John slowly turned his head in the same direction. He could see nothing. The haze from the headlights dulled his vision and made the shadows blur into swirling shapes that disappeared into the vortex. He was about to look away again when a low, malevolent grunt emanated from the trees. The sound hit him in the gut like a punch. As he flinched instinctively at the noise, he felt his stomach spasm in readiness to dispel his dinner.

Melinda was looking at him in terror, her head snapping back and forth between John and the darkness.

"Get in the car," John ordered.

She was about to protest, when a rock appeared out of the gloom. About the size of a cannonball, Melinda had just enough time to duck back into the car before it would have smashed into her head. Then, John saw there definitely was something out in the gloom. Whatever it was, it crossed the track behind the car in a single, fleeting rush of movement. Now, there was nothing between it and John. It had purposefully moved around the car to get around the obstruction. John only had to contemplate its possible intentions for a moment before he was running full tilt towards the open driver's door of the car.

He grabbed at the keys in his panic to get the car started again, stamping on the gas and throwing it into reverse as it roared into life. The engine screamed at the abuse as he yanked the steering wheel round. The car pirouetted through a slush of mud and debris, scattering it across the trail in an untidy arc. John shifted into drive and felt the back-end shudder as the rear tires fought for grip. For a second, they were immobile before the big car catapulted forwards, bouncing precariously along the track. Just before he swerved back onto the asphalt of the main road, the rear window shattered as a spruce limb jettisoned into the car's interior.

Neither Maggie's nor Melinda's screams were enough to make him stop, or even look back.

Printed in Dunstable, United Kingdom